continued . . .

Lord of Lightning

"Intriguing . . . the story of a strong-minded woman who seeks to dominate the pattern of her life . . . and the brave man who has the strength to let her be strong."　　　　　　　　　　　　　　—Edith Layton

"Janet Lynnford has a magical gift for drawing readers into the story, and into the hearts of her characters. . . . *Lord of Lightning* is a captivating tale, rich with detail, brimming with adventure, and sepll-bound with a love not to be forgotten."
　　　　　　　　　　　　　　　　　　—Patricia Rice

Pirate's Rose

"An impressive debut that captivated me from the very first page. Ms. Lynnford captures the lush sensuality of the Elizabethan period with effortless skill. Rich in passion and intrigue and blessed with a bright, vibrant heroine and a winning hero, *Pirate's Rose* is a delightful romantic adventure that kept me turning pages long past my bedtime."　　　—Teresa Medeiros

"Just the kind of dynamic, spirited, richly detailed romance I love to read. I expect great things from this author."　　　　　　　　　　　—Linda Lael Miller

"Makes the battle of the sexes fresh and exciting . . . sweeping in scope and intimate in detail . . . a book to treasure."　　　　　　　　　　　—Karen Harper

"A vivid tale. . . . Enjoy!"　　　　　　　—Kat Martin

SPELLBOUND
SUMMER

Janet Lynnford

AN ONYX BOOK

ONYX
Published by New American Library, a division of
Penguin Putnam Inc., 375 Hudson Street,
New York, New York 10014, U.S.A.
Penguin Books Ltd, 80 Strand,
London WC2R 0RL, England
Penguin Books Australia Ltd, Ringwood,
Victoria, Australia
Penguin Books Canada Ltd, 10 Alcorn Avenue,
Toronto, Ontario, Canada M4V 3B2
Penguin Books (N.Z.) Ltd, 182–190 Wairau Road,
Auckland 10, New Zealand

Penguin Books Ltd, Registered Offices:
Harmondsworth, Middlesex, England

Published by Onyx, an imprint of New American Library,
a division of Penguin Putnam Inc.

First Printing, August 2002
10 9 8 7 6 5 4 3 2 1

Copyright © Janet Ciccone, 2002
All rights reserved

 REGISTERED TRADEMARK—MARCA REGISTRADA

Printed in the United States of America

PUBLISHER'S NOTE
This is a work of fiction. Names, characters, places, and incidents either
are the product of the author's imagination or are used fictitiously,
and any resemblance to actual persons, living or dead, business
establishments, events, or locales is entirely coincidental.

BOOKS ARE AVAILABLE AT QUANTITY DISCOUNTS WHEN USED TO PROMOTE
PRODUCTS OR SERVICES. FOR INFORMATION PLEASE WRITE TO PREMIUM
MARKETING DIVISION, PENGUIN PUTNAM INC., 375 HUDSON STREET, NEW
YORK, NEW YORK 10014.

This book is dedicated to:

My husband, who is a wonderful potter and,
like my heroine, makes pots of beauty and grace.

Connie Rinehold,
a mentor of rare talent and caring.

Cecilia Malkum Oh,
the best of the editors.

My e-mail authors loop,
thanks for always being there for me.

The members of my local Romance Writers of
America chapter,
Central Ohio Fiction Writers.
Many thanks for your friendship and support.

Chapter 1

Geddes MacCallum, fifth Laird of MacCallum, wagered that a battle could have raged around the Englishwoman and she would pay it no heed. She stood knee-deep in the rushing water of the burn, looking happier than any woman had a right to, given what she was doing.

Her spade flashed in the summer sun as she wedged it into the gray muck of the bank, levered a chunk loose, and dumped it into a waiting bucket. With her rapt expression and her dirty clothing, she reminded him of a child making mud cakes.

She was no child, though. The womanly curves beneath the drape of her clothing made that plain. She had tucked up her practical brown kirtle skirt to reveal slim, enticingly bare legs. Though the fabric of her simple bodice was brown linen, its excellent cut emphasized her small waist and graceful movements as she bent and straightened, harvesting muck from the bank.

Geddes frowned as she paused to push back an errant lock of shining brown hair. Her gesture streaked her creamy cheek with mud, though she didn't seem to notice. Nor did she seem to realize that she was in danger. The burn ran between his land and that of Angus Kilmartin, Master of Fincharn. Everyone in the area knew that only five months past, he had vanquished the Kilmartin in a deadly battle over the right to Duntrune Castle, but the Englishwoman was not from this area. She could not know that his four men, stationed along the burn, watched for marauding Kilmartins, anticipating their attack. Or if someone had told her, she didn't care.

She was more interested in digging clay.

It was a dangerous attitude for a young gentlewoman, traveling with naught but a young male escort and an old man to protect her. Dangerous—but intriguing to find such daring in a female.

He moved closer, intent on seeing more of her.

As he approached within hailing distance, Geddes stared at her hair. Glinting with highlights of rich cinnamon, it was bundled in a careless knot at the nape of her slender neck. It sagged as if it were about to tumble down, yet its dishevelment did not lessen the provocative quality that held his interest.

Her manner fascinated him most of all. With single-minded concentration, she riveted her gaze on the bank, as if her entire future lay before her.

Two old men and a bairn just learning to toddle stood above her on the bank, seeming equally interested in the work. Geddes recognized one man as Magnus the Potter, who lived with his son in the village of Duntrune. The old man usually spent his days dozing in the sun at his son's doorstep, uninterested in anything around him. The Englishwoman's arrival had apparently changed that.

Geddes would not have believed it possible for Magnus to be so animated. With his wizened face full of color, he gestured and barked orders to the other old man, who must be the Englishwoman's teacher. The doddering old fellows, reportedly acquainted, were in their element as they each claimed a full bucket of gray muck from her. The Englishman lugged his to a waiting cart.

"Come, Jamie," Magnus ordered his grandson as he trudged toward the cart as well. "I'll no' have ye fallin' into the burn."

The child, unsteady on fledging legs, ignored his grandsire. Fascinated by the flashing spade, he toddled to the edge of the steep bank and stuck his head too far over the edge. His balance failed him. Both arms flailed. As he realized his peril, his face crumpled and he emitted a wail.

The Englishwoman dropped her spade in the burn and leaped forward, arms outstretched to catch the child, but Geddes was closer. He swooped down and scooped the lad into his arms.

Startled, Jamie yowled at the top of his lungs.

"I've got him," Geddes assured the Englishwoman, whose anxious gaze widened and locked on him. He patted the bairn on the back, feeling awkward but triumphant. Yowl as he would, Jamie would have disliked a tumble into cold water far more than being snatched to safety by his laird. "Och, wee Jamie, ye dinna fancy a dunking, do ye?" he quipped, jiggling the bairn in his arms, hoping to soothe him.

Jamie bellowed louder.

Geddes's confidence in his child-tending skills sank lower.

"James Malcolm, shame on ye," his grandsire muttered, stumping up to relieve Geddes of the lad. "I told ye to stay away from the burn. Thank ye, MacCallum. 'Tis good o' ye to look out for the laddie."

The child quieted at once in his kinsman's arms. As Magnus put distance between his grandson and the burn, Geddes noted how the Englishwoman's gaze followed the old man, an appreciative expression lighting her features.

Geddes stepped forward, thinking it high time she attended to the ruling chieftain as closely as she did the local potter.

"Greetings," she called, shifting her gaze back to him and waving in a salute. "You must be the other local laird." She smiled, and a sparkle danced in her eyes.

Despite the mud streaks on her cheeks, that smile nearly bowled him backward as she offered him the same friendly appreciation she had bestowed on Magnus. The charming dimple that appeared in her rosy cheek accentuated the good-natured humor in her face.

Geddes didn't know what to make of her. Women didn't look at him with impersonal friendliness and appreciation. Nor did they refer to him as "the other local laird." Women behaved in a seductive or obsequious manner, depending on what they hoped to gain from him. He was known, after all, as the Rakehell of MacCallum.

He glanced at his men to see if they'd noticed. The four members of his garrison studied the meadow opposite and the wood behind him, as they should. But he didn't doubt they were listening to his exchange with the Englishwoman. By nightfall, every word he and the maid uttered would spread around Duntrune.

Geddes watched her as she fished for her spade in the burn and retrieved it, further wetting her skirts in the process. Seeming untroubled by her dripping garments, she hoisted a load of gray sludge aloft and waved it at him. "Look! I told you I would find the clay, and I did. Isn't it wonderful?"

Strictly speaking, she had not told him. She had told his tacksman, Dougal Dunardry, who had questioned both her and her young Scots escort last night, then told them to clear off. But here she was still. The hump of blanket reclining under yon tree was, he judged, her young escort. Not much protection just now, though by all accounts they'd been here all night. His wish to sleep might be understood.

As they had not obeyed Dunardry, he had decided that someone with more authority must send them on their way. He would do it now, whilst the young man, who was reportedly tall and muscular and might have been the reason for her resistance, slept on. "This was my grandsire's favorite place to fish. I dinna appreciate yer digging it up without my leave, Mistress Cavandish." He adopted a curt manner that most people found intimidating.

She dropped the gray chunk into her bucket, propped the spade against the bank, and shaded her eyes against the sun with one slim hand. "My apologies, but the Kilmartin laird said in his letter that this land was his. He gave me permission to dig, so I did."

His impatience dissolved, replaced by incredulity. "You exchanged letters with him?" The villain had written to her and said she might dig, so she had come? How naïve could she be? Worse yet, how naïve were the pair who served as her protectors?

She seemed to sense his concern. "Of course I exchanged letters with him. I first learned of the clay from Master Magnus, who had the local scrivener write to our mutual friend, Master Stone. Once I knew about the clay, naturally I sought the permission of the owner to dig. I wouldn't come all this way without his consent."

Geddes found the story odd. Why would Magnus, an untutored villager, write to a distant acquaintance he hadn't seen in years? He immediately suspected Kilmartin, knowing the permission he had granted would not be free. The sixty-year-old Master of Finch-arn had usurped MacCallum lands and tenants after killing his father in battle while Geddes had been away soldiering. Geddes had personally fought the wily old wolf and his men to regain Duntrune Castle. Now that he had reasserted his authority, he would have the Englishwoman understand what belonged to whom.

"That side belongs to Angus Kilmartin. This side is mine. If ye take clay from here"—he stabbed one finger at the bank where she dug—"ye mun have my permission first."

She turned her attention to where he pointed. "I do apologize for trespassing. I learned of the change in landowners yesterday, but truly, I thought it did not matter who owned it, since neither of you is interested in the clay. If you would but look at it, you would understand why 'tis critical that someone put it to use. Look how lovely it is." A dreamy expression transformed her features from attractive to beautiful. With her gaze locked on her heart's desire, she beckoned him with the spade.

Geddes had never had a reason to look at raw clay at all, let alone notice the match to this particular specimen. But her obvious fascination intrigued him.

Against his better judgment, he moved closer to study what appeared to be little more than mud.

"It took us half the night to uncover it," she said, caressing the pale gray muck with gentle fingertips, ignoring the fact that it was laced with tree roots and stones. "Because we took care not to erode the bank into the stream. We wouldn't want to dirty folks' water down the way." She shot him a glance, as if to see whether he appreciated her concern for the land.

He did, though he would rather she not dig at all.

"Have you ever seen the like?" She took a chunk of the clay in both hands, wet it with water from the burn, and began to roll it between her palms. Despite the mud beneath her short, pearly nails, Geddes realized she had the hands of an artist. They were lithe and clever, clearly accustomed to molding natural materials to her will.

He had always appreciated artistic skill, whether in males or females. Just because he lacked such skill himself didn't mean he couldn't enjoy it in others. Her clever hands were the perfect complement to the idealism shining in her eyes.

A pang of regret twisted through him as he remembered how he, too, had once been similarly idealistic, hoping to achieve the impossible, ardent in his efforts to convince his father to believe in his dreams. How painful when his tower of hope had come crashing down. If only hers did not have to do the same . . .

Geddes crushed the idea in midthought. Though he had won the fight with Kilmartin, his troubles were far from over, which made this location dangerous. He must not encourage the Englishwoman to stay. Not for any reason. Determined to distance himself, he concentrated on the gray muck.

"There are many kinds of clay," she said, sprinkling the chunk she held with more water and continuing to work it. "The finest is pure white kaolin. It isn't found in many places, nor did I expect to find it here. Besides, 'tis very soft and undesirable when shaping especially large pieces."

She glanced his way again, as if gauging his response. Seeming satisfied that she had his attention, she turned back to the clay. "There is also white clay, which is very pretty, but again, hard to find. What potters need and want is a reliable source of this." She displayed the chunk, which now held together in a cohesive roll instead of crumbling. "This is excellent clay. It has a splendid texture and is perfectly malleable. 'Tis greatly coveted by those who make and sell pottery."

Geddes moved closer. He was unimpressed by the clay, but the graceful swell of he bosom, rising and falling with excitement beneath her brown bodice, drew him against his will. The luminous flesh of her face and throat glowed with vitality. Her enthusiasm warmed him in a way he hadn't expected.

He felt like a freezing man who had just stumbled upon a magical fire burning in the wilderness.

Leaning over the bank, he allowed himself to absorb her warmth. It was rare to meet someone in Duntrune with such a zeal for life. As he stared, transfixed, she caressed the clay, and he recognized the nature of that touch. It had all the reverence of a lover caught in the throes of a passion that consumed her. Her fingers trembled slightly, and he sensed the excitement in her, quivering just beneath the surface. She couldn't wait to make this clay hers.

He also recognized that he was becoming aroused. Perhaps it was not surprising. He hadn't had a woman since returning to Duntrune. He'd been too busy fighting battles. Small wonder that he enjoyed the sight of an engaging female.

The Englishwoman tilted up her face and offered him an angelic smile, totally oblivious to the lustful direction of his thoughts. " 'Tis some of the best clay in the country you have here. You possess a treasure, sir." She beamed up at him with a joy that was contagious.

That smile was undoubtedly what had allowed her to travel safely across the whole of England and half of Scotland. When confronted by her innocent, trusting air, people probably found it difficult to disappoint her expectations.

"Do I possess it, or do ye?" he asked wryly, forcing himself back to reality. He glanced at the barrel into which her associates had packed the clay between layers of damp hemp.

She had the grace to duck her head in seeming embarrassment. "I do beg your pardon, sir. As I said, I heard of the change in property ownership after I arrived and meant to speak to you, but I was so excited about the clay, I didn't. I cannot wait to put it on a wheel. 'Twill make a glorious vase. Or perhaps a beautiful bowl, depending on what you prefer. Just wait till you see." She smiled at him, radiating exuberance. "I promise not to be avaricious. I'll share the clay with you, pay you for it in coin, or trade finished goods for the raw material. Anything you like."

The offer was interesting. Given his reputation, the proposals he had received from females since returning to Duntrune were of an entirely different nature. "Anything I like?" he asked, filling the words with innuendo to test her.

A color like the blushing dawn suffused her cheeks.

"Anything as it relates to clay or clay objects," she amended, refusing to simper or break their eye contact. "My work is exceptional, I assure you. If you will allow me to set up a pottery wheel, I will demonstrate my skill. All I need is a reliable water source, a stout table on which to prepare a sample of the clay, and a shed to shelter my equipment and materials. After you see the results, you can decide."

This woman was definitely an exception to the rule. Rather than trying to ingratiate herself into his good graces, rather than offering him her body, she offered him clay vessels.

The change was refreshing. Still, there were problems.

"Mistress Cavandish," he said, "ye dinna seem to comprehend, though Dunardry tried to warn ye. Ye canna dig here."

"If Kilmartin doesn't mind, why should you? He said he did not yesterday morn, after I'd been his guest for the night. Nor did he think you would mind." Happily she pried out more clay and dumped it into a waiting bucket.

Nonplussed Geddes shifted on his feet. Dunardry hadn't mentioned this. "You stayed the night as the guest of the Kilmartin?" His enemy minded everything, including his neighbor's business. If he said he didn't, he was lying. Until recently, the Kilmartin and his men had occupied Duntrune Castle. "He said he didn't mind your digging for clay on"—he cleared his throat to emphasize the last words—"his land? Those were his exact words?"

She paused and tapped her rosebud lips with one finger, thinking. Her gesture soiled her chin anew with clay. On most people it would have looked absurd, but it lent her a disarming air.

"I don't suppose those were his exact words," she admitted. "A rather depressing gentleman, is Master Kilmartin. He keeps a gloomy hall. If he would but clean the windows, the light might shine in and make the chamber more cheerful, but I suppose his ill health prevents interest in cleaning. Perhaps a difficult life has also given him a gloomy nature. At any rate, I believe his exact words were 'I dinna give a braw damn fer it, nor does the MacCallum. Dig away.' "

Her amusing imitation of a man whom Geddes knew to be a cutthroat villain didn't reassure him of her good judgment. The response was typical of Kilmartin, though, especially since the bank she dug in was on the disputed MacCallum side. "He didn't frighten ye?"

"Good heavens no, sir. I'm sure he can be a daunting enemy. Given what I've heard, I revised my first estimate of his character. On arrival, I thought him sly and untrustworthy. When I later learned he killed your father in battle, usurped your land, and fought to keep it when you returned, I concluded he is also violent and covetous. But I was no threat to him, so he was little more than gruff toward me. I wanted nothing he valued, nor do I have anything of value to him. I ascertained that before I accepted his invitation to stay the night at Castle Fincharn."

Perhaps she wasn't so naïve, Geddes thought, surprised by how well she had summed up Kilmartin's character after such short acquaintance. She was also correct in stating that she had nothing the neighboring laird valued. Except for one thing. He wondered why it hadn't occurred to her that Kilmartin might value her virtue and decide to relieve her of it.

Apparently, she hadn't thought of that. Nor had

Kilmartin, though perhaps he had been too confounded by this wee bit of a lassie marching up to his hall and claiming the right to dig in the burn.

Perversely, Geddes wished she'd come months earlier, when a pitched battle had raged between his and the Kilmartin's forces to reclaim his heritage so rudely usurped by the neighboring clan. That would have frightened her away. Now she saw nothing except the clear boundaries that he had reestablished with great effort.

"Do we have an agreement?" she urged.

He snapped his wandering attention back to her. "I wasna aware we were discussing one."

"I dig the clay. You share in equal parts as you wish."

"The only bargain I want is you out o' that water. You're playing with fire."

She smiled up at him. "I would appreciate a fire. This water is chill," she said with cheerful aplomb, concentrating on wedging her spade into the gray clay. She looked the picture of health, her cheeks rosy from the exercise of digging. Her gracefully arched eyebrows framed inquisitive eyes, from which she shot him an inquiring glance.

Geddes swore beneath his breath. He shouldn't get involved with her, yet she was in a vulnerable position. "Ye canna stay here, digging another night away," he said.

"I'll take that as an invitation to stay the night at your castle. My thanks. I'll join you there as soon as I finish." She gazed affectionately at the clay bank and patted the bottom layer, not seeming to notice the twisting of tree roots snaking through it. "I should take only what I can use straightaway. I'll save the rest for later." She raised a last chunk to the man she called Master Stone, who reverently accepted it with his bare hands and stumped off to pack it between layers of damp hemp.

Geddes wrestled with the dilemma. If he brought her to Duntrune, she would consider it permission to stay as long as she wished, which he had no intention of permitting. She must return home as soon as he could arrange for her to travel with a safe escort.

On the other hand, she would be safer with him for the time being than with the Kilmartin. The old badger had some trick up his sleeve, writing to her and encouraging her to dig in the burn.

"Why the devil did ye come all this way for clay?" he couldn't resist asking.

She looked up, surprise written all over her expressive face. "Didn't your man tell you? Master, er . . ." She trailed off, as if uncertain of the name.

"Dunardry."

"Yes, pray forgive me. I have difficulty with Scots names. So many of them start with Mac or, around here, Dun, and I get them confused. But yes, Master Dunaudley." She pronounced it wrong with charming surety, at the same time incorrectly raising Geddes's relative several levels by adding the English title of master. "I told him to say that you have the finest bed of clay in all of Christendom, and I'm going to make it into the most splendid pottery this part of the country has ever seen. I'll take on apprentices, especially female, and we'll turn this into a vigorous trade center. The women in the village could use a decent form of employment. The local economy will improve. Buyers will obtain high-quality vessels for everyday and special uses. Everyone will benefit."

Geddes swore some more and turned away abruptly.

Workshops for females? Benefits to the economy? She'd come the length of two countries into dangerous territory with the vain hope of starting a business? This woman was as daft as they came.

"Be at Duntrune Castle within the hour," he ordered brusquely, overcome with distaste by the prospect of having to shatter her dreams. "My servants will see you to a chamber where you can wash and change into dry clothing."

Without another word, he strode away.

She was not in danger at the moment, but it wouldn't last. He had more men patrolling the area for Kilmartins. Numerous sightings had been made. Little wonder. The MacCallums and the Kilmartins had been feuding for half a century. The old man at Castle Fincharn wouldn't give up now. He would do anything to injure his enemy, which made her a perfect target if Angus Kilmartin believed her under MacCallum protection. Nor could her two escorts, the one an old potter, the other a young lad snoring under the tree, be of much use.

Someone had to protect her, and Geddes knew the Kilmartin wouldn't do it. If she stayed at Castle Fincharn, his enemy would take advantage of her in some unsavory manner.

Then Geddes remembered his reputation. Was he better suited than the Kilmartin to shelter her?

Hell, yes, he decided after the barest consideration. She would be safer with him. And unlike the Kilmartin, he would give her all the clay she could carry. She could take it back to England when he packed her up and sent her on her way.

He was sorry her hopes were doomed, but he was better equipped than the Kilmartin to tell her so. After all, he knew what it meant to look into the future and see nothing but a hopeless, empty path. He would let her down gently.

He was definitely a better choice than Angus Kilmartin.

Chapter 2

She had met a rakehell at last. How interesting.

Curiosity about the man called Geddes MacCallum teased Angelica Cavandish as she watched him stride away, his dark plaid kilt swinging around his knees. He had extremely well built legs, bound though they were by Highland legwear—strips of leather wrapped around cloth. In truth, all of him was well put together, especially his classically chiseled features and sapphire eyes that suggested a quick intelligence and forthright nature.

Angelica cataloged the information for later review. Since Geddes MacCallum owned the land that held her clay, she must make a study of him. Her eldest sister, Rozalinde, with her years of experience in the family textile trade, had taught her to handle people with care in matters of business.

"Study your prospects well," her sister had advised. "Discover what they need; then see if you can provide it in exchange for what you want. Your chance of success increases with this approach."

It sounded simple, yet Angelica knew a difficult task lay before her. She must win the MacCallum chieftain to her way of thinking so she could continue to dig clay and set up her pottery.

She gripped her spade, determined to persevere. She could never have her own business back home in Dorset or anywhere else in England. English guilds did not accept women, especially not gentlewomen. Nor did Scottish guilds, most likely, but she had gambled on the fact that this land lay far from cities and towns where the guilds were. The local chieftains were the law here. If she could discover what Geddes Mac-Callum needed that only she could supply, she would succeed.

Unfortunately, they had gotten off to a bad start. She sighed, sorry for her ill fortune but unable to change it. The Master of Fincharn had written, saying the land was his. Believing him, she had come to Scotland. How could she know he had just lost the land in a clan war? He had lied to her, plain and simple, for some reason she couldn't understand.

So she should have asked the MacCallum chieftain's permission. He had a right to be angry, to find her digging on his property without so much as a by-your-leave. She had been too eager to find the clay.

Once again, her impetuous nature had gotten her into trouble.

Except that Angus Kilmartin had played on her eagerness. He had told her the MacCallum wouldn't care. Mayhap he had even believed this was true.

Fortunately for her, the MacCallum laird was willing to discuss her use of the clay. That meant he was a reasonable man. She added the trait to the list she had compiled in her head, ticking them off one by one.

Intelligent.

Possessive of his land.

Reasonable, except perhaps when unduly opposed.

A rescuer of children.

A rakehell.

The last item she had heard from Angus Kilmartin. Although Kilmartin's lie about the land turned him into an unreliable source of information, others had reinforced the idea since she arrived. A serving maid at Castle Fincharn, the stable lad, and her friend Magnus had all said that Geddes MacCallum seduced women by the score. True, he had been away for some years, but half a dozen youngsters in the vicinity were said to claim him as father, a visible reminder of his past carousing. He was set in his dissolute habits, and they had warned her to beware.

Angelica pushed back her knot of heavy hair and began to clean her spade. Despite the warnings, she had sensed no danger. The MacCallum chieftain hadn't seemed inclined to seduce her. He hadn't even looked at her in an unacceptable manner. That seemed promising. She would move forward with her plan to reap the clay.

Angelica stroked the damp material, remembering the moment when she had crossed into Scotland. She had fallen in love with this wild, beautiful country. Its rugged peaks and shadowy green glens, its glittering lochs bordered by bee-loud meadows enchanted her, but none held as much allure as this chuckling stream with the rich cache of treasure buried in its bank.

How she loved the clay's raw texture beneath her fingertips. Visions of the wondrous vessels she would make arose in her mind. Tall, graceful vases that belled from pedestal feet, soaring to symmetrical rims. Great bowls that bloomed beneath her hands as she shaped them, like flowers opening to the sun.

Her own source of clay. Her own workshop. The right to sell her wares where she would. These were her goals. She would focus all her skill on convincing

Geddes MacCallum that she was the person to develop the resource he held.

At the same time, she thanked heaven that her future no longer lay in the hands of Angus Kilmartin. A good thing, that. Given the choice, Angelica would do business with a rakehell rather than a liar any day.

She paused, wondering how she had come to such a conclusion. She had known liars in her life, but never a rakehell. Her sister and mother had refused to allow her near the ones at Queen Elizabeth's court, and there hadn't been any in Dorset, where she grew up. Dorset had been a quiet place, the men boring. Praise heaven that Master Jacob Stone had taught her to work with clay.

When she was ten, pottery had seemed like a new kind of play, but by fourteen, she had seen it through new eyes. She had set her heart on making it her life's work. But once she had found it, the few men she had fancied disapproved of her aspirations. One, in particular, had let her down.

Against her will, Angelica recalled that day some five years ago, just hours before the banns announcing their marriage were to be called. In a special gown, with a special flutter in her heart, she had met James Selbourne for a last romantic tryst before their love was announced to all.

He'd been seated beside the spring, waiting for her. His blond hair shone in the early morning sun; his smile was winning, as always.

"I've made a special cup for us," she'd said, dipping water from the spring and holding it out to him. She had fashioned it especially for this day. "A loving cup with two handles and two spouts. One for each."

It hadn't worked as well as she'd hoped. As they

had struggled to drink from it together, the handle she held broke off.

"Never mind," she had said with a laugh. "I'll make a new one, better designed than this."

"Then you'd best hurry." He'd checked the sun. "We are but hours from church."

"I'll make it after church." She had smiled up at him, loving him so, ready to forget the cup and concentrate on his kisses.

But his expression had changed. "That you'll not. No wife of mine shall labor like a peasant. Once the banns are cried, you will give up this nonsense and concentrate on our life together."

She had stared at him, stunned. "Making pottery is not labor. Or 'tis a labor of love."

"It is work, and my wife shall not work," he had said firmly. "Besides, you will soon be too busy tending our children and keeping our home." He smiled indulgently and slid an arm around her waist, pulling her near. "I know you fancy it, love, but you'll forget it, especially once you have my son in your arms." He had bent to kiss her.

Angelica had pulled away, rage flowing through her like a swarm of wasps. "I do not intend to forget it. 'Tis my life's work."

His face had clouded. She had never seen him angry, and it transformed him. Gone was the sunny smile, the good humor. In their place, a stubborn, inflexible expression reigned. "My wife shall not work at a dirty, grubby occupation, and there's an end to it. Not as long as I have two shillings to rub together. What would the neighbors say?"

"Hang the neighbors, James," she had cried, wanting to sob. "This is you and me, and you want to see me happy, do you not? I cannot give up working with clay."

"Clay does not make you happy, Angelica. 'Tis a childish pastime, left over from your youth. I'm older than you and understand such things. As your husband, you must let me guide you."

Looking back on her pain, Angelica couldn't think why she'd ever believed herself in love with James. She'd thought he cherished her, clay and all. Now she knew he'd never understood her, never supported her dreams. She had been a fool not to talk to him about them from the first.

Nor could she think why he had believed he loved her, if he disliked her working with clay. Could it have been her sister's marriage to an earl and her brothers' titles that had attracted him? Could it have been her connections and her dowry, not her?

Whatever it was, he had refused to yield on what he termed "her foolishness," and she had broken the betrothal. She would not make such a mistake again. In truth, she did not think the man existed who approved of her making pottery, except for Masters Stone and Magnus.

So be it. She would keep company with old men who shared her enthusiasm. With little time left on this earth, they understood the necessity of pursuing the heart's desire.

Seeing things in such a light, she puzzled over why women succumbed to a man like Geddes MacCallum. What could illicit passions of the flesh offer that passion for her craft could not? Her skill put bread and meat on the table, as well as satisfaction in her soul. Her success was her own, owed to no one.

As far as she could see, a woman gained nothing

from a liaison with a rakehell and risked everything. What was the attraction?

True, Geddes MacCallum was pleasant to look upon, wrapped in that exotic wool kilt, with his length of plaid shot through with thin bands of pale blue, red, and yellow and pinned across his broad chest. He had kindly rescued the child, Jamie, then agreed to let her stay the night at Duntrune Castle. But in his presence, she had felt no overwhelming urge to beg him to ravish her.

It mystified her that other women did. How did a rakehell inspire such feelings in females?

"Mistress Cavandish, are you not freezing in that cold water? Let me take a turn."

Angelica was jolted back to the present to see the wizened face of her teacher smiling down at her. Years ago she had convinced Master Stone to take her on as his "apprentice." Since he'd been too old to work, his workshop operated by his son, he had had the time.

At once, he'd agreed to coach her in earnest. Each day she had bloomed under his tutelage, refining her ability to prepare the clay, shape it on the pottery wheel, mix glazes, and fire her ware in the kiln dug in the hillside behind the workshop. His friendship was ever dear to her.

"No need for you to take a turn. I believe we have enough clay for now." She slogged through the knee-deep water and clambered up the bank to grasp the gnarled hand he offered. "I must go to the castle so I can coax his lordship to let me continue digging. Since he agreed to shelter us for the night, I expect I'll be able to convince him. He seems reasonable."

"Reasonably interested in you as a female." Iain came to life as she wrung out the hem of her wet skirts. He

threw off his blanket, straightened to his full height, and
sauntered over. Though a mere eighteen years of age,
he was an imposing figure, well schooled in fighting by
his half brother Drummond Graham, as well as by his
clan chieftain, Alex Graham. "You'd best have a care
with that one." Iain nodded toward the trees where the
MacCallum chieftain had disappeared.

"You were asleep. What do you know?" Feeling
serene, Angelica sat on the grass to clean and dry her
feet. She appreciated the fact that her brother-in-law,
Alex, had asked Iain to accompany her north. Though
he was gloomy at times, like now, his stalwart presence and friendly courtesy were definite assets. Her
sister Lucina said he'd once actually been jovial and
full of fun, but a ruined romance had changed him.
What a shock to hear the lad had fallen in love with
his own half sister before learning his mistake. "I'm
sorry you had such a terrible experience with love,"
she said, pulling on her stockings, then her shoes. "But
no parallels exist here."

"I am not referring to my own experience." Iain
raked his fingers through his red hair, which was tousled from his nap under the tree. "I saw how he
looked at you. Men understand each other, ye ken."

"Heed 'im. Heed 'im. Best watch yer step with the
MacCallum," Magnus the Potter urged, stumping up
to stand beside Master Stone and Iain. Little Jamie
trailed after him, keeping a respectful distance from
the edge of the bank. "He's a canny one with the
lasses," Magnus said. "Casts a spell over 'em, they
say. Holds 'em in his thrall so that he can pluck
their virtue."

"There. You see, Angel," Iain persisted. "I promised your sister no harm would come to you, and I
intend to keep my word."

Angelica surveyed her three guardians—Master
Stone with his solemn expression, Magnus looking as
if he were predicting doom, and Iain, his youthful
forehead puckered with concern. She wanted to laugh
in their gloomy faces. They had found the most wondrous resource in the world, and they were foretelling
the world's end. "I'm interested in his clay, not him,"
she insisted, "except for the fact the clay is on his side
of the stream."

Magnus's thick salt-and-pepper eyebrows met as he
frowned. "They've feuded fer fifty years over that
land, the MacCallums and the Kilmartins."

"Which do you prefer as chieftain? MacCallum or
Kilmartin?" She grasped the chance to change the
subject. The dismal party trailed after her as she
packed her spade on the cart and checked the clay a
last time, tucking the hemp around it more tightly.

"I've lived in the village o' Duntrune all my life,"
Magnus grunted. "We're MacCallum folk, but it hasna
been easy. These last years were the worst, after the
Kilmartin killed our chieftain, then helped himsel' to
our home. I'm glad tae see the tail end o' him. The
MacCallum is more civilized, if ye take ma meanin'.
Ye saw it yersel'. He didna throw ye off his land."

"Of course he didn't. I offered any terms he likes
for the clay. We shall all share in it equally, of course,"
she added, gazing at him with gratitude. "Thank you
ever so much for your aid in finding it. When your
letter to Master Stone arrived, 'twas like a gift from
above. Nowhere in Dorset could I claim my own
source of good clay. It all belongs to men who laughed
at me, a weak and inferior woman."

"Ye're no' weak from the look o' ye," Magnus said,
missing the irony in her voice as he eyed the barrelful
of clay she had helped dig. "An' yer comin' is a

blessin' to me, mistress. I've wanted to dig that clay fer an age, but I couldna do it alone. Ye're brass bold, ye are."

"That she is," Iain chimed in. "I traveled with her. Never sick on the ship or whining about the discomfort, like most females."

"Is that what I am? Brass bold?" Angelica liked the idea. The clay had sat here in the stream bank for centuries. No one had cared to dig it from the disputed territory over which wars had been fought. Didn't that all but guarantee it would be hers?

"Aye, ye're brass bold to come all this way," Magnus said. " 'Tis a valuable trait to have now that ye've angered the Kilmartin. Though ye'll have the MacCallum's protection, ye're to watch yer back."

Iain's face tightened with concern. "By the saints, I was so busy watching the MacCallum take in your charms, I didna think o' that. We canna stay at Duntrune."

Angelica puzzled over this. "But we must, for I want his clay. And why have I angered the Kilmartin?"

"Ye were on his side of the argument afore," Iain said with conviction. "Now ye're on the MacCallum side."

"But I'm not on any side in the argument," she protested, feeling faintly alarmed. "I don't know a thing about who has the most valid claim to the land. I'm neutral in the matter."

Iain gestured in exasperation. "Explain the way of the Scots to her, Magnus. Mayhap she'll listen to you."

Magnus shook his gray head ponderously.

Iain mirrored the motion, looking remarkably like the old man, though he was five decades younger.

"If ye stay at Duntrune Castle, ye're fer the Mac-

Callum side o' the argument," Magnus intoned. "That's our way. Kilmartin will want revenge."

Angelica's stomach tightened with discomfort. Surely this couldn't be right. The Kilmartin seemed too old and ill to spend his time trying to kill visiting maidens. Yet he had fought a fierce battle against the MacCallum clan only months ago, and had bested the former MacCallum chieftain in battle before that. Appearances must be deceiving. Still, she hoped . . . "The Kilmartin is not in full health, from the look of him," she pointed out. "Perhaps he hasn't the strength to take revenge on me, if he even wishes to."

Magnus stepped between the traces of the cart, prepared to trundle it away. "Ill or in health, he's a force to reckon wi', an' dinna forget it. Enough jawin', now. We'd best move this clay." He lifted the traces of the cart. "And mistress, ye're to use my workshop and my pottery wheels. There's nay need to depend on the laird."

"Truly, Master Magnus, I could not impose on your son. His work requires the entire workshop space now." Angelica knew that Magnus lived with his married son, who'd had no skill with clay and instead transformed the pottery into a woodwright's shop.

The old man tugged up his trews with one hand and sighed at her words. "Guess I'm livin' in the past."

"But I will want use of your pottery wheels. As soon as I can find a place, perhaps we can move them to it. Then you can work with us all you wish." She felt a glow of pleasure as hope lit up his eyes. "Your experience with the local fuels for firings and the use of your kiln will be most welcome. Believe me, as soon as I establish a place, we will be eager for you to join us."

His expression of hope faded, to be replaced by skepticism. Obviously he did not believe her likely to find a place. Despite his praise for her boldness, he did not think the MacCallum would grant her wish.

Angelica knew better. Other women might be held spellbound by the handsome chieftain, but she intended to use her full powers of persuasion to get her way. If he tried to seduce her, she would not succumb. She was single-mindedly devoted to the clay, and when she wanted something related to clay, she generally got it.

True, people had attempted to discourage her ambitions. Her mother had tried to shame her out of the desire, insisting that life as a master potter was inappropriate for a gently born lady. Her sister Rozalinde had tried issuing tempting offers to Angelica to join the family textile trade.

"What makes textiles more suitable for a woman than pottery?" Angelica had argued.

"Making pottery is so . . ." Rozalinde had hesitated, searching for the right word.

"Dirty," Angelica had finished for her. "Everyone thinks so save me."

She looked down at her kirtle skirt, the hem of which was soiled from dragging up the side of the bank. It wasn't as if she were entirely covered with clay. Nothing that a session with a washbasin couldn't cure. But perhaps the MacCallum didn't care for a woman who dabbled in clay. Had her interest protected her from his lustful nature?

Gingerly, she touched her face and realized it was streaked with clay from her toils. She must look like a wild Indian from the Americas.

A sudden urge to laugh seized her. She knew little

of rakehells, but if this one found clay unappealing, perhaps she should coat herself with it and stay that way.

But meeting the MacCallum *had* proved a theory of hers. A rakehell outside the bedchamber was the same as any other man: demanding and cross when one didn't obey, and always expecting to be in charge.

Yes, her work with the MacCallum was cut out for her, but Angus Kilmartin was an entirely different matter. If Iain and Magnus spoke truly, she had made an enemy, and Rozalinde had taught her that enemies complicated things. Had she been right to come here?

For the first time since arriving in Scotland, Angelica felt a tiny twinge of doubt.

Chapter 3

Geddes returned to Duntrune Castle, preoccupied by his latest problem. A stubborn, outspoken, clay-streaked problem it was, too. Not to mention most tantalizingly female.

He admitted that the clay hadn't detracted in the least from Angel Cavandish's attractive face, nor from her enticing legs revealed by tucked-up skirts. Then there had been the way her bodice outlined her swan-white throat and led the eye down to the tantalizing swell of her breasts.

Heat pooled in his groin at the memory, and a haze threatened to settle on his brain.

Concentrate on the problem at hand, he warned himself. She must depart from Duntrune.

What had Dunardry said of her? She came from a merchant family of comfortable means? Well, then, her family would take her back again.

Her sister, the wife of a Border Scot, had arranged for her to sail to MacCallum land on one of King James's ships, bound for the island of Jura. That spoke of high connections. Fine. Geddes would see that the same ship escorted her in the opposite direction. He needed his men to fight off Kilmartin attacks. They could not be spared for an extended journey south.

He refused to dwell on her marital status. Unwed and unafraid to travel with naught but an aged potter and a young Scot for escort. Outrageous.

He lingered over the last detail. She was called Angel by those who knew her. A fitting name, as something of the angelic certainly lurked in her smile.

That smile had stirred something in him: memories of long summer days when he was a boy, wading in that same sparkling burn, chasing frogs and catching fish. Free of his oppressive parents, he had basked in the sunshine, reveling in the pleasure of being young and alive.

Two decades later, the sight of the muddy angel splashing in the water had reawakened feelings from that idyllic time. Fair memories added pleasure to today's fair vision. Like a water selkie, she'd blended with the lush meadow and the whispering trees of the nearby glen. Droplets of water had sparkled like crystals on her flesh, a fitting adornment for a magical female who valued clay above all else. She was like a gleam of hope, sparkling in the burn.

For one impossible moment, he'd believed anything might be possible.

Then he'd remembered. He was fresh from the battlefield. Several clansmen were just recovering from wounds and one had died. How could he even imagine that peace was possible?

Just as he had once learned about the bitter side of life, so must Angel Cavandish. He was sorry. He wished to spare her the pain. But she must give up her dreams and return to England. The land where her coveted clay resided would always be in dispute.

As he entered the castle gate, he spied his seventeen-year-old sister, Lilias, whispering to one of his men—a clansman who had been posted at the burn. Word of the Englishwoman's presence would be everywhere by nightfall. His name would be linked with hers.

Scowling, he stalked toward Lilias, but she spotted him and raced off. The guard slunk away.

Annoyed by the inescapable gossip, Geddes strode into the kitchens. Five off-duty men lounged around the huge hearth. At his appearance, they snapped to attention. He motioned for them to sit again, his attention trained on Muriel McCloud, who had been cook and housekeeper ever since he could remember. "Lay the high table for four tonight. We have guests," he said.

Muriel planted both hands on her ample, black-clad hips. "Dirt in my clean kitchens," she accused, thrusting a forefinger at the offending footprints he had tracked across the stone floor. Grasping her mop, which was never far away, she attacked the insult dealt to her pristine territory.

Suppressing the urge to chuckle, Geddes feigned annoyance and sank onto a stool vacated by one of his men.

"Ye tracked dirt in my clean kitchen as a lad, and ye do it still, though ye be chieftain," Muriel muttered as she mopped. "Dirt is the enemy of the Lord, though ye never listened to me."

Geddes ignored her. She was asking in a roundabout way for him to remove his boots, as the others had. A few of them ducked their heads with chagrin as he eyed their stockinged feet. They must bow to Muriel's edict of no dirty footwear in her kitchens, but as chieftain, he did not.

He had laid down the law on his first day home. Though he disliked playing the tyrant, his kin had been impossible to rouse upon his return. They had been living in caves, unwilling to oust the Kilmartin from Duntrune because they lacked the Faerie Flag. The blasted family relic supposedly had magical powers, ensuring victory to those who carried it into battle. But it had disappeared a good fifty years ago.

Geddes cared nothing for the flag. He believed in himself, not a scrap of tattered cloth. But the clan, what was left of it, swore by the ancient relic. They left him no choice. He had demanded they follow the rules set down by his father, and by his grandsire before him.

Obey the chieftain without question.

Fight when and where decreed.

Never meddle in the chieftain's private affairs.

Geddes didn't like the last edict. It distanced the chieftain from the bonds of affection with his kindred, but that had been his father's intent. Euan MacCallum had lived for his whores and his hounds, in that order, so the rule had served him well.

Despite this, Geddes let the rule stand. He had his own reasons for keeping to himself.

"One is a female guest, I hear, MacCallum," Muriel persisted as she mopped and remopped the floor. "What sort o' female would that be, in these parts?" She sounded suspicious, as if Geddes were bringing a harlot to dine.

"An English gentlewoman is visiting Duntrune with her Scots escort. She will keep company with my sister." He sent her a threatening glance. She was walking the edge of one of his rules.

Muriel perceived his displeasure and altered her tone. "Ye surprised me, 'tis all." She put away her mop and bustled over to motion for Ross, the new kitchen lad, to turn the spit more slowly. "The Lady

Lilias dinna seem to be suffering for company o' her own kind."

"Has she been out again at night?" he demanded, concerned by the hint.

"That I doubt, since ye locked her in her chamber after her last midnight foray. But she's languishin' fer someone, and 'tis no one to yer likin', or she'd tell ye of him." Satisfied with Ross's speed, Muriel grumped and grunted her way to her cutting board and sliced into a heap of onions, leaving Geddes to wonder.

His sister had changed a good deal since he'd seen her last. No longer a silent child with huge dark eyes, she was a woman, with a woman's interests and a woman's needs. It was his duty as chieftain to guide her into matrimony. But how could he, if she refused to discuss the subject?

Her very refusal suggested that Muriel was right: Lilias had something to hide. Two nights running, she had slipped into the castle after midnight. He'd confronted her, demanding to know if she'd been trysting with a lover. Her stubborn silence in the face of his questioning convinced him she had. So he'd locked her in her chamber the next night. He'd let her out come morning, but she had refused to speak to him that entire day. Still, as he'd seen no evidence of midnight wandering since, he hoped she understood his message. She could not meet with some ruffian behind his back. He would see her wooed in a proper manner or not at all.

"Rhuri, take a man to Fincharn to fetch Mistress Cavandish's things," he ordered, determined to get on with his task of protecting the Englishwoman until he could see her gone.

Rhuri Dunardley, his war captain, winced. "Er, now, MacCallum?"

Geddes stared down his nose at his second cousin, who sat on a stool lower than his own. He knew that morale in the garrison wavered. "Aye, now," he ordered, incensed that his men believed more in a scrap of cloth than in their own fighting skills. "Take a dozen men if ye like, but dinna let the Kilmartins ken ye're afraid."

Rhuri unfolded his considerable height from the stool and stood at attention. Tallest of the garrison, he had to duck his head to pass through most doorways. "With all respect, MacCallum, I dinna trust the Kilmartin. Face-to-face, he'd cut me down."

Geddes hated acting the imperious laird, but when his men showed misgivings, they drove him to it. "I dinna ask ye to offer yourself as a sacrifice, ye bampot. Give a message to the first Kilmartin you see. Order her things brought to the new boundary I established between our lands."

"Aye, MacCallum." Rhuri bowed hastily and backed away, clearly unsettled by his error.

Geddes turned back to the fire, depressed. He drew out his dirk and began to sharpen it on the cook's oiled whetstone. The scrape of steel against stone honed his foul mood. Before Geddes had left seven years ago, Rhuri had been one of the most stout-hearted warriors of the garrison. Now even he stumbled into stupidity.

As Rhuri left the kitchens, he collided with Lilias, who swore in a most unladylike manner and swatted him away.

"Yer pardon, my lady," Rhuri apologized.

"Great lunkhead." Lilias flounced into the kitchens as Rhuri departed. "Och, the whisper is all over, brother mine." She sidled up to him, not troubling to lower her voice. "'Tis said ye're hot for a new lass."

He frowned at her. Her luxurious black hair, falling in a wild tangle about her face, hadn't seen a brush in days. Despite that, her pouting red lips and willowy frame rendered her far too sexually appealing for her own good.

Why had he let her return to Duntrune? Her virtue had been safer under their aunt and uncle's rigid supervision at Inveraray, where their father had sent her before his death. In the strictly devout household, Lilias would have been forced to spend her days in prayer. When she had written, begging to come home, Geddes had agreed. But instead of behaving like the obedient child he'd known, she defied him at every turn. Now she imagined herself in love with some lad.

"That means aye," she accused, pouncing on his silence.

"Dinna bait me, Lilias." He grasped her arm and thunked her down on Rhuri's vacated stool before the fire. Remembering Muriel's hint, he resolved to question her again.

Sensing a quarrel in the offing, his men retreated to the far end of the kitchens to finish their ale and tease the kitchen maids.

"I took pity and brought you home," Geddes began, frustrated by his inability to break through Lilias's reserve. "And how do you repay me?"

"If your idea of pity is locking me in my chamber, I am indeed in luck that you've returned, brother mine," she said acidly. "I ken it well, so dinna threaten me with return to Inveraray to get your way. I'll be civil to your new doxy."

At her taunt, he applied the dirk to the whetstone with savage intensity.

She held up both hands. "Dinna tell me she's no' your doxy," she mocked, recalling the denial he'd flung at her yesterday when she had accused him of lusting after a village lass. "But she will be. I know you of old."

Geddes clashed stone against steel as she wrinkled her nose at him. He hated her goading, yet Lilias refused to leave off. She hadn't been this way when they were young. Her behavior puzzled him. "Is that what you told Georgie Dunaudley in the yard?" He looked up from his sharpening.

"Oh, aye." She toyed with her skirts, smiling a crafty smile. "That and more."

Geddes subdued the urge to throttle her. "Stop it, Lilias." He slapped the stone on the hearth and thrust his dirk into its sheath. "You're doing this to hide who you met the other night. 'Tis no use. I'll find out who it is, so you might as well confess."

At the mention of her midnight trysting, Lilias glowered at the fire, refusing to meet his gaze. "You dinna care what I do."

Geddes smoldered inside. He'd never had to play the role of parent, nor had their parents set good examples of how it should be done. His father had kept his children at arm's length, seeing them only at table. There, he'd clouted them for misbehavior and otherwise ignored them. Ingiborg, his disappointed, deeply religious mother, had spent her days in embroidery and prayer, consigning her children to the care of a nurse.

But Geddes was determined to care for Lilias, with or without good examples. And just now, his sister had all but admitted that someone did interest her. He pounced on the hint. "Lilias, if you're mooning over the wheelwright's son, you're to stop, for he's betrothed to the shoemaker's lass. 'Tis fitting, as he got her with child."

"Och, so the pot's callin' the kettle black," Lilias flung at him. "How many bastards did you spawn, yet you've no' visited a one since your return."

"I've been fighting a war, in case you didna notice." He hated the reference to his neglected duty. "They've had to wait."

Lilias smirked. "Ever a MacCallum. Battle comes first, people, a distant second. You havena changed one jot, brother mine."

"Battle *must* come first when your home is usurped. What would you have me do? Hide in the library with you, sketching plants?"

She stared into the fire. "Father mocked my love of drawing, too." Her gaze seemed fixed on the distant past. "He never saw what I wanted. 'Do yer duty to ycr clan.' 'Twas all he knew how to say."

As she muttered the phrase that had fallen so often from their father's lips, Geddes recoiled. Unwelcome memories sluiced through him.

The clan was all. Except for the chieftain, the individual had no rights in the face of clan needs. Not even if what one wanted was for the good of the clan. Not if it broke with tradition.

His last, terrible quarrel with his father on this very subject had obliterated any wish to remain in Duntrune. With his dreams in tatters, he had fled, swearing never to return. But now, with his father dead, he must take his place and fight the interminable clan wars. If he wanted a home, he had no choice.

But he could do one thing differently: He could protect his sister from a disastrous marriage such as his mother had made. She need not become a broken spirit, incapable of caring for anyone, going about her few activities without a shred of zeal.

"I'm no' mocking you." He attempted a gentler

tone. " 'Tis just that I'm no' our father. Dinna compare me to him."

"Nay? He liked a doxy or two. As do you."

By Saint Columba, the lass would drive him mad. "You evade the question, Lilias. Who is this lad?"

"Well . . ." Lilias flashed him a sly glance and drew out her answer. " 'Tis no' the wheelwright's son. He kisses like a sloppy pup."

"He kissed you whilst he was involved with the shoemaker's daughter?" he demanded.

"Nay, but the lass talks, ye ken," she snarled, seeming glad to catch him in an unwarranted suspicion. "And why should I no' listen to what she says?"

He despaired. What was he to do? He understood little of Lilias. He'd been twelve when she was born and had seen little of her, having escaped from the nursery himself. He'd fled the onerous atmosphere of Duntrune Castle, preferring the company of his granduncle Simon. Under his kinsman's kindly tutelage, he'd learned to ride, hunt, and love the land of his birth.

By the time Lilias could walk and talk, Geddes had avoided the castle. With no one to encourage sibling affection, he, his brother, and Lilias had never discovered common ground. Little wonder that she now resisted his efforts to gain her confidence. He must try another approach.

"What pastimes can I provide to cheer you? I could purchase linen and embroidery silks," he proposed. "Or would you prefer to spin and weave?"

"Is that the best you can do?" Lilias shot to her feet, glowering. "Offer embroidery?"

Geddes grasped her wrist and hauled her back to her stool. "I have no skill at mind reading. You'll have to tell me what you want."

Lilias averted her face, sulking. "No' embroidery, that's sure."

"What, then? You stay up half the night, wandering the castle or scribbling on paper by candlelight," he accused, exasperated by her stubbornness. "The other night you fell asleep and knocked over the candle. You'll set us afire if you keep on."

"I'll do nay such thing," Lilias contradicted.

"I agree. You'll do your drawing by sunlight and stop wasting valuable wax. 'Twill also keep you from sleeping half the day away. And you're to stop neglecting your appearance. Look at you. You're not wearing shoes. Your smock is torn." He indicated a rent in the white linen through which her bare shoulder showed. "Your hair needs combing."

Defiant, she shook back the mop of hair that foamed about her face. "Some people say I look like a faerie queen, as wild and fair as the wind."

"Some people are filling your head with rubbish," Geddes exploded, sure her mystery lover had told her this. "Next he'll be cozening the faerie queen into his bed, and I'll no' have it, Lilias. Do you hear?"

" 'Tis better than what you offer. You don't even talk to me. You let me come home to Duntrune, yet you ignore me for days."

Geddes sucked in air as insight into her problem surfaced. Lilias needed attention. She'd never gotten it from their parents. He knew enough of their mother's sister to guess that she'd not been affectionate. Lilias had been abandoned by everyone of importance in her life.

Everyone save him.

The enormity of the responsibility he had assumed daunted him. He knew nothing of raising a female.

How did he fulfill her needs while protecting her from those who would take advantage of her?

Yet he must find a way.

Rising, he pulled her to her feet, noticing that Muriel was watching them from her cutting board. A perplexed expression creased her broad face.

"Loose me, Geddes," Lilias hissed, fighting him. "You'll no' lock me in my chamber again. I'll run away first."

"*If* you behave, you'll no' be locked up." Ignoring Muriel, Geddes shifted his grip, drawing Lilias's arm through his. Although the gesture was courtly, he kept a firm hold on her. He must deal with his sister, and the wily wench could be as canny as a rabbit when she wished to escape.

"What do you want?" she asked with downcast eyes and petulant mouth.

Geddes considered, then tried a new tactic. "A game of chess," he proposed.

Lilias's head bobbed up. "Chess?" She narrowed her eyes to suspicious slits. "You never liked chess. You like chasing skirts."

Geddes tightened his hand on her arm as he fought off a burn of anger. "I'm offering to play. Do you accept or no'?"

"You think to buy me off with a game?" She pulled, trying to break away. "You expect to redeem yourself so easily?"

Geddes expelled a frustrated breath as he guided her out of the kitchens, through the screens passage, and into the great hall, deserted at this time of day. She stopped struggling as they crossed the expansive flagstone floor.

"I dinna suppose you've thought o' finding the Faerie Flag," she nagged as they neared the entry. "You promised you would."

He stiffened. Since her arrival, Lilias had led the household whispers about the flag. "Why do you value that infernal piece of cloth?" he demanded. "There's naught special about it."

Interest kindled in her dark eyes, and all sullenness fell away. "You *did* see it once," she cried in triumph. "Was it much damaged by age? Could you make out the designs embroidered on it?" She shook his arm, as if hoping to shake information from him. "Geddes, did you feel its power?"

Geddes sighed, despairing at her interest in a tattered relic "I never saw it, nor do I believe in it. You credit it with a capacity it canna have."

"Nay." Lilias hung heavily on his arm, stopping him. A look of longing softened her features. "Mother saw it carried into the Battle of Dunardry before it disappeared. It was as big as a man when unfurled, and its many colors shone in the sun as the MacCallums triumphed. If we had it, Duntrune could never be retaken. Who do you think stole it, Geddes?"

Geddes hunched his shoulders, displeased by the entire subject. "Kilmartins. Who else would want it save those who fight us and our Campbell kin for our land?"

Lilias heaved a breath of gloomy resignation. "If they took it, they dinna have it now, or you couldna have recaptured the castle. As long as we canna find the flag, 'twill be an ongoing battle, the castle taken and retaken, back and forth."

Geddes shook his head. It was perfect nonsense. He had reclaimed his home and he would keep it.

Still, if his people believed the story, it could come

true. Men's nerves in the garrison were on edge, despite the recent victory. The servants ran for cover at the least disturbance. At this rate, the household would soon be as bad as in his youth—an unbearable cauldron of seething unrest.

"I dinna need a blasted scrap of fabric to hold Duntrune," he said. "Nor did Father die because he lacked the flag. He was old and easily overcome in battle."

"How would you know? You weren't here."

Lilias's accusation burned through him. So his suspicion was correct. She held a grudge because he had left Duntrune, as had their brother. Their mother had then died, and their father had sent her to Inveraray to the north.

For the first time, Geddes realized how it must have been for his sister, abandoned by those who should have loved and cherished her.

"I regret that life was unpleasant for you in Inveraray, Lilias." Though he meant what he said, the words felt stiff and unnatural as he forced them out.

"Unpleasant doesna begin to describe it." She laughed harshly, a sad sound from one so young. "But I doubt you'd have done a thing, had you known."

He guided her across the entry hall and up the spiral staircase built by his great-grandsire. "I canna undo what's done," he said. " 'Tis over. We'll start anew."

She stopped on the stair and regarded him with disdain. "I'm to forget the past like that? Be placated with a game of chess and keeping company with your new doxy?"

Geddes's patience stretched as thin as a taut piece of cloth, threatening to tear. The only way to overcome the ugly past was to bring change to Duntrune, but no one would let him. Not even Lilias. "You'll be civil to her, regardless of what you think she is." He forced her up the stairs. "After she's arrived, you'll entertain her in the solar until the supper hour."

"Entertaining sluts." Lilias regarded him through speculative, half-lowered lashes. "What are we coming to? Still," she mused, "you havena lived up to you name since you arrived. I suppose 'tis time you got under way."

Geddes struggled not to silence her with a roar. "She is our guest."

"She'll be your *doxy* soon enough."

Geddes wanted to box her ears. Unlike the rest of the household, Lilias cheerfully broke the rule of not meddling in his private affairs. Over and over she insulted him. Violence wasn't the answer, but what was he to do?

Sensing his silent fury, she wrinkled her nose at him, then broke free and raced up the stairs.

Geddes clenched both fists. Despite his friendly overtures, she still preferred to provoke him. He despaired of ever reaching her.

He hoped the Englishwoman would not be as difficult to manage, though everything he'd seen thus far suggested she would be. He would have to send her back to Dorset as soon as possible.

He wondered what had possessed her to leave her safe, orderly home in England. Her country had no wars within its borders. No families feuding against families. No unexpected attacks rousing you from sleep, terrifying you and yours, ending in death.

If he'd lived a peaceful life, as she had, he would have valued it. He would never have left home.

Tonight he would lecture her on the importance of what she had relinquished. Peace was a precious thing, and he intended to have it at Duntrune, regardless of his own personal cost.

Chapter 4

"She'll be your *doxy* soon enough."

Angelica stood in the entry hall of Duntrune Castle, shaking her head in disbelief as she listened to the people above her on the spiral stair. She hadn't meant to eavesdrop on what must be the MacCallum chieftain speaking to a female companion. She disapproved of eavesdropping as a rule.

Unfortunately, she had been unable to avoid it. The pair, though out of sight, were audible as she and Iain were led into the entry hall. The carrot-haired serving girl who had answered their knock stood frozen before them. Her face was scarlet with embarrassment, her gaze riveted on her shoes.

"She cannot call you a doxy." Outraged, Iain whipped out his dirk. " 'Tis an insult not to be borne."

Angelica placed a restraining hand on his. "You cannot fight a maid, Iain. Save your anger. She cannot be referring to me personally. She refers to the chieftain's most common company. He *is* known as the Rakehell of MacCallum, is he not?" she asked the girl.

The red staining the girl's cheeks flamed brighter. "Aye," she choked, taking an intense interest in her feet. "I wouldna tell ye a lie. He has an uncanny way with the lasses."

"There. You see." Despite the girl's mortification, Angelica turned to Iain with a brisk smile. "You must not fear for me. I shall set the record straight regarding my reputation."

Iain seemed only marginally reassured. "I'm still no' convinced we shouldna return to the Kilmartin. At least he doesna deflower every female that interests him. Even this young lass acknowledges her chieftain's ways." He nodded to the serving girl.

"I cannot think he has his way with every female alive." Angelica turned to the girl. "He has not touched you, has he, child?"

"Good Lord, Angel," Iain protested. "Such a thing to ask."

Angelica stilled him with a hand to his arm. "Pray answer," she urged the girl. "I must know."

The girl, whom Angelica judged to be perhaps twelve or thirteen, had jerked up her head at the question, her eyes as wide as serving trenchers. "Och, nay, mistress. He wouldna look at the likes o' me. I'm no' of age."

Angelica turned to Iain in triumph. "You see? He has discretion and some honor, at least. He does not trouble the maidservants," she said.

"Well, hardly," Iain huffed. "Most like he prefers more exalted company."

"He does like some o' the maidservants," the girl contradicted, as if she wished to be helpful. "He fathered a child on Marion seven years past, afore he went off. An' he takes women whenever the urge comes on him. I heard tell he had Marion in the stillroom, the dairy, and even in his mother's chamber." She ticked off the places on her fingers, looking proud of her knowledge, though obviously repeating what she'd heard from the older servants.

Iain's face tightened. "Lucina would not like this, Angel. I insist that we—"

Angelica held up a hand, struck by a seeming contradiction. The man who tumbled serving maids had also rescued wee Jamie from the stream. Perhaps something else explained his lusty behavior. "He must have been in love with Marion, to be so eager," she said to the girl. "Was he not?"

"With my lady's chief handmaiden? I doubt it. He got her with child and went his merry way." The girl tossed her head with a self-important air, clearly pleased to be privy to her elders' gossip. "Marion wed someone else later, and lucky she was, too, that he would have her."

"That does it. We're leaving." Iain grasped Angelica's hand and hauled her toward the door.

Angelica dug in her heels. "Iain, I wish to stay."

"I promised your sister that naught would endanger you," he said in low tones.

Angelica regarded him calmly. "I know what you promised, but do you wish to return to Castle Fincharn and the hospitality of Angus Kilmartin? To dine on burned meat and hard bread among lousy dogs? And don't forget sleeping on a bed like a rock."

Iain looked stymied. "That thing the Kilmartin called a bed *was* more like a rock, but I dinna fancy angering him, which we will if we dinna return."

"Nor I. But if we do return to Fincharn, I cannot get the clay. I, for one, will try my fortune here. I told you, the chieftain seems honest to me. We're choosing the best side of this quarrel, I'm sure."

"You're making this difficult, Angel." Iain scrunched up his youthful, freckled face in a pained expression. "Would that Master Stone had not stayed in the village with Magnus. You might listen to him."

"*I* am not making it difficult. The chieftains are. We've made the best choice of the two."

"You might fall under his spell," Iain warned glumly, "and then were will we be?"

"I will be here, enjoying the marvelous day," Angelica said firmly. Though she'd been disappointed by the girl's answer about the maidservant Marion, she supposed a rakehell must have good traits as well as bad. He had definitely rescued Jamie. He had also been shocked to learn that she, a lone female with only two escorts, had spent the night at Castle Fincharn. "What is your name, child?" she asked the girl.

"Jenny Marie."

"Pray tell me one thing more, Jenny Marie. How, in your judgment, does the laird select the females he wishes to, er, enjoy?"

"If they're no' too young or too inexperienced," Jenny Marie said promptly. "And if he takes a fancy to 'em."

"There, you see? I am completely inexperienced. He'll have no interest in me," Angelica informed Iain with relief. "Even rakehells have boundaries beyond which they do not pass. I think we are best off here. MacCallum may like women, but he is honest. I see it in his face. The Kilmartin does not seem nearly as trustworthy. Just think, he usurped the MacCallum land and abused the tenants. Now that MacCallum has reclaimed it, he's setting things to rights with his people. I admire that."

" 'Tis true, he's been generous with the villagers since his return," Jenny Marie chimed in.

"Show Angel a cliff and she'll jump off it," Iain muttered dismally. "Just because the man has admirable qualities doesn't mean he'll be honorable with you."

"But you must admit that sleeping here will be safer than in the woods." Angelica dodged his protest. "And much more comfortable." She had already seen enough of Castle Duntrune to approve. It contrasted markedly to the Kilmartin's castle. Here, all was immaculate, with polished glass windows and no refuse littering the floors. The pink marble floor of the vast entryway shone. As they had crossed the yard, she had even noted a lad planting flowers in a big stone urn to one side of the door.

The laird might be a rake, but he saw to his responsibilities, as well as the amenities. The MacCallum would suit her purpose far better than the Master of Fincharn.

She nodded to the girl. "Do take us to our chambers, Jenny Marie. We are tired from our labors and wish to rest. We've been up most of the night."

Jenny Marie nodded and headed for the stairs.

"I would enjoy a real bed," Iain acknowledged, peering into the great hall as he trailed after their guide. "Impressive," he said to Angelica. "Take a look."

Angelica paused to admire the magnificent chamber, complete with an elaborate beamed ceiling and rows of windows with generous panes of glass. It was much nicer than the Kilmartin's hall, with its open fire, smoke-blackened ceiling beams, and grimy windows. As a final flourish, brightly colored tapestries lined the walls, and the MacCallum flag with its huge stag's head hung over the dais.

Well satisfied, she hurried after Iain, who was just disappearing around the first bend in the spiral stair.

"Dirt!" A stout woman in black serge and a creamy kertch and apron confronted Angelica, brandishing a mop. "I'll no' have it in Duntrune."

Angelica stepped backward in surprise. "I beg your pardon?"

"Ye heard me. Dirt is the enemy of the Lord." The woman attacked the floor with her mop.

Angelica saw a path of footprints trailing from the door, marring the pink marble floor. Mud from the stream bank must still cling to her shoes.

The woman returned to confront Angelica, her broad face stormy. "Take off yer shoes at once."

Astonished, Angelica removed her footwear. "They're not so very dirty," she began as the woman snatched them from her and handed them to a lad who appeared at her elbow as if by magic. "I would clean them at the pump or well if you'd but show me—"

"Ye'll do nay such thing. Ye're a guest," the woman declared haughtily, blocking her way with the mop. "Ye, too." She gestured at Iain, who had come back down the stairs. "Take off yer boots."

Iain sat down at once and tugged at his right boot.

"Och, yer pardon, Mistress McCloud." Jenny Marie hastened to help Iain remove his boots. "I forgot to check fer mud."

As the boots came off, a chorus of female giggles filled the hall. Angelica saw a gaggle of maids huddled at a far door, sneaking furtive peeks at the guests.

"Bring 'em to the back door next time, Jenny Marie," Mistress McCloud barked as she took the boots. "If they're going to be covered in mud, they can use the back stair." She handed off the boots to the lad, then narrowed her gaze at Angelica's clothing. "Ye'll wish to change out o' that filthy kirtle, I'm sure."

"But I have no other to wear in its place," Angelica protested, wondering if the incensed housekeeper would confiscate her clay-splattered clothing on the spot before all and sundry.

"Nay?" The woman stared at her with bright blue eyes that seemed more inquisitive than hostile. "Where is yer baggage, I'll be askin' ye?"

"I left my extra clothing at Castle Fincharn, as I thought I would be sleeping there again tonight." Angelica was determined not to be embarrassed that she had slept in enemy territory. "But as your laird has kindly asked us to stay here, I must—"

"Ye slept at Castle Fincharn and awoke to see the light o' day?" the woman interrupted, her eyes round with amazement. "The Lord and Saint Columba preserve us. The lass is watched over by the angels, fine."

The maids and Jenny Marie stilled. Everyone stared at Angelica as if she had just announced that she had flown to Scotland rather than sailed on a ship.

The real miracle, though, was the way Mistress McCloud's attitude changed at her words. "Susan, fetch Mistress Cavandish some clothing from Lady Ingiborg's chambers," she ordered one of the maids. "Ye're of a size with the MacCallum's lady mother, bless her departed soul. We'll find garments to fit yer station whilst I see to the washin' of yers. Then ye may sit with Lady Lilias in the solar until the supper hour. Now then, dinna stand here gawking, Jenny Marie. Take 'em above stair." She gestured with imperious dignity, clearly accustomed to being obeyed.

At her order, the maids dispersed. The diversion was done. Jenny Marie raced up the stairs, beckoning for Angelica and Iain to follow.

"Is she always like that?" Iain asked as Mistress McCloud disappeared after the maids. "The laird lets her order guests about?"

"Oh, aye," the redhead said with surety over her

shoulder. "Muriel McCloud makes the most heavenly apple tart with chestnut cream that ye've ever tasted in yer life. The MacCallum lets her do her will, fine."

Angelica absorbed this. Either the MacCallum was a man singularly fixated on the needs of his stomach, or he thought other people were. But then she remembered how her mother had often told her that a belly full of fine food could turn the most difficult men into lap dogs, and she resolved to do her best to spare Muriel McCloud exposure to "dirt," as she termed it. Though clay dust had a way of getting everywhere when she made pots, she would try to keep it out of the castle.

As they reached the first landing, a young serving lad appeared to guide Iain to his chamber. To Angelica's relief, she saw no sign of the MacCallum chieftain or the woman to whom he'd been speaking. Bad enough that she had heard their conversation. Worse still if they knew she had.

With a last smile of thanks to Iain for his company, Angelica followed Jenny Marie past several closed doors. "Who is Lady Lilias?" she asked as Jenny Marie swung one portal wide.

Jenny Marie rolled her eyes and grimaced. "Lady Lilias is the MacCallum's younger sister," she said in dramatic tones. Kneeling at the hearth, she opened a tinderbox and proceeded to kindle a spark. Within minutes, a welcome blaze crackled amid the dry kindling stacked on the grate.

Angelica wasn't at all sure what Jenny Marie's dire tone implied about the MacCallum's sister, but it didn't sound promising. Added to that, she had an uncomfortable feeling that the female she had overheard calling her a filthy name on the stairs was this same Lady Lilias.

* * *

Clad in an out-of-date though still elegant kirtle skirt and bodice of golden-brown velvet, Angelica stood at the entry to the solar, smoothing her newly coifed hair. Jenny Marie left her with a satisfied smile, apparently pleased with the fit of the clothing that had been unearthed.

Angelica studied the cozy solar with its soaring oriel window facing south, comfortable upholstered furniture, and bright tapestries hung on the walls. A fitting chamber for the private hours of the highest-ranking family in the land. Angelica took a deep breath and stepped over the threshold, feeling self-conscious in the elegant borrowed clothes.

"So you're here to be seduced by my brother." A young female seated by the crackling fire hurled the accusation at her in icy tones.

Angelica fastened on the dark, snapping eyes, the angry tilt of the chin, and the perfect oval face crowned by a mop of ebony hair. The hair might have been beautiful had it not been in wild disarray. Bare, soiled toes peeped from beneath a tattered black skirt.

Angelica understood the pleasures of feeling the earth beneath one's feet, the freedom of being unconfined. Yet she guessed that by meeting her without shoes, the girl meant to convey something other than a love of the outdoors.

She returned to the eyes. They seemed defiant, and something else Angelica couldn't name. A hint of bare shoulder showed through a rent in the young woman's sleeve, transforming her wild air to seductive. Here was a female of tender age, poised on the brink of womanhood, feeling the strength of her sexual powers but uncertain what to do with them.

This, Angelica decided, must be Lady Lilias, Geddes MacCallum's sister.

The girl stared at her, not the least ashamed of her outrageous question and manners.

Her greeting was worrisome. From Angelica's experience, verbal attacks like this one hid a lack of confidence. She sent the girl a winning smile to show she was not offended. "Do you greet all female visitors to Duntrune Castle this way?" she asked in a neutral tone.

The girl squinted at her, as if taken aback by Angelica's unflinching response. "You're the only female who has been invited to stay here since my brother's return," she said, "but those who used to come always sought to share his bed. So my question is justified. Is that your plan?"

Wondering if she could dissuade her of the idea, Angelica stepped into the chamber and crossed to stand before the cheerful fire. "The only bed I want freedom to seek is the streambed nearby," she said with friendly candor. "I'm here to dig clay." She sat across from Lilias and studied her. Heavens, the girl was scarcely old enough to be out of the schoolroom, yet she appeared to flit about without any supervision, judging from her dirty feet and ragged skirt hem. Angelica leaned near. "You can set your mind at ease," she said in her kindest tones. "I won't steal your precious brother from you."

Lilias recoiled as if Angelica had stung her. "He isna precious to me."

"But of course he is," Angelica insisted. " 'Tis the most natural thing in the world to love your sibling. I hated it when my sister Rozalinde fell in love with the Earl of Wynford and married him. It took her away from me, and I loved her so."

Lilias tilted her chin haughtily. "I hate it when I mun be civil to my brother's new doxy, 'tis all. It has nothing to do with him, save that he's forced ye upon me."

Angelica didn't believe the girl's denial, but she found the revelation interesting. The brother had instructed his sister to entertain her. A proper role for a chatelaine, but the sister was not obeying him as became a gracious hostess. "I'm sure you know him best, as he's your brother," she said. "But I must tell you that from my experience, men cannot tolerate my liking for clay. Your brother didn't seem to appreciate my interest much either, so I think I'm the better judge when I say I am unlikely to become his doxy. In fact, I suspect he would prefer to wring my neck just now. You should recognize the urge in him. You have undoubtedly inspired the same response."

She paused, and the girl shifted, looking uncomfortable. So she was correct. Lilias had been the female arguing with the chieftain on the stair. The pair had sounded as if they clashed often. Perfectly natural, since Lilias was the baby of the family. Having occupied that same position at home, Angelica understood the need to strike out against the overprotection often lavished on the youngest. Though Lilias had fewer siblings, they had much in common.

Lilias leaned forward in her chair and snatched up the poker, plying it to the fire. Sparks flew and the logs shifted dangerously, threatening to tumble from the grate.

"Ask me another question," Angelica coaxed, hoping to end the antagonism. "I'll answer as honestly as I can."

The girl flashed her an angry glance as she put down the poker. "I dinna believe you're here to dig clay.

When I was a child, women came from far and wide in the hopes o' marryin' my brother. As chieftain, he's coveted as a mate. I'm warnin' ye, he seduces the females who interest him, but marry?'' She scoffed and shrugged. "Never."

Angelica wanted to laugh out loud at the girl's insistence on an impossible seduction. "I thank you for your warning, but I promise you, I have no such interest in your brother, and no man I've known has had the power to hold me spellbound. I'm here to dig clay, as I said."

The girl snorted. "Why do you keep saying that?"

"Because 'tis true." Angelica spread both hands on her knees and leaned forward, eager to share her excitement. "I've spent most of the time since I arrived digging clay. I have a barrel of it in the stable. After I have dined and thanked your brother for food and shelter, I intend to begin working with it."

The girl stared at her skeptically. "In truth?"

"Yes," Angelica said staunchly. "In truth."

"Why?" Curiosity finally displaced disdain in the girl's dark brown eyes.

They were fine eyes, full of a quick intelligence, but Angelica recognized the need to proceed with care. The girl didn't appear to trust anyone, and Angelica didn't need another enemy. "I dig clay because I adore making poetry," she said. "Bowls. Basins. Vases. Pitchers. Drinking vessels. I make them and sell them. 'Tis the craft I was taught since I was a child."

"If you're a gentlewoman, why do you practice a craft?" Honest bafflement shone in the girl's eyes. "They say you are. Doesna your family have the funds to keep you?"

Angelica smiled, warming to the girl's first show of

true interest in her as a person. "They have enough funds, but I grew bored. I had nothing to do until I discovered I had a special skill I could develop." She waved her hands for emphasis. "I'm sure you understand that, being a girl and the youngest of the family. How can our elders expect us to be satisfied with nothing but embroidery all day?"

The girl flinched.

Angelica made a mental note: Lilias didn't like embroidery. Another thing they had in common. "Would you like to try making a pot with me after we dine?" she urged. " 'Twould be my pleasure to show you how 'tis done."

The girl studied her in silence, seeming uncertain how to respond to a friendly overture. "It sounds boring to me," she said at last in noncommittal tones.

"Oh, no, making pottery is extremely exciting, especially if you have a good teacher. Master Stone has taught me for years. He still shows me new techniques each time I encounter a problem. I don't claim to have the same experience as he, but I'm patient. It would be my pleasure to instruct you, if you like." She leaned forward and caught one of the girl's hands in her own. "You have perfect hands for working with clay. Strong, sensitive fingers. Short nails. You would do very—"

The girl leaped to her feet, snatching her hand away as if she'd been burned. "I dinna want to work wi' yer dirty auld clay. I dinna like it. My brother says I dinna like anything. He calls me impossible."

Angelica sat very still, realizing the girl was on the verge of a personal confession. "And are you impossible?" she asked softly.

"Aye."

"Why?" Angelica asked.

The girl stomped one bare foot on the wood floor. "I'm supposed to be questioning you, Mistress Cavandish. No' the other way around."

Angelica's heart went out to the girl. Clearly something troubled her. "Did your brother send you to question me?" she asked.

"*I* decided to question you and report back to him. 'Twill make his task easier," the girl informed her.

"And what is his task?"

"Seducing you."

They had come full circle, and Angelica had had enough of the seduction nonsense. She had been a little sister far too long not to recognize the annoying wish of the youngest to be embroiled in the elder's affairs. Besides, perhaps the man really did mean to seduce her. "As I said, he'll not succeed because I'm not interested. Nor will he wish to once he knows me better. Let us talk about you instead. We haven't been properly introduced. I'm sure you know that I am Angelica Cavandish. What is your name?"

A sulky expression crept across the girl's face as she rose without a reply. She flounced to the massive wood table in the middle of the chamber and poured a cup of some beverage from a pitcher. Deliberately, she failed to offer any to her guest.

The clay vessels appeared to be poor specimens, and Angelica made a mental note to tell the chieftain so. "I see that you're not ready to engage in polite formalities," she observed. "That's understandable. We're strangers who were not properly introduced by family or friends. But I need to call you something, so I believe I'll call you Lucina. She's my older sister and I love her dearly. Though the name doesn't quite fit you, 'twill do for now. So tell me about your schooling, Lucina.''

"Dinna call me that." The girl frowned in annoyance. "I am the Lady Lilias of MacCallum. Lucina doesn't suit me at all. And I dinna like seeing you in my mother's kirtle."

"Hmmm. I got the *L* right." Angelica pretended to be pleased to learn the name and ignored the comment about the kirtle. "Well, Lilias, I am happy to meet you. Pray call me Angelica, and do tell me about your education. I'm guessing you had a tutor. Am I right?"

Lilias looked startled. "How did you know I had a tutor?"

"I've heard that many Scots chieftains' children are well educated, and you look intelligent, so I guessed you'd had one," Angelica said with candor. "Did you like him?"

Lilias nodded with reluctance. "My brothers didna like their studies, so I was oft his only pupil. He taught me the Latin names for many plants and flowers and how to draw them with pen and ink."

Angelica smiled, delighted that the girl had shared a hint of who she was. "What else do you like?"

Lilias regarded her slyly. "When I'm not drawing plants, I like to ride like the wind across Highland meadows and sleep in a shieling at night."

She was supposed to be shocked by the unladylike interest, but Angelica had too many unladylike interests of her own to be appalled by such tame things as horseback riding without an escort and sleeping in a hut on the mountain slopes. "I suppose a sheep or two joined you in the shieling at night. How nice for warmth," she said blandly.

"They're not dear when they're born, all wet and

slimy," Lilias snarled, clearly incensed that her daring had failed to impress or outrage the newcomer.

"Oh, have you seen lambs born?"

"Aye. I like them when they're covered with blood. I like to see their dams lick it off."

Angelica nodded as if this were the most natural subject of discussion in the world. "Isn't it wonderful how the miracle of birth causes females to do things they would never consider otherwise, save for love of their young?"

The girl's face darkened. She smacked her cup on the table. "Not in this family. Our mother never did a thing in her life for love of her young. She stuck me with a nursemaid when I was born and I scarce ever saw her again."

With that, Lilias pivoted and glided to the door, then paused. "My brother *will* seduce you. He loves seducing women, and you'll be a challenge. He loves a challenge. You'll see. You won't be able to resist him. None of the others could." Having issued the dire prophecy, she disappeared through the door.

Angelica stared after Lilias, full of sorrow for the girl. Little wonder she behaved like a wild thing, rude and unrestrained in her speech. She'd been deserted at a tender age. Probably brought up by this nurse or that, the parents not realizing it was important for the child to form loving emotional ties. Lilias needed the warmth of familial bonds.

Angelica wiped away the moisture gathering in her eyes. She knew how it felt to be loved by her family, both mother and father and all six siblings. She wouldn't trade their caring for anything. But the previous MacCallum chieftain and his lady hadn't seemed to understand such things. Could the present chieftain know the depth of his sister's pain?

And what of the chieftain himself? She stared into the fire, scarcely seeing it. Geddes MacCallum had been reared by the same parents as Lilias. As with his sister, might untold anguish lurk behind his grave, handsome face?

Chapter 5

"I know you wish to send me home, sir, but first you must hear me out. There are excellent reasons why I should stay."

From the depths of his favorite chair in the solar, Geddes MacCallum studied Angel Cavandish as she spoke. They had supped in the great hall with little exchange, separated as they'd been by her youthful escort, whose name he'd learned was Iain Lang. Now he had granted her request for a private audience.

With her seated in the chair opposite, though, he couldn't concentrate fully on her words. The distraction of her presence at close range was too unsettling.

She had cleaned up a good deal. No trace of clay remained on her person, and in place of her drab clothing, she wore a velvet skirt and bodice that matched the rich tones of her cinnamon-brown hair.

The garments had been his mother's and seemed a bit too long for Angel, yet their elegance transformed her into a tantalizing princess, fit to reign over a kingdom of her own. Now that she was out of the burn and within reach, he was acutely aware of how small-boned and delicately formed she was. How enticingly female.

Never would he have thought, from looking at her

lithe form clothed in velvet, that she could cross the whole of England and half of Scotland in order to dig the night through, filling a barrel with clay. She was an intriguing mix of daintiness and strength.

The daintiness was emphasized by a creamy silk-and-lace smock framing her milk-white throat. The glowing brown velvet, embroidered in the same color, hugged her shoulders, swelled over tantalizing breasts, then plunged to a vee just below her waist. A pair of sleeves in matching brown velvet, slashed and embroidered in gold, revealed puffs of the creamy silk beneath. Lace at the wrists emphasized her slender yet capable hands.

It was a masterpiece of a gown, but like the best of gowns, the eye was not drawn to it, but to its wearer. It clung to her, accentuating her every move. The velvet also echoed the color of her marvelous hair, which, though looped and bundled at the nape of her neck, strained against the pins, as if eager to escape at the first opportunity. He suspected it would, too. It was like the rest of the woman: vibrant, full of life, and unwilling to do as bidden.

He felt an unreasonable urge to remove the fabric and discover if the glowing flesh of her throat and neck led to equally ripe secrets beneath.

Damn her desirability; she was out of place here. Beauty and delicacy could not survive at Duntrune. He shifted and cleared his throat. "You will depart as soon as I can arrange escort for you and your friends, Mistress Cavandish."

"Oh, but I fear I cannot." She had the temerity to smile as she defied him, offering only a hint of an apology. "I cannot leave behind that wonderful clay." She rose and moved to the table, the swaying kirtle skirt offering delicious hints of feminine hips and thighs. Her petticoats must have been too wet to wear, and Muriel had not provided others. She appeared to be wearing no more than the silk smock beneath the gown.

The idea sent a charge of interest to his loins, far more insistent than his reaction at the burn. There they'd been separated by a wide gulf of land and water. He'd been conscious of people listening and annoyed by her refusal to leave at his command.

Here, they were wrapped in the cocoonlike privacy of the solar. She was so close, he smelled the intoxicating scent of roses on her silky flesh. The scent came from the soap reserved for ladies of the castle. Lilias used the same thing. But on Angelica, the scent beckoned like a heady bouquet, promising seduction.

By Saint Columba, what made him think that? Had all the talk of his rakehell nature convinced him to act on it with the first available female? Annoyed by the power of people's gossip, he returned to the business at hand. "What of your reputation? Did you think of that? An unwed woman, living under my roof?"

"Everyone says you expect to seduce me," she said in matter-of-fact tones. "However, I must warn you that I have never in my life been interested in seduction. I'm interested only in the clay."

"In truth?" He quirked a questioning eyebrow at her. Judging by her behavior in the stream, she spoke truly, but he couldn't quite believe it.

"In truth." She regarded him from the table, her head held high with confidence. "Tell me, pray, were these cups made by Magnus the Potter?" She held aloft one of the castle's common ware.

"No' by him. By one of his apprentices. The lad took to shoemaking in the end. He had nay skill for pottery."

"*That* is for certes." Angelica gazed at the cup with a mixture of contempt and pity. "I did not wish to say anything until I knew it was not Magnus's work. Now I shall tell you what is wrong with it. Do you see this lump?" She brought him the cup, tilting it so he could see the bottom. " 'Tis an unbroken air bubble and reflects shoddy work," she said with crisp precision. "Clay must be worked thoroughly to remove air bubbles before it is formed on the wheel. I will make you a superior set of cups using the clay from your stream. They will be truly fit for a laird." She brandished the cup, her excitement clearly growing. "My cups will have thinner walls. A more delicate shape. More graceful handles. Yet they will be solid. Good for everyday use. Just think."

Seeming carried away by her plans, she fell to one knee before him in a flurry of velvet skirts, holding the cup. "Your clay bed will produce some of the finest pottery in all of Scotland. If my set is better than this set, you must let me stay. You cannot pass up such an opportunity." She placed one pleading hand on his as she spoke.

Geddes was too stunned by the gesture to think clearly. Of all the arguments she might have offered, he hadn't expected this. The sudden revelation of her dream, the sweet earnestness in her face, the warmth of her touch left him speechless. But more than that, he saw in her a need: the stark, raw need to fulfill her desire.

Here was a woman who, when she wanted something, wanted it with a passion that defied barriers.

She thought nothing of traveling the length of nearly two countries to follow a chosen path. Without hesitation, she stood in cold water and toiled through the night. When she desired something, she reached for it with a certainty that was inspiring.

Yet he must consider more than her desire. He must point out the danger she would encounter in attempting to fulfill it. Though he was loath to disappoint her honest wish, if he denied her now, he would spare her the torment of loss after heroic effort had been wasted. He had promised himself to let her down gently. The best way was to be firm and clear. "No," he said.

She did not crumble. She withdrew her hand and gazed at him, an unwavering look of determination in her eyes. "What do you need from me to say yes?" she said.

"I dinna need anything from you." He lunged to his feet, brushing past her delectable form. Did she have any idea how she inspired his lust?

Of course she did, he told himself angrily. She said she didn't. Yet she was setting a trap, using herself as bait. Well, he would not taste the tidbit, much as he would like to. He had far too many problems as it was. He had no needs that she could fulfill.

Even as he formed the thought, he knew he lied. He had a need: an illogical wish to taste her lips with his own. A female of such passionate nature was unlikely to be passive and boring in the bedchamber. Her ardor would be as dazzling as the brightest jewels in a crown. The idea of being the focus of such potent emotion captured his imagination.

But lust, he warned himself, must not be fulfilled simply for its own sake. "You came from a peaceful land," he said, swinging around. "You have no idea what you've given up. Peace is precious. Return there and reap the fruits of your heritage."

Her expression tightened, and she rose to her feet, the velvet skirts forming a graceful column. "There was nothing for me in Dorset anymore, nor anywhere in England. You have no idea what you're saying."

Moisture sparkled in her bright eyes. Tears? The idea baffled him even as he felt the urge to assuage her pain. How could she have suffered in a peaceful land? "I would think your country a fair haven compared to the strife of the Highlands. How could you not be fulfilled there?"

Her dry laugh cut him short. "How? Imagine having a professional skill but being refused the right to practice it as anything other than a lady's pastime. An occasional indulgence. An amusement to pass the time of day. Imagine men who think you're insane for wishing to do anything other than embroider all day. Imagine being ridiculed when you explain your goal, which would benefit others as well as yourself. But you're treated like a child and told to run along and play rather than trouble those older and wiser than you. I was never, ever able to practice my skill in Dorset in a meaningful way."

Geddes winced as her description hit home. *He'd* had a skill. With it, he could have brought prosperity to Duntrune, but everyone had ridiculed him. They hadn't listened. They still didn't.

"Try to see what I see," she whispered, moving closer, her hands clasped around the cup, her face as reverent as if she were in prayer. "Everyone will wish to buy high-quality MacCallum ware, which will be created by your people once I teach them. Imagine your shabby village transformed into a prosperous center of industry."

He winced. The village *was* shabby. He hadn't wanted to admit it in the months since retaking Duntrune, but the lack of leadership before his arrival had clearly strained the villagers' resources. Cots begged for new roofs. Garden plots had not been planted due to lack of seeds.

"Of course you don't want it built up too much or with too many people," she continued. "It would be a shame to ruin Duntrune's beauty. You want just enough work that people will prosper, be able to repair their homes, clothe their children, and put food on the table."

Geddes winced again. So she had also noticed the pitiful plight of the villagers. He had tried to remedy the situation, but he was continually pressed by Kilmartin attacks. "And you think you can accomplish all this?" He tried to keep the skepticism in his voice to a bare minimum.

If she noted it, she gave no sign. "Not immediately, but given time, yes." She settled both hands on her hips and nodded briskly. "We will begin by establishing the production of fine-quality ware. Once we have a reasonable stock, we can sell in neighboring towns. Later, we will send out a few men to find markets. They will use what they carry as samples to take orders. In the meantime, I will train people to fill those orders. We will grow quickly, I assure you. But not so much that the village loses its purity. We don't want that."

We. He marveled at how easily her enterprise became theirs. "What will you do when you run out of clay?" he asked, testing her with a realistic problem.

She only laughed, tossing her head, her eyes sparkling as if he'd made a jest. "Once we prosper, we will search for new beds of clay. You have so many streams and shady glens, this area must be ripe with it. Moisture and rock ground down over time give rise to beds of clay. We'll find more.''

She made it sound so simple. Temptingly simple. It fired his imagination. He saw his clansmen and tacksmen, in Duntrune and beyond, well clothed and happy, their faces filled out from satisfying meals rather than haggard with hunger. He saw peace in the land.

Unexpectedly, he yearned to agree. To give her what she desired because his heart desired it as well. He ached to say yes.

Yet the clan feud would always ruin his hopes. *Kilmartin willna let me,* he thought, then realized he'd said it aloud.

Angel smiled engagingly. "He'll have to join us."

Geddes stalked to the windows and gazed out, needing to put distance between himself and her tempting idealism. "He'll never join us," he stated. " 'Tis no' a possibility."

"Then we must let him know what he's missing. At least let me make the cups." She followed him, as if sensing he teetered on the brink of agreement and eager to press her advantage. "Wait until after you see what I can do."

"I canna wait that long."

Her high, clear forehead drew into a frown. "My, you are impatient. How long do you think 'twill take?"

He remembered how long it had taken Magnus to fill orders. "An age."

Angelica clucked her tongue in disparagement. "Nonsense. I can make a set like this in no time at all. The only delay will be in setup. Let me see." She had put down the ugly cup and gestured freely as she aired her thoughts aloud. "I must move Master Magnus's pottery wheels to a suitable location. Then I must weather the clay to get it wet enough to mix to a malleable consistency. But once that's done, I can make a set of drinking flagons and a pitcher like this— better than this," she corrected, "in an hour or so. It won't be fired yet, nor the feet trimmed, but you'll see the finished shape so you can judge my skill. Is that too long?"

Geddes stared at her. She could make a full set of pottery cups *and* a pitcher in an hour? He couldn't believe it. Magnus's idiot apprentice had taken weeks to make this misshapen set.

"Of course we must assemble enough ware to fill the kiln before firing, so you cannot use the pieces right away," Angelica said, as if it were all settled. "And Master Stone and I must consult with Master Magnus regarding local glaze materials. But in terms of giving you a sense of what I can create, I can make a half dozen vessels in an hour, easily."

She returned to the chair and retrieved a small fabric pouch that he hadn't noticed earlier. "I brought this for you, to demonstrate my work and show my goodwill." She opened the pouch, removed a small bowl, and held it out. When he made no move to take it, she caught his right hand, pried it open, and placed the bowl in his palm.

Surprised by her wish to make him a gift, he stared at it. It was the most marvelous, minuscule work of art he had ever seen. The sides of the bowl were thin and delicate. Its shape, a perfect circle, spoke of unity and harmony. A robin's egg–blue glaze suggested birds in flight, soaring through sunlit skies, home to their nests. It was a thing of enduring beauty. Ethereal, yet hard enough to withstand the demands of time. It reminded him of the woman who had made it with her fine, strong hands. "Did you bring many of these with you?" He glanced up to find her watching him intently.

A rueful smile tugged at the corners of her mouth. "This one alone survived the journey. The three others are chipped, broken to pieces, or cracked."

Another surprise. "If you had only the one, why did you no' give it to the Kilmartin? You thought he owned the clay."

She shook her head, and his gaze strayed once more to her shining hair, straining against its pins. "I meant to, but I couldn't bring myself to do it," she said. "I didn't think he would appreciate it. But when I met you, I knew. . . ."

Her gaze rested on him, eyes alight with interest. Had she not been unwed, he would have thought she assessed more than his ability to appreciate her work.

That wasn't her purpose, he warned himself. She was inexperienced, judging by her marital status and her general demeanor. But she seemed as concerned for his people as her own needs, including them in her plans. She was unselfish, willing to give as well as to take.

His body responded to her in a manner that was impossible to ignore. "You thought I would appreciate your handiwork more than Angus Kilmartin?" He moved to the other side of the table, needing to place its width between them.

She grinned, suddenly impish. "I know you won't use it for feeding the dogs."

He couldn't conceal an answering smile. Unbidden, his thought from the burn returned: She had beautiful, clever hands. Such female hands could give a man great pleasure. Everyone expected him to seduce her.

But rumor did not necessarily become reality. In

this case, it must not. He placed the bowl on the table and stepped back. "Mistress Cavandish, you are in danger, digging in the burn," he said. "You are in danger here at Duntrune if Angus Kilmartin believes you are one of us."

She stepped up to the table, directly across from him. "Sir, I saw no danger as long as your guards stood nearby."

He thought of the battle to win back the castle, of the man who had died, and hardened his heart. "Danger does not dare challenge my guards at the moment. It is there, nonetheless."

She planted both palms on the table and leaned forward, her face flushed with sincerity. "We'll have to deal with it, then, won't we? We cannot give up now. Not if the land at the burn is yours."

We. That word again. He tried to feel indignant at her stubbornness, but he liked the sound of solidarity. None of his clansmen spoke in such stalwart terms. They had rallied behind him and fought to regain the castle because he demanded they do so. But he feared they lacked the will to hold it. They certainly did not have the confidence of this woman. "The Kilmartin will want to kill you," he challenged.

She paled and straightened. " 'Tis what Master Magnus said. But I did him no harm, nor do I mean to."

Geddes leaned toward her. "*I* mean him harm."

"Only if he claims your land, no?"

"Aye, but he *will* claim it, for he considers the land his."

She swung away from the table. "How annoying. Can you not share?"

He stared at her, dumbfounded by her ignorance. "Highlanders? Share land?"

" 'Tis only a bit of grazing land. The clay is an important resource, but there's plenty if Kilmartin wants some. We share in Dorset all the time."

"Ye dinna," he contradicted, "else you wouldna be here, looking for clay."

"Men exchange things with one another all the time. One needs grazing land; the other needs access to water. They make an agreement. Not the same as sharing, I suppose, and you are correct, women cannot take part. The men would rather die than let me near their clay."

Pain suffused her voice, and once more she allowed him a glimpse into her soul. He saw a personal deprivation so powerful, it seared him.

She slammed the door shut, cutting off the intimate view before he could respond. "I will convince Angus Kilmartin that I, at least, have no quarrel with him," she said briskly. "Then I can remain here in safety."

"You will have a quarrel with him once he tries to kill or abduct you," Geddes warned.

"Surely if I explain to him my neutrality, he will understand."

Geddes thought of his family's age-old dispute with the neighboring clan and shook his head. " 'Twill do you no good. You are now a MacCallum ally."

For the first time, she seemed to hesitate. "I, er, thank you for letting me be your ally. I truly wish to offer you a service. You must need something that only I can provide."

She spoke with a straight face. Not a hint of innuendo. His mind rushed at once to the bedchamber, while she, no doubt, imagined other tasks—women's duties about the household or in the kitchens. He fought to subdue his sexual interest, driving his mind in other directions. The image of his difficult little sister sprang into his head. The girl had not come to sup in the great hall, as she had been bidden. "Lilias," he said slowly.

"Your sister did meet with me before supper," Angelica said hurriedly, as if sensing his displeasure with Lilias and seeking to protect her. "We discoursed for some time. She is a young women with great potential."

He squinted, surprised to hear his ill-mannered sister termed in such a manner. "I have not noticed that she was inclined to put that potential to good use."

"I'm sure that's true just now, but you must be gentle with your sister, sir. She needs you so. Truly."

The effect of her dignified and surprising defense of his sister was destroyed by the lock of unruly hair finally springing loose, as it had been threatening to do. The metal pin clattered to the floor.

"Goodness." She grasped the long lock as it tumbled over her shoulder, and fumbled to recoil it. It sprang free again, flopping like a beached fish, though infinitely more lovely.

He acted on the sudden urge to touch that glorious hair. Her wish to help the villagers, her plea for his sister, had both surprised and touched him. That, mixed with her innocent sensuality, formed an irresistible combination. "Allow me." He retrieved the pin and straightened, facing her.

She stilled, staring at him, an odd expression in her eyes.

What was it? Not the wish to act the siren and entice him. He would recognize that in a woman. Nor did she seem the opposite—frightened and ready to bolt.

As he moved closer, she cocked her head and gazed up at him with questioning brown eyes.

Interest. That was it. She was interested in what he would do next. Perhaps she even wondered how she would feel about what he did.

An innocent, indeed. She was the most unusual female he had met in an age. More than unusual—fascinating. As he circled to stand behind her, she closed her eyes, as if preparing to submit to his touch. She stiffened momentarily as he handled the loose tress.

Pleasure spread through him as the silky texture of her hair caressed his fingers. So soft, smelling of roses. He wanted to know if her flesh felt equally soft. As he secured the pin, his fingers brushed her neck.

A visible shiver shook her slender frame. Tipping back her head, she released a surprised, exalted moan.

So his nearness did affect her. The knowledge awoke his own response. She seemed so tender, yet so full of vitality, he could not resist. He settled one palm on her bare flesh, just at the smooth curve of her neck.

She sighed, tipping her head, rubbing her cheek against his hand.

Exhilaration shot through him. She liked his touch. Wanting more, he settled his right hand on the other side of her neck.

A tiny gasp of pleasure broke from her lips.

Enchanting. He leaned over, his lips nearly brushing the nape of her neck. "Shall I stop?" he breathed.

In answer, she clasped her hands over his, holding them in place. Her breath quickened.

Ah. Permission. He welcomed the desire washing through him, bypassing his mind and pooling in his loins. He let the tension build as he traced the vulnerable nape of her neck with his lips.

Her answering murmur of appreciation pleased him

as much as the softness of her skin. She felt much too good beneath his lips.

He eyed the graceful line of her spine, falling to the swell of her rounded bottom beneath the velvet. His hand itched to explore that forbidden territory.

Easy, now, he cautioned himself. He did not want to frighten her.

But in his mind he disrobed her, removing the form-fitting bodice and the velvet skirts, then the smock. From experience, he knew the flesh of her thighs would be as white and swan-feather smooth as the flesh behind her ear. He nipped her neck lightly, then smiled wolfishly as she wrapped both arms around her middle and sucked in a breath.

How he relished her response. She had said she was interested only in the clay. How he enjoyed disproving that determined little lie. He didn't doubt that clay had been the center of her life before they met. Otherwise she would not be unwed at her age. Nor would she be traveling on her own.

But now that they had met . . . Anticipation filled him as he savored the knowledge. She was definitely interested in something he offered. Something besides his clay.

Chapter 6

Excitement cascaded through Angelica as Geddes brushed his lips against her neck, then turned her gently to face him so he could explore her throat. His powerful hand settled at her nape; the other closed on her shoulder, making her his willing captive.

From the moment she had heard that he was a notorious rakehell, she had set her expectations of him very low. Yet he had surprised her by rescuing Jamie, and now he surprised her again. He didn't grasp her roughly and have his way with her. Instead, his questing mouth against her neck was unexpectedly tender.

Tilting back her head, she released a sigh of enjoyment, dazzled by the gleaming waterfall of sensation he inspired in her. His broad shoulders blocked the rest of the world from view, wrapping her in his masculine warmth. The potent scent of horses and leather teased her nostrils. She yearned for more of him. More warmth. More touching. More Geddes.

Was this how it felt to be spellbound by a rogue?

She couldn't quite believe it, though how would she know, having never met one? As she had concluded at the stream, a rogue must have both bad and good traits. Anyone could have the weighty task of rebuilding his heritage placed on his shoulders. To Geddes's credit, he did not shirk the responsibility but set to work with courage. He had admirable traits, and just now, one of them seemed to be pleasing her.

Opening her eyes, she glimpsed his face. His expression shocked her. His eyes were glazed with a passion that turned her knees to the consistency of limp washing. Yet farther above the knees, she felt decidedly more lively than anything to do with laundry. As his rapid breath warmed her neck, flames shot through her body like renegade fireworks, exploding deep in her belly. Through the haze of pleasure, one thought stood out: She had never felt this way with James.

An equally intriguing idea glimmered at the edge of her mind. She, though clay-loving and practical, interested this experienced rogue. He had liked her gift of the bowl. She had seen appreciation in his eyes as he received it. Now he appreciated her as well.

Tension built within her as Geddes's tongue anointed the hollow at the base of her throat, then dropped lower. Her breasts tingled, and she realized with shock that they ached for his touch.

With deliberate slowness, his palms moved to cup her shoulders, then slid sensuously down her arms. Her heart thudded like a crazy thing, wanting to escape her chest. If only he would . . .

He raised his head and settled his grip around her waist. Pleasant . . . but disappointingly far from the parts of her body that clamored for more.

She gazed at him in wonder. What in heaven was next?

The sensual quirk of his mouth, the tightening of his hands on her waist, suggested he wanted more, too. Still, he did nothing. Perhaps he expected her to shriek or sob or run away.

But why should she do that? He wasn't forcing himself upon her. He was offering himself, and she found a smile springing to her lips. "That was an amazing demonstration, sir."

He blinked, as if caught off guard. "If that is all you have to say, Mistress Cavandish, then you failed to understand the point of the demonstration. If you dinna keep away from me, there will be more of what you just experienced."

The idea left her breathless. She wet her lips in anticipation, then realized his glittering gaze was locked on her face, on her mouth.

"There must not be more," he warned.

But his voice had thickened to a sensual growl, rough with unspoken desire. His sapphire eyes had darkened to the color of a stormy sea. Nervously, she moistened her lips, then realized she was doing it again.

"Are you deliberately trying to arouse me?" he demanded.

"No, I . . . that is—" She broke off, staring with fascination. "Do I arouse you?" she dared.

He regarded her with eyes half-shuttered. "If you're uncertain, why dinna you look?" he drawled.

He was a master of provocation. Holding her breath, she glanced down. Sure enough, his kilt tented at the juncture between his thighs. As she returned her gaze to his, he kneaded her waist and raised his eyebrows meaningfully.

She wanted to melt into his embrace. Pleasure spread through her, pooling between her legs. She felt incredibly feminine, soft against his hard masculinity. In some ways, she felt the way she did when molding clay. An unnamed desire stirred within her. She wanted . . . She must . . .

With a small cry, she gave in to it. Locking both

hands around his neck, she rose on tiptoe and kissed his warm, inviting mouth.

He grunted in astonishment but hesitated only an instant before responding. His arms wrapped around her, crushing her to him in reply.

His grasp flattened her breasts against the muscles of his chest. The hardness beneath his kilt pressed against her lower belly. The tingling she felt escalated, and she softened her mouth beneath his.

With a groan, he accepted her invitation, tasting her lips with swift movements that sent her blood spinning in a delirious frenzy. He knew about her love for clay, he knew she wished to establish a pottery, yet he still wanted to kiss her.

More, she wanted to moan. *Don't stop.*

A sharp cry interrupted from the doorway. "Kilmartins, brother—"

Angelica looked up to find Lilias staring at them with angry, frightened eyes.

"They're firing the village," Lilias cried. "When they're done, they'll attack the castle, and all you can think of is your doxy. Fool! How could you even imagine they would leave us alone?"

With a roar of rage, Geddes released Angelica and raced for the door.

Unbalanced by the sudden withdrawal of his support, she sagged against the table, feeling dazed by both the kiss and its sudden end.

Lilias stepped aside as Geddes reached the door, then prepared to follow him, but he pushed her back into the solar. "You will remain with Mistress Cavandish, Lilias. Do not, under any circumstances, go beyond the gate, or I'll lock you in your chamber again. Do you understand? Dinna do anything rash, like last time."

Lilias stuck out her bottom lip and moved toward the door again.

"Do as I bid," he roared. "And you, Mistress Cavandish." He turned on Angelica so suddenly, she jerked to attention. "You will remain here as well, or I warn you, I cannot be responsible for your life. The pair of you, dinna move or I'll . . ." He paused and shook his head sharply. " 'Tis not what I'll do to you but what the Kilmartins will do. Heed me, or you'll pay the price." His orders finished, he raced for the stairway, shouting for his war captain.

With the magic of the kiss wearing off, Angelica's stomach knotted into a hard lump of fear. The roof of Magnus the Potter might be burning above his family's heads at this very moment. Master Stone could be in danger as well. She had spent the last hour imagining a rosy future for the village. She hadn't thought the Kilmartins would dare attack. This was more serious than she had realized.

"We must do something. We cannot sit here, idle," she said to Lilias, wondering what rash thing the girl had done last time. And what "last time" did the MacCallum chieftain mean?

Lilias hurried to the window and flung wide one of the panes.

Shouts and screams from the village pierced the darkness. The smell of smoke floated to them on the chill night wind.

Lilias gave Angelica what seemed like a speculative glance. "There *is* something we can do, *if* you're willing."

Angelica wanted to agree at once, but the warning in Lilias's tone caused her to hesitate. "Is it something rash, as your brother said?"

" 'Tis something that will rout the attackers. What could be rash in that?"

Angelica suspected that Geddes would object to this line of reasoning, but it appealed to her own need for action. "Lead on," she ordered grimly, determined to do whatever was required. "I'm willing to try your plan."

For the first time since Angelica had met her, Lilias smiled in approval. "Verra well, follow me."

As they left the solar and hurried down the corridor, Angelica noted that the vast castle seemed unusually quiet.

"The men are in the stables, arming and mounting up to defend the village," Lilias flung over her shoulder, as if sensing her question. "The women are hiding. They've nay doubt barricaded themselves in the storage cellars." She halted before a heavy oak door and tugged it open with considerable effort. Despite the pitch-dark interior revealed beyond the door, Lilias plunged forward, moving upward.

Angelica followed but bumped her toes against a solid obstacle. Upon exploring with her foot, she found a barely visible, winding stair. With hands on cold stone walls, she navigated the dark, dizzying path. The stale air suggested that it was little visited. After an interminable climb, she emerged behind Lilias into a tower chamber.

The full moon shone through a window, revealing a large room with a high, vaulted ceiling but little else. A table but no chairs stood in the middle of the room. A stand with a washbasin crouched beside a plain bed. A huge, ironbound trunk reposed at the bed's foot.

Lilias knelt and flipped open the trunk. Out came a long pole and a bundle of homespun linen that looked to Angelica like little more than a sheet.

Bed linen would save the village?

Lilias gave her no time for questions. She raced for the door with her bundle, shouting instructions. "There will be a guard at the gates. You must engage him whilst I slip past. Hurry. There's no time to lose."

Angelica pelted down the tower stairs after Lilias. "But I should come to the village with you."

They emerged from the tower stairway into the castle corridor. "Follow if you can. Old Dunardley will have orders to keep us here." Lilias banged the oak door shut, then headed for the next staircase and descended in a flurry of tattered black skirts.

Angelica raced after her, determined not to let her go alone.

In the castle yard, chaos reigned as men raced past, fastening weapons at their hips and pulling on leather jackets studded with metal. The excited whinny of horses issued from the stables, and mounted men emerged, one by one, into the chilly spring night. Iain appeared among them, riding a well-muscled garron, his sheathed sword on his back. Angelica froze in place, shocked until she remembered: A Scot stood by his host when danger threatened. With his generous nature, Iain would not hold back.

Certain of MacCallum success, Angelica questioned Lilias's plan to follow the cavalcade into the besieged village. Surely it was not only rash but unnecessary. "Lilias," she began, "perhaps you should—"

"The Kilmartins believe they can overcome us, and every MacCallum, to the man, believes it as well," Lilias hissed. "I mun do this. Now talk to him." She pointed at the approaching gatekeeper, then slipped away, leaving Angelica to face him.

The old man bristled with daggers, and his sword's

scabbard clanked against his thigh as he walked. He paused to watch Lilias as she disappeared behind the shrubbery.

Angelica stepped forward to distract him. "She intends to watch her brother's departure from a safe vantage point," she lied. "What is happening? Where are they going?"

"Best remain inside the castle walls, where 'tis safe, Mistress Cavandish," he admonished. "There's trouble in the village tonight." Despite his stooped posture brought on by advanced years, he drew his sword partway from its scabbard and tested the blade with his thumb. Clearly he intended to use it if necessary to defend the gate and his home.

"How terrible." Angelica dredged up a calm she didn't feel. She must keep him engaged while Lilias made her escape. "Is it the Kilmartin clan?" she asked, knowing full well it was.

"Aye, Kilmartins." He bit off the name with savage ferocity as he slammed the sword back into its scabbard. "Firing the thatched roofs of the cottages, nay doubt. Stealin' and killin'. 'Tis ever the way o' the Kilmartins."

Angelica's stomach churned with anxiety at the thought of killing, but she kept her composure as she spied Lilias inching toward the gate. The gatekeeper, Dun-whatever-his-name-was, had his back to the gate and couldn't see her. As Angelica racked her mind for something to hold his attention, Lilias slipped through the gate and disappeared among the trees beyond.

"Clear the way," a man shouted at Angelica and the gatekeeper.

Angelica whirled to find the mounted men bearing down on them. The MacCallum garrison charged to

the rescue of Duntrune village. Geddes, their chieftain, rode at their head on a black stallion, his hair
flickering like black flame in the wind. His face was
set and grim.

The gatekeeper yelled for Angelica to move and
leaped to one side.

She leaped the opposite direction, flattening herself
into the yews. They prickled the backs of her arms
and neck as the straining bodies of the horses thundered past, their pounding hooves and mighty bodies
as dangerous as their riders' swords.

Angelica's mind spun as she considered her next
move. It was unwise to become involved in a battle,
but she couldn't forget Lilias's earlier words. The Mac-
Callum clansmen didn't believe they could overcome
the Kilmartins, and Lilias was going to do something
about it. Add to that what Geddes had said about the
girl's being rash. She could be hurt. Two were better
than one in such a case.

Making her decision, Angelica hiked up her velvet
skirts and raced after the last horses as they thundered
through the gate. The gatekeeper shouted and gave
chase, but she did not stop. If she got far enough away
from the gate, he dared not follow. His duty was to
defend the castle entrance if it was attacked.

Relieved by the ease of her escape, her heart ham-
mering in her chest, Angelica stumbled in the dark
after the mounted men, hoping to find Lilias. The girl
had been on foot. She couldn't be too far ahead.

As she approached the village, she spied the girl's
slim figure, lurking among the trees. "Lilias, wait,"
she called.

Lilias halted at the point where the trees ended.
The village beyond was a scene of horror. Women
herded crying children into the woods as mounted

men raced after them, brandishing swords. Villager men with pitchforks leaped to their defense. Mounted MacCallum warriors charged at mounted Kilmartin attackers. Swords clashed. The shrilling of frightened horses throbbed on the air, and the acrid smell of smoke rose above it all, accompanied by the crackle of fire. Angelica spied the leaping flames in the distance. Some would lose their homes tonight.

"Here. Help me," Lilias ordered. She thrust the end of the sheet into Angelica's hands. The other end of the cloth was attached to the pole in her hands. "I'm going to run so it unfurls and all can see. You follow. Dinna let it touch the ground."

Without further warning, Lilias raced forward, unfurling the voluminous fabric. "The Faeric Flag," she shrieked at the top of her lungs. "MacCallum, awake. Your flag has returned. Death to the Kilmartins."

The vast field of fabric billowed in the night breeze. Startled by Lilias's sudden move, Angelica ran after her, holding a corner, raising both arms high to keep it aloft.

A mounted Kilmartin took one look at Lilias bearing the flag, dropped his sword with an oath of horror, and turned his horse.

"The Faerie Flag is returned from the grave," he cried, riding hell-bent among his clansmen. "Retreat."

A stampede ensued as the Kilmartins, to a man, fled. The MacCallum garrison, heartened by the turn of events, chased their attackers with roars of triumph.

Lilias raced after them, waving the banner above her head with all her might. The end whipped from Angelica's hands, leaving her to stand, panting in wonder.

The village cleared, leaving MacCallums to swing down from their horses and begin helping the villagers. Women straggled back from the forest carrying bawling babes and leading frightened bairns by the hand. Older boys and girls chased loosened goats back to the village green. Women bent over the injured to examine wounds. Men hurried with buckets of water to pour on blazing straw thatch.

Angelica stared at the degradation, her elation at the triumph fading. Ahead of her, Lilias stumbled in a rut.

"Ouch. My ankle." Lilias slumped to the ground under the weight of the pole.

Angelica relieved her of the burden. "Why are they afraid? 'Tis a plain linen banner, is it not?" She fingered the fabric, puzzled by the men's reaction on both sides.

"Dinna let it drag on the ground." From her sitting position, Lilias caught up the edge of the banner. "The Faerie Flag belonged to the MacCallum clan for nigh over a century. Those who carry it into battle are promised victory. Enemies who face it flee in terror, knowing its power."

Angelica regarded the plain banner in surprise. " 'Tis magic, then?"

Lilias shrugged. "Some say 'twas given to the clan by faeries. Others say 'twas brought from the Holy Land by an ancestor, where 'twas blessed by a saint. Kilmartins believe in it, as you saw. So do our men. Look how fiercely they attacked, believing its power on their side. But magic?" She shrugged again. "I couldna say for certes. It has been missing since before I was born."

Angelica frowned at Lilias, then at the cloth. "If the Faerie Flag is missing, what is this, pray?"

"Nothing. 'Tis a piece of cloth I hemmed and sewed

to this pole. But we mun keep up the appearance that 'tis the true flag."

At Lilias's stark admission, Angelica understood all. "Well, well, my friend." She favored Lilias with a conspiratorial smile. "Your ruse succeeded in frightening the Kilmartins away from Duntrune. I would call that Highland ingenuity."

Lilias met her gaze with a grim smile of her own. "I succeeded this time, but I'll no' be able to use the trick twice. And Geddes hates any mention of the flag, which is considered irrevocably lost. There'll be hell to pay because I pretended it has been found. I took another risk."

"What risk did you take before?"

Lilias grimaced. "I went to Castle Fincharn and tried to talk to Angus Kilmartin. Thought I could reason with him, but I couldna. He intended to hold me for ransom. As luck was with me, I managed to escape."

Escape from the ruthless Angus Kilmartin? Though Angelica had walked into and out of Castle Fincharn with no one to stop her, she knew how impossible leaving would have been if the Kilmartin had held her captive. She studied Lilias, wondering.

Was the girl simply very clever? Or was there more to her story than there appeared?

Chapter 7

Angelica received Geddes's summons to the solar early the next morning. With resignation, she dressed in the velvet gown once more. It was inappropriate for morning wear and had not fared well in the melee last night. But she had nothing else to wear as she met with Geddes to defend what she and Lilias had done. It wasn't a pleasant prospect. Not when she recalled his stony expression when he'd ordered her back to the castle last night.

Sure enough, as she approached the chamber, she heard raised voices. Geddes and Lilias were arguing.

She wanted to retreat, to wait until the storm blew over, but she could not desert Lilias. She also wanted to know about the Faerie Flag. Though she wasn't certain she believed in magic, last night had proved the flag's effect on the men of both clans. If it could be found, would it not help protect Duntrune? Why would Geddes be opposed to that, as Lilias implied?

Drawing a fortifying breath, she entered the solar. Geddes stood by the hearth, his head bowed, his saffron shirt creased, as if he'd slept in it. She cleared her throat, and he glanced up.

With a pang, she took in the fatigue in his eyes and the shadow of unshaven beard on his jaw. He must have spent most of the night helping the villagers, as well as directing the patrols to ensure that no new attack was planned. He would have slept little or not at all.

Words of comfort and sympathy rose to her lips, but he averted his face, cutting her off. Lilias sat in a chair, staring at the fire, her expression like a storm cloud. Neither of them greeted Angelica.

Determined to keep her composure, Angelica crossed the chamber and took a seat opposite Lilias. "Good morrow, Lilias," she said evenly. "Good morrow, MacCallum. How are the villagers this morn?"

"Well enough," he growled, "considering what they've been through. About time you answered my summons." He clasped the poker and attacked the burning logs as if they had done him a wrong and required rebuke. They shifted and flared in seeming resentment.

"I was not overly eager to respond because you appeared furious with your sister's success last night," Angelica began, hoping to shame him for his unreasonable attitude. "And what I meant by my polite inquiry was, did anyone die?"

He glanced up at her blunt question, his expression suggesting she had no right to ask.

She stared back at him. It was her right to know after she had been so intimately involved. She, too, had spent part of the night toting water buckets and binding wounds.

"Nay," he said at last. "None died." He immediately rounded on his sister. "But they might have. What did you think you were doing, Lilias, pretending you'd found the flag? If the Kilmartins had realized it was false, you could have been killed."

"But they didna realize," Lilias pointed out. "They heard my shouts, panicked, and ran."

"I warned you to stay here in safety. You were injured."

Lilias's eyes burned with indignation. "I twisted my ankle by falling in a rut. 'Tis no' a mortal wound. Mistress McCloud bound it up, and I can walk. 'Twill be fine."

" 'Tis your punishment for disobeying me. You are fortunate it isna worse." Geddes put up the poker and strode to the windows, communicating his displeasure by turning his back on them.

His tactic raised Angelica's ire. "I don't see why you are angry with her." She sat forward on the edge of the chair. "She meant to help and she did. Pray, what is wrong with that?"

"I'll no' have interference from you, mistress," he snapped without turning around.

"Then why did you summon me?" she asked reasonably, amused, in spite of the situation, at the vagaries of men. Her brothers were much the same.

"You're just angry because I saved the castle," Lilias interjected, her voice rising. "And I proved that everyone, MacCallum and Kilmartin alike, believes in the Faerie Flag. Now are you convinced? Now will you search for it, as you should have the moment you returned?"

"I'll hear no more of this foolish flag," Geddes roared. He pivoted and strode across the chamber. "And you, Mistress Cavandish, I expected more discreet behavior from you." He loomed over her, the anger in his eyes seeming to burn through her. "You disobeyed a direct order. I told you there was danger, but you refused to listen. You put yourself in the thick of it."

Angelica rose to meet him, insulted by this slight to her judgment. "I may have miscalculated the extent of the danger, but you err as well in your hasty conclusions. You are angry with your sister because she, instead of you, routed the attackers and saved many lives. That is pigheaded and stupid."

Lilias nodded in silent agreement, looking smug.

Geddes glowered down at Angelica. Standing toe-to-toe with him, she felt dwarfed. He filled her vision and her senses until she knew of nothing in the room but his fury.

"I dinna think it wise or polite to call your host pigheaded," he growled.

"Nor was it wise to punish success. Not when you need it so badly." She crossed her arms to block his powerful effect on her. "It appears that you've been avoiding an important issue. What is the Faerie Flag?"

He jerked away, pacing to the windows. "It doesna exist, and everyone kens it. After the retreat last night, the garrison saw your flag, Lilias. They ken it isn't real, for all that you've made such a show of locking it away in the tower chamber. Some of the villagers might have seen as well. The word will be all around."

"But it existed once." Lilias stamped her foot, nearly crying in frustration. "Dinna you see, brother? You mun find it. Everyone believes in its power."

He turned, his face set in grim lines. "*I* dinna believe in it," he said, "and what the chieftain believes is law for the clan."

Being the youngest in a large family, Angelica understood all too well the patriarch's belief in his own superiority. But family matters were rarely so clear-cut, as he seemed to wish. "I'm sorry you're angry, sir, but your sister is correct. As long as your people believe in the flag, it exists, even if only in their minds. You will continue to have trouble."

"We would have rescued the villagers last night with

no difficulty," he said. "You and Lilias need not have interfered."

So his manly pride was hurt. "But you didn't rescue them. Lilias did, thanks to her make-believe flag."

Geddes squared his shoulders, blocking the light from the window. "That is the trouble. How long can we keep a secret like that?"

"As long as necessary, I hope," Angelica said, "at least from the Kilmartins. In the meantime, it seems all the more reason to find the real one. I understand you are insulted that your people believe in the flag more than you, but if it inspires their will to win, let them have it. 'Tis harmless enough."

She felt as if she were talking to a tree trunk. He fixed his gaze out the window, becoming even more distant. " 'Tis no' harmless. Clan MacCallum once reigned supreme over this region." He spoke as if to the faraway hills. "My ancestors never doubted their right to hold the land until the Faerie Flag was lost in my grandsire's time. Belief in the ability of the clan died. If we are to survive at all, we canna base our strength on an object that may be stolen, lost, or burned. We must believe in our own fighting strength." His chin dropped to his chest in seeming defeat. "But no one does. At least no one has in my lifetime. 'Tis why I left Duntrune seven years ago."

This quiet confession hit Angelica like a wet load of clay. His disagreement with Lilias had never been based on pride or mere resentment. The pain was older, went deeper into clan history, and she was humbled to recognize her error.

But Lilias was having none of it. "The clan isna why you left," she muttered into her lap. "You left because of Susan Kilmartin."

"She was part of it." Geddes's gaze fired sparks of

displeasure. "An important part, but the flag was always at the root of the trouble. Have you any idea what it's like?" He swung back to Angelica, suddenly focused on her again. "Trying to lead men who believe they will fail unless a bit of cloth flies above their heads?"

Angelica flinched at the anguish in his eyes. "I am sorry. I now understand your opposition to finding the flag. But—"

"I was scarce able to rouse enough men to retake Duntrune." The words came from him faster, like a newly released deluge. "Only after my ceaseless campaigns to rally their courage did they fight for their home. The men were living in caves along the coast. Like animals, they were, and content to remain so. We would never have retaken the castle if the Kilmartin hadn't become lax. We caught him unawares, 'twas all."

Lilias muttered and shook her head in disagreement, stubborn as only the young could be with the certainty of their convictions.

Angelica waited, urging Geddes with her gaze to continue. Painful though it was, she must hear all.

"You saw them last night." His voice dropped to a penetrating whisper, clearly audible over Lilias's mutterings. "Clan MacCallum will fight to exhaustion as long as that flag flies over their heads. They will chase after their foes as they did last night with the strength of a thousand dragons. The Kilmartins were terrified. Yet had anything changed?"

"Not practically," Angelica said, "but both sides believed it had, and beliefs are very strong."

"Useless beliefs must be changed," Geddes shouted, as if he would enjoy personally ramming change down everyone's throat.

Lilias ceased her muttering and fixed him with a suspicious gaze. "That sounds like something Lachlan would say."

Geddes shrugged, appearing uncomfortable. "Lachlan said all manner of things. Some of them were idiotic, others sensible. I'm sure he would agree that these lads can show some spirit and fight, no' mewl in their milk for the blasted flag."

"It *is* something Lachlan would say," Lilias insisted, giving her brother a sly smile.

"The devil with Lachlan," Geddes said. "He's no' here."

Angelica watched brother and sister, puzzled by this exchange. "Who is Lachlan?"

"No one you need ken," Geddes snapped. "He hasna the grace to come home, Lilias. Dinna bring up his name." He swung away from the windows and stationed himself by the hearth.

"I'll bring him up if I like," Lilias flung at him. "Lachlan is our brother," she explained to Angelica with a trace of apology. "He's older than me, but younger than Geddes. Lachlan the Peacemaker, we called him. He didn't want to fight for any reason. He thought the clans should live in harmony. He went off to Paris to pursue his studies. We haven't heard from him in years." She eyed her brother. "He and Geddes were born only a year apart. They looked a good deal alike, but Geddes was always a fighter. He used to trounce Lachlan and me daily before we broke our fast, just to prove he could."

Geddes frowned. "You exaggerate, Lilias. You were naught but a child."

Lilias shrugged. "You *were* a bully."

"I was training to be chieftain."

"You enjoyed hitting us because we were smaller

and weaker." Lilias delivered this accusation with relish, as if knowing it would provoke him. " 'Tis a wonder you've changed."

"I havena changed. I've learned what's important, as will you with maturity. I've Kilmartins to fight. You have a future to prepare for." Geddes pounded his fist against his open palm, as if he would like to pound Kilmartins, and perhaps Lilias if she didn't behave.

Lilias pursed her lips and made a disparaging sound.

Angelica almost smiled at the memory of how, in her youth, she had also believed the future less important than the present. But as she gazed from one sibling to the other, she became more puzzled than ever. Lilias did not behave in the least like a smaller, weaker sibling. "Let us be practical," she intervened when neither spoke. "Where can you begin to look for this flag? Where was it last seen?"

"We're no' searching for the flag," Geddes said succinctly. " 'Tis a waste of time."

"You see? He'll no' even try." Lilias turned to Angelica, pouting. " 'Twill be difficult to trace after so many years, but no' impossible."

Geddes shot his sister a harassed look. "I have explained my will on the subject. I expect to be obeyed."

"I shall search for it if I like." Lilias screwed up her face, daring him to prevent her.

Brother and sister seemed so much alike, with the same ebony tresses, the same fierce expression on their faces as they confronted each other, driven by the same determination that sprang from the Highland blood flowing in their veins.

"Why not compromise?" Angelica proposed, feeling it was time to stop the bickering and make some decisions. She appealed to Geddes. "We can talk to people to learn what they know. If they know the flag is false, we can ask them to keep the secret, assuring them that we intend to search for the real one. 'Twill appease them while you encourage them to have more faith in you and themselves. What is the chance that I might find it?"

"Nigh on nil." He strode up and down the solar, seething with restless energy, as if eager to lead but stymied by a clan that was afraid to follow. "My mother searched for close to two decades with no success." He cast Angelica a look of curiosity. "How do you expect to find it, when she could not?"

"That depends on where she looked and where she failed to look," Angelica said. To her, it seemed of little use to dwell on past failures. "I can but try."

"It was last seen at a battle on the coast at Dunardry," Lilias put in. "After the MacCallum and Campbell victory over the Kilmartins and the MacDonalds, it disappeared."

Angelica thought this over. "Is anyone still alive who might know where it went?" she asked finally.

"I dinna ken." Lilias cast a baleful glance at her brother. "*I* was never permitted to ask."

"I shall make some inquiries," Angelica said briskly. "As an outsider, I may discover something that a long-time resident overlooked."

"If the blasted thing really exists, 'twould be so old by now, 'twould be rotted to a few threads," Geddes all but roared. He clamped his mouth shut, obviously reining in his temper. "You will be busy starting this clay enterprise of yours." He narrowed his eyes. "When will you have time for this asking, and why should you wish to?"

Her heart beat faster in sudden excitement. "Does that mean you agree I should stay?"

His expression soured as he seemed to realize what he had said. "Only until I can get a message to the captain who brought you, so he can take you back again. I cannot spare an escort to accompany you now. Not after last night. We have two wounded men."

Angelica asked after the men, concerned for their welfare. But even as she did so, joy radiated through her. He would let her stay. She was so happy, she wanted to sing. "You won't be sorry, letting me stay." She struggled to contain her relief as he moved toward the solar door.

"If you're going to stay, I'll expect you to make yourself useful, as you offered to do last night." He paused to eye her speculatively, as if an idea had occurred to him.

Useful? Trepidation swept up and down her spine as she endured his perusal. He had just granted her ultimate wish, but now his eyes flickered with passion, and she shivered, remembering their kiss last night. "In what way useful?" she dared.

"I expect you to supervise Lilias. See that we have no repeats of last night's performance, or of anything else inappropriate." He glanced at his sister. "And the sooner she gives up that wretched black skirt, the better I will be pleased."

"What?" A howl erupted from Lilias. She had been watching them with alert, eager eyes, but now her face reddened. She clenched her fists and confronted her brother. "I'm no' a babe, needing a nursemaid to follow me about. How dare you even think it." Her pride was clearly wounded. "And she's your doxy, for heaven's sake. Why should she have anything to say about my clothes?"

Angelica noted that she applied the foul name with

less conviction than in the past. The tiniest seeds of doubt must have been planted after their collaboration last night.

"She is an older, responsible female," Geddes said, "who is capable of minding her manners and ensuring that you mind yours. And she is no' my doxy."

"She will be, Geddes MacCallum. You always bedded females as fast as you could. And you canna make me obey her. She went with me last night. She's as unruly as I." Lilias cast him a look of triumph, having found the perfect argument.

The unruly part was true enough, Angelica had to admit, so she let it go. But she took exception to being argued over like a Christmas pig. "Listen to your brother. I am not his doxy." She scowled at Lilias. "Nor do I appreciate your calling me such." She whirled on Geddes. "But I agree wholeheartedly that I should not take on responsibility for your sister. That belongs to close kin, not a stranger."

Geddes seemed unwilling to listen. "As long as you obey Mistress Cavandish," he continued as if she hadn't protested, "*I* will search for the flag. I will take on that responsibility. But the minute you stop, so will I."

Lilias grimaced, stymied by this threat. "Black rent, brother?"

"If required," he said calmly.

"But *I* object to the arrangement," Angelica interjected. "Even if you search for the flag instead of me, I must start my clay business, as you pointed out. I cannot make much progress if I must supervise your sister."

"Lilias can help you with the clay. The pair of you can keep company. 'Twill help protect your reputa-

tion, Mistress Cavandish. I'll no' have it said that you
are my leman."

More howls of fury and objection issued from Lilias.
"I dinna like clay," she said, sobbing. "You are cruel
and unnatural."

Geddes ignored his sister's tantrum. He fixed his
gaze on Angelica and waited for her reply.

Frustrated, Angelica wanted to dissolve into a tantrum along with Lilias. As a child, she would have.
But as an adult, she knew such behavior would not
help, so she straightened her shoulders and faced Geddes. "You have granted me my wish to remain in Duntrune, and for that I am grateful. I appreciate your
concern for my reputation, and I see that Lilias needs
supervision, but this is a weighty obligation. I am not
sure I am qualified."

He stepped near and stroked her cheek. His smile
was warm, his eyes snapping with suggestion.

The world suddenly whirled in dizzying hues around
her. The subtle touch of his roughened hand against
her cheek spoke of a thousand desires. She sensed
them in him, then felt the answering response within
herself. She was powerless beneath his touch.

"Mistress Cavandish, you will do as I command, and
if you step out of line even once," he crooned in seductive tones, "you will be forbidden to dig any more
of *my* clay."

Chapter 8

At Geddes's threat, Angelica exhaled sharply and drew back, her expression shocked. Though it was no laughing matter, he had to suppress a grin. She looked as if he had just voiced aloud his desire to seduce her.

He would like nothing better than a fiery affair with this strong-willed, passionate female. His tone, which she had understood, implied as much. But he had chosen to threaten her clay instead, knowing it would be more effective. Looking as alarmed as the nymph Daphne fleeing the unwanted amours of Apollo, she dashed from the chamber.

Geddes's wicked pleasure faded as a great weariness consumed him. He should not have agreed to let her stay. Everything she hoped for would be crushed in the end. But the difficulty of sending her away just now was real, and he did need help with Lilias.

His sister stood staring at him, her forehead furrowed into a field of perpetual discontent. So she had bought them a onetime victory. If the deception could continue, they might have some breathing space from Kilmartin attacks that would give them time to rebuild. He needed that time to gather strength.

What he hated was gaining it through deception. He

had too much of it in his life. Deceit was like a treacherous bog. You set foot in its dangerous territory for one reason only: to get to where you were going. But you took great risk in choosing that direction. One wrong step and the lies could entrap you like thick, black mud. They sucked you down with slow, relentless strength.

He raked back his hair with one hand, exhausted. It had been a wretched night, and he had barely slept an hour. He wished to seek his bed. "Lilias, you will go to your chamber and remain there until the noon dinner hour," he instructed. "Mistress Cavendish will take up her new duties as your companion at that time."

Lilias scowled at him.

"Must you frown so? I should think 'twould hurt yer face."

With the suffering expression of a martyr, Lilias disdained to answer. She swept from the chamber, her tattered black skirt fanning out behind her. It ruined her dramatic exit by catching on a nail in the lintel and tripping her. With a hiss of annoyance, she jerked the skirt free, regained her balance, and flounced away. A moment later, Geddes heard her chamber door slam.

Geddes resolved to be rid of the skirt. She knew it annoyed him, and it certainly did nothing to enhance her charms, tripping her as it did. Yet she flaunted it and her dirty feet as signs of her rebellion against his authority, which annoyed him all the more.

Sinking into a chair, he tried to sort through recent events. Both women were displeased with him for different reasons, and he could get through to neither of them. He had more injured men, despite their unexpected victory last night. Then, this morning, a new difficulty had reared its ugly head.

Opening his sporran, he drew forth a black-sealed parchment and smoothed it on his lap. Though he had read the message earlier, he scanned the lines once more.

The Englishwoman is mine, Angus Kilmartin had written in plain, bold letters. *Surrender her or pay the price.*

What bravado, to demand her return after losing last night's battle. And why did the Kilmartin want her? Geddes refolded the letter and smacked it against his thigh as he considered. The old man had exchanged letters with her, invited her north, then urged her to dig for clay.

The answer must lie in the burn. Angus was looking for something. Before Geddes had returned, someone else had been digging. The evidence was plain for anyone to see.

But Geddes had interrupted the old man's search by retaking the land, so he had set someone else to the task. Had Angel Cavandish been his idea or that of Magnus the Potter?

Whatever the answer, if something of value lurked in the burn, it now belonged to Geddes. The land was MacCallum land. He decided not to reply to the letter. Knowing that Clan Kilmartin would not attack again as long as they believed he had the Faerie Flag, he would wait. He must count on the ruse, much as he hated it.

Firm in his decision, he reached under his chair and hauled out Angel Cavandish's travel pack. He'd meant to return it to her, but their discussion had been too turbulent. He would get it to her later.

Rising, he placed the pack on the table and eyed it speculatively. If the Kilmartin claimed the lass, why had he returned her things at Rhuri's request yesterday? Puzzled by the contradiction, he undid the buckle and peered inside, hoping for a clue. Three clean white smocks lay on top, each embroidered in designs of white thread and embellished with rows of white lace.

An unexpected vision arose in his mind of that same white linen molded to Angel Cavandish's breasts. The lace at the neckline would lie against her radiant flesh, rising and falling with each breath she took.

Unsettled by his body's response to the image, he put the smocks aside.

Several pairs of clean stockings appeared next, followed by a simple but well-cut green kirtle skirt and bodice. He fingered a dark blue shawl shot through with pale blue threads, a stack of linen handkerchiefs, and a gray traveling cloak with a hood. An ivory comb and a wooden box of hairpins were next. A huge work apron emerged last. The stiff, heavy canvas was clearly meant to protect her gown while she worked with clay. At the very bottom of the pack lay a sack of gray powder. Geddes sniffed but could not identify it. The pack contained nothing more.

How telling the contents were of their owner. No useless baubles or personal mementos cluttered the pack—only essentials, except for that odd sack of dust. Geddes felt certain it was related to the angel's passion for clay. He just did not know in what way.

Discouraged by the lack of clues, Geddes shoveled the items back into the pack. As he refastened the buckle, he sensed a presence behind him. Turning, he found Iain Lang staring at him from the doorway, his green eyes fierce with distrust.

"That is Mistress Cavandish's pack," the young man accused, storming into the chamber.

"So it is," Geddes said blandly, though he was annoyed that he hadn't thought to examine the pack behind closed doors. "I had it fetched for her from Castle Fincharn. Did you see any signs that Angus Kilmartin intended to wed the lady under your care?"

The lad slammed to a halt. "Wed her? Nay. How could you suggest such a thing? He's decades older than she."

"I agree. Yet the old laird seems overly interested in her. I was seeking clues as to why." Geddes slung the pack into Iain's hands.

Iain caught it, looking as surprised by the statement as by the unexpected receipt of Angelica's baggage. "I'll throttle him if he touches her."

I, too, Geddes thought. "His son may want her. Did he seem enamored of her? Or she of him? He's a brawley lad, well liked by the lasses."

"No' by Angelica," Iain swore with vehemence. "Brian Kilmartin seemed well enough, but he's younger than she. No more than twenty. And the old man is a ruffian. She would no' consider such a family, with their interest in feuding. Nor would I let her, if she did."

Relief filled Geddes to hear Angelica's disinterest in Brian Kilmartin confirmed. At the same time, he saw an opportunity to gain information about his enemy. "Brian Kilmartin is never at the raids on us, nor was he there last night. Only the Kilmartin war commander. Did the lad voice an opinion about the feud while you were there?"

Iain's expression shifted from hostile to curious. "You dinna ken where he stands?"

Geddes saw the chance to win an ally and reached for it. "Nay," he confessed, "the old master rules Fincharn. I can only guess at his heir's position. But you were there. What do you think?"

"Brian spoke up only once, but he seemed against the feud." Iain shared his knowledge with disarming eagerness. "His sire snapped at him and bade him be still."

" 'Tis good." Geddes sank into his chair, digesting this welcome news. He motioned Iain to the seat opposite. "Can you tell me aught else?"

Cradling the pack in his arms, Iain sat. "The old man is unwell. If you could reason wi' the heir, you might someday have peace. I wished for it for years, growin' up in Lockerbie, where the Grahams and the Maxwells were always at one another's throats." Regret crept over Iain's youthful features, apparently inspired by bad memories.

Now Geddes understood why the young man had joined them so readily last night. He felt an instant bond with the young Lowlander. "So you understand feuds."

"Aye, though we dinna have them on my stretch of the border now. My chieftain and his wife ended them."

Not just the chieftain. The wife, too. If Geddes had it right, the wife was Angel Cavandish's sister. He winced inwardly as he imagined an entire family of such strong-willed women. "And you would like to do the same? End feuds?" Geddes fingered the hilt of his dirk as he sized up Iain. Perhaps this was the key to this likely lad with the pleasant, open face and fiery red hair. He was searching for his place in the world, and he would like nothing better than to emulate his chieftain. And the wife.

"I would like to spread peace if I could."

With the opportunity beckoning, Geddes reached for it. "I have not yet thanked you for joining us last night," he said with quiet courtesy. "Or for working into the wee hours to douse the fires and set things to rights. You went beyond mere politeness. I am in your debt."

Iain flushed and looked self-conscious. "I canna stand by and watch raiders burn and kill members of any clan. They were no' provoked."

"I thank you for your faith in us, but how do you ken Kilmartin doesna have legitimate complaints against me or my father?"

"I dinna ken," Iain replied with candor, "but he killed yer father, yet ye dinna seek revenge. Whatever wrong was done to Kilmartin is avenged. After staying a night at Castle Fincharn, I see the feud promoted by a bitter old man, living in the past. 'Tis time to let it rest."

Geddes was liking Iain better and better. "I appreciate your view of our situation. Still, you need not have ridden with us and I thank you for doing so. My people are weary from continual attack. How are we to rebuild if we canna even sleep, unafraid, in our beds at night?"

"I've seen enough of it, too. Senseless raiding out of greed or misdirected revenge."

Geddes nodded, judging the lad to have a caring heart as well as a wish for justice. "So you understand that you and Mistress Cavandish are now a part of our feud." He fixed Iain with a stare, urging him to recognize the choice he had made last night.

Iain shifted uncomfortably. "I had thought only to protect Angel on her journey."

"*She* chose sides, did she not?"

"She says she is neutral, but she has the utmost faith in you as a chieftain," Iain said a mite stiffly.

"Does she now?"

"Aye, she is vehement on the subject. Says you are honorable." Iain thrust out his jaw, a gleam of belligerence in his eye. "Are ye?"

Geddes fixed the lad with a sardonic frown meant to intimidate him. "If you mean, did I take advantage of Mistress Cavandish, you had best ask her. She seems inclined to tell you all."

Iain sighed, seeming oblivious to Geddes's desired effect. "She assured me last night that you hadna, so I suppose she chose rightly between the two lairds. We both did," he murmured, as if to himself. "Angel is single-minded, though. I never know what she will do next."

Geddes thought of how the selfsame Angel had kissed him last night and had to agree.

"Ye say Kilmartin takes an unusual interest in Angel?" Iain asked.

"Aye. I've word that he wishes her to return to Fincharn."

"For no good purpose, I'll vow." Iain played with the buckle on the pack, frowning. "I'd ask yer support in protecting her. 'Tis my duty, but the Master of Fincharn has many men. I may need help. In return, I am willing to ride with you, fight with you, as long as she is safe."

Geddes experienced a rush of satisfaction as the lad made his position clear. Not only was he honorable, but also wise beyond his years. In any case, Geddes needed every hand he could recruit, and Iain had a strong one. "I am pleased to accept your support, though I do not wish to endanger you unnecessarily. I will call on you only if our need is dire. You should most like confine yourself to assisting Mistress Cavandish with her clay enterprise."

"Nay, Angel is the one who loves getting filthy. I personally hate the stuff." Iain held up both hands, as if to fend off the unwelcome substance.

Geddes concealed a smile. He doubted the lad would escape as easily as he hoped. Not if the single-minded Mistress Angel decided she required his aid.

He dismissed Iain Lang a few minutes later, sending him off to return the pack to Angel. Still, he had troubles. Could his people possibly keep the ruse of the false flag hidden from outsiders?

He doubted it, but he must sound them out, as Angelica had suggested. Such a ruse could buy them valuable respite from raids, which they desperately needed. Some would call him foolish not to grasp the opportunity eagerly, but he had an aversion to deception and misplaced faith.

All this led to one thing. Much as he hated to do it, he must search for the true flag, as he had promised his sister and Angel. If the Kilmartins ever learned they had fled from a false flag, there would be retaliation with no quarter granted. He must also double his diligence to ensure that no Kilmartin spies penetrated his household.

Disliking his chosen path, he twisted and turned, looking for alternatives. Nothing seemed clear this morn. Nothing save the way Angel Cavandish aroused him. She inspired in him the desire to behave in a most inappropriate manner.

A rakehell was supposed to behave inappropriately. People expected him to take her if he wished.

It would complicate matters. Iain would protest.

It would bring superb enjoyment in trying times.

He would owe the Englishwoman something.

He was sheltering her, giving her the clay she desired. It was a fair trade. Once she returned to England, no one would know.

Save he would know, and he had already asked her for help with Lilias in exchange for the clay. He couldn't do it. Nor did he relish the idea of ruining the virtue of this particular female, with her clever hands and admirable will. She had been like a pearl yesterday, gleaming in the burn.

No, not a pearl. An angel.

As she had stood the water, her skirts tucked into her waistband, passionate joy had radiated from her face. She had been like a marvelous discovery, giving him hope for the future, making him want to believe.

An angel, without doubt. In both her person and her name.

Back in her chamber, Angelica found her own brown kirtle skirt and bodice, washed and pressed, lying on the bed. Eager to feel more herself after the clash with Geddes MacCallum, she took off the velvet skirt and hung it in the wardrobe.

Half-clad, she paused to stare out the window. What had she gotten herself into? The chieftain would let her stay at Duntrune, but, oh, at what a price.

Groaning under the weight of the new responsibility, she yanked at the laces of her bodice to untie them. As the youngest girl in her large family, *she* was the one who teased her older siblings and enjoyed their spoiling and pampering. With the money and backing of her family, *she* had the luxury to act on her desires. In many ways, she had always behaved like Lilias, as the girl had so aptly pointed out.

Now she must guide the young woman on a safe path to maturity. It would force her to reconsider her own behavior. Lilias would not make it easy for her, despite their agreement last night. In fact, Angelica should have forbidden last night's activity.

That was the problem. She was a poor substitute for the loving mother that Lilias deserved, but she vowed to do her best by the girl. She could certainly offer genuine friendship and caring, for the girl's pain had touched her.

Other tasks pressed on her as well. She had seen Master Stone last night and been assured that neither he nor Magnus and his family had been harmed in the raid. Today, though, they would require food, which she meant to supply. Jenny Marie had come, telling her Lilias was in her chamber until the dinner hour, when Angelica was to take up her responsibilities. For a few more hours, she was free.

Seating herself before the looking glass, she began to redress her sagging hair. The sparkle of light on the glass reminded her of the Scots coastline, a watercolor of glorious blue water meeting pale blue sky. Surely the beauty of the land would more than make up for the added duty. The mild summer weather, though chill and misty many a night and early morn, offered gleaming hours of daytime sun. Alder and oak in green abundance surrounded the castle, which overlooked Loch Crinan to the south. Wide-open meadows replete with grazing sheep and Highland cattle stood to the north.

She also loved the old Norman tower house of Duntrune, with its protective curtain walls. Under the direction of Muriel McCloud, the stone castle was kept scrupulously clean. The magnificent great hall, the herb-scented kitchens, the personal chambers were all well proportioned and comfortable. Willingly, she would make this her home.

As she coiled and wrapped her hair, Angelica added extra pins, remembering how unruly it had been last night. An added attraction at Duntrune flared in her mind. Although unwise, she had indulged in an experiment last night, sampling the wares of a Highland rogue. Concerned by her action, she reviewed the mental list she had compiled of his traits:

He had proved that he was intelligent.

Possessive of his land.

Reasonable, though after this morning's interview, she would call him quick-tempered.

A rescuer of children.

A rakehell.

She must modify the last item. A puzzling rakehell. Had he been an ordinary rogue, openly seducing every female alive, she would find him boring. Yet she had not seen him seduce any females since her arrival. Indeed, he had not attempted to seduce her, though the opportunity had existed. True, he'd been fighting Kilmartins, but he could have found a way to ravish her. She knew enough about men to realize that.

Instead, she had been the one to initiate their kiss.

Closing her eyes, she remembered that moment of folly. Why had she done it? Because she had no clay of her own, had been deprived of clay for weeks, and he had let her dig some of his?

That must be it. She was grateful. The ecstasy he stirred in her soul had much to do with her guess that he would let her stay.

Yet it was far too simple an explanation for the power he exercised over her senses. She wasn't that greedy, to be moved by material gain, even if it was something she desired. No, he had done no more than put his hands on her, and she had been transported by pleasure. Such a response both fascinated and mystified her.

It hadn't been seduction. Geddes MacCallum had behaved too honorably. A rogue would seize his pleasure and wring it dry.

Instead, he had waited for her tacit approval before even repinning her lock of hair. In the kiss they had shared, though his lips had demanded, he had also given. Wasn't a rogue incapable of generosity?

He was desire counterbalanced by restraint. How unexpected and appealing. Not what she expected in a man, though she had seldom interacted with any men except stolid Dorset workingmen. Respectable, boring men.

Geddes managed to be respectable without being boring. He cared about his sister's reputation. He cared about her, Angelica's, safety. She could trust such a man. He would not overwhelm her with his mesmerizing ways unless she invited him, as she had last night.

She must not seek such sensations in future, she told herself. Her workshop would be ready soon. She would concentrate on the dependable stimulation of her art.

Eager to get to it, she left her chamber and descended the back stair to the kitchens. Carrying her shoes, which were dirtier than ever after last night, she padded into the chamber in her stocking feet.

Muriel McCloud wiped her hands on her voluminous white apron and nodded with approval as she noted the shoes in Angelica's hand. "What can I do for ye this fine morning, my lass?" Her smile was warm and welcoming.

Had she heard aught of the agreements made in the solar that morning? Was she friendly because of that?

Geddes had warned Angelica that everyone here knew everyone else's affairs.

"I must go to the village," she began, not sure how Muriel would receive her plan, "to the family of Magnus the Potter. Though they were unharmed in the raid, many of their supplies were destroyed. May I take them some food?"

"Help yersel' from the larder and buttery." Muriel lifted a large wicker basket from a hook and passed it to her. "The MacCallum always sees tae the villagers. He'll be glad of yer help."

"Magnus will be moving his pottery wheels to the castle today," Angelica said. "I noted a small outbuilding by the stable that would be a good location. May I use it? And can a pony and cart be spared?"

Muriel fell to kneading bread dough at her worktable. "I dinna ken. Ask Sim Dunarchy, the head stableman."

Another of those Dun names. Was this the same or a different man from the one who had questioned her upon arrival? She struggled to remember his name but couldn't. After a second, she gave up. "Could you say that name again?"

Muriel squinted at her. "Dunarchy? Why?"

"Who was the other man I met?" Angelica asked. "Dun something else." Muriel continued to squint at her, as if she'd suddenly become half-witted. "All the Dun names confuse me," she admitted sheepishly. "And all the Mac names. I've learned MacCallum, but I need to write the others down."

Muriel threw back her head and brayed with laughter. "Ye'd best be learning them all if ye're going to bear a MacCallum babe. Yer child will be kin to them." She chortled.

Angelica stared at her. "But I am not going to—"

She was interrupted by four great men in MacCallum kilts who clattered into the kitchens, laughing and talking. They grasped wooden bowls and spoons from a table and crowded around the kettle bubbling on the hearth.

"Night patrol, here to break their fast," Muriel informed her. She winked at Angelica as she moved to serve the men.

The boy who had taken Angelica's shoes yesterday sat on a stool, cleaning footwear and soaking up the fire's warmth. "Move, laddie. Ye're in the way." One of the garrison tapped the lad on the shoulder, then gestured him aside with a jerk of his thumb.

The lad took his work and moved. But as he settled in a new spot, he scowled and put out his tongue at the group's turned backs.

Angelica stifled a laugh, recalling how she and her siblings had done the same more than once.

The lad saw her. Grinning, he sidled over, gesturing to let him carry her basket.

"I thank you, but I see that you have many pairs of boots to clean," she said. "I should not keep you from your work."

Instead of answering, he reached for the basket again.

"Here, here, dinna trouble the lady, Ross." Muriel bustled over, clucking her tongue. She caught up a boot and the cloth and, putting them in the lad's hands, gestured for him to get to work.

He fell to again.

"He's a deaf mute," Muriel explained to Angelica as they moved toward the door. "Poor homeless laddie. He was found on the road no' so long ago. He wants to help."

Angelica felt sorry for the lad. "Does he have no family?"

"No' that seems to want him. For certes he looked as if he hadn't lived indoors for weeks. Ragged and lousy, he was. If he's run away, I couldna blame him. Still, the MacCallum is asking about to see if he has any kin. In the meantime, he says 'tis only proper we take him in. Crude little urchin, but he kens how to clean boots and shoes."

Glad to know of the MacCallum's generosity, Angelica bid Muriel farewell and left by the back door. At the stables, she spoke to the first person she found, a young man pitching refuse from a stall. "I'm here to see Sim Dun, er . . ." She floundered, at a loss.

"Dunarchy. I'll fetch him." The lad put up his pitchfork and walked off.

Angelica breathed more freely. Somehow, she reminded herself, she must learn those Dun names.

Her meeting with the head stableman went smoothly. After arranging for a donkey cart to follow to the village, she returned to the kitchens, slipped behind the eating men and into the screens passage, and crossed the great hall to meet Iain in the front entry.

She was making progress, but she still had much to do.

Chapter 9

"You've been busy this morn, I trow. Everyone in the household is whispering."

Angelica accepted Iain's greeting in the front entry. He looked rested this morning. Despite his having been up half the night, his green eyes were alert. But it seemed he'd been listening to tittle-tattle. Resigning herself to the new role gossip would play in her life, she rolled her eyes. "What did you hear?" she asked.

He bent over and whispered in her ear. "I didna just hear. Last night, I saw. That flag was never an ancient relic. I could tell as soon as I saw it up close, which I did, despite Lilias's attempt to bundle it up after the retreat."

Angelica shivered, wondering how many others had seen and whether they would tell. "What are people saying?" she whispered back.

"The household is thrilled to know the Faerie Flag is returned," he said aloud.

She took his hint. Some clanspeople and villagers thought the flag was real. Those who knew otherwise were keeping the secret to themselves. " 'Tis wonderful, though the chieftain is displeased with me and Lilias for going out last night. He did not want us involved."

"I wouldna have wanted it either, but as I went,

too, I canna chide you." Iain grinned with sudden puckish humor.

"Most like you to take the part of the downtrodden." She patted his arm in appreciation of his caring.

"Indeed, I pledged my support to the MacCallum while we're here," Iain said, looking sheepish at the praise. "In return for his help in keeping you safe, o' course."

Angelica grimaced at this revelation. "Was that truly necessary? To pledge your support?"

"Aye. There are more Kilmartins than the one of me," Iain pointed out. "And you chose sides when you insisted we stay here."

She sighed, sorry to admit it, but they were digging their way ever deeper into MacCallum affairs. She was far from neutral; in truth, her recent decisions had made her a MacCallum ally. "You are correct, and now I've done more than choose sides. I will be keeping company with Lilias in exchange for the right to start my pottery. Beginning at noon today, I am responsible for her conduct and reputation."

Concern flashed across Iain's face. "Lilias will be a handful," he warned.

Angelica indicated her basket. "Which is why I wish to accomplish as much as possible before I take charge of her. I have food for Magnus's family, and Master Stone. Let us visit them at once."

Obligingly, Iain opened the heavy oak door for her.

As he stepped aside to let her pass, Angelica saw that he had her pack, and she pounced on it. "Oh, I've wanted my shawl."

Iain held the pack steady while she searched for the wrap.

"How did you manage to get it from Castle Fincharn?" she asked.

"The MacCallum had it fetched for you. A model of courtesy, eh?" His sly glance intimated many questions.

Angelica merely nodded in agreement as she pulled forth the shawl and draped it over her head and shoulders. A soft mist hugged the ground as they ventured forth, and she hid in the shawl's depths, refusing to respond to Iain's hints.

The aged gatekeeper looked chipper that morning, though Angelica was certain he'd been up half the night. Perhaps he thrived on being needed. Or might he be happy about the flag?

He operated the winch that raised the metal yett as she and Iain drew up. "Everyone's celebrating the return o' the Faerie Flag," he said with a jovial smile, confirming her belief. "Ye did a great deed, helping wi' it and routing the enemy, Mistress Cavandish."

So he believed the deception. "I could not hang back with so much at stake," she said.

The gatekeeper winked at her. "The MacCallum and his lady ken what's best for our clan."

His answer was partly heartening, partly annoying. Angelica shot a glance at Iain to see how he would take it. First Muriel, now the gatekeeper, thought she and Geddes were intimate.

But Iain apparently hadn't heard this part of the gossip, or else he trusted her word from last night. He said nothing.

"The MacCallum is a gentleman," she said firmly to set the record straight. "I am not *that* sort of influence on his decisions."

The gatekeeper nodded his grizzled head with a sage expression. "Geddes MacCallum was always one for the lasses, begetting babes as he went. But ye'll be different, I trow. Ye're nay serving maid to be set aside."

Angelica struggled with confusion. Despite Geddes's reputation, she could not see him playing the churl, even as a younger man, casting aside one girl after another, especially if children were involved. There had to be some other explanation.

Putting the puzzle aside for later study, she bade the gatekeeper good day. She and Iain continued toward the village. A rider approached as they reached the trees. He passed them at a canter, clearly in a hurry. Angelica glimpsed the features of an old man, weathered by years. The gatekeeper seemed to know him, for he saluted the rider as he entered the castle yard.

Scolding herself for being curious about the MacCallum's clansmen, Angelica took Iain's arm and they walked on. At the village, full order had been restored to the rows of daub-and-wattle cottages. Goats were back in their pens. Men and boys stood on ladders, rethatching two cottages whose roofs had been burned. Everyone looked tired, but they still smiled and nodded in greeting. They must be pleased with her and Iain's role in routing the Kilmartin attackers.

Magnus's daughter-in-law, Agnes, greeted them with great cordiality and bade them enter, though Angelica saw at once the fatigue in her eyes. She stirred a cauldron on the fire while balancing Jamie on her hip. The child grinned at Angelica.

"Hello, laddie." As she tousled his hair, she remembered how Geddes had rescued the child from the burn, then tried to comfort him. Such a man had warmth and caring. "Have you a smile for your Angel?" she asked.

Jamie buried his face in his mother's shoulder, too shy to answer.

"Come now, say good morrow to the lady," his mother scolded lovingly. "You were bold enough yesterday, nearly falling intae the burn."

Jamie kicked his legs and hid his face in his hands, peering at Angelica through his fingers.

Angelica chuckled. "Never mind, Jamie. When you're ready, I'll let you play with some clay. You'll like rolling and shaping it." She turned to Magnus's daughter-in-law. "Is all well with the family?" she asked.

The woman pushed back her straggling hair. "As well as can be expected. Our cot is no' in the main path, so we have our roof." She jerked her head upward to indicate the intact timbers with thatching above. "Everyone's thanking ye for what ye did, ye and Lady Lilias, and ye, young master." She nodded to Iain.

"We are glad to be of service," Iain said, picking up a wooden windup top and waving it at Jamie.

Agnes set the child down, and Jamie crowed with pleasure as Iain set the toy spinning for him.

Agnes inched close to Angelica as the pair played. "Mayhap the MacCallum will find the true Faerie Flag soon," she whispered. "Ye did an amazing thing, convincing him tae search. Till then, we've been sworn tae keep the secret from the Kilmartins. And from those at Duntrune who dinna hear."

So many knew the truth, yet they joined the conspiracy to hide it from the Kilmartins. For the first time, Angelica felt a glimmer of hope. They believed enough in Geddes to keep a secret for him. At the same time, she understood his irritation. Ultimately, they still pinned their hopes on the supposed magic of the flag rather than on themselves.

"Mistress Angel. Lang. Welcome." Magnus stumped in, his rusty black breeches and jacket still streaked with yesterday's clay. Master Stone followed. They both looked tired from the harrowing night, and less refreshed from their brief sleep than the younger folks. Magnus eyed the basket Angelica had tucked under her arm.

She hurried to present it, having forgotten as she talked to Jamie and Agnes.

As Jamie and the men enjoyed fresh wheat buns, Angelica questioned Magnus. "Your son is well?"

"Aye," he confirmed. "He went off tae work this morning. He's building a gentleman's house over by the coast."

"Well, then." She rubbed both hands together, reassured. "Shall we look at the pottery wheels?"

Between the four of them, they wrestled the wheels from a small shed built against the back of the cottage. Angelica ran an assessing hand over the large wooden wheel of the first, then worked the treadle.

The wheel twirled smoothly. The wooden disk on top spun, connected as it was to the bottom wheel by a metal pole. It was in good condition, the perfect platform for molding clay.

"I oiled and repaired 'em from time tae time. They're no' in bad shape," Magnus said. "Couldna let them go, though I wasna using them anymore." He worked the treadle of the next wheel, a loving light in his eye. "When I heard from ye, Stone, I kent they would be back to work right enow. 'Twas my dearest wish."

Angelica wanted to hug him, she was so filled with

happiness. The wheels would return to use. She, Stone, and Magnus would serve as masters, teaching the apprentices. Their pottery would thrive, brightening all their lives. What more could one ask?

By the time they finished admiring and dusting the wheels, the donkey cart had arrived, driven by a lad. Angelica smiled as Stone, Magnus, and Iain loaded the first wheel without dismantling it. She would have the workshop set up in no time.

An hour later, Angelica bent over a huge mortar, crushing a lump of dried clay to a fine powder with a pestle. Magnus, Stone, and Iain had delivered the first two wheels and returned to the village for the third and fourth. The stable lad had helped her clear the straw-thatched building of tools and farming implements. The single chamber seemed quite spacious, once it was empty. At its center, the stablemen had placed a large workbench where she could prepare clay.

Now she hummed an English dancing tune, feeling content. What bliss to see the high-quality clay crumble to a fine powder. It would mix beautifully with water for a sample. Despite the rocky beginning of her arrival, despite the attack last night, the belief in the Faerie Flag would keep them safe. All would be well.

The sun had burned away the last traces of morning mist. Light poured through the windows and at the entry, drenching the workshop in golden light. In the midst of her happy thoughts about clay and pottery, a shadow crossed the entry. She looked up.

Lilias limped in, favoring her sprained ankle. "He burnt my kirtle skirt," she fumed, shaking her fist in the air. "I am so angry, I could spit in his face."

Angelica stared at Lilias, surprised by this tirade. "Who burned your skirt? What do you mean?"

"Geddes burnt it." Her scowl was enough to frighten a Kilmartin. "I hate him."

For the first time, Angelica noted that Lilias was wearing a dark blue kirtle skirt instead of the usual black one. She groaned inwardly as she realized that Geddes must have acted on his dislike for the ragged black skirt.

"He's a tyrant." Lilias faced her across the workbench. "He tolerates no difference in opinion from his own."

Angelica put down her pestle. "I thought we agreed to a truce this morning. We need time to work this out."

"You agreed. I did not," Lilias announced flatly. "And I shall not agree as long as he acts like the king of swine."

Angelica decided to ignore Lilias's new name for her brother in favor of more pressing matters. "I understand that you are angry." She glanced out the door, hoping no one was listening. "But he bought you a new skirt, did he not?"

"I didna want a new one," the girl insisted. "I hate him. He pretends to be nice, but then he burns my personal things. He's a swine, and I intend to tell him so."

Angelica sighed in frustration. "I am in the midst of an important test, Lilias. I cannot think clearly about the matter just now. I would like to discuss it later, if we may."

"You dinna want to discuss it at all. Admit it." Lilias pivoted on her good foot and stalked to the door, limping. "Duntrune will never change. Everyone is set in their ways."

Angelica knew she had said the wrong thing and cursed her insensitivity. "Don't go, Lilias. Stay and talk to me about it."

"I dinna wish to talk about it. I hate Geddes. I just wanted you to ken why."

"You *do* want to talk about it, else you would not have come," Angelica called after her. "Let us talk more after dinner. Why don't you work on your sketches until then? The plants you were telling me about. I should love to see them."

Lilias harrumphed loudly and disappeared through the door into the yard.

Angelica picked up the pestle and pounded the clay with a vengeance. By heaven, another problem. She hadn't handled it well, either. She should have agreed with Lilias, should have said she would speak to Geddes about destroying his sister's property. But she hadn't, and now she would have to work even harder to repair the damage. Would this pair never quit?

A full hour passed before Angelica recovered her calm and formed a rational plan. By then, she had pulverized a quantity of clay and picked out all the roots and pebbles. It was ready to mix with water for a test batch.

Hoping that Lilias was also calmer by now, she poured a measure of water into the mortar and mixed the contents with both hands. As she worked, another shadow fell across her workbench like a bad omen. She jerked to a stop.

The MacCallum chieftain filled the entire entry. He had donned a clean, pressed saffron shirt since she saw him last. With his plaid pinned at the shoulder by a silver brooch, he was a well-formed specimen of a man, standing silent, silhouetted against the light.

The sight of him sent a twinge of unorthodox excitement spiraling downward in her belly. The madness of last night seized her. She wanted to drop the clay and taste his masculinity once more.

She straightened self-consciously instead. "Greetings, sir." She waited, wishing he would speak. Was he aware that he had upset his sister? Was he displeased that Angelica had appropriated the outbuilding?

He strode forward to tower over her, staring down at her work and clay-covered hands. Then he shifted his gaze to stare at her.

Feeling more self-conscious than ever, she tugged at her apron, wondering if her bodice gaped in front. From the way he looked at her, she might as well be naked. Was he thinking about last night?

She ought never to have kissed him, but she had been unable to help it. He knew how to increase the pulse of any female on whom he concentrated his attention. She should be excused for reacting. It was the surprise, that was all.

"The clay is performing wonderfully well," she began. "I'm preparing a sample for test purposes. Allow me to show you—"

"Lilias is missing," he interrupted tersely.

"Lilias? Missing? What is the hour?" Angelica clasped her hands together, filled with dismay. Had she missed the noon dinner? Had time gotten away from her, as happened so often at home?

" 'Tis eleven of the clock. I ordered her to remain in her chamber until the dinner hour, but she has disappeared and cannot be found."

This seemed impossible to Angelica. "The castle is large. Surely she's tucked out of sight somewhere."

"By all reports, and according to my personal search, she is not."

Angelica bit her lip and tried to think. For certes, Lilias had been upset and wanting to upset her brother in return. "Perhaps she has a place where she hides to annoy you."

"She likes to annoy me, aye, but she is not hiding in the castle."

"Mayhap she's at the village," Angelica offered, hoping this was true. "Or in the stables. Yes?"

"No. All have been searched. To no avail."

With growing distress, Angelica wiped her wet, clay-covered hands on a cloth and untied her work apron. "Then we must search for her at once."

"Indeed. I have horses being saddled even now."

Angelica scarce had time to hang the apron on a peg before he propelled her across the stable yard and boosted her into the sidesaddle of a small garron mare. His urgency transferred itself to her, and a frightening idea stabbed at her like points of angry needles: Had Lilias been kidnapped? Were they on their way to negotiate ransom for her?

The pace Geddes set didn't suggest it. Once they splashed across the stream at the ford and entered the woods beyond, he let his stallion trot beside her gray mare at a reasonable pace. Yet he shifted with restless agitation in the saddle, checking his many dirks, his sword. She sensed a grimness in him, a dark brooding. Could the clan elder she saw earlier have brought bad news? If so, Geddes didn't tell her. He mentioned only his sister. So why weren't they racing to her rescue?

"This is *your* fault," he accused without even looking at her.

"Mine?" Angelica straightened in the saddle, disoriented by the unexpected charge. How had she aided a kidnapper?

"You encouraged her to disobey me last night, so she has gone off on her own," he said. "She thinks you will take her part every time she does so."

"She hasn't been kidnapped?" Angelica searched his rigid profile. "Do you mean to say she hasn't been stolen away?"

"How could you think that?" He shot her a shocked glance. "No one has ever been kidnapped from the castle proper. Even if Lilias had, by some remote chance, been kidnapped from beyond the castle, we would ken it. There would be a ransom demand."

Angelica pulled her mare back to a walk, vastly relieved. But hard on the tail of relief came annoyance. "Shame on you, Geddes MacCallum, for frightening me. From the way you behaved, I thought she'd been carried off by some villain."

He slowed his stallion to a walk to match her mare's, rolling his eyes heavenward. "I never said that. I am told Lilias headed north through these woods. I lay the blame with you. Your approval last night emboldened her to defy me."

"Then I'm not a proper guardian for her," Angelica suggested, hoping he would withdraw the order.

He failed to take her hint. "You are entirely proper if you put your mind to it. So you'd best do so, else I have no need to keep you at Duntrune. I should ship you home."

"You cannot ship me home just now," she pointed out, dismayed by his renewal of the threat, though she had brought it on herself with her impetuous remark.

"I can do so later."

Angelica sighed, knowing this was true. Yet just now, he turned to her in his concern for Lilias. The idea was so gratifying, she wanted to steep in it like a long, hot bath. But it did not help find the missing girl. "Where do we search for her?" she asked. "Do you know where she went?"

"No' where, but I ken why." His angry intensity returned, clearly arising from his concern about his sister.

"Why are you worried about her if you're sure she's unharmed?" Angelica prodded, no longer afraid of an unnamed danger. "She's gone to visit a friend, yes?"

He fastened his gaze on a distant point, offering her a fine view of his clean-shaven, tightly clenched jaw, but nothing more.

Her compassionate feelings dissolved as a kernel of suspicion formed in her mind. "Has this happened before?"

"Of late, far more than I like."

"You might have mentioned that fact to me from the start," she snapped. So this was why he wasn't galloping to rescue his sister. "I feared for her life, and all along you knew she goes off somewhere. Somewhere of which you disapprove. And of late, she's done it more frequently?"

"Aye," he admitted without apology.

Angelica waited for him to elaborate on where Lilias might have gone. Their horses trudged along the sunlit path, their hooves thudding on the hard-packed soil. She might have waited until doomsday. He yielded none of his secrets.

"I will not play this game with you, Geddes MacCallum." She leaned back in the saddle and signaled the mare with the reins. The responsive mount halted. "There is no use looking for Lilias," she said to Geddes's back as he rode ahead on the path. "You just told me you have looked everywhere. There is nowhere left to search. She will return when she's ready and not before."

Geddes and the stallion froze on the path. Then they erupted into motion, wheeling as one to dash back to Angelica and her mare. Anger blazed in Geddes's eyes as the stallion skidded to a halt, the horses parallel.

To Angelica's relief, her mare stood firm, ignoring the two males as if their sudden action was commonplace and of no concern.

"She canna continue this way," Geddes raged.

"What way?" Angelica longed to demand that he tell her all. Yet he was not accustomed to sharing. She must draw it out of him bit by bit. "What is wrong with where she goes?"

" 'Tis indecent. Immoral," he shouted. The stallion tossed his head and shifted on restless feet, seeming to agree.

Angelica studied the bleak despair in his eyes. Surely his sister did not visit a house of ill repute. But could she be friends with someone who owned one? Or was she . . . Insight loomed on the horizon. Lilias's transgression had nothing to do with bawdy houses. She had a sweetheart, and Geddes hated the idea so much, he refused to admit the possibility, let alone consider the man's identity. "She's *your* sister," she said quietly. "You know her better than I. Tell me whom she sees."

He raised a clenched fist as if to strike someone, anyone. The stallion half reared, then skittered sideways, full of his master's mood. "I will kill him for trifling with her."

"He's trifled with her? How dare he have less than honorable intentions toward your sister—" she began, then halted, realizing the obvious. "Lilias must love him, else she wouldn't go to him. If he's trifled with her, she has trifled with him in return. It was by mutual consent."

Geddes nodded stonily. "So I suspect."

Angelica hurt for him. She knew how it felt to have a sibling involved in danger. Her eldest sister, Rozalinde, who had been like a second mother to her, had had the most unorthodox dealings with the neighboring earl. Though only three at the time, Angelica had still felt the tension and anxiety in the household. Yet her sister had wed her earl in the end and both were now happy. Lilias might settle well. "Could he be someone from the village?" she ventured.

"Impossible."

"Impossible because you consider the villagers too humble?" She crossed her arms and surveyed him up and down.

"She is a chieftain's daughter and a lady."

Angelica wrinkled her nose at his haughty reply. "I see. Cool your temper." She reviewed what she knew of the local people. "Who lives to the north?"

He drew his mouth down into a scowl. Kilmartins lived to the northeast. Angelica had stayed at Castle Fincharn and knew where it lay. They both knew.

"It could be one of her distant cousins." Geddes seemed beside himself, casting about for possibilities. "A Dunardy. Or a Dunaudley. Or a—"

"Kilmartin?" she finished, raising her eyebrows.

She thought he would explode into a million pieces. His distorted visage would have frightened even the savage Kilmartins into a retreat.

"Just what are you suggesting, Mistress Cavandish?" He nudged the stallion closer, a dangerous edge to his tone.

Angelica patted the gray mare's neck, glad she did not even turn her head in the stallion's direction. "I met Brian Kilmartin," she began. "I thought him a nice lad. In truth, he does not seem to support the feud—"

"Never," Geddes bellowed, his face reddening. His hands clenched like death on the reins. "Nay MacCallum has ever wed a Kilmartin, do ye ken? No' in one hundred years."

Angelica recoiled, unaccustomed to being shouted at. "I've heard that such marriages between rival clans happen often in Scotland to end feuds. The king is said to order it done."

"No' here." His voice sank to a growl fraught with pain. "No' this feud."

She felt the stark agony twisting his expression. As if they were bells, tolling in a steeple side by side, she quivered with the vibrations emanating from him. She wanted to reach out, to help and to heal. "Why?" she asked more gently. "What is the feud about? Is there something besides land?"

His anguished gaze bore into hers for a long moment, as if the answer were too horrible for him to utter.

"Ho, MacCallum. Greeting to ye, sir," a female voice interrupted from ahead on the path. A thin woman in a faded green apron and white kertch waved to them. "I told ye he'd come, an' here he is," she called to someone behind her.

Angelica glimpsed a clearing ahead, dominated by a thatched stone cottage and a garden.

Geddes turned to the newcomer as if welcoming the excuse to escape.

Angelica chafed. She had been so very close to learning more of this complicated man and his affairs.

Within a short acquaintance, she had discovered that a rakehell was far more than the term implied. As chieftain, he had many virtues, as well as many burdens to bear, and he had almost shared one of the weightiest with her. Why she wished him to open his heart, she did not know. She knew only that she longed to have his confidence.

He seemed eager to avoid such sharing. Turning to the woman as she advanced on the path, he nodded politely. "Goodwife Dunangley."

Another Dun name. As the woman bowed her head and dipped in a semblance of a curtsey, Angelica fumbled for the elusive second half of the name. It slithered away like a wily fish, too clever to be caught.

"Will ye no' visit our humble home, MacCallum?" She beckoned to the chieftain, then to Angelica, including her in the invitation.

"O' course." The rage in Geddes declined, as if he had drained it to a holding chamber for later retrieval.

The woman's wrinkles tightened as she broke into a smile and led the way into the clearing. The cheerful cottage sat surrounded by flowers, herbs, and various outbuildings. An old man in nondescript, baggy clothing worked in a neat garden filled with bean and cucumber vines, lettuce, and green plants that were likely turnips and beets. A dark-haired lad of perhaps ten years, in a soiled tunic and leather-bound leggings, worked at the old man's side.

The youth straightened and stared at them as they entered the clearing but did not come forward. As she drew nearer, Angelica saw the man's gray hair and wrinkled face. The pair must be the child's grandparents. So where were the parents?

"MacCallum." The old man straightened with great

effort, clutched his back with one hand, and hobbled forward to doff his cap.

The lad continued to stare. The goodwife snatched off his cap, stuffed it into his hand, and propelled him forward. The lad moved like a sleepwalker, squeezing the dark wool between his palms.

After a moment's hesitation, Geddes dismounted, releasing his horse to graze on the lush grass.

Angelica slipped one leg over her mare and jumped down.

"Dunangley." Geddes nodded to the old man. "You've no' been troubled by Kilmartins, have you?"

"Nay, MacCallum," the old man grated. "Thanks to yer patrols, we've had nay trouble from them since yer return."

The goodwife sidled up next to her man. Hooking her arm in his, she nudged him.

"About those chickens we owe you, MacCallum," the man jerked out in obedience to her reminder. "I, that is, we—"

"Forget the chickens," Geddes said. "Ye dinna owe me a thing. 'Tis I who owe you for the lad. I've been meaning to pay ye a visit." He caught up the leather sporran at his waist and yanked it open. Feeling inside, he removed some coins and held them out.

The man gawked at him, his face a puzzle of awe.

His wife tickled his ribs, and he hastened to take the coins. "Thank ye, MacCallum. Ye are kind." He bowed many times as he spoke.

"I told 'em all in the village that we could count on ye," the goodwife said with obvious pride. "Ye're a true laird." She offered him a dazzling smile of appreciation.

Angelica liked the smile, despite the woman's missing teeth.

Geddes apparently did, too, though he looked thoroughly discomfited by the old dame's praise. He moved toward the child. "What is yer name, lad?"

"Euan, sir."

Geddes winced.

Angelica saw the lad's eyes were as blue as sapphires, with thick, black lashes. A handsome lad, a tiny image of the chieftain standing before him. She sucked in a breath as she realized who this child must be: the spawn of the rakehell.

"Have you learned your letters, Euan?" Geddes asked the lad.

"Nay, MacCallum. I help grandsire with the gardenin' an' the huntin', and grandmother wi' the milkin' and the churnin'."

"And do you like this milking and churning, Euan?" Geddes said the name clearly, despite his prior reaction.

The lad regarded him with unaffected candor. "No' so much, but I ken where ma duty lies."

"And where does it lie, lad?" Geddes asked softly.

"With ma kindred and ma chieftain."

Geddes smiled, clearly well pleased by this answer. "And what is the duty of the kindred to the chieftain?" he quizzed, as if the questions and answers were a ritual.

"To serve with loyalty and fight to preserve the clan."

A curve of his lips transformed Geddes's face into the picture of pride. "Well spoken, lad. I am proud of thee." He turned to the grandparents. "You have reared him well. I am obliged to you. In return, I shall see that he develops his fighting skills. He shall serve among the best of Clan MacCallum. When the cold weather sets in, he will be tutored at the castle. You can count on more coin to see to his needs and yours. You have bred loyalty in him."

"Thank you, MacCallum. Ye are good tae us." The man fumbled in his haste to perform his bow.

The woman was more collected and gracious. "MacCallum, we are yer loyal kin always, in good times or bad."

Geddes's smile had the brilliant quality of a rainbow after cloudy skies, it was so radiant with appreciation. Here were people who believed in him. Angelica saw at once it was his heart's desire and was glad for him.

"Tell the other kindred that as chieftain, Geddes MacCallum cares first and foremost for his clan," he said. He moved toward his horse.

Angelica nodded to the family and followed him.

"I knew from the moment ye returned. Ye're a changed man," the goodwife called after them. "God's blessings on ye and yer lady friend."

Angelica stubbed her toe on a stone and nearly sprawled in the grass. Geddes caught her elbow, steadying her.

With a proprietary smile, Geddes tightened his grip on her arm. Clearly, he liked the idea implied by the goodwife.

"That makes me cross." She deliberately removed her arm from his grasp. "I wish to stay at Duntrune, but I will not be assumed to occupy a position I do not, nor will I be lorded over by you." Quickening her pace, she marched to the mare and mounted before he could assist.

Despite this, he grinned as they rode out of the clearing, seeming well pleased with himself.

Angelica didn't like his attitude one bit. As they

left the clearing, she retaliated by asking the question nagging her. "Why did you wince at the lad's name? Do you dislike it so?"

He bristled like a cat rubbed the wrong way, from tail to head. " 'Twas my father's name."

"Is that a sign of kinship, to name the child after the recent chieftain?"

He pretended great interest in a distant bird, and she knew she had guessed rightly. The child was his, though he did not wish to admit it. Yet he had done right, providing for the lad, which proved her point. He was a man first and a rakehell second. A man put his responsibilities first.

"Where is the child's mother?" she asked. "Is she provided for as well?"

"She died at the birth of the lad."

A cold wind seemed to blow at Angelica's back. Had Geddes loved this woman? Did her death explain why he'd taken other women at random? Because he'd lost the love of his life?

"Am I to understand from our earlier discussion that you will not help me find Lilias?" he demanded, interrupting her thoughts.

"Lilias will return anon," she insisted. "I will speak to her when she does."

"What can you say to her that I have not already said?" Geddes halted the stallion on the path.

Angelica halted her mare as well, steeling herself for another quarrel. "I expect that to remain private between her and me, sir, else I cannot vouch for my success."

"And if it remains a secret, you expect to succeed?" His laughter held no mirth. "I find that rather unlikely. Lilias is an ungovernable child."

"You forget that she is no longer a child," Angelica

reminded him. "Though she is not yet a woman, either, I intend to treat her with respect. I believe she will respond favorably to my proposal, but we shall have to see. I will keep you informed of how matters stand."

He assessed her for a long moment, as if considering how likely she was to succeed. "I dinna ken what you're up to, but it had best be good," he said at last, gathering the reins. The stallion came to attention, his long tail switching, betraying his eagerness to move. "You will remember what I said. If Lilias thinks she's in love, you're to dissuade her. I will expect regular reports from you."

At his signal, the stallion leaped forward.

As Angelica watched man and beast move as one, she felt the weight of the burden Geddes had transferred to her. But he would not shift all responsibility so easily. He would play some role in helping his sister find happiness. She would insist on it.

"Well, then, friend," she said to the mare. "Shall we return to the castle?" As she followed the path back to Duntrune, she realized that the man who interested Lilias might not be Brian Kilmartin, but her brother clearly suspected it was. And if Lilias believed she was in love, no one on earth could dissuade her from it.

But Angelica could end the illicit trysts. And to do so, she knew only one specific cure.

Constant supervision. An arduous and unending task.

Chapter 10

Geddes let his stallion have his head on the return to the castle. Sensing his dark mood and eager for a run, the animal launched into a canter along the hard-packed woodland track.

Weary in both mind and body, Geddes welcomed the wind in his hair and his steed's power. He'd meant to find Lilias, but instead he'd given the responsibility to the Cavandish lass.

Idiot. Fool. Why had he done it?

He called himself a hundred names, yet no rebuke awaited him back at Duntrune. His people seemed pleased with him since last night's triumph. In the stable yard, he dismounted, and the stable lad darted up to loosen his mount's girth, smiling at him.

"Allow me, MacCallum," the lad offered as he began to walk the stallion to cool him down.

Geddes relinquished the reins to the lad with reluctance. He felt less than useful, being waited on by others. As he turned toward the castle, he found Rhuri doffing his bonnet before him.

"A word with you, MacCallum."

Geddes pasted on an indifferent expression. "Aye?" This would be it. Word that the false flag had been recognized and news of it had spread everywhere.

Rhuri inclined his head toward the kennels. "In there, where we can be privy, if you dinna mind."

Thinking it odd they should talk among the dogs, Geddes led the way to the wooden structure just off the yard. The dim interior smelled and sounded of dogs. Close to two dozen hounds raised a clamor as they entered. Geddes caressed a head here, ruffled ears there as the dogs stood on their hind legs in their straw-lined boxes, demanding attention.

In the open area where dogs were groomed or their wounds tended, six men of the garrison stood at attention. Geddes eyed them in surprise. Three were Mac-Callum cousins on his father's side of the family, one a Campbell on his mother's side. One was a Dunardley on his grandmother's side. The last was a Dunaudley cousin from his great-aunt's side of the family.

"What's this?" He swung around to Rhuri.

Rhuri ducked to avoid hitting his head on a beam. " 'Tis only that we've taken counsel, MacCallum." Rhuri stood straight and tall as he announced the men's intentions. "We're prepared tae follow yer lead and pretend the Faerie Flag has been found."

"Are you, now?" Geddes kept all reaction from his face and voice, not at all sure what this meant. He couldn't believe they understood what they were proposing.

" 'Twas an ingenious idea, tae fool the Kilmartin intae believing ye'd found the relic." Rhuri seemed to take his chieftain's abbreviated reply for permission to continue. "The Lady Lilias was brave tae undertake yer direction. We respect yer decision and will keep the secret tae a man. We swear."

Geddes didn't like their thinking he would ask Lilias to do such a thing, or that the false flag was his idea, but it seemed a poor time to say so. "I thought you believed in the flag and its power."

"Twice now, we've won battles without it, have we no', lads?" Rhuri looked to the others for confirmation.

"Aye, we have." Alex MacCallum nodded. "Twice is somit."

"Indeed. Gives us hope," put in Georgie Dunaudley.

A general chorus of agreement ensued from the others.

Rhuri waved his hands for silence. "If you'll search for the true flag, MacCallum, we'll no' breathe a word."

So they still wanted the true flag, but they were willing to believe in him, at least temporarily. It wasn't what Geddes wanted, but it was, as Alex put it, something. "I dinna think the secret can be kept," he challenged, putting forth the main problem. "Who else saw last night? Villagers? The household? Everyone gossips here. Word will leak and spread. The Kilmartins will know within a sennight."

"We've agreed there's to be nay gossip," Rhuri said with conviction. "We've talked to everyone all round. Among those who ken, we've made a pact. All have sworn to silence. 'Twill work. Ye'll see."

"Aye. A pact." They all nodded, their faces serious.

Rhuri looked to Geddes for approval.

Geddes scanned their faces, some bearded, some clean shaven, their eyes alert and enthusiastic. He wanted to believe in them, and to have them believe in him. This was what he'd worked for since coming to Duntrune. He nodded slowly, stunned to recognize the incredible step forward they were taking. Even if they did not succeed, the very fact that they wanted to try touched him. He felt a sudden rush of hope.

Without full awareness of what he was doing, he lunged forward and found himself grappling with Rhuri in a massive bear hug. "Aye, o' course I approve." He pounded his war captain on the back, relishing the pounding he received in return. "By Saint Columba, you have my blessings."

But moments later, as he crossed the yard, mixed feelings churned within him. Gossip had always been rampant at Duntrune. Could they suppress it if they were determined?

He didn't know, but they wished to try. They were beginning to trust him. He must trust them in return. And he did trust their good intentions. With all his heart, he did.

The supper hour had come and gone and still no Lilias.

Angelica sat in the dark on a low stool in the upper passage, her back against the wall, the tapestry above just brushing the top of her head. No light illuminated her solitary vigil except the moon shining through the window at the top of the spiral stair. With the household abed, she intended to take Lilias by surprise when she returned to her chamber a few doors away.

Angelica nodded with drowsiness. Already her new duty hung upon her. If Geddes would only take responsibility for his own sister, she need not sit here late at night, longing for her bed. Instead, he had let her volunteer for the task, sure that a woman could handle it better than he.

That was the trouble. She *could* handle it better. Left to his own male devices, he would bungle it and force Lilias into open defiance. She was trapped into helping him—an impossible, annoying situation. If her eyelids hadn't felt as if two rounds of heavy clay pushed them down, she would have been angry. If he were here right now, she would find a way to make her point.

A door creaked open at the far, dark end of the passage. The mysterious form of a man glided forth.

She'd known Geddes's chamber lay at the opposite end of the passage, but she hadn't been aware of which door was his. Against her will, she shivered with awareness as he approached.

He had put aside his plaid and sporran and wore only a linen shirt and his kilt. He padded along the wooden floor without a sound and stopped before her. With his feet bare and the shirt unbuttoned to his waist, he looked the picture of a devil-may-care rakehell. Yet the silvery light of the moon illuminated something more. He was not a boring rogue who tarried with any female available. He was a provocative sorcerer who seemed solely interested in her.

Unsettled and just a little annoyed by his effect on her, she gazed up at him. Her position offered her an unparalleled view of his heavily muscled calves, the firm flesh flecked with dark hairs. How beautifully sculpted he was. Intrigued, she let her gaze travel higher to where his kilt brushed his knees. Higher still beneath the kilt would be . . .

Appalled by the direction of her thoughts, she drew back on the stool. But instead of ending, her erotic fantasy deepened as he sat on the floor beside her, crossing his long, muscular legs.

Despite her stool, his head topped hers. In the intimacy of the semidark, his shoulder brushed her arm. His hair smelled of wood smoke, and his breath, as he turned toward her, of fiery spirits. What did they call it here? *Usquebaugh,* the water of life? After a day like this one, she felt as if she, too, could use reviving waters. She seemed to be wandering in a medieval dream where the knight of the castle controlled her every response.

He spoke no greeting, so she remained silent. He knew why she was here, and she thought it appropriate he should join her vigil. After his anger earlier in the day, he seemed subdued. She hoped he felt guilty as well.

"Tired?" he asked.

"No," she lied, struggling to prop open her drooping eyelids.

"Odd thing. Some of my men approve of the ruse that the flag is real. They have found out all who know it and sworn them to silence."

It was just as Agnes had told her, though she was pleased to hear that the garrison had thought of it. Geddes's wish to share the news with her pleased her even more. "If they thought of it first, all the better," she agreed.

"Aye, 'tis good." His voice resonated with satisfaction.

His men had given him a gift of trust, and she was glad for him. Her anger ebbed.

More silence followed, now almost companionable. He seemed to trust her so thoroughly to handle Lilias, he no longer feared for his sister. She appreciated his confidence in her, yet he would not escape his responsibility so easily.

"One problem," he interrupted her reflections.

"No more problems," she protested. "I've had enough for one day."

"We'll have more when Lilias learns that folk think the false flag was my idea, and she merely the bearer."

Angelica groaned inwardly. "You want me to tell her," she stated.

"You ken how she would take it from me."

The idea of assuming yet another task rankled, yet she had to agree. "I'll tell her gently."

"I knew you would. Ye have a way wi' her that I do not."

"You'll not avoid being a brother to her, for all that."

"Nay, nay, I wasna trying to do that."

"Good, for 'twill cost you. Dearly, I should add."

"Eh? How do you mean?" He looked clearly uneasy with her threat.

How satisfying to know she had this power over him. "I expect you to admit you care for her," she said.

He was silent for a long moment, looking at his hands.

Angelica imagined his inner turmoil as he struggled against his family upbringing that forbade words of caring. She should have felt compassion for him. If she hadn't been so tired, perhaps she would have, but just now, she felt smug to see him squirm.

How wicked of her.

"I do care about her," he admitted at last.

"What was that? I didn't hear you."

"I care about her," he repeated gruffly.

"About who?" she pressed, lifting her eyebrows.

"About Lilias," he shot back, catching the fact that she was provoking him. "I care about Lilias, my sister. I care about her very much, in case you thought me incapable of such a thing."

"Well done." She liked to hear the rakehell speak of his heart. "Next, you must tell *her* how you feel."

He stared at her. "She doesna want to hear that. She'll tell me I'm an idiot."

Angelica nearly laughed outright at his discomfort. " 'Tis the chance you must take—your punishment, if you like—though you might get to know her beforehand so you'll recognize when she's ready to hear it."

To her surprise, rather than contradicting her, he nodded in agreement. She felt a twinge of remorse. Because of his reputation, she had been hard on him, yet he rose to the challenge, just as he'd risen to defend his clan. She should have known he had the guts and determination to do anything he set his mind to.

"What will you say to Lilias to keep her from venturing out?" he asked, jolting her back to the issue at hand.

"I'll think of it once she's here." She would not tell him her plan. He would disapprove.

"No' sooner?" He seemed to sense she was holding back.

"If I think of it now, I'll smack her when I see her, I'll be that cross."

"Aye, there's that." He chuckled. "She's one tae raise yer ire."

Another understatement. His arm was so close to hers, she could almost feel the warmth of his flesh through the fabric of his shirt and her smock. She wanted to reach out and touch him, to make contact, as she had that first night.

"She's missed three meals today," he worried aloud. "The lass doesna eat. She's too thin."

"I'll wager she ate something, wherever she went."

"She didna eat as well as we. I ordered Muriel's barley broth and dried apple tart especially for her, as I ken she likes them. You liked them as well," he observed, shifting to study her. "But ye didna care much for the pickled eels. I'll see they're no' served again."

This surprised her. The last thing she expected was for him to notice her eating choices, let alone try to please her. "My mother didn't care for eel, so I never developed a taste for it. But I wouldn't wish to spoil anyone's pleasure. Let Muriel serve eel if she likes."

"But you would like more apple tart?"

"Cherry when the season is right," she said, naming her favorite.

At her choice of words, his eyes lit up with mischief, and she felt her face flame.

He leaned closer, seeming to relish her embarrassment. "I should bid you god'den, though I feel guilty, leaving you alone."

"Guilty you are." Her resentment flared, and she rearranged her skirts, deliberately tantalizing him with a glimpse of bare leg. "Let guilt keep you awake for hours. 'Twill serve you right."

"It will, without a doubt. You must let me take something of you to my chamber. 'Twill remind me of the debt I owe you for attending to my sister."

Was he going to kiss her? Angelica fervently hoped so. She had been angry with him, but he had responded well to her discipline. So well that as he studied her face, seeming to memorize every nuance of her, she shivered with excitement. His gaze dropped lower to caress her throat, her breasts, her waist.

As he looked his fill, a telltale heat stole over her. The hint of a smile, the gleam of passion in his eyes, said he liked what he saw. She could not move for the singular pleasure of being devoured whole by his gaze.

All too soon, it ended. He rose and bowed to her.

The muscled calves were once more at eye level, more intriguing than ever.

"Was that enough to take with you?" she could not resist asking. "You will not forget your debt?"

"Nay, neither of us shall forget it." He moved down the passage on silent feet. "As you shall learn in time."

Angelica sat in the dark, realizing he was right. He owed her a debt for her help with his sister, and she owed him a debt for giving her the clay. Each was repaying the other, yet the exchange did not seem to end their obligations. Instead, the feelings that resulted seemed to bind them together more tightly than ever, and she found she liked it that way.

How confusing. Even frightening. For what would happen if she did not succeed with Lilias? What if the clans continued to feud? She was investing so much of herself in this endeavor, yet there were dark forces working against her. And she could not tell how it all would end.

Angelica faced Lilias across the darkened solar. As predicted, the girl had slipped in well after midnight. Angelica had popped up from her seat in the shadows, used the element of surprise to overpower Lilias, and steered her into the solar.

Caught in her transgression but unrepentant, Lilias shook back her cloud of hair. "I'll no' tell you where I've been, and you canna make me."

"You don't have to tell me. I know where you've been," Angelica countered, smiling gently. "You've been with your sweetheart. So why do you not bring him here for your brother to meet?"

Lilias stared at her as if she had gone mad. "I canna bring him here."

Angelica nodded. "So he is a Kilmartin, as I suspected. Brian Kilmartin. I met him. He seems a likable lad." She reached for the tinderbox and lit a candle on the table between them.

A mixture of dread and wonder shone in Lilias's eyes.

Angelica felt like a fortune-teller who had just astounded her client by revealing her deepest secrets. "Your brother will know eventually," she said, hoping to use her advantage to convince Lilias. "Truly, you might as well have Brian woo you properly rather than create such worry over your disappearances."

Lilias drew back. "You dinna understand anything about us. My brother will ne'er permit Brian to woo me. No' under any circumstances."

"On the contrary, if you truly love Brian, you must *wed* him to heal the breach between the clans. Brian's father will not live forever. The feud will end someday if his son refuses to carry it on. Nor, I suspect, will Geddes continue it if the Kilmartins agree to peace."

"But Brian's father is in power just now," Lilias pointed out, "an' he willna permit us to wed. Nor will Geddes, if ye ask him."

"So you want the feud?" Angelica challenged. "Is it more exciting when you see Brian, knowing that you are breaking your brother's heart?"

Lilias stiffened. "He doesna have a heart. He burnt my skirt. I hate him." If her words had been acid, every piece of fabric in the chamber would have been eaten through.

Angelica gripped the edge of the table. "That was wrong of him, and I shall tell him so, but he does have a heart. Everyone does when they're young and innocent. But that heart cannot be broken and successfully mended over and over. Think of how your mother and father broke your innocent heart as a child, over and over, and tell me otherwise."

At this stark truth, Lilias clapped her hands to her temples, clearly reliving her childhood pain when both parents had ignored her.

Angelica wanted to embrace her, to tell her she wasn't the worthless female her parents had thought her, unimportant and undeserving of notice. But she realized that pain was more effective than words in forcing change.

As she waited for Lilias to reach understanding, the light of the candle flickered. The single, thin taper illuminated only a tiny segment of the table, making scant inroads into the dark. It was like the problem of the MacCallum family looming before her. Angelica felt like that small flame, fighting to bring a blessing to a vast, oppressive night. "Your clan's future rests with you, Lilias," she said quietly, willing the girl to understand the power she held in her heart. It would not be the first time love had healed a feud, yet love could also cause war. What she proposed brought with it great risk. "You must help bring change to your clan."

"*I* must change Duntrune's future? Me, a lowly female? Are you mad?" Seeming to recognize the risk, exhausted by her emotional trials, Lilias groped her way to a chair and dropped into it.

"If you truly want to be with Brian, Lilias, things cannot continue as they are."

" 'Tis hopeless, it is." Lilias's voice was a deadweight. Her shoulders slumped, her defiance crumbling. "There is no way out of this trouble. 'Tis the curse of Duntrune. Things never change, except to get worse."

Angelica hated this kind of talk. "They *will* change.

We will change them. Others may not like it, but we can change what *we* do. That alone will make a difference. So I tell you now, the first change I intend to make is to end your sneaking out to see Brian and returning in the dead of night. I cannot permit it anymore."

Lilias rallied at this, flinging back her ebony hair and sitting straight in the chair. "You canna stop me from seeing him. You canna watch me all night, every night. I'll elude you."

"That isn't what I had in mind." Angelica suppressed a smile. "I'll be coming with you when you meet with Brian. You may see him, you may kiss and embrace him, but I must always, always be there with you. Do you understand me, Lilias? I want no babe to come of your love for Brian. Not until after you've wed him properly at church."

Lilias's jaw dropped. Her lips moved, but nothing came out.

Angelica wanted to laugh aloud, so profound was the girl's astonishment at this unorthodox plan. "And while we're with him, he can advise me in finding some new sources of clay. Or mayhap in establishing some markets for my pottery. So you can see, we'll be going during the day, not at night."

"B-but 'tis a terrible risk. You can be caught by the Kilmartins," Lilias spluttered.

"So could you. In fact, you were once. Tell me, Lilias, how did you really manage to escape?" Angelica had sensed from the start that there was more to Lilias's story about being held by Angus Kilmartin but managing to depart Fincharn Castle without difficulty. "Did Brian arrange it for you?"

Lilias looked mortified, and Angelica knew she'd guessed aright.

"Why do you want to do this?" Lilias complained. "You have no reason to care."

"But I do care." Angelica fought the impulse to embrace Lilias to show how much. The girl was not yet ready for demonstrative gestures. "I believe this the best path for everyone," she said quietly. "I made a bargain with your brother and I intend to keep it. If I do not, I could lose access to the clay. But more than that, I see people causing each other misery for no good reason. If I can help end it, I will, and make you happy in the bargain."

Lilias sagged back into the chair, seeming overwhelmed by her argument. "What of my brother? He'll forbid your plan."

"Your brother will not know of it. He will trust my judgment when I tell him that we are off on business. And we will be. The business of the clan's future."

"He'll insist on hearing the details," Lilias predicted gloomily. "He wants his finger in every pie."

"We shall see."

"How will you manage?"

"*You* will manage, my dear. With a little help from me. We must do this together, for your clan depends on you first and foremost."

"I canna believe it." Lilias sounded disgusted, as if she'd never believe anyone in her clan would rely on her, let alone accord her the honor or responsibility of saving them.

"A lass can have great power," Angelica said with asperity. "In fact, several clansmen have told Geddes they know the flag you carried is false, but they admire you for what you did. They believe you and Geddes acted together in the idea, and they have sworn to keep the secret. They will support the idea that the true flag has been recovered." This version of the facts seemed to silence even the impossible Lilias. "You are becoming a woman now," she continued. "You must exercise your gifts to care for your people. I will also need your help in the pottery."

Lilias wrinkled her nose. "You may play at mud cakes, but since I am becoming a woman, I shall not. If I mun be present during your disgusting enterprise, I shall watch," she announced.

"You'll get bored, so you might as well make yourself useful. But we'll see to that later." Angelica halted Lilias's protest. "There are other requirements to this arrangement. You will take three meals a day with your brother. After supper each evening, you will keep company with him in the solar. No sneaking off."

"That man is no' worth my time."

"He is your chieftain, he is all the immediate family you have, and he loves you."

"You know nothing of how things are at Duntrune, of how things have been for years."

Angelica was undaunted. "I grew up with four brothers and have helped with half a dozen nephews, not to mention dozens of other waifs adopted or fostered by my brother Charles and his wife, Frances. Pray trust me when I say I understand males better than you, my dear. And I understand how family matters should be managed. My loving parents and siblings taught me well."

"Ha," was all Lilias would say, though she looked impressed at Angelica's description of her family.

Angelica had confidence in herself, but she knew she had a difficult course to steer. There would be rough sailing ahead.

Chapter 11

"I'm to say nothing to Lilias about her absence? Nothing at all?" Geddes stood on the other side of Angelica's workbench the next morning as she stated her latest proposal. He'd slept but little last night. With Angelica waiting for Lilias in the passage, he'd been unable to doze off. As she'd suggested, guilt—and lust—had kept him awake. Leaving his chamber door open a crack, he'd listened for his errant sister to return.

He'd heard Lilias creep up the stairs at a ridiculous hour. Angelica had surprised her, and the pair had retreated into the solar, closing the door.

Relieved to know that Lilias was unharmed, he had slept at last, but this morning he required an accounting—and a promise that no more midnight wandering would occur. Since Lilias had not come to the hall for the morning meal, he had sought Angelica and found her in the shed, covered with clay to the elbow.

He narrowed his gaze on her. "I await an answer. How am I to accept such an outrageous proposal without knowing more?"

"She and I have an agreement." Angelica kept her attention locked on her work. She pushed the clay with the heels of her hands, flattening it as if she were kneading bread. "I would prefer the chance to try it before you speak to her. We shall see if it works."

He shifted on his feet, disliking the idea. "I dinna like secrets," he warned. "I fail to see how my silence will improve her behavior."

Angelica paused in her work with the clay. "She will no longer slip out at night," she announced. "That is the improvement. Lilias promises to be in her chamber each night, all night. Does that satisfy you?"

"All night, every night?" It was an incredible step forward. He could not disagree. "There mun be more to it," he muttered, turning the proposal over in his mind. "Has she agreed to stop going wherever she goes?"

"She has agreed to take three meals a day with you in the hall," Angelica said.

"She was no' there this morning," he pointed out, unable to curb his resentment.

Angelica seemed to take no offense at this accusation. "I judged that she needed more sleep, having been out half the night, so I told her to stay abed. I apologize for making that decision without your approval. She will be in the hall for noon dinner, and at evening supper. Beyond that, I have another requirement."

She had hinted of this last night. "What?"

"I wish the two of you to pass an hour in one another's company each evening after supper. Engage in some pastimes in the solar. Play chess. Read together. The like." She fell to kneading the clay again.

Geddes watched her deft hands as she flattened the clay, then folded it back on itself and flattened it again. "But the gloaming is the prime hour when Kilmartins tend to attack," he objected. "I should be working with the patrols."

She dug out a piece of tree root and tossed it into a bucket. "Surely Kilmartins cannot attack every night." Seeming undaunted by his argument, she gathered the clay into a ball, then cut it in half with a wire. "On the nights they do not, Lilias requires your presence, else I cannot keep her in hand during the day." Without a glance in his direction, she combined the two pieces of clay and slammed them onto the work surface.

He snapped to attention at the unexpected explosion.

Grasping the slab in one hand, she pounded it on each side until it formed a block. The piece she was working probably weighed two stone, and she looked formidable, her lip caught between her teeth in concentration. As she worked, the muscles in her bare forearms rippled below her rolled-up sleeves.

"What in the devil are you doing?" Geddes watched in fascination as she recut the clay, dug out more rubble, then slammed the pieces together again and reshaped the block.

"What I would like to do to you at times." She glanced at him, a hint of mischief glinting in her eyes.

Unexpectedly he relaxed, catching her humor. The secrecy of her plan concerned him, yet she might succeed if Lilias did not sneak out at night. "Is this one of those times?"

She flashed him a covert grin. "Aye."

"And what am I to do to avoid being slammed against a workbench by such pretty hands?" In truth, he would prefer that those pretty hands performed other acts on his body.

She seemed to realize it, for she slanted him a coquettish glance from beneath fluttering eyelashes. "All you need do is agree to my proposal and fulfill it. If danger threatens, of course you must respond. Lilias and I will understand. But the rest of the time we will keep company, along with Iain, as a family ought. And you will make every effort to be entertaining and to get to know your sister."

A family keeping company together. She said it severely, as if it were a prison sentence, yet the idea ignited a pleasant glow in his mind. He'd meant to spend more time with Lilias, the baby sister he'd never known. Iain was practically one of the clan now, at least in loyalty. And if Angel were present . . .

He imagined her at his side, the firelight glinting off her glossy hair. He would slip one arm around her shoulders, and she would not object. . . . "Verra well, an hour each evening. Now tell me what you are really doing to that clay."

She smiled her approval, and a charming dimple dented her cheek, accenting her moist mouth.

He liked looking at her soft, bowed lips.

Two nights past, he had liked doing more than looking.

She slammed the clay down hard, as if reading his thoughts. "I am removing air bubbles from the clay before I throw it on the wheel." She arranged her expression in stern lines, as if she were lecturing to a pupil. " 'Tis called wedging."

He suspected she was thinking of the kiss, too. And whatever she thought, it didn't seem likely to lead to more. Not just now.

"You must also apologize to Lilias for burning her kirtle skirt," she said.

"Rubbish." Taken off guard, he said the first thing on his mind. "The skirt was the next thing to lousy. It needed burning. I gave her a new one just before you arrived. She can wear it."

"Is that what your mother or father would have done? Burned her skirt?"

The question brought him up short. Though he hated to admit it, it was, but the feelings behind the action were not like those of his parents.

"If you wanted to get her out of the skirt, you needed to win her trust first." Angelica punched the clay for emphasis. "Your timing was terrible."

"Why does she wish to look like a beggar? It makes no sense."

Angelica regarded him with wide, accusing eyes. "She wants you to accept her despite her flaws, and you showed that you do not."

Renewed hope filled him as he saw the direction of her thinking. Lilias was testing him. True, he had failed the test, but now that he understood her better, he might try again. Last night Angel had made him admit he cared for his sister. He would go the next step. "I will tell *her* I did it because I care about her. Our parents never did that."

"Oh, excellent." Seeming surprised by his decision, she presented him with a smile fit to dazzle the sun itself.

A warmth spread through him, beginning in the region of his chest and moving swiftly to vitalize his entire body. "Our mother was self-centered and unloving," he elaborated, spurred by her response. "If she wasn't making tapestries, she was bemoaning my father's loss of the Faerie Flag."

"I thought your grandfather lost it fifty years ago." Having gained his agreement, she reached readily for the forbidden topic.

He kicked himself mentally for introducing it. "He did. But everyone blames the present laird for not recovering it. 'Tis one and the same to them."

"No wonder your father hated the mere mention of the flag. It divided your family." She studied him as she worked the clay.

"You are most perceptive, Mistress Cavandish," he said dryly.

" 'Tis time to let it unite you instead of divide. If you stopped fighting the idea of the flag—" she began.

"I'm no' fighting it." He thought of his talk with his clansmen yesterday.

"Then where will you start the search?"

Her probing annoyed him. As if he would renege on his promise. "It has been only a day."

"Why don't you go south on the morrow? To the town of Dun . . ."

He waited for her to finish. And waited. Then he realized she didn't know the name. "Dunadd," he supplied.

"That's it. Tell the men who are keeping the secret. 'Twill satisfy them."

He grinned at her. "You dinna ken the name."

She reddened and slammed the clay especially hard on the bench.

"You dinna." He chuckled. "The names confuse you. Dunardy, Dunaudley, Dunarchy, Dunable."

"I've never heard that last one. I think you made it up," she accused.

"How would you ken if I made it up or no'?" he teased. He enjoyed the way she blushed to the roots of her hair.

Looking steadily at the clay as she worked, she avoided his gaze. "And I thought you had no sense of humor."

"Who said I have no sense of humor?"

"No one said it. You've just acted morose and cross since I arrived."

"These are no' exactly happy times." So he was morose and cross. Not very appealing. Except she had found him appealing two nights past. He leaned toward her across the workbench. "Was I cross two nights ago? When 'twas just you and me in the solar?"

She glanced at him, a quicksilver, darting look that carried an entirely different message from her earlier teasing or her quiet determination. "Nay," she admitted. Her blush crept back as she directed the single word to the clay.

With satisfaction, he recorded the hunger haunting her cinnamon-brown eyes. "What was I that night, eh?" he urged, restraining the surge of lust between his legs.

She squirmed. "I . . ." She kneaded the clay, her hands suddenly restless and uncertain. "You were . . ." She paused in her kneading, then suddenly punched the clay. "I cannot say it."

"Why ever not?" Fully aware of her dilemma, he pretended ignorance.

"Because you want me to admit how I feel about a certain gentleman who is seasoned in . . ." She paused and swallowed hard, her cheeks blooming the prettiest huc of pink he'd ever seen.

"In . . . ?" he encouraged, widening his eyes.

She bit her lip, glancing at the clay, then at him, then at the clay again. "In congress with the ladies," she finished in a rush.

"Congress?" he echoed in bewilderment. "Such a complex word. What sort of congress do you mean?" He was enjoying this immensely.

"You know what sort."

"I confess, I do not. Pray enlighten me."

She captured a deep breath, as though it would elude her if she wasn't quick enough. "In matters of a sexual nature," she said in a gasp.

"Ah." He nodded, keeping his expression serious, though he wanted to laugh aloud. More than that, he wanted to put his lips against one of her soft, lush cheeks and sample her sweetness. "If you wish to tell me how you feel about a gentleman who is seasoned in matters of a sexual nature, pray do," he said instead. "Who is the gentleman?"

"You know very well who he is. Who else have I kissed?"

He grinned wolfishly. "I canna guess. Who?"

She huffed with indignation. "No one but you."

He clasped a hand to his heart. "May I take that as a compliment?"

She smacked the lump of clay. "You may take it however you wish. But the fact remains that you kiss many lasses and I kiss none save you."

This caused him to wonder. "You've kissed none save me? Ever?"

"Well, not for many years. A great many years."

His heart picked up speed, racing with the idea. He savored being the only man she had kissed in some time. "And how did you feel when we kissed?"

She clasped her hands and looked up, her brown eyes suddenly full of warmth. "I was inspired," she confessed. "I felt as I do when I've . . ." She paused to bestow a smile of blinding radiance on him. "When I've created the perfect pot."

It wasn't at all what he'd expected.

"I felt as if I could make a hundred pots," she rushed on before he could comment, "magnificent, every one of them. I tell you truly, you are positively inspiring, sir."

He squinted at her. "Am I hearing aright? The feelings I inspire in you are being compared to what you feel when you handle this . . . this muck." He jabbed a finger at the block of clay.

She smiled tremulously. "You must not take offense. Next to my family, my work is the most important thing in my life. I've paid you the highest compliment I know how."

He straightened his plaid, then scratched his head. He'd never known a woman who found kissing him like making pottery.

"Despite this, I want to assure you that since I now have my wheel again, I will be inspired by my clay alone," she continued, her clay-covered hands still clasped earnestly before her. "I promise not to assault you again."

"Nay?" He cursed this turn of affairs. "Despite the fact that I am inspiring?"

"Indeed. I experienced a moment of weakness. It was no doubt caused by my long separation from my art during the journey. Now that I again have my work, you must have no fear. I promise not to be so rude again." She reached down and caressed the block of clay. With her gaze locked on him, she was clearly unaware of what she did with her hands.

Her long, slender fingers flexed and smoothed over the slippery substance. He would give anything for her to—as she put it—assault him again. Those hands could work miracles, he was sure. "What a relief," he said. "I vow, I was quite concerned about your intentions."

"Do not mock me, sir. I am entirely serious."

"So am I, my dear Mistress Cavandish. Are you certain you will be able to keep such a vow?"

"Entirely certain."

"I am not. We Highlanders live dangerous lives. As you saw two nights past, we are subject to unexpected attacks. Life could end on the morrow, so we tend to live it fully each moment. I warn you, in the face of such uncertainty, you will have moments of doubt."

"I do not think so."

"And what of me?" he continued, ignoring her avowal. "What if I cannot control myself? What if, in the midst of danger, I am compelled to kiss you entirely against my will?"

Her smile had a hint of tolerance in it, as if she knew he was teasing her. "Some rogues have control over their roguishness. I believe you are one." Her expression suggested they shared some secret understanding.

He blinked, thrown into shock. Did she know his secret? Could she possibly suspect?

"At any rate, have no fear," she said with assurance. "I've made up my mind."

He sighed with relief, realizing she couldn't know. No one could, he was certain. If none had guessed by now, surely they never would. And she wouldn't drop the subject so easily if she had such a formidable source of blackmail. He was safe for now. "One can make up one's mind, then unmake it," he said, returning to his former teasing. "I sense such will be the case for you."

"Do you always have such strong intuition?"

He would not risk answering that question. Instead, he bowed and took his leave.

He did not need strong intuition to recognize that this strong-willed woman had an unexpected interest in him. As for him, his lust for her was growing. It lay in wait for him like a latent tropical fever, flaring up and consuming him when he least expected it. He admitted now that since he'd first seen her in the burn, he had wanted her.

He had devoured her last night with his gaze, fueling the need within him. *Is that enough to take with you?* she had asked.

Of course it wasn't.

A flood of angst besieged him as he relived the destruction of his dreams as a lad. He'd left Duntrune, crushed in spirit. Hope had died.

The intervening years had deadened the pain just enough that he'd forgotten. Fool enough to try again, he'd returned to Duntrune.

Whether she meant to or not, Angel reminded him of his youthful dreams. She fueled the conflagration of male-female heat building between them. If she wasn't careful, she would learn soon enough that such heat was typically resolved in only one way.

Except it was his duty to ensure that it did not.

To his torment.

Chapter 12

Two days of rain and relative quiet passed with Lilias refusing to speak to Geddes. She came to meals, as promised, but that was all. With Angelica, she said little unless addressed.

On the second night, Angelica sat at the solar table after supper, the fire crackling cheerfully in the grate. Lilias sat opposite her with a book of blank pages and ink. Iain stood by the window, looking out at the rain.

"Beautiful work, Lilias." Angelica leaned across the table to view the flowers Lilias was creating with ink and a narrow-tipped brush. An intricate tracery of stem and leaves rose to a pristine cluster of mountain bluebell buds. "Though you use only black ink, it looks so real, I can see the blue."

Lilias's mouth twitched as she struggled to contain a smile. Clearly the praise pleased her.

"Will you show me more?" Angelica asked, encouraged to discover a positive asset she could nurture.

With a show of reluctance, Lilias turned the sketchbook and held it up. She folded back one page after another.

Angelica studied each one with growing appreciation as blooming heather, lily of the valley, and purple sedge came to life before her eyes. "Marvelous," she said softly. "You have a gift for capturing the soul of each plant, Lilias. How long have you been drawing like this?"

"Since I was old enough to hold a brush," Lilias said with ladylike modesty. "My tutor taught me to use both pen and brush. I also memorized the Latin names for each plant."

"What a wonderful skill." Angelica clasped her hands together, thinking of the many ways such skill could be applied.

"You've won her trust if she's showing you her drawings." Geddes entered, carrying a bundle in one hand.

Lilias closed the sketchbook and glowered at him.

Uncomfortable to be caught in the middle of their quarrel, Angelica joined Iain at the window. If only Geddes would do as he had promised and apologize. The tension between the two was growing unbearable.

"Aye, I'm remiss," Geddes said gruffly to Lilias, as if reading Angelica's thoughts. He set the bundle on the table before his sister. "But I fear you're stuck with me, the churlish, thoughtless brother." He put a hand on her shoulder.

Lilias flinched and tried to twist away, but Geddes held her firmly in place.

"Come, Iain, we should say our god'dens." Angelica moved toward the door.

"I wish you to stay." Geddes put out his other hand.

"We should not intrude." Angelica halted, uncertain what to do.

"Aye, this is a family matter," Iain added. "We'll leave ye in peace."

"As Lilias's companion, Mistress Cavandish is all but family now," Geddes contradicted. "And you, Lang, are of the clan into which her sister married.

Ye're kin by marriage, so you're involved as well. Hear me out." He pinned Angelica with a burning stare.

He seemed to be promising something. Something she wanted. Angelica nodded, unable to refuse his appeal.

Taking a deep breath, he turned back to his sister. Apprehension shone for an instant in his eyes, but it fled at once, replaced by the warrior's determination. "I was wrong to burn your kirtle skirt, Lilias," he said. " 'Tis only that I like to see you dressed up fine, but I went about it wrong. I hope ye'll accept my apology and this gift."

Angelica gripped Iain's arm. What it must have cost the chieftain to make such a confession. He must have labored for the last two days over the choice of words and the time to say them.

Lilias seemed stunned by her brother's words. She stared at him as if she couldn't believe her ears. "Geddes MacCallum never apologized to anyone in his life. Nor did he make gifts."

"Nay?" Geddes shrugged. "An' what are ye gang to do about it, if the old Geddes is dead?"

An odd expression crept over Lilias's face. One moment she seemed about to smile; the next, she hovered on the verge of tears. Her mouth trembled.

"Open the bundle," he urged in gentle tones.

Lilias eyed the bundle as if she hadn't received a gift for a very long time and scarce knew what to do with it. Slowly, she unrolled the canvas fabric, revealing the contents. Three long-handled brushes lay inside.

"These are the finest of brushes." She picked them up and stroked their tips against the palm of her hand. "Are they sable? From Italy, mayhap?"

"According to the seller, aye on both accounts," Geddes agreed.

"Italian goods are no' easy to find in Scotland. No' even in Glasgow."

"They have all manner of things in Glasgow."

"Our brother Lachlan could buy Italian goods more easily in Paris, yet I receive them from you and Glasgow, instead. Mayhap I should demand more such gifts from there," Lilias said with a ghost of her usual cheekiness.

"Mayhap I should make ye settle for a kiss on the cheek instead."

Lilias's answering grin had a fragile quality.

For a moment, Angelica thought she would go to her brother to claim the kiss. Instead, the grin wavered, and Lilias suddenly averted her face, one hand pressed to her mouth.

With a pang, Angelica realized the girl was holding back sobs. "Did you live in Glasgow long?" she asked Geddes, edging toward the door, pulling Iain with her. Though she had instigated the apology, she had never meant to be present when it happened. This was their time, not hers.

"Aye, for seven years," Geddes said.

"That's where he went when he left us, to soldier for the king," Lilias choked out. "And Lachlan went to Paris. We heard nothing from either of them. 'Twas as if they were both dead."

"I'm no' leaving you again, Lilias," Geddes said. "I care about you too much."

Lilias burst into tears. Geddes moved toward her, but she backed away, clutching the brushes against her chest. Muttering something about going to her bed, she stumbled from the room.

Angelica clung to Iain's arm, stunned. The apology

had been a monumental undertaking for a hardened warrior. But words of tenderness and caring? Little wonder Lilias was shocked to tears. Having had parents with hearts of Highland granite, she had probably never before heard an expression of love from a family member in her entire life.

Geddes stood gazing after his sister, his chest heaving, as if he were stirred by great emotion. The stark expression on his face wrenched at Angelica, and his eyes had a moist quality about them.

Iain disengaged his arm from Angelica's grasp and tactfully moved toward the door. Angelica remained where she was, caught in the web of emotions filling the room.

How she admired Geddes for what he had done. She admired him even more when he turned and met her gaze, silently seeking her reaction. She let a smile curve her lips. Suddenly she felt like one of the candles burning in the sconces. Warmth and light kindled within her, spreading through her body until surely her glow could be seen by everyone in the room.

He had spoken of his love, and the earth had seemed to shift beneath her feet. Never mind that his sister had not responded in like manner. Never mind that he had a wicked reputation.

The warrior had a heart. She had heard him speak of it with sincerity, and that mattered more to her than anything else she could name.

Late that night, Geddes lay abed, looking at the canopy above his head, and wondered if he'd done it wrong somehow. It hadn't ended the way he'd envisioned. Lilias wasn't supposed to weep and run away when he declared his affection for her. It had been hard enough to do it. Why did she make it harder for him, not even returning the gesture when he knew she felt something? And what had she meant by her sly comment about where he'd bought the brushes?

He couldn't be sure, but nothing was sure in this life. You took chances when you reached out to others, which was why he'd done it so seldom.

He had taken other types of chances daily for many years, but they had been military in nature, not family related. So he had hesitated to take this risk. But he wasn't sorry he'd done it. He wished Lilias to feel cared for and protected. Mayhap she needed time to adapt to using words to express herself. Words certainly came hard enough to him.

The only way to make it easier was to use them more often, just as he must do with his clansmen. They must all behave as if they trusted one another, and eventually the feelings would become genuine.

A tap sounded at his door, and he sat up, reaching for his shirt and pulling it on. It was unusual for anyone to come to his chamber this late.

At his command to enter, the door opened. Lilias stood in the entry, holding a candle, her hair a dark cloud against her white linen night smock.

He beckoned for her to come in. "What is it, Lilias?"

She padded over to him, still favoring her bad ankle. Placing the candle on the bedside table, she sat on the edge of the bed. Her eyes were red and her nose swollen from crying.

He patted her arm, wanting her to know his concern for her.

"Tell me where our brother is." Her voice was as stark as the highest mountain crags at night.

It was the question he'd been dreading. Because of his expression of caring in the solar, she had guessed everything. Her tears had been due first to confusion, then grief. "He is very ill, Lilias," he said quietly. "Granduncle Simon has gone to be with him. He didna want me."

"That's why Uncle was here the other day but left without a word to any of us?"

He nodded, feeling as bleak as she looked. "He agreed to have Uncle with him, but not until he sent for him. I offered to stay, but he had me thrown out and threatened to murder me if I came back. He didna want any of us to see him. He looks terrible."

"He's ill from drinking." She tossed her head, clearly understanding more about it than he wished her to. "Dinna pretend otherwise," she interrupted as he sought to deny it. "It was always drink with him."

"Aye," he admitted. "But we must not judge and condemn him. We've each had our hardships and sought solace in our own ways."

Lilias took this in silence, seeming to recognize it as the truth. "Will you tell them?"

"Aye, but no' just now. The men don't believe in me yet. We've been beaten down by Kilmartin attacks for months. At the moment, all we have standing between us and destruction is a false flag. Without the clan's will to fight, we'll lose Duntrune."

"You should be ruthless with them. Push them brutally. They would understand that and do whatever you command."

The vehemence of her anger shocked him. "It wouldna win their loyalty, nor would they be strong in their own right. I must do things my own way."

She lost her composure at that. "Your way could be our undoing." Her face contorted, and tears tracked down her cheeks. "I'm sorry. I shouldna have said that, but I'm afraid."

He put out his arm, offering his embrace as comfort, but she jumped up, backing away. "Nay. I'm still angry with you. For staying away so long. But I . . ." She fought to hold back renewed sobs. "I am glad you're home." She limped to the bed, kissed him swiftly on the forehead, snatched up her candle, and hurried from the room.

At last, the response he'd wanted. Geddes swung his legs from the bed, thinking to go after her, but stopped. She needed to be alone, to grieve and adjust. He sank back against the pillows.

The deception between them was over, and she had said the words he longed to hear. She was glad he was home.

Trust. They must behave as if they trusted one another, and eventually the feelings would follow. They must use words to tell one anther their feelings, despite the risks and the discomforts.

He had received two rewards tonight for making the effort. One just now from Lilias. The other was the light in Angel's eyes after Lilias had left the solar. He had touched and moved her by expressing emotion.

And when she was touched and moved, her eyes shone with a joy that rearranged his universe, not to mention certain sensitive portions of his anatomy.

He didn't want her solely out of lust. Any woman could be lusted after. He wanted Angel Cavandish because she had wise instincts and infinite tenderness. They were good reasons for lust, to his way of thinking.

Settling beneath the sheets, he drifted off to sleep,

feeling better than he'd felt since his return to Duntrune. As Lilias had said, she was still frightened and angry with him. It would take time for her to heal, but he had to trust that she would, in time.

But it was hard waiting, and he was impatient. It had always been his worst fault.

The next day, everyone behaved as if naught had happened. Lilias was silent at table, saying little to anyone, keeping to her chamber when Angelica didn't require her in the pottery. Geddes spent scant time at each meal. He had mustered the villagers as well as the garrison to weapons training. From early until late, clansmen and tacksmen made bows and arrows and practiced shooting at targets both near and far.

If Angelica had hoped for everything to be different between the family members, she was disappointed. Lilias didn't become sunny-tempered. Geddes was still morose. She, Angelica, was still English and an outsider to the Highlands. Things couldn't change overnight. She had expected too much, too soon.

On the bright side, she heard no whispering about a false flag. Those who knew the secret seemed to be working together, keeping it contained. Geddes had directed Muriel to tell the household that the flag must not be discussed as if it were an everyday object. He could not even reveal where he had found it or where it was now stored, so secret was it. In keeping with tradition, it was a revered relic that could be brought forth only in moments of danger. The rest of the time it must lie out of sight. His one concession was to permit prayers in the castle chapel now that the flag had returned.

Angelica praised heaven for the momentary lull in the storm and concentrated her energies on making clay. She wanted a goodly supply prepared before beginning to throw, as she, Magnus, and Stone could go through large quantities in a short time. She didn't want to stop the moment she'd begun.

They had put the clay out in weathering troughs to soften in the rain. For the next two days, she helped Magnus clean and repair his old mixer, which stood in a clearing near the village. The huge wooden barrel was bisected by a wooden pole that bristled with metal mixing blades. The pole was, in turn, rotated by a large attached beam.

On the morning of the fourth day, Lilias walked away from the donkey harnessed to the mixer beam. "I dinna want to lead Sebastian anymore, Angelica. I'm tired. Canna we stop?"

Without her guidance, the donkey stopped in the path that circled the mixer and lowered his head to graze. Grasping a large mouthful of grass, he munched it happily.

Angelica looked up from the trough where she, Magnus, and Stone were pulling roots and stones from weathered clay before it went into the mixer. "Don't stop now, Lilias. You're doing so well," she called through the wet handkerchief tied over her nose and mouth to keep out the dust.

"But 'tis boring," Lilias complained. "The dust makes me sneeze." She punctuated her complaint with a vigorous demonstration.

Irritated, Angelica beckoned to Iain. "Will you get the donkey going again? We need to finish that batch if we're to be done by sundown."

Iain put down his shovel and left the barrel from which he'd been digging clay to go into the picking trough. He took Lilias's place leading the donkey.

"What's the use of having a donkey if he has to be led?" Lilias complained. She sneezed again.

"He pulls the beam, which is very heavy. Try turning it without Sebastian's help and see," Angelica reprimanded. "And you're to wear your handkerchief to keep out the dust. Without it, of course you will sneeze."

"My lady is no' used to such work," Magnus said. "Ye ought to rest, Lady Lilias."

Angelica frowned. "Her ladyship can get used to doing whatever is required to fulfill her people's needs. This clay will eventually provide work for many of her kinsmen and kinswomen."

"Then let them do it," Lilias said with a flippant air. "You promised to take me riding, and now you've gone back on your word," she accused Angelica. "It's been days now, an' we havena been anywhere but mucking about in the dirt."

Angelica felt guilty. She had promised that Lilias would see her lover, but she hadn't wanted to leave the clay. "If we go riding, Iain must accompany us, and the clay will take doubly long." She sighed.

"Stone and I can finish the clay," Magnus offered, rubbing his nose and streaking it with clay. "We'll get a few men from the village to help. If ye can pay them with a few loaves o' bread each, they'll do it gladly."

"I could ask, I suppose." Angelica smiled her thanks to Magnus. "If Muriel says we may pay workers in bread, then after the noon dinner hour, Lilias, we shall ride out."

Lilias brightened. "Promise?"

Angelica nodded, though she hated to leave the clay so soon. "I promise."

Lilias grinned. "Come here, Jamie," she called to Magnus's grandson, who sat on a hillock nearby,

watching them. "Would you like to ride the donkey?"
She chased Iain back to his shoveling, then returned
to seat Jamie on the donkey's back. "Now tickle his
sides with your heels and he'll walk for you."

Jamie obeyed and screeched with joy as the donkey
moved forward. Within minutes, the animal was walking at a steady pace, young Jamie whooping and
laughing.

"There," said Lilias with satisfaction, having escaped her duty by delegating to another. "Now I can
get a cool drink of well water."

"Bring some for the rest of us," Angelica directed
as Lilias sauntered away. She grinned wryly as she
watched the girl pause to exchange pleasant banter
with a village maid. Lilias was becoming friendlier and
more outgoing. And her drafting of Jamie into the
work proved that she could be an enterprising young
woman if she wished.

In the early afternoon, Angelica made her way back
to the castle, prepared to keep her promise to Lilias.
The clay was almost done. On the morrow she could
begin throwing on the wheel. Exhilarated by the prospect, she pushed open the kitchen door and entered.

Muriel greeted her with a frown. "Dirt," she said,
pointing to the flagstone floor.

Angelica looked over her shoulder to see the trail
of dusty footprints she had left on the pristine floor.
"By heaven, I am sorry." Annoyed that she had forgotten, she removed her shoes.

Ross came forward and took them, giving her a re-
proving look. Even the kitchen lad reprimanded her.

"Jenny Marie, go up to Mistress Cavandish's chamber and put out the bath," Muriel ordered.

Angelica shook her head. "Thank you, Muriel, but

Lady Lilias and I are going riding. I do not have time
for a bath just now."

"Dirt is the enemy of the Lord," Muriel said firmly.
"I'll forgive the error this time, but be warned. Next
time take off yer shoes before you enter my kitchens,
or there will be a price to pay." She signaled to two
kitchen maids. "Hot water, pray. Mistress Cavandish
will have a wee bath while Ross cleans her shoes."

Muriel's word was law when it came to matters of
cleanliness. Rather than provoke a quarrel, Angelica
resigned herself to soaking in a hip bath. It would be
pleasant, sure, but she had scant time, and what was
the purpose? She could expect to become dusty and
windblown during the afternoon ride. But Muriel
seemed to have her heart set on this punishment for
soiling her floor, so she let it go.

As Angelica climbed the back stairs, the two maids
followed her, each bearing brimming buckets of
steaming water. Jenny Marie had pulled the brass hip
bath from its place in the attached tiring chamber and
set it before the hearth. One of the girls started the
fire while the other filled the bath and Jenny Marie
went down for more water. Ross came in with two
buckets of cool water for adjusting the temperature.

As the chamber door closed at last behind the girls,
Angelica glimpsed the lad lingering in the corridor.

Wondering what he was up to, she opened her door
a crack. Ross had entered the empty solar and stood
before an oak chest that sat against the wall. He had
the lid open and was rummaging through the contents.

She crossed the corridor, wondering what he was
looking for. He didn't behave as if he were stealing.
He picked up one article after another, studied it, then
put it back. Mayhap he was curious. She entered the

solar. "What are you doing, Ross?" she asked, coming up beside him and touching his arm.

He jerked at the sight of her and backed away, clearly frightened at being found in the family's private solar without invitation. His dark eyes darted this way and that, as if he were a cornered animal seeking escape.

" 'Tis all right," she assured him. "Would you like to see what's in the chest? Come, we can look together and 'twill not be taken amiss." She picked up a blanket and gestured for him to examine it with her.

He took to his heels and ran as if he were the hart pursued by a wild boar.

She had frightened him, Angelica thought, moving to the door. Looking into the corridor, she was just in time to see him scamper down the back stairs.

The child must have lived in fear in his past life, especially since he could not hear people's words or speak in return. That would explain his fear of her.

She returned to her bath, but as she soaked away the morning's clay, she puzzled only briefly about Ross. She preferred to unleash her mind onto the subject of Geddes MacCallum.

He had studied her face and body the other night, memorizing what he saw. Each part of her had been touched by his molten gaze and set on fire. Relaxed in the bath, she touched her lips, her cheeks, her throat, and felt beautiful. How did he manage to make her feel this way?

Out of habit, she mentally reached for her list of his traits, then stopped, losing interest. He was far more complex than a mere list.

Geddes MacCallum was a unique combination of

the tough and the tender, the sensual and the sincere. He fascinated her.

But not to the point where he rivaled her interest in clay.

Some hours later, washed and dressed in an out-dated but attractive blue brocade riding costume brought by Muriel, Angelica rode the gray garron mare whose name she had learned was Lucy. Iain, mounted on a darker gray gelding, rode close at her heels. They both followed Lilias and her chestnut mare up a steep slope.

The three horses navigated the rough path with surefooted swiftness, despite the stony way. At the top of the hill, they plunged into a thick wood.

"Might we slow down, Lilias?" Angelica pleaded, disliking the branches that slapped her as they pressed through the dense trees.

Lilias did not respond. If anything, she rode faster.

"Are we almost there?" Angelica called to their guide, whose mare seemed to know the way, despite the lack of path.

"Nearly." Lilias flung the answer over her shoulder. "I have to give the signal to Brian."

They followed as she burst into a clearing. Ahead lay a shining loch, glittering like a silver platter in the afternoon sun, stretching away to the northeast where Ben Cruachan reared its craggy head. Lilias kicked her mare into a canter, riding straight toward a gaggle of geese foraging for food at the water's edge.

The frightened geese rose into the air, squawking and honking as they flew east along the shore of Loch Awe. And to the east, Angelica knew, lay Castle Fincharn.

"Brian sees the geese and knows you're here?" Angelica reined in Lucy as she and Iain caught up with Lilias and her mare.

"Aye." Lilias fastened an ardent gaze on the shoreline, clearly eager for her love to appear.

"What if something else alarms the geese and causes them to take wing?" Angelica asked, unable to resist the question.

"Brian brings his bow or his fishing line and the castle has something fresh for supper that eve."

"Quite the strategists," Iain commented as he reined in beside them.

"Angelica has shown me my duty and I intend to be faithful to it." Lilias sat straight and proud, her black hair whipping in the breeze. "I must unite our clans." She signaled to her horse, and the mare bore her at a trot along the edge of the loch. For the first time, Lilias looked and carried herself like the chieftain's daughter that she was.

Angelica caught Iain's eye and nodded toward her retreating charge. "At last, we see her true colors emerge."

"Aye," he agreed. "Let us hope this plan of yours succeeds. You've given her a dangerous permission. You could have knocked me over with a feather when you told me what you'd planned."

"She'd have continued to meet with Brian with or without anyone's permission," Angelica pointed out. "At least this way, someone is looking out for her."

"You womenfolk think alike," Iain groused, guiding his gelding after Angelica's mare. "Gemma Sinclair used the same tactic with me when I first met Rowena. She insisted on being with us when we trysted. Good thing she did, too. 'Twas bad enough that I kissed my own half sister. Think what might have happened if Gemma hadn't been there."

"How terrible for you," Angelica agreed. "But at least we have no such circumstances here. We shall see if they are compatible, and if they are, marriage is in order. But they'll have to have great courage to defy their clan leaders. They could both be cast out from their clans."

A short time later, a dark-haired young man rode into view. His brown gelding had a white star on its forehead, and he sat as tall and proud in the saddle as Lilias, wearing the tartan of the Kilmartin clan. His plaid was pinned with a brooch that caught the light of the sun.

Lilias kicked her mare into a canter and raced to meet him. The horse had scarce slowed to a trot before Lilias slid from the saddle. Brian reined in, dismounted, and turned toward her. The impetuous girl catapulted into his arms.

Their embrace spoke of a joy so expansive, Angelica felt it, despite the distance. Moisture sprang to her eyes. Having met Brian during her stay at Fincharn, she had hoped her instinct was correct, that the pair were suited. Now, seeing them together, she felt sure they were.

Wanting to give them a moment of privacy, she reined in Lucy and dismounted, motioning for Iain to do the same with his mount. She looped the reins so the mare could graze. By the time she glanced back, Brian was nodding toward her and Iain, speaking to Lilias. Without a doubt, he was asking why they were there.

Iain joined her, and together they approached the young lovers. Though Angelica regretted breaking the magical spell surrounding them, she must fulfill her charge as a companion.

Lilias performed the introductions with consummate grace, a sharp contrast to her first meeting with Angelica.

"To what do we owe the honor of your visit?" Brian Kilmartin bowed over Angelica's hand, his gesture polished and gentlemanly but his expression still perplexed. He saluted Iain with a small bow.

"Angelica and Iain are my nursemaids," Lilias announced before Angelica could begin the speech she had rehearsed to answer this inevitable question. "She says we may meet as often as we wish as long as she and Iain are present. She wishes us to wed and unite our clans."

"After the last raid, it seemed a possible solution to me," Angelica said. "*If* the two of you truly love one another, that is. I know of only one way to be sure of that."

"Time together, Brian," Lilias interjected. "Angelica says a couple who are courting mun have time together." So huge was Lilias's smile, Angelica thought it would split her face in two.

Brian's smile rivaled hers. "I willna risk my good fortune by asking too many questions on that score. I'll simply say welcome, Mistress Cavandish. And to ye, Lang." He bowed again.

The hour that ensued was one of idyllic beauty by the lochside. The sun shone on the water, creating diamond points of light on each flickering wavelet. A bounty of fish leaped to capture insects hovering just above the water's surface.

Angelica strolled with Iain, appreciating the changing blues and greens of the palette spread out before her. She felt closer to her life's goal than she had ever been, and she felt a flutter of hope. In contrast, Iain seemed morose.

"This mun be my path in life. I'm good for naught but ruining romances," he complained. "I'm a blight on romance. A romance destroyer. The part fits me, I suppose."

"A romance destroyer?" She chuckled, trying to make light of the matter, hoping to cheer him. "What exactly do you mean?"

Iain shrugged. "I mean since I destroyed my own romantic future, I'm adept at destroying that of others. Just watch." He cast a critical stare at Brian, who was facing him as he kissed Lilias. "The kiss is becoming rather too heated for my approval."

Brian apparently sensed Iain's gaze upon him. He looked up, guilt written all over his expressive face.

Iain sent him a warning frown.

Gently, Brian put Lilias aside.

"There. You see." Iain bent to pick up a smooth, flat stone and skipped it across the water. "I frightened him. He'll no' kiss her again during this visit. At least not with such passion."

Angelica patted his arm and turned the subject. Though it seemed a bit extreme that he should consider all his chances for romance ruined, he was unquestionably scarred by his painful experience with Rowena. Who wouldn't be, believing he had found his beloved for all time, only to discover they were siblings? "Look, there's a deer," she whispered, shaking his sleeve, trying to distract him.

They both stilled so as not to frighten the doe and her fawn that had come to the water's edge. The doe regarded them warily with huge, limpid eyes as her youngster drank its fill. She lapped only a few times at the water before giving the signal to flee the unpredictable humans, who were as likely to give chase as to admire them. The pair bounded away into the woods.

Humans *were* unpredictable, Angelica realized. A desired response that one cultivated in another was not always forthcoming. Witness what had happened to Geddes the other night, offering his brotherly heart to Lilias and receiving naught tangible in return.

"How do things fare with you?" Iain asked kindly as they resumed their stroll.

"Well enough," Angelica conceded, unwilling to commit to more.

"No better than that?" He raised his red eyebrows in question.

"I'll feel better once I've made a pot or two."

Iain chuckled. "Or a dozen or more. So you have your pottery, as you vowed you would. But what of him?"

He did not specify whom he meant, but they both knew. "The pottery will prosper under his protection. 'Twas my goal from the first." Angelica plucked a wildflower and tucked it into her hair.

"The pottery. You speak of naught but pottery." Iain rolled his eyes toward the blue sky. "What of Geddes, the man?"

"He loves his sister. He works hard to care for his people. I admire that." She hoped to escape further questioning.

"But you're attracted to him."

"I'm sure you feel it your duty to point that out."

"O' course it is. I'm a destroyer o' romance, ye ken." Iain plucked a long blade of grass to chew on. "Attraction often overwhelms good judgment, so I'm warning ye. Dinna forget his reputation, 'tis all."

Angelica shook her head. "I haven't forgotten what they say of him, but he was gone seven years, just at the time when the youth was changing into a man. I believe he is not quite the way they remember him."

Iain *tsk*ed. "He may have changed, but that doesna mean he would offer marriage to the woman he gets with child."

Angelica snorted. "Really, Iain, I am in no danger of becoming with child. *I* kissed *him*. Once. Just to see what it was like, you understand."

"*You* kissed him?" Iain wrinkled his freckled nose. "You didna tell me that. You're sure 'twas no' the other way around?"

Angelica felt a vast superiority. "Very sure. He didn't try a thing until I initiated the kiss. It was an experiment, of sorts."

Iain looked doubtful. "An' what did ye learn from yer experiment?"

How could she admit that Geddes MacCallum had made her feel as if she could touch the stars? "I learned that I am in complete control," she insisted, which was true, despite the excitement. "And that he would never press himself on me."

"Ye dinna need me to ruin yer romance for ye?" he asked, chewing on the grass blade.

"Truly, Iain, 'tis not a romance. 'Tis a business proposition. That is all," she told him firmly. It was true, she told herself, even if she wished with all her heart that it were otherwise. Attraction was a pleasant thing, but it was not the same as love, no matter how much she admired him. No matter if he touched her emotions. Love must be felt by both parties in equal measure and be accompanied by agreement in basic choices about life. Although Geddes didn't mind her pottery, although he didn't find her unattractive when she was streaked with clay, it didn't mean he wished to marry her.

Even if all the requirements were met, there were still risks to love, and she knew from experience that not all love stories ended happily ever after. She had already taken her risk, and one heartbreak was enough for a lifetime.

Chapter 13

Geddes sat across from his sister that evening, the chessboard between them. Wax tapers burned in sconces on the solar walls and on the table to light their play. Iain was riding patrol, a duty he claimed to want that night, being bored with sitting indoors. Geddes thought it more likely he wanted to avoid another scene like the one several nights past.

Angelica sat alone at the far end of the table, immersed in a book. She looked clean and demure in her green kirtle skirt and bodice. The clothing was well tailored and serviceable but Geddes preferred her in the brown velvet. It set off her tawny brown hair and willowy form to perfection. In fact, with candlelight gleaming on her hair, he wished it were unbound. He wagered it would fall to her waist in a river of cinnamon silk.

" 'Tis your move," he said to Lilias, unable to keep his gaze from straying to Angelica time and time again.

"Mine? Oh, aye." Lilias seemed to be daydreaming, a bemused smile on her face. She had been quiet all through supper, neither complaining nor whining, as she usually did. Geddes found the change most welcome. Mayhap their brief talk the other night had cleared the air between them. But he must not expect her to change completely. At his admonition, she studied the board for a moment, then moved a pawn.

Geddes took it with his bishop. "Check. You're not paying attention, Lilias."

"I am. I'm going to castle." She switched her queen and a castle, saving the queen from attack.

How like life. You sacrificed one thing of value to save another. If only it did not have to be. Geddes took the castle with his bishop. "You lost a valuable piece," he admonished.

"It was the only choice left to me," she complained, moving another pawn with little forethought.

He refrained from pointing out that her careless play had caused the loss in the first place. At least she was no longer angry with him or wary. She seemed contented in a way she hadn't been since his return. He could only assume it was caused by their talk the other night. "Who would like to hear of my search for the flag today?" he asked as he considered his next move.

Instead of pouncing on the promised news, Lilias kicked her crossed foot and stared at her shoe. She was shod for a change and wore clean stockings. "You didna find it, else you would ha' told me straightaway." She smiled at her footwear instead of at him.

Geddes snorted. "I would like some show of appreciation for doing as I promised."

Her smile widened as she continued to gaze at her shoe. " 'Tis good, brother," she said.

"I expected a bit more enthusiasm," he said crossly, feeling he deserved as much attention as her foot, if not more.

She glanced at him, as if he'd finally roused her attention from something more engrossing. " 'Tis verra, verra good. Did you learn anything of use?"

"One old woman told me a story of how it was carried into the battle, but that was the last she saw it," he admitted, still not appeased. "But I shall not give up. I'll return to Dunadd again in a sennight and urge old men and women to tell more rousing tales of the past, particularly the Battle of Dunardry."

Lilias leaned across the chessboard and kissed him on the cheek. He warmed at her show of approval, but as she resettled on her stool, her gaze wandered to the ceiling, her expression bemused.

"You're in an unusual mood tonight," he observed. "What's on your mind?"

No answer.

"Where did you ride today, Lilias?" he tried. Could that be the key to her behavior?

She kicked her foot and regarded the board as he made his move. "Oh, nowhere in particular." A smile tugged at the corners of her mouth, as if she were savoring a precious memory.

"That's no' an answer. Where did you go?" They were going to drive him mad tonight. He could not even get Angelica to look at him. The book on the table held her complete attention, though the writing in it looked like little more than chicken scratchings. "I asked where you went," he prompted again. "Down the coast? Along the burn? Where?"

Lilias jerked a thumb at Angelica without looking up from the board. "I was with her and Iain the entire time. I was perfectly behaved."

"But where?" he pressed.

"I showed her all the views." Lilias waved a hand, indicating nothing in particular.

Geddes gave up on his sister. Clearly he would get no sensible conversation from her tonight. "What are you reading?" he asked Angelica.

"Nothing much." She turned a page with great care, seeming unable to spare him a glance. The paper appeared brittle and crinkled, as if it had once been wet. She smoothed the new page with care.

"You appear fascinated with your 'nothing.' Such engrossing reading must have a title," he said. "What is it called?"

She closed the book and looked up at him. " 'Tis a book of glaze recipes." She caressed the leather cover as if it were holy. "Magnus's father collected them over the years, then passed it to Magnus when he died. 'Tis a valuable collection that will benefit us greatly when we are ready to do glaze firings, but it would interest no one else."

"I do not have to be interested in reading it myself to wish to hear about it. What does it tell you?"

She smiled and fixed her gaze on a distant point, her expression becoming much like Lilias's, preoccupied elsewhere. "Some things I already knew. Others I did not."

"Fascinatingly vague," Geddes muttered. Why was everyone so closemouthed tonight? "Checkmate," he informed Lilias.

His sister stood up. "You trounced me again. I hope you're happy."

" 'Twas your idea to play."

"I was trying to be polite."

"You're not succeeding."

"When did you become so interested in manners?" Lilias planted both hands on her hips. "You never were in your wicked, wicked youth." She sniffed and arched an eyebrow at him.

He didn't like her sly comment. Her reference to his past irritated, like a splinter he couldn't remove. "Dinna start on me, Lilias." He dodged the guilt that insisted on rising. She had best leave this subject alone.

"Lilias, you are being rude," Angelica reproached. "Pray stop at once."

"I want to ride again on the morrow, Angelica." Lilias turned suddenly sweet as golden honey. "May we not?"

Angelica smoothed the cover of her book with deliberate care. "I wish we could, but on the morrow we must continue preparing the clay so Magnus, Stone, and I can begin making pots."

Lilias rolled her eyes. "You're mad to work so hard over that muck," she complained. "You drive yourself like a slave."

Geddes had had enough. He loved his sister, but he wouldn't tolerate rudeness from her. "Lilias, you will no' insult Mistress Cavandish. Apologize at once."

"I shouldna be surprised that you take her part," Lilias countered. "But she does work like a slave, and I shall say so if I wish."

"Lilias," Angelica admonished, "you promised to help me with the clay if Iain and I went riding with you. I also expect you to be civil. You must keep your part of the bargain if you wish us to keep ours."

Geddes waited for Lilias to fly into one of her tantrums, but surprisingly, this seemed to subdue her. She stood in silence, gaze lowered, fingering the linen fabric of the blue skirt he'd given her. "I canna bear it," she said at last, casting him a sidelong glance, "seeing you so besotted with her, brother. Some speculate about when you'll do the deed. Most are convinced you already have. How is it to end?"

"Lilias," Geddes barked, stunned by her audacity.

"I will not tolerate such speech about my personal affairs. No' from you or anyone else."

Lilias threw up both hands. " 'Tis only what everyone says. Geddes MacCallum has always had lasses. Why should this be any different?"

Was that a challenge he heard in her voice? An odd pairing with the plea he saw in her dark eyes. What did she want of him?

She wants the truth, his conscience whispered.

He shook his head to clear it. He had felt sure she wouldn't tell anyone of his deception. She wouldn't dare. He must silence his conscience or it would betray him, and they would all be lost.

He glanced at Angelica, who had fallen silent, her expression perplexed and questioning. His heart sank. Even she seemed to be probing, yet she couldn't know what he'd done.

"If you're concerned about the future, pray keep faith with me," he said with more conviction than he felt. "I will find a way to make things right."

"I dinna see how." Lilias was as blunt as a rusty old dirk. "We grew up together. I ken how ye were then, and how ye are now. So do others if they'd stop and look."

Geddes labored to remain impassive. By Saint Columba, she *was* threatening him. Not with her own betrayal, but with that of others. It was as obvious now as being struck by a claymore. She was telling him so. "Lilias," he warned, concerned that she might blurt out the truth, "you go too far."

"No, *you* go too far. I can sew a false flag, but I canna do more." Lilias scowled her angriest and stamped her foot. "Has he seduced you, Angelica?" she demanded, swinging in their guest's direction. "Has he even tried?"

Angelica's eyes widened in surprise. "Of course not. He's a great leader. He has too much integrity to do such a thing."

"Aye, he does." Lilias's face crumpled and she burst into tears. "Which is why we're headin' for disaster. And no one will listen to me." She rushed from the room.

Geddes bit back a curse as he stared at the door through which Lilias had bolted. She had seen through the mask he wore, but why must she bring Angelica into it? "I regret that outburst. I canna imagine what she was thinking, to say such things," he apologized, not wanting to think about it just now.

Contrary to his expectation, Angelica seemed not the least embarrassed. She regarded him with a calm, concerned gaze. "She knows something you do not wish her to. What is it?"

The depth of her perception unbalanced him. "I'll not be harassed by the both of you," he growled, scrambling for a defense. He hadn't thought she would follow a word of his exchange with Lilias, let alone approach the truth so quickly.

" 'Tis as clear to me as the nose on my face that she's worried about something. Something you're hiding, and Lilias has guessed what it is."

She'd summed up the circumstances far better than she could imagine. "You displayed a great deal of confidence in me, despite that," he countered, relishing her faith in him.

"I *am* confident in you," she acknowledged with a gracious nod. "I am pleased to see your relationship with Lilias changing. But I'm baffled that she sees this change as threatening, or that she sees me as involved. I don't understand. What did she mean?"

She was too persistent. He should leave the room to avoid her questioning. . . .

But he didn't want to.

He could change the subject. . . .

But she would return to her questioning again and again, giving him no peace.

He could kiss her. Or encourage her to kiss him. That would distract her.

Liking the last option, he crossed the chamber to stand at her elbow.

She twisted to look up at him, suddenly wary.

"Thank you for having faith in me," he said to convey his heartfelt appreciation.

"You need not thank me. The honorable deserve our faith." Her chest rose and fell rapidly as she spoke, betraying her awareness of him.

"Why are you so sure I am honorable?" Few people troubled to question what they were told. Why was she any different?

Her expression turned pensive. "You told your sister you care for her. Your men are coming to see that you devote all your attention and skill to clan interests. I believe you have a generous heart."

Her avowal caused a stirring in his chest. At that moment, he yearned to strip away the mask he hid behind, yet she seemed to see *him*, despite the facade. She, an outsider, offered him recognition like a gift.

He dropped a light hand on her shoulder.

At his touch, her chin sank to her chest, and she released an audible sigh. Her eyelids flickered. For a second, he feared she was going to faint.

But she braced both arms on the table and straightened her spine with obvious effort.

He pulled over a tall stool and sat, looping a supportive arm around her shoulders. The chamber was warm, so he threw off his plaid and loosened the cord at the throat of his shirt. "Are you feeling unwell? 'Tis close in here. I can open a window if you like."

"No, no. I am fine." She shivered as she spoke, a delicate flutter like that of a bird as it settled on a branch.

He loved the feel of her within the circle of his arm, as if she had come home to where she belonged. "Lilias did not mention where you rode today," he said by way of conversation. "Will ye no' tell me what you saw?" With his free hand, he toyed with the lace lining the neck of her bodice, loving the sensual feel of the fabric, loving the idea of the sensual feel of her flesh a mere finger's width away.

She gulped a deep breath, as if the air would be all gone before she got enough. "I saw such beautiful views of . . ." She turned to look at him and faltered, her gaze dropping to his chest.

He glanced down and realized that his shirt hung open, exposing a wide swath of his chest. So she liked what she saw. "Beautiful views?" he prompted. "Of what?"

The darkness at the center of her eyes grew larger, turning them a rich, smoky color that spoke of hidden fires.

He grinned at the sight of her arousal.

She closed her eyes and turned her head away, as if in deliberate denial. "Views of lochs and forests," she breathed. " 'Twas wonderful. I couldn't wish for more."

He inhaled her softness, enjoying her appreciation of his land and his person. "What else did you do besides enjoy the views?"

With a stern expression, she clasped both hands on

the table and stared at them, as if they wished to wander and required restraint. "We looked at a glen where there might be deposits of high-quality clay."

"Did you speak to anyone along the way?"

"Indeed. A kind woman named Jean Dun . . . er . . ." She hesitated, blinking in confusion as she floundered over another of the Dun names.

"Dunaudley, descended from Dunardley, descended from Dunadd," he supplied, unable to resist teasing her. He put his free hand over hers.

Her eyes glazed over, and he wondered if the names alone were muddling her mind. He hoped not.

She shook her head as if to clear it, then carefully removed her hands from beneath his. "Yes, well, Jean with the Dun name let us sit beside her well and drink cool water. We met her daughters and her son."

"Go on." He loved her confusion. This woman thought she knew exactly what she wanted in life, and it did not include a man. The thought of trying to change her mind, of perhaps succeeding, exhilarated him.

Geddes stroked the backs of his fingers along her jaw. She was so alive. So tender. Her nearness sent urgent messages to the lower part of his body. Messages he hated to ignore. "Who else did you see?"

The flutter shook her once more, and she closed her eyes, as if seeking strength to fight it. "No one much." Her voice had sunk to a whisper, low and uncertain.

Geddes was pleased. She was thoroughly distracted, seeming so susceptible to his touch, so responsive to his desire. If he was going to kiss her, it should be now.

He leaned close, then closer. His lips were mere inches from hers. His body tightened in anticipation of the pleasure.

Her eyes flew open. She saw him and jerked back. "What are you doing?" she cried.

He kept his arm firmly around her shoulders. Words were not his way of dealing with women, but she seemed to want them. "Lilias implied earlier that I hold you in some regard." He could not bring himself to say *besotted*.

"I would never believe anything so extravagant."

Her choice of words took him by surprise. Yet it was fitting. Practical, hardworking Angel would naturally think that enjoying his interest was extravagant.

But even the hardest worker was entitled to an occasional extravagance. Her kiss that first night had suggested her wish to indulge. If he knew nothing else, he recognized the signs of a woman's liking for a man. "You would never believe such a thing on your own, I agree." He leaned even closer, as if to whisper in her ear. "But what if I confirmed that Lilias was right?" Wanting a taste of her sweetness, he touched the soft shell of her ear with his tongue.

A blush crept over her face. It was like a sunrise, changing her soft skin from ivory to pink, beginning at her hairline and spreading all the way to where the scooped neck of her bodice displayed an inviting expanse of throat. She stared at the book on the table, both hands gripping it as if her life depended on it.

He touched her again. Gently. Experimentally. Savoring her as he never had a woman. What an effort to do no more. "Angel?" He enjoyed her name on his tongue, as if it were sweet marmalade.

She closed her eyes and tilted back her head. "Yes?" she breathed.

He touched her again.

"Mmmm," she purred, reminding him of a kitten. A delightful bundle of warmth, though he must not forget that such bundles had strength, agility, and claws. Still, he had never met a woman so responsive to his slightest touch. Passion seethed through him, and he had little doubt that it was playing havoc with her, too, given the way she clung to the book. It took an act of supreme will to subdue his desire.

With visible effort, she pushed back the stool and stood. "I must bid you god'den." She refused to look at him.

He stood as well, knowing he must let her go. But not forever. Here was a woman of pure tenderness, and he wanted her. He would just have to convince her that she needed him.

But what then? the insidious voice in his mind nagged. *She is a virgin.* He'd been through this dilemma before. He could not sully a virgin without wedding her after.

Aye, and what was wrong with marriage?

There was the danger Lilias warned of. Grave danger. He might draw Angel into it with him if he wed her.

But it was a danger he would like to ignore, given the opportunity.

Chapter 14

Angelica labored over her clay the next day. The batch mixed up beautifully, becoming slick and malleable in Magnus's mixer, but she couldn't appreciate it properly.

She felt odd and unsettled as she worked, unable to concentrate. It was most unlike her. Anything to do with clay usually held her enthralled.

But surely under the circumstances, it was perfectly natural. She couldn't expect to feel as comfortable and at home as she had in her Dorset workshop. This wasn't Dorset.

Yet today she felt as if she'd traveled to another world, not another country. She felt as if she were someone else.

Maybe she was. Her mind kept returning to the solar where she had been last night with Geddes.

He had said that he held her in some regard. He had meant to kiss her, and she had welcomed the idea. But it wasn't just because she liked his kisses. He was an enigma she felt compelled to understand.

How unusual. The old Angelica would never have been interested in discovering what lay behind a rake's mask. She would have accepted what others said of him and kept away.

But she doubted what they said of him. She had tried and failed to reconcile the image of a thoughtless rake with this hardworking chieftain. She looked beyond his perfectly formed sensual lips to how he chose to use them. She had stared last night at his gaping shirt, wanting to explore his muscled chest with her hands, but not just because he was attractive. She had wanted to touch his heart.

His clansmen said he was a rake. How could they be wrong?

Her instinct told her he had changed. They saw what they expected to see, what they wished to see. All save Lilias, who saw something else but refused to share.

Angelica cut off her thoughts with a silent curse. Had she lost her mind entirely, to get involved in this coil? She had come here for clay and had gotten it. *It* was her source of happiness. Clay was more reliable than the chieftain of a feuding clan.

But for the first time in her stable, sensible life, clay failed to hold her attention. In her mind's eye, she kept seeing *him*.

Geddes dismounting from his stallion with a fluid grace that outshone the most accomplished dancer.

Geddes leaning over her, holding her hairpin, with passion's fire in his eyes.

Geddes making a place for her in his household.

It was disconcerting in the extreme.

By the end of the day she was exhausted. The struggle to leash her imagination, which persisted in elaborating on these images and taking them in new, titillating directions, had worn her out.

Glad to stop work and prepare for supper, she went upstairs to wash and change. As she mounted the back stairs and stepped into the corridor, she saw the door at the far end close.

It couldn't be Lilias or Iain, for she had just left the pair sitting under the great oak in the stable yard. An animated Lilias had been regaling Iain with a tale of Highland selkies. Geddes had not yet returned from the village, where he and every able-bodied man drilled in archery. At this time of day, all the household servants were either in the kitchens helping to prepare the evening meal, or gathered in the great hall until it was served. The men of the garrison were there gaming with dice or otherwise passing the time. None of them came to the chieftain's private living quarters except to deliver messages or when summoned to the solar. It couldn't be one of them.

As Angelica approached the door, she thought through the assignment of each chamber along the corridor. Jenny Marie had one day indicated which belonged to whom. This one had belonged to the lord of the castle. She touched the latch lightly as she passed by, knowing Geddes had chosen not to occupy it. He had his reasons, she supposed. The next one had belonged to the lady of the castle. On the left side of the corridor was the chamber assigned to Iain, and beyond it, the one belonging to Geddes.

As she stopped before the last door on the right, the one in question, she recalled that it had belonged to Lachlan, the absent MacCallum sibling. The heavy oak door yielded no answers as she examined it. It could not tell her who had ventured upstairs at the gloaming and gone inside. If she wished to know, she would have to look, risking a confrontation with an unwanted intruder. Should she fetch one of the men first?

It could be no one dangerous, she decided, unwilling to wait. Placing a hand on the latch, she pushed the door open, glad that it didn't creak. Someone cared enough to keep the hinges oiled. Inside, books lining a shelf greeted her, neatly arranged by size. No dust graced them. Muriel apparently extended household cleaning to all parts of the castle, used or unused.

A window with no drapery admitted light, illuminating the surface of a desk set before it. Papers were strewn over the worktop. How odd. Had Lachlan MacCallum left them there seven years ago, and they had sat there undisturbed all this time? It seemed unlikely.

Less surprising were the few articles of clothing visible in the wardrobe. No doubt Lachlan had left behind items that were too old, too small, or inappropriate for a journey. She made out some tunics and a leather jerkin as she moved cautiously into the chamber, seeing no sign of who had entered . . . until she spied a small leather-clad foot. It was just visible beneath the high four-poster bed. Ross, the boot-cleaning lad.

She smiled but made no sound to reveal her discovery. The young rascal must be curious about the castle, and she saw no harm in his looking. Not as long as he avoided thievery, and she had heard no complaints on that score. Rather than get him into trouble, she would leave him unmolested. She had frightened him before, finding him in the solar. He would be terrified if she confronted him while trespassing again.

As she moved toward the door, she noted a book lying open on the desk, as if someone had been reading. The title was French. Though she could read little

of the language, she recognized the word *amour* in
the stanzas ornamenting the page. French love poetry?
Had Lachlan been a romantic as well as a scholar?

The idea of the book sitting untouched for seven
long years haunted her. It awaited his return, as did
the people he had left behind. Lilias seemed to miss
him, given the way she spoke of him, yet he had sent
no word for many years.

At the thought of the family's loss, an unexpected
wave of homesickness engulfed her. How she wished
she were sitting in the airy dining chamber of her
childhood home with her aged mother, her sister Rozalinde, and her husband, the Earl of Wynford, her
brother Charles and his wife, along with each couple's
many children. Good food would be shared all around,
and after, her nieces and nephews would coax her to
play. She yearned for people who trusted and understood her as only family could.

But she'd chosen to settle in another country, to
nurture her sense of belonging in a place of her choosing. To do so, she must win people's trust. She wanted
one man's trust in particular, but if she won it, would
he share the secret that Lilias had guessed?

Geddes obviously did not wish her to know it. He
had exerted all his charm last night to divert her from
asking. To her folly, his tactic had worked. She had
had to quit the chamber before she succumbed to
his kiss.

As she returned to her chamber, she imagined the
pots she would make. Beautiful. Reliable.

As she closed her door all but a crack and waited
for Ross to emerge, she imagined the people she
would teach to make pots. Delighted. Prospering.

She saw Ross come out of the chamber and tiptoe
toward the stair. He wore a woolen cap.

The child must be roaming the castle in search of clothing, for she had not seen him wear a cap in the past. Now that she looked more closely, his tunic was tight and too heavy for the season, poor thing. He needed new clothes.

Halfway to the stair, he paused, then retraced his steps to stop before the door leading to the tower. With a swift movement, he grasped the handle and pulled.

It was locked, of course, and Geddes kept the key. Only a few people knew that the false flag lay secreted in the tower. Angelica doubted that Ross even knew of the flag, since he couldn't hear. He undoubtedly hoped to find more clothing in the tower. Summer was upon them. He might already be feeling the heat of the kitchens.

She might not be able to leash her rampant imagination that insisted on roving to Geddes MacCallum every other moment, but she could speak to Muriel about Ross's need for some summer clothes.

"Muriel, Ross's tunic is rather heavy for this weather," she said, pausing on her way to the pottery the next morning. "Mayhap he needs a new one."

Muriel puffed as she kneaded a great mass of barley bread dough, a task she and two maids performed daily. "I hadna thought of it, mistress." She pulled the dough toward her and slammed it on the wooden table with vigor, as if it had had the impudence to resist.

"I took the liberty of peeping into Lachlan's chamber and noted that some of his old clothing remains in the wardrobe. As he doesn't need it, could something be cut down to fit Ross?"

"I suppose. Lachlan will no' need it." Muriel thumped the dough, as if she would like to thump the absent MacCallum for staying away.

Angelica pulled up a tall stool and sat, leaning both elbows on the kitchen worktable. She liked the clean, cozy kitchen. It reminded her of when she'd been a tiny girl watching her mother and the head cook prepare dainties for the family. It had been a place of trust and confidences. "Where did Lachlan go?" she asked.

"We dinna ken. Always a scholarly sort, was Lachlan." Muriel punched down the dough. "Loved books and reading. Wanted to be a physician, or so he said. Went away to Paris to enter the university. My lady had a letter or two, but then nothing more."

"I would hate to lose contact with my family." As she spoke, Angelica realized she yearned to write to her family and receive their letters in return. But she could not send a letter just now, given the lack of messengers. "Is there a way to contact Lachlan?" she ventured. Surely the clan would be glad of tidings of him.

"I would leave it alone," Muriel warned.

"Why? Lilias seems to miss him. Were others fond of him?"

"Aye," Muriel admitted in her gruff way. "Near in looks to his brother, he was, but a different sort o' lad, a good lad. Did little tasks for me without my askin'. Brought pheasant or trout in season for roasting. Full o' odd ideas, he was, like wantin' to end the feud. But he's long gone now. Leave it alone, I tell ye."

"What was the feud about, Muriel?" Angelica asked softly, saddened for both families "Why do they fight over the land?"

Muriel shrugged and gathered the dough into a ball. She sprinkled her worktable with more flour, then flattened the ball, pushing it away with the heels of her hands. "We need the burn to water our sheep in pastures near the castle. The Kilmartins have their own burns aplenty. Why should they have it?"

"If Angus Kilmartin has his own land with his own streams closer to his castle, why does he want ours? I mean the MacCallum's?" Angelica corrected her error. How quickly she had come to identify all too closely with her host's clan, seeing their battle as her battle.

Muriel noticed as well, for she shot Angelica a grin. "The pasture's always greener on the other side o' the loch," she quipped.

So it seemed no one had a good reason to claim the disputed land. No one could remember who had owned it first. The idea depressed Angelica. "Who was that older gentleman who visited a few days past?" she asked, wondering why she had never seen the man again after that morning.

Muriel squinted at her. "What older gentleman?"

"He rode in the morning after the raid. An older man, wearing the MacCallum tartan. I never saw him at meals, so I suppose he didn't stay."

"Och, that would be Simon MacCallum, the Mac-Callum's granduncle." Muriel kneaded the dough with renewed vigor. "He's earned his rest, so he lives at a MacCallum holding near Inveraray, up north and out o' harm's way. Most like he was reporting on the spring planting or such."

The man hadn't looked to Angelica as if he were reporting on the spring planting. He'd looked weighed down by sorrow. "Does he not customarily stay?"

Muriel shrugged. "If he likes," she said noncommittally.

Angelica knew she would get no more from Muriel on this score and gave up. "You would be a champion at wedging clay, Muriel. You have strong hands."

Muriel snorted, though humor sparkled in her eyes. "You tend to the pottery, mistress. I'll tend to the kitchens. And dinna trouble the MacCallum about his brother. He has enough to worry him, as 'tis."

Angelica busied herself in the pottery the next day, forcing herself to shut out thoughts of the missing MacCallum sibling, the feud, and Geddes. The welcome respite offered by the false flag held, allowing the tranquillity she required. The people of the household went about their duties with their usual calm. The village was peaceful. It could mean only that the unthinkable was happening. Those who knew about the flag were keeping the secret. Not a whisper had passed about the flag in the usual gossip rounds.

First they kept the secret of the false flag. Then they kept the secret that Geddes was searching for the true flag. It was a major step forward in clan solidarity, and she was glad for them.

The clay was a delight, yet she felt anxious now that the time had come to throw it. She hadn't touched a piece of clay for nigh on two months. It was as if a different person had taken up residence in her skin and she was no longer the girl who had left Dorset. Time had passed. She was in a new place, living among new people, working on a different wheel.

Rhuri entered the pottery as she was wedging up a nice ball of clay. He bowed and tendered her something in his large palm.

It was a wooden rib for shaping pots. "Thank you, Rhuri. 'Tis good of you."

"Made it mysel'. We like to carve when we're not

on patrol, so the MacCallum showed us how to make
'em. He's a fine leader, he is."

Angelica didn't follow how teaching rib-making related to leadership, but clearly Rhuri was thinking well
of his chieftain, which she wished to encourage. "He is
using all his skill to protect the clan's lands," she said.

Rhuri nodded adamantly. "Aye, he's a canny one,
he is. You would ken it better than the rest o' us."

"Rhuri, you are mistaken about me," she stated,
deciding to address the rumors about her and Geddes
directly. "Things between me and your chieftain are
not what you think."

He nodded in friendly fashion, his long red hair with
its warrior's braids swaying. "Ye dinna have to dress
it up fer us, Mistress Cavandish. We respect ye, and
we're glad ye've come among us. My second son is
near beside himself wi' excitement at the idea of wor-
kin' wi' clay. Would you teach him?"

She hadn't known Rhuri had a son, but like the
other clansmen, he must have a wife and family farming and herding on nearby clan lands. "Stone, Magnus,
and I would be glad to teach him. How old is he?"

"Nigh on sixteen summers," Rhuri said proudly.
"And verra clever with his hands. He carves all manner o' things—tiny animals and such—for the wee
ones. And pretty things for the lasses, o' course," he
added, pulling a face.

"Bring him to us," she invited, pleased at the idea
of having their first apprentice. "He can try some of
the duties and see how he likes them."

A smile lit Rhuri's homely face. He stepped back
and bowed. "I will do that. Thank you, my lady." He
swung jauntily away.

Angelica sighed, glad to be respected for her effort
to help others but disliking what Rhuri thought of her.

Bad enough to be imagined a mistress when she wasn't, but to be respected anyway? The value of virginity dwindled in such circumstances. Why guard against enjoying Geddes's caresses if she could accept them and still be liked and esteemed?

The temptation to act on such a bold idea set her mind ablaze.

Appalled by her daring, she focused on centering the ball of clay on her wheel. But the last thing she felt like doing just now was working. She wanted to be with Geddes.

It was not time for a meal, though, and seeking him out in the middle of the day would look odd. She must work. More unsettled than ever, she took her place on the seat.

Magnus stumped in, wearing a large apron over clean clothing. Angelica guessed that Agnes must have pried him out of his clay-covered garments at last and washed them.

"Ready to throw clay, mistress?" He was all aglow with excitement at the prospect.

"Indeed," she nodded, pretending she was. "Is Stone coming?"

"Aye. He wouldna miss the chance." Magnus removed the damp hemp cover from the clay barrel in the corner and dug out a huge chunk. Handling it like a sacred object, he began to wedge it on the table.

Stone joined them and fell to work. Taking a deep breath, Angelica pumped the treadle of her wheel. Soon the three wheels hummed as they turned the clay they had harvested. Stone and Magnus transformed it from lumps of marvelous material into even more marvelous crocks, basins, pitchers, and drinking vessels.

But as Angelica worked, the rhythm of the wheel

spoke unfamiliar words to her. *Geddes MacCallum,
Geddes MacCallum,* it whispered over and over. Why
could she not still the turmoil of her emotions so she
could concentrate?

An hour later she slowed her wheel, dismayed as
she surveyed the six ugly bowls she had made. This
wasn't her customary work.

Surely it was only that she hadn't thrown anything
for two solid months. It was the longest interval she'd
ever been away from pottery since she'd learned the
skill. She needed a day or two to get her hand back.
She needed time to learn the new wheel's capabilities
and the material's strengths and weaknesses. She
needed time to adjust.

The morrow was the same though. Worse, in fact.
The superior clay wedged up well, as always. She centered the ball on the wheel and pumped the foot treadle that propelled it. With care, she coned the clay,
drawing it up, then flattened it with the heels of her
hands to ensure that all bubbles were gone. The clay
was perfection. . . .

Her work was not. Since her youth, she had not
produced mediocre work. Now the sides of her pieces
were too thick. The shape was uninspired. When she
tried to improve a bowl that showed promise, the top
collapsed, unable to bear its own weight.

Ashamed of her unusual failure, Angelica hurried
to rewedge the clay and try again. The mortifying re-
sult was repeated. Stunned, she stared at the grotesque
object she had created. It had all the grace of a pud-
ding crossed with a pig.

Was she sentenced for the rest of her days to creating utilitarian pieces that were little more than acceptable?

Looking up, she caught Stone watching her. He said

nothing, returning his gaze to his own work, but she had seen him studying her bowls. They both knew she was not producing her best.

Angelica dragged her feet as she entered the kitchens that night, tired from the strain of trying to concentrate, discouraged by her humiliating failure to produce her usual stellar work. A niggling fear ate at her. Had she left her skill in Dorset? In coming north to another country, had she forfeited her ability in order to find the clay?

Nonsense. The idea had no logic. She was still the same person. Skill did not leave one overnight.

But it wasn't overnight. She hadn't thrown a piece of clay for sixty days. She was in foreign territory, no longer the same person she had been while living at home under the protection of her family. She felt anxious and uneasy, full of unsettling desires and unaccustomed yearnings. She wanted to go home.

But she couldn't return to Dorset. She would be stifled in the home of her youth. With nothing expected of her and nothing to do, she would stagnate and grow old. She would miss the beauty of this wild landscape, the stalwart clansmen and women, the handsome face of Geddes MacCallum. Warring sets of emotions tormented her.

"Dirt in my clean kitchens," Muriel fumed, heading toward her with the mop, her mouth thinned into a tight line.

"Oh, I am sorry." Angelica looked over her shoulder and saw she had forgotten to remove her shoes once more. She had been too busy wallowing in her woe.

Muriel jerked to a halt just behind her and applied the mop to the flagstone floor. "Ye ken my rules, but ye think nothing o' breaking 'em. Twice ye've done it, now."

Angelica felt a twinge of annoyance. A terrible problem dominated her thoughts, and Muriel was concerned about her floor. But that was unfair. The floor was Muriel's daily duty, and she should respect the woman's wish to keep it clean. "I said I was sorry and I am. Shall I help mop?"

"Nay, 'tisna fittin'." Muriel swept her mop back and forth over the dirty footprints, indignant and unapproachable.

Angelica sighed. " 'Twas not intentional. I forgot. What can I do to make it up to you?"

"Nothing. But ye'll no' forget again. Where's that Ross?" Muriel grumbled at the absence of the lad. "I havena seen him fer hours. Leave yer shoes on the hearth for him to clean."

Shrugging, Angelica did as bidden and went to change out of her clay-spattered clothing. She was sorry she had offended Muriel, but she had truly forgotten. She would never intentionally track clay dust on Muriel's kitchen floor, knowing how the woman felt about it.

A gown of wine dark brocade greeted her in her chamber. Out of style but unmistakably elegant, the ells of silk spread across her bed, demanding her caress. She stared at it in awe, then hurried to wash in the basin and put aside her dirty clothing so she could run her hands over it.

The luxury and softness of the silk set her sighing with pleasure. Rich bands of black velvet accented the skirt, the bodice, and the long belled sleeves. The brown velvet gown that Muriel had provided had been beautiful but far less formal. Clearly she was meant to wear this more elaborate gown. Did she dare?

The idea of entering the great hall in this extravagance caught her imagination. She would be like the lady of the castle, appearing before the clan, sitting at Geddes's side. The skirts were to be belled by layers of the frothy white petticoats heaped on the bed. She wasn't sure she could resist.

A tap sounded at the door and Jenny Marie entered. "May I help ye dress, mistress?"

Angelica looked up from the gown. "Who sent these clothes, Jenny Marie? Muriel?"

"Nay, 'twas the MacCallum. Chose it himself from his mother's wardrobe. Said he dinna like ye havin' only two changes of gown, an' those suited only fer work. Said he wanted to see ye dressed up fine, to show off yer beauty, like."

He thought she had beauty? Since she'd ended her betrothal years ago, Angelica had never thought of herself as a beauty, but Geddes MacCallum thought her beautiful. Suddenly she felt like a princess who had spent years under an enchantment, forced to dress as a drudge. Now the spell was broken. She could dress in silk velvet and feel beautiful for an admirer. And not just any admirer. Geddes was a warrior prince.

It was indeed the stuff of daydreams.

Her good sense argued against it. Wearing the gown would reinforce the idea that she was his mistress.

Except that no one seemed to care if she was. No one save Iain, who was supposed to protect her. Yet being a mistress did not threaten bodily harm. Her reputation couldn't be damaged more than it was. She was already considered an immoral woman and not shunned for it. If Geddes wished to adorn her in silk and admire her, why resist?

Determined to enjoy the gown, she accepted Jenny

Marie's offer. The girl proved most adept at dressing hair, creating an elegant bundle of braids at the nape of Angelica's neck, holding it in place with jeweled hairpins—another extravagance provided by Geddes. The bodice was cut low and laced tightly, partially revealing her breasts. Though her waist was not especially small, the many petticoats propped the skirts to enormous proportions, shrinking her waist to nothing. The wine-colored overskirt was slashed in front to reveal a silver tissue underskirt. As she descended the spiral stairs, she felt both enchanted and enchanting. At the entry to the great hall, she paused.

Geddes rose at once from his seat on the dais. He must have been watching for her. With his gaze locked on hers, he crossed the open expanse of floor. The world around her receded. The crowd in the hall quieted as he approached her.

She stood rooted in place as he halted and surveyed her up and down. Dark passion radiated from him, enveloping her like a Highland mist that made her faint with excitement. She luxuriated in the feeling, even as she doubted the wisdom of enjoying it. The scars of past wounds made him a complex man, not given to straightforward emotions. She could not think his passion amounted to love.

But when he offered his arm, she took it, choosing the pleasure he offered.

"You look as exquisite as your name, Angel," he whispered, leaning over her.

The warmth of his breath against her cheek reminded her of their shared passion the other night. His huskily uttered compliment lit fireworks in her blood, making her giddy. She could barely find her voice to reply. "Thanks to you," she forced out, "spoiling me with lavish gowns."

His devilish gaze caressed her. "Dare I hope that you like it, despite your usual preference for adorning yourself with clay?"

"Of course I like it." She more than liked it. She loved the way the wine-colored gown displayed her body for him to admire, loved the way he ran his gaze over her. It filled her with a fever of anticipation.

He led her across the great hall, and she felt as if she floated on his arm, smiling and nodding to those who greeted her. When had folk resumed their normal chatter? She marveled at their calm acceptance of her as Geddes escorted her to the high table and pulled out her stool.

There was something to be said for the Highlanders' code of behavior, their apparent respect for and tolerance of nature, particularly human nature. She had a sudden insight into the precarious quality of their lives from one day to the next. It must account for their lack of judgment of her. Who had time or energy to waste on vicious gossip when life was full of danger? As Geddes had hinted the other night, one might be pressed to live life to the fullest when danger threatened, as it did their clan.

She arranged the voluminous skirts and sat, acutely aware of his presence as he joined her at the high table. The delicious scent of roast capon with sage tempted her. Trenchers heaped with it, roast turnips, and onions stood before Lilias, Geddes, and Iain. They had already begun eating. A serving maid brought a bowl and placed it before her, then stepped back.

None of the others had bowls before them. Angelica examined its contents. It was filled with what appeared to be thin gruel. How odd. Taking up her spoon, she stirred it. It looked like gruel. It stirred like gruel. It tasted like . . .

"What *is* this?" She squeezed her face into a grimace as she put down the spoon. She glanced from her meager bowl to the heaped trenchers before the others, then at the girl who had brought the bowl. She stood a pace behind Angelica, her face arranged in a neutral expression.

"I dinna ken. Let me see." Geddes leaned over to look in the bowl.

Lilias craned around him from the other side.

Geddes shot her a bemused glance. "Did ye do something to earn Muriel's wrath?"

"I forgot to take off my shoes and tracked clay dust in the kitchens. But I apologized to her," Angelica said. "I offered to help clean it up."

Lilias smirked.

Iain grinned.

Geddes threw back his head and guffawed. "It makes nay difference to Muriel. You'll suffer the same fate as any other who breaks her cleanliness rules. Gruel for supper if ye canna obey."

Angelica stared at the contents of the bowl, then at the maid who had brought it. The girl's mouth twitched to hide a smile. Mortified, Angelica wanted to slide beneath the table. "Did you ever suffer her wrath?" she demanded of the girl.

"Oh, aye. 'Tis as the MacCallum says. We all have, except fer the perfect Lachlan."

Mention of his name surprised Angelica. "Did you know Lachlan?" The girl would have been a child seven years ago.

"Nay, but I heard he was perfect. He ne'er forgot one o' Muriel's rules. So she never lets us forget him."

"And what of the MacCallum?" She let frost creep into her tone as she nodded at Geddes, who had not offered to override the rule for her. "Must he do as Muriel says, as well?"

"Och, he's the chieftain. Muriel lets him do as he pleases." The girl had edged away during this exchange. As Angelica turned back to the table, she raced away, no doubt to regale her friends in the kitchens with tales of how the punishment had gone down.

Angelica rose from her seat, chagrined.

"Nay, stay." Geddes grasped her hand and tugged her back.

"Did you never get the gruel punishment?" she demanded of him, humiliated past bearing.

"Aye, in my wicked, wicked youth. We all did, save for the perfect Lachlan." He winked at Lilias. "Once you suffered Muriel's wrath, you were far less likely to forget."

Brother and sister grinned at her.

Angelica burned with shame. Every one of nigh on fifty pairs of eyes seemed to laugh at her. From the dais down to the bottom of the table, people stared and whispered of her foolishness.

Geddes squeezed her arm. "Ye're one of us now," he said softly in her ear.

He rose and drank to her health, embarrassing her further. But when he finished, every person in the hall cheered her.

And cheered.

And cheered.

Amazed by this unexpected show of affection, Angelica stared out at the range of faces. Men from the garrison threw up their bonnets and shouted with glee. Rhuri thumped the table and loosed a wild whoop of approval. Matrons, girls, and lads applauded her more sedately but with equal approbation. They thought she was having carnal relations with Geddes MacCallum, yet they appreciated what she was trying to do for them, as Rhuri had said.

She looked at the gruel and felt a smile growing on her face. Geddes elbowed her gently and sent her a conspiratorial grin. She began to chuckle.

"Eat," he urged her. "Show them you're made o' stern stuff."

She picked up the spoon again, and the hall fell silent. Everyone watched as she once again tasted the contents of the bowl. It wasn't bad for gruel, now that she gave it a chance. Not fatty or burned. She took another spoonful. Then another. Suddenly she put down the spoon, picked up the bowl, and drained the entire contents.

The hall went wild with approval. Cheering, shouts, and happy bedlam broke out. Somewhere, a piper began to play a reel, and several men and women leaped up to dance.

"I drank it all," she announced to Geddes amidst the clamor, putting down the bowl.

"I'll give Muriel a good report of ye," he said with solemn approval.

"Do so, but I swear I will never, ever forget to remove my shoes in Muriel's pristine kitchens." She felt a little better. No, she felt much better. She smiled down on the raucous crowd that accepted her as the chieftain's woman.

But all the approval in the world couldn't make her forget the crude bowls she had made, sitting on a board in the pottery. She had come to Scotland to make beautiful pots, and she had made ugly ones.

Chapter 15

They seemed as thick as thieves today. On her fourth day of making hopelessly ugly pots, Angelica watched Geddes and Lilias through the window of the pottery. They sat beneath the shade of the great oak, their heads together, laughing over some jest.

Lilias had changed since Geddes had given her the brushes. No longer sullen and angry with her brother, she had taken a bath that morning and dressed in a clean kirtle skirt and bodice. Her ankle was as good as new, and she no longer limped. Now she smiled at Geddes and tapped him on the arm as she made a point. In response, he put an arm around her shoulders and delivered an affectionate squeeze.

The new closeness between brother and sister was just what Angelica had hoped for. So why was she restless and anxious?

Her mind skipped back to Lilias's explosion the other night in the solar. She had spoken of disaster. Despite this, she seemed very happy about something now. Mayhap Geddes had managed to calm her fears about the feud.

Taking off her apron, Angelica gave up throwing clay for the day. Her pots were too much like yesterday's, with thick sides and uninspired feet. Instead she would help Magnus and Stone prepare the kiln in the woods.

Finding a broom, she left the pottery, avoiding Geddes and Lilias. Though she dearly wished she were the one receiving Geddes's affectionate squeezes, he needed time with his sister. She needed to concentrate on her enterprise.

The kiln sat deep in the greenwood, built of brick, half-tunneled into the side of a hill. The firebox stood in front at ground level. Air drew through vent holes bored into the hill from above. Working with Stone and Magnus, Angelica cleaned away old birds' nests and brushed the inside of the kiln with her broom.

At last the kiln was ready, and they loaded their clay ware, piece by piece. Though her work was less than stellar, Angelica allowed that most of her crocks were worth firing. They weren't excellent, merely acceptable. Stone and Magnus had turned out an excellent batch of basins, mugs, and bowls. All told, the results would sell.

Still, Angelica's heart was heavy as she helped the two men build up brick across the opening. Magnus kindled a spark and lit the tinder in the firebox. They fed it fuel for hours as night settled over the land.

Nigh on midnight, Angelica sent her friends home to sleep. At their protest, she insisted. "I wish to stay. The garrison is on patrol. As you return to the village, let them know I'm here."

She sat by the kiln in the dark, feeding the fire. Summer stars flickered among the leaves overhead, the light of their cold fire augmenting the roar of flames in the kiln. In the presence of such a conflagration, she burned with desire. To be complete. To be whole.

Yet no matter how she reached, completion eluded

her. Was this her fate? Each time Dame Fortune gave her a piece of what she wanted, she snatched away the rest?

Angelica rose to place more kindling in the firebox, a tunnel of brick that opened to the inside of the kiln. Flames danced and leaped, mystical orange and yellow, drawn through the earthen cave inside before seeking escape. How she wished to escape as well. But she must face her difficulties to overcome them. Groping her way back to the board set on two boulders for kiln watchers, she sank down and buried her face in both hands.

"Good even, Angel."

She jumped as the voice of Geddes MacCallum penetrated her misery. When had he begun calling her Angel? She couldn't think, but it comforted her just now. Despite her surprise at his appearance, she was glad he had come. She needed a friend. Or mayhap she hoped for more than a friend.

"Geddes." She nodded, pretending she had not been crying. Her tears would be invisible in the dark.

"May I?" He indicated the seat beside her.

She nodded and made room for him. Though fully garbed in kilt and plaid, he was barefoot, a state he and all the men at Duntrune seemed to adopt when they weren't riding or fighting. The board bench accepted his weight with only a slight give.

His presence gave her courage. The curtain of velvet night draped them in privacy. As always, she felt acutely aware of his masculinity, her untutored senses responding to his slightest move. A pity she must be a mistress in name only.

She stole a glance at him as he leaned forward to pick up a faggot. The blade of his dirk bit into the wood as he began to whittle. His broad hands moved deftly, shaping, sculpting.

At length, she discerned the handle of a pin tool coming to life. He was making another implement for her to use in working clay, and she appreciated the kindness. Her troubles were trivial compared to his, yet he took time to distract her from her gloom.

"How goes the firing?" He nodded toward the kiln.

"The kiln hasn't been used in years, but we cleaned it out, filled all the chinks we could find, and unblocked the vents. It seems to be performing well."

He nodded and whittled in silence. Within minutes the handle was finished. He presented it to her.

She took it, wincing.

"Does it not suit?"

"Oh, yes. You are kind to fashion tools for me." She didn't want to admit to him, of all people, her misgivings about her skill. Not after he had agreed she should remain in Duntrune and start the pottery. "I've had a touch of homesickness, but 'tis only natural. 'Twill pass." She forced brightness into her voice.

He put away his dirk, casting her a sidelong glance. "You didna sing over your work today, as you did while mixing the clay."

She could not respond to this observation, only marvel that he had cared to notice. He must have watched her in silence; she had not even known he was nearby.

"You were going to make me a set of drinking vessels, if I recall." His gaze penetrated. "May I hope you will find time soon?"

Her stomach knotted. The thought of having to form anything on the wheel just now flooded her mouth with the taste of bile. She would produce more miserable failures. "At the moment, I would be fortu-

nate to make a chamber pot fit to sit under a bed,"
she blurted.

He eyed her keenly. "That bad?"

She nodded, full of misery.

"Has this ever happened before?"

"No, never." Which made it a double misery. She
had no experience in getting around such an obstacle.

His arm crept around her shoulders, offering friendship and comfort. It felt so good to be comforted. She
leaned against him, her head nestled against his arm,
her face hidden as she struggled against the tears. She
would not display weakness, even though she felt as
weak and vulnerable as a piece of kindling tossed to
the flames of the kiln.

He squeezed her shoulder, then rubbed her back.
Reassurance spread through her, flowing from his fingers and palm. He had a firm, masterful touch that
was . . .

She blinked as she remembered what she had said
to him the other day. His touch was as inspiring as
working with clay had once been. She desperately
wished to recapture the feeling, yet it wasn't that
alone. The promise of intimacy with him was like a
light in the forest, drawing her to a place of comfort
and strength. "Would you . . ." She jerked to a halt,
appalled that she had almost asked him to make love
to her straight out.

"Would I what?" he asked.

"Er, have you ever wanted to be or do something
and others wouldn't let you?" she amended, tenta-
tively taking a roundabout way to her goal.

His expression darkened. "Aye."

"And what did you do about it?"

He cast her an assessing glance, as if to determine
whether this was idle chatter or if she truly wanted to

know. "In my youth, I did nothing about it," he said at last, apparently deciding she asked an honest question. "I obeyed my elders and was the person I was expected to be."

The pain in his voice was like night falling, and not a pleasant night, like tonight. Darkness emanated from him, creeping over her like a suffocating fog. Anguish lurked in its shadows, waiting to leap out and smother the unwary. Though the oppression that had ruled her life had never been this severe, she understood the agony of keeping silent when forbidden to speak, the torment of aching to grow but being stifled by society's rules.

"Excruciating sums it up nicely." He had apparently noted her quickened breath, her distressed expression. "Yet I did nothing to stand up for my beliefs."

"You were young. You had no choice but to obey your elders." She could scarcely catch her breath, she hurt for him so. The pain was like a physical pressure, squeezing her lungs. "But later?"

He shrugged. "Later, I ran away. I left Duntrune because I saw no hope of change."

She, too, had run away, but her suffering couldn't compare to his. Mayhap it wasn't surprising that he'd been a rake and a womanizer for a time. "But settling in a new place allowed you to change?"

"Aye, I changed." He spoke so low, she had to lean closer to hear him. "I was able to make my own rules, and to serve someone whose rules I could accept."

This she understood. Even now, she struggled to become someone new, to both herself and others, yet it was possible only because the person she served agreed with her choices. "I see you are different now," she observed.

His head snapped up. "How can you? You didna ken me before."

"I didn't, but everyone tells me how you were, and I don't see that you fit their descriptions. They're not really looking at what's before them, but I am." She leaned forward, both hands braced on her thighs as she made her point, shaking her head with vigor. One of her annoying hairpins slipped and a braid flopped loose.

His gaze shot to her bare throat, now surrounded by loose hair.

She shoved the hair over her shoulder, growing hot and uncomfortable as she sensed his rising interest. It reminded her of how distracted she had been all day. "This is your fault, you know, Geddes MacCallum," she admonished. " 'Tis your fault I've made the ugliest pots in my life for the past days."

"My fault?" The darkness that had dominated him slid away. Curiosity and surprise took its place. "Tell me what injury I have done you, and I shall repair it straightaway." His tone became lighter, like eiderdown.

She didn't want to dampen his mood, yet she was entirely serious. "I see now why I've been unable to concentrate. I'm looking at this odd disparity that no one else cares to notice. 'Tis most distracting. I cannot think straight after I've been with you."

He arched a brow, turning suddenly cynical again. "That's what a rogue does. He makes a woman think of only one thing."

His sarcasm annoyed her. "I'm not thinking of that one thing, at least not the way you mean it. I'm thinking the things that Lilias thinks."

She took a blind shot in mentioning Lilias, but she hoped it would yield results.

Sure enough, he seemed taken aback. Cocking his head, he narrowed his gaze on her. "If you can figure out what my evasive little sister thinks, you're a better person than the rest o' us at Duntrune. I'd say you'd have to read minds." He paused, eyed her speculatively. "Or has she *told* you what she thinks?"

Guilt formed like a black cloud over Angelica as she thought of the secret Lilias had shared. The girl had admitted her love for Brian Kilmartin, but she had revealed nothing about Geddes. "I don't know *everything* Lilias thinks," she answered honestly, "but she knows you're not a rogue, and I agree."

He smiled with indulgence, as if she were a child who had never seen a globe and guessed the world was square. "How would you ken?"

"If you were a rogue, I wouldn't want to kiss you."

Surprise flashed across his face. "You wouldn't?"

"Of course not. Rogues are boring compared to a man like you." She took pleasure in pointing out the difference. "They have a limited repertoire of conversation and experience. They are shallow and dissolute in every way."

His eyes widened in what seemed to be genuine astonishment. "You dinna think me shallow?"

"Of course not." The idea that others thought so outraged her. "You know you are not shallow, nor are you dissolute in any way at all."

He gazed at her, seeming to relish her declaration. "Well, well, I didna ken ye were so adamant on the subject. I wish my people believed in me as thoroughly as you do."

"Oh, but they do. At least they are learning to believe." She delighted in sharing this with him. "They need time to become accustomed to your good qualities, but Rhuri thinks well of you. Very well, indeed."

"And just how would you ken that?"

"He told me as much when he gave me a new rib."

His gaze whipped to her midsection in seeming alarm.

Angelica loved his proprietary concern. It created a delicious warmth deep in her belly. "He gave me a wooden rib to shape my pots," she explained, "as you taught him and the others to make."

Geddes recovered his humor, even chuckled at his error. "So Rhuri thinks well of me. And *you* want to kiss me?"

Was it her imagination, or did he state it tenderly, encouragingly? She nodded, touching her tongue to her lips. "Every minute of the day."

His gaze riveted on her mouth, and a slow grin lit his face. But it wasn't the predatory leer of a rake who anticipated taking advantage of her. No, he was charmed to know she liked him, pleased because he felt the same in return. And mayhap he was touched as well?

Whether he was or not, the prospect of passion flickered between them, as fiery as the heat blazing from the kiln. It drew her relentlessly to him.

He wasn't a rogue. He might have been once, but he wasn't any longer. If he wished to kiss her as much as she wished to kiss him, why must they play at games? Why should she wait for him to invite her first?

Mayhap if she kissed him, thoughts of him would no longer overwhelm everything in her life, even the instinctive movement of her hands on the clay. Mayhap she could still the turmoil of her emotions so she could concentrate. Mayhap giving in to one desire would free her to pursue the other. She had to find out.

Driven by the strength of her logic, she reached for him. Sliding her fingers into the rich warmth of his thick hair, she turned his face to hers and sought his lips with her own.

Chapter 16

Geddes was ready for Angelica this time. The first time, when she had kissed him in the solar, she had caught him by surprise. Now he knew her better and had waited, with eager anticipation, for this moment. Drawing her onto his lap, he deepened the kiss she had initiated, and she responded.

Oh, how she responded.

The taste and feel of her mouth sent the fires of passion roaring through him until he felt he rivaled the kiln. Her lips melded to his, the perfect complement to his need.

She believed he wasn't a rogue, and that made her want him.

How entrancing.

Her powers of observation defied that of most men he knew. It made him want her all the more.

Nay, he stated his desire too mildly. He *lusted* for her.

How insane.

Her strong, sure hands felt so good in his hair. Catching one of them, he guided it to his bare throat, inviting her to explore as they kissed. Her fingers caressed his flesh, moving to the nape of his neck, then back to his throat. Her touch nearly blinded him with its tenderness.

She saw past what was said of him to who he really was. Her instinct was like an arrow, flying straight and shining to the mark. She exposed his heart, which he had hidden for years. She wounded him in the process.

Yet even as he bore the pain, her trust brought him new life. It flooded in with her healing touch. Moved by her generosity, he crushed her against him and explored her moist mouth until heat roared through him.

Wood shifted in the firebox, snapped, popped. Angelica jumped, twisted on his lap, and stared at the kiln.

"Is aught wrong?" The movement of her thighs on his inflamed him beyond bearing. Yet he retained just enough presence of mind to know he shouldn't say so if the kiln were about to explode.

She studied the kiln a moment, then shook her head. "I've learned the signs of trouble in a firing. I see none here." But instead of returning to their kiss, she pushed forward to the edge of his lap and stood. "I must feed the fire."

She was already doing that. He stifled a groan as he watched her choose logs and angle them into the firebox. The flames roared deep within him. She'd best be careful, else he would be hard-pressed to stop at tasting her lips. His body clamored to devour the rest of her—her throat, her shoulders, her breasts, the secret place between her legs.

But he must not make love to her. He knew the consequences of such an act. Marriage would be necessary, and he should not marry while living under the veil of deception.

He would enjoy what he could, though, especially

looking at Angel. She knelt before the kiln like a primeval goddess who served a higher power, building the sacred flame. The greenwood whispered around her, the trees sheltering their secret meeting place. Higher and higher rose the heat in the kiln until it roared in the vents, the flames of passion rising white-hot in him as well.

She returned to him, eyeing him with what seemed like appreciation. "Am I invited back?"

His throat tightened with emotion as he reached for her.

She settled in his lap, her bottom firm and marvelous against his thighs. She entwined sweet, welcoming arms around him, trailing kisses across his cheek to his ear. "Geddes, I need you," she whispered. "I wish you to make love to me."

The area suddenly seemed to lack air. Geddes gasped and found nothing to fill his lungs. "You . . . canna mean that," he managed, feeling half-strangled.

She caressed his cheek, her strong, agile hand so gentle. "I know what they say of you, but they're wrong. You are too honorable to be an indiscriminate debaucher of women, and honor is learned young."

The depth of her perception held him spellbound.

She traced his lips with one finger. "I have thought on it long and hard. Since I arrived, I have not seen you once behave with dishonor toward a woman. People are mistaken about you. If you ever did take advantage of women, you've changed."

Her show of trust was an amazing gift, yet he must refuse her invitation. "Lilias hinted at disaster," he reminded her.

"Yes, that puzzled me. What did she mean?"

"I canna tell you, but know one thing, sweet. I would like to make love to you if circumstances per-

mitted." The refusal sounded hollow, yet he knew all
too well that Lilias's prediction of disaster could come
true if things went wrong.

"You see," she said in triumph. "You're no womanizer. And you pay heed to your sister, though no one
would fault you if you did not. But you must change
your mind, because I cannot work, and 'tis all your
fault."

He blocked her lips with one hand as she stretched
to kiss him. She seemed to think that by accommodat-
ing her desire for him, she would be free to pursue
her creativity. Yet it was too romantic a notion, and
he could not make love to her for such a reason.
Though he knew how it felt to be distracted by sexual
urges, logic must overcome desire. "Angel, I'm no'
the answer to your trouble with the clay."

"I'll be the judge of that, Geddes MacCallum." Her
smile was confident, illuminated by the glow of the
kiln. "When you kissed me just now, the stars seemed
to grow brighter. I feel as if I could reach out and
gather them with both hands, yet never be burned by
their heat."

She almost convinced him, but not quite. Still, the
stars did seem brighter since her lips had joined with
his. The points of light glittered on high among the
leaves, seeming to pulse against the black velvet of
the sky. He felt as if his veins were filled with their
fire, but he must not give in. "You cannot give up
your virginity. 'Tis important to a maid."

"I'm too old to be considered a maid."

"You're too bonny to be thought anything else."

Her smile had a modest, tentative quality about it.

"Ye dinna believe me." He swore inwardly. "The
men in Dorset were bampots, or they'd have compli-
mented you enough to convince you." He kissed her

throat, then sampled her flesh with his tongue. A vein pulsed beneath his touch, so full of life. "Ye have beautiful hair." He ran his hands through the thick tresses, untwining her braid that had sprung loose earlier, igniting his desire. "Beautiful eyes." He anointed each of her closed lids with a kiss. "Beautiful shoulders." He lowered his head, eyeing her breasts.

As if sensing his wish, she caught his hand and brought it against her lush fullness. The weight of her breast in his palm filled him with a need so raw, so urgent, he could scarcely contain himself. Sweat trickled down his back and chest, tormenting him as he held back.

"If I'm so beautiful, why don't you do as I ask?" She searched his face for an answer.

He groaned, unable to form words.

"I need you," she whispered.

"No."

"But Geddes—"

"You canna say a thing to change my mind."

"Nothing whatsoever?"

"Nothing," he said. "I canna help you with your art."

"But Geddes . . ." She drew a ragged breath, as if suffering from the same air deprivation that had choked him earlier. "I think 'tis more than my art. 'Tis something else. Geddes . . . I . . ."

She seemed to struggle with some internal conflict. "Oh, dear." She sighed deeply, as if in defeat. "It isn't my art at all. I think I love you."

Everything in his world stilled. Through a confusing haze, he tried to see her more clearly, sure he had misunderstood. "I seem to have become hard of hearing. What did you say?"

She tilted up her chin and met his gaze boldly. "I

said I love you. I only just realized it. I can't work for thinking of you. I just haven't wanted to admit it until now."

The stars ceased their pulsing in the sky. The planets halted in their spheres as her words seared their impression into his brain. Angel Cavandish had said she loved him.

He'd lied when he'd said nothing could change his mind. Her words held such power—the power to change his mind, the power to rob him of all in his head save those wondrous words and the woman who uttered them.

Still, he fought the haze of desire that engulfed him. She must be mistaken, but she didn't hesitate to put her words into action. Pulling aside his shirt, she nuzzled his chest with incredibly erotic lips. His mind turned muddled. He was blind to anything but the stunning surprise of what she had said.

"Everyone believes we take our pleasure together and thinks not the less of us," she reasoned aloud as he stared at her, dumbstruck. As if sensing his befuddlement, she caught his chin with her fingertips and turned his face to hers. Her eyes shone with an innocent sincerity that was disarming. "Why should we not, when I want you, and you want me?"

She overwhelmed his reason. When she talked like that, not even Saint Columba could save him. Layers of tension that had plagued him since arriving at Duntrune fell away, and for the first time in his life he felt in command in his home, beloved by a woman for who he really was. She was balm to his wounds, and he would gladly be her inspiration for shaping mud or anything else she required. Despite his wish to protect her from possible disaster, he could not refuse.

He eased her around to straddle his lap, raised her

skirts, and pushed them back to bare her thighs. "You're enough to drive a man mad, Angel."

She eyed his kilt and the evidence of his arousal. "You don't look mad to me." She kneaded him through the wool fabric. "You look magnificent."

The merest touch of her agile fingers almost pushed him over the edge.

Grasping her wrists, he dragged away her teasing hands. "Dinna touch me, Angel. I canna take it just now."

The wickedness of her grin suggested complete understanding. "Mayhap later?"

He groaned. "How do ye ken so much for an innocent?"

"Five of my siblings are married and I ask many questions."

"And they all answer you?"

She nodded. "I refused to leave them alone. So you see, I'm no angel."

He was all too familiar with her persistence, but he could scarcely fathom such a family, so open with intimate details. If only he had grown up in such a circle of trust.

"Geddes," she said softly. "Though I'm no angel, and though I was once betrothed, I know not how to proceed. Will you show me what to do?"

Her earnest entreaty was his undoing. Protest fled, honor following. He grasped one lace that fastened her bodice in back and pulled. It knotted, refusing to come undone. Blast. He wasn't sure he could last long enough to disrobe her.

He wore fewer barriers. Her eager fingers stripped away his kilt with ease. She settled her soft, bare thighs against his larger ones, making him rigid.

But the thought of coupling with her, sitting upright

on a board, displeased him. "Angel, if we're to do this, I want it to be the most pleasurable experience of your life." He lifted her up and set her on her feet. "We should have a bed with clean sheets and a fire in the hearth."

"A bed? Let me make one." With nimble fingers, she unpinned his plaid. Unlooping it from around his body, she shook it out and spread the heavy wool fabric on the grass. "I love it here in the woods, with the stars overhead. With the kiln nearby, we have all the fire we need."

She was right that they had enough fire, both in the kiln and raging within him. As she sat to pull off her shoes and stockings, then beckoned to him, his mouth went dry from the heat kindling within him. She was all too inviting.

He rose, leaving his kilt on the bench. Clad only in his long linen shirt, he knelt on the plaid beside her. Catching one of her bare feet in his hand, he caressed the silky flesh of her calf, moving upward to her thigh.

She caught her breath, clearly sensitive to his touch, and her pleasure drove him on. Her head fell back, her legs parted, and he hurried to search for the sweet bud of desire hidden at the juncture of her thighs.

Like a magic flower, she bloomed at his command. For him. Only for him. Compelled by her laugh of pleasure, he knelt between her thighs and sought the flower with his tongue.

"Oh, Geddes." Her cry of surprise tore through him.

The joy in her voice filled him with raw need.

"Is this usual?" She panted, giggling and twining her fingers in his hair, her grip almost painful to his scalp.

Yet he cherished her display of excitement. "It depends on what you call 'usual.' " He chuckled between lavish applications of his tongue. "If you mean do all men and women do this together, the answer is no. But when I am with you"—he anointed her increasingly slick flesh with another deep kiss—"it will be usual from now on." He followed his words with action.

"Oh, heavens, Geddes." She trilled her delight, her hips writhing.

Her response fueled his determination to take her to the heights. She had been unable to work because of him. He would show her exactly why her innocent senses had refused to comply.

He stroked.

She sighed.

He swirled with his tongue.

She sang.

And when at last she convulsed with the spasms of fulfillment, he suddenly knew that if he took her now, it must be forever. He would have it no other way. His desire refused to yield to any argument remaining among his scattered wits.

"What of you?" she asked, struggling up on one elbow. Though her eyes were languid with satisfaction, her first thoughts were for him.

"Aye, what of me?" He lifted his brows and awaited her invitation, because he knew the hardest part for her was yet to come. She must truly want him.

Despite her languor, she cast him a teasing grin and dived for him. Her hand closed around his swollen flesh, and this time he did not discourage her.

She was astonishingly adept at learning to please him. At his slightest direction, she complied with increasing skill. At length, when he thought he would go entirely mad with need, she pushed him onto his back and straddled him, guiding him between her legs.

"Are you sure, Angel? Very sure?"

"Of course I'm sure. I wish to please you."

He had lost track of all arguments long ago. "Very well. Hold yourself up," he urged, his hands on her waist, lifting.

She obeyed with a virginal eagerness, bracing one knee on either side of him, gripping his shoulders. With care, he guided himself between the damp, delicious folds awaiting him. She settled on him.

Geddes felt as if the searing heat of the kiln had enveloped him. She held him so tightly, so sweetly. He shifted in ecstasy as she worked her way deeper.

A long, sensual purr of appreciation escaped from her throat, fueling his excitement. Her body melded to his, and she bent over to lean against his chest, seeking his mouth with her own.

"Take it slowly," he cautioned, wishing he could fling away caution and ride with her on the wind.

"I don't want slowly." She moved against him, beginning to pant.

She had no idea what she was doing to him. He was half-delirious with arousal.

"What is this resistance?" She worked harder, twisting and writhing with obvious pleasure.

" 'Tis natural for your first time. Easy, my sweet," he cautioned. She had sworn that no man could hold her spellbound, nor did he. It was the other way around. He was mesmerized by the feelings she sent crashing through him.

She did seem enthralled, though, thrusting against him. "Geddes, I cannot seem to get enough of you."

He welcomed her wish for more of him. He tugged

at her bodice, and she slipped it from her shoulders, baring her breasts. She was so perfectly formed, she was like springtime, opening infinite possibilities to him. As he cupped her soft flesh, he swore to protect her. With his last breath, he would fight for all she held dear.

Her moans of elation lifted him to another plane. When she sank to the hilt on him, crying out in pain as her maiden's flesh rended, he rocked and comforted her, holding back his own need.

He would not move until she was ready. He vowed he would not. But it was too stern a promise, and she, too sweet a delight. He stiffened within her, flexing.

She straightened and looked at him, an expression of shocked wonder on her face. "My heavens." She moved against him experimentally. "Do you mean there's more?"

"We've hardly begun." He encouraged her to seek her pleasure. Anything that pleased her, pleased him. His excitement mounted as she moved, sending him soaring on tides of feeling.

Urgency opened up unexpectedly, like an unavoidable chasm. He struggled against it for a moment, but she thrust against him with increasing speed, her head flung back, her breathing rapid. He realized he could no longer hold back against the rising ecstasy. Nothing existed but the moment and the desperate friction of their bodies.

Her cry of fulfillment sent him soaring to his own completion. He drove upward, his body racked by spasms as he achieved a shattering completion. It seemed to go on and on. All boundaries between them receded, and he felt at one with her—both understanding her and understood.

In the end, they collapsed against each other, arms

entwined. He inhaled the scent of satiated woman and realized that her analogy had been right. Touching her was indeed like touching the highest stars. Except that in this case, he knew for a certain that he had been burned. Seared to the heart. And he didn't care.

He was willing to go through hell to keep her.

And he expected he probably would.

Geddes awoke at first birdsong, wrapped in his plaid, lying on the forest floor. A deep, abiding contentment spread through him as he felt Angel snuggle against him, still wrapped in slumber. She had jumped up once after their lovemaking to plug the kiln vents with moss as the fire died down. But she had returned quickly to his arms, and he had wrapped them both in his voluminous plaid, holding her as they drifted into sleep.

Now he wished they could stay here forever, just the two of them, free to enjoy one another without the interference of daily affairs. Satisfaction filled him at the memory of her words. He felt complete with her and at one with himself for the first time since his youth.

Yet when she shifted against him, the lower part of his body was no longer contented. It indicated a distinct interest in her.

As if sensing that interest and reciprocating, she awoke and rolled against him, turning to cling to him with both hands.

Her lips looked delightfully swollen from the night's kisses. They beckoned to him, and he dipped down to sample her nectar. His groin tightened.

"Oh, my." She stared down in surprise. "Can it happen again so soon?"

"I thought you were no' an innocent," he said gruffly.

"I believe my siblings left out a detail here and there." She looked sheepish. "So is it possible?"

"If the pair wishes it, aye." He eyed her meaning-fully.

"I most certainly wish it. Do you?" She nuzzled his cheek.

"I believe you already have your answer, as my in-terest is plain to see," he said dryly.

She chuckled, wrapping one hand around his arousal and seeking his mouth with her own.

The second time, their lovemaking was gentler and more leisurely. Heat and fire were splendid, but so was the slow build of pleasure fueled by tenderness. He explored her responses with great interest, bring-ing her to the brink gradually, then gathering her in his arms and pushing them both off from the edge.

As his body shook with release, he felt as if he were flying. They soared together. He would never have enough of her.

At length, he held her in his arms, staring up at the green canopy forming their roof, and wondered. "Do you suppose it worked?" he mused aloud.

She stirred drowsily. "If what worked?"

"The remedy. If you can now make perfect pots."

Catching his meaning, she cuffed him lightly on the arm. "As if you were a medicinal, meant to cure me."

He laughed. "But I do wonder. If you know you can come to me at any time, will you feel more con-tented at your work? How can you wait to find out?"

"Do you mean I should go to the pottery now? And leave you here alone? Never."

He kissed her. "I wish we could stay here all day and into another night, but we canna. We shall be missed, if we havena been already."

She understood his hint at discretion and sat up.

With obvious reluctance, she rearranged her clothing. Each gesture, each sensual movement, reminded him of how much he had enjoyed her.

"Oh, dear." She held up his plaid to display a smear of her virgin's blood.

" 'Twill rinse away with cold water. I'll stop by the burn on the way back."

"We've missed the breaking of fast in the great hall." She pulled on her stockings and tied the garters. "So I'll stop by the kitchens for a bite, then go straight to the pottery." She seemed inordinately pleased about something. "Now that you mention it, I am eager to try my hand at the clay again."

"Ever summoned by the call of the muck. May you enjoy it." He swept her a gallant bow.

"My thanks, sir. I hope I shall."

He swung around. "You'll tell me one thing before you go. How were you named Angel if it didna fit, which it clearly does not?"

"My mother grew herbs, among them angelica. The name was an understandable choice for her last daughter. She and my father shortened it when I was still in swaddling bands and looked an angel, all sweetness and good behavior. Only later, when I was mobile and into everything, did they realize their mistake. By then, the name had stuck. It was too late." She offered an impish grin.

Too late. It was that for him, as well. He had vowed to resist her, but he could not. "Get thee to the pottery, Angel." He turned her around and smacked her lightly on the bottom to send her on her way.

She hesitated.

"Go," he barked. "I'll come to you later to see your work." Though he would rather be buoyed aloft on his passion for her, he wanted her to go, for a niggling

curiosity teased him. Would she now make splendid
pots? Could he have inspired her art as well as her
body? An intriguing question.

At his determined order, she trotted off in the direction of the castle, visible through the trees. He looped
his plaid and headed for the burn. Of all the boons
he might have hoped to gain upon returning to Duntrune, the love of a beauteous Englishwoman had
been beyond his imagining. Everyone thought she was
his mistress, but unfortunately, he couldn't let that belief continue. She must become his wife. And he knew
very well that if he wed her, his deception would become an even greater burden to him.

Geddes went about his morning's affairs as if nothing had happened, but he guessed that someone must
have seen him and Angel at the kiln. The maids in
the kitchens cast him more saucy glances than usual,
giggling and chattering. Muriel studied him with concern in her aged eyes, though she asked no questions.
She served him a portion of bread and bacon in silence. As Rhuri and the men assembled in the stable
yard for archery practice, they exchanged more ribald
jests than usual. All were in high humor, casting him
sly glances when they thought he didn't see.

By the noon dinner hour, he decided to look in on
Angel. She was still in the pottery, working with a
large piece of clay on the wheel. As he watched, she
brought the clay up into a mountainous shape, then
pressed her thumbs into the top, beginning the inden-
tation that would form a pot.

Like magic, the piece took shape before his eyes.
Her strong hands guided the viscous material with
surety, the rising power of the vessel's sides thrusting
to full strength and dignity. He closed his eyes and

sucked in a breath, remembering the feel of those same deft hands on his body. Skilled hands. An artist's hands. Made for giving pleasure and creating beauty.

As he stood with eyes closed, he heard the wheel slow. He blinked, feeling as if he were awakening from a dream. She stood staring at her work, the beauty of her expression transfixing him. She had created a bowl so exquisitely formed, he ached inside as he looked at it. Its sides were so thin, the piece seemed all but translucent. Even he recognized its artistic value, untutored as he was in the art.

She must have sensed his presence, for she looked up, seeming unsurprised to find him watching. Their gazes met.

Dazzling happiness illuminated her face as she glowed with the joy of achievement. Suddenly he understood with full clarity the drive of the artisan that filled her. It put her next to the angels, as she brought order to chaos. She created harmony in the world, in his world, and with all his heart, he was glad.

Never mind the chaos that could destroy their future. He must wed with her. The elation of meshing with her assured him that he was no longer alone in the world. It was a priceless gift.

He would willingly take any risk for her, go to hell and back to fight for her future. Anything to make her his.

Chapter 17

Angelica's lovemaking with Geddes didn't remain secret for long. She could tell that Iain knew about it as soon as he entered the pottery that afternoon. His frown cut into his usually sunny expression like a cutting wire through clay. Someone must have come to the kiln and seen her in Geddes's arms.

Pumping the wheel's treadle at a steady pace, she ignored Iain. Just another moment of bliss before she must face the consequences of her actions. As the wheel spun, she immersed her mind in the texture of the clay. The mouth of a tall drinking flagon widened beneath her fingers, flaring to a dramatic finale. It was one of the set she had promised Geddes, and she wanted it to be perfect. But even the rhythm of the wheel nagged at her as she worked, reminding her of what she had done during the enchanted summer night.

What folly.

What foolishness.

What absolute joy.

She hadn't meant to tell Geddes she loved him. She hadn't known it herself. But in the midst of a heart-stopping kiss, the realization had come to her. Caught off balance, she had taken a reckless plunge.

She had offered her body, her heart, everything.

Geddes had offered only passion.

Yet she could not regret what she had done. The tenderness of his touch made her feel vibrant, alive. His acceptance of every facet of her, including her love of clay, made her know she was appreciated. She was happier in his arms than she'd ever been in her life.

Reality refused to go away, though, as Iain cleared his throat.

Please, another moment. Her skill had returned like magic. She wanted to feel nothing but the moist texture of clay spinning beneath her fingers. Balanced and centered in the aftermath of Geddes's lovemaking, she had set aside the fear that she might not succeed. With single-minded concentration, she had poured the passion he aroused in her into her work.

The results were all that she could wish for. She had made close to two dozen excellent pieces in the last hours. She hadn't slept more than six hours in the woods with Geddes, yet she felt so full of energy, she could work forever. Her passion for her art and for Geddes meshed into one.

Iain cleared his throat even more loudly and shifted with impatience.

Resigned to an argument, she removed her foot from the treadle and let her wheel slow. The earnest concern in his expression reminded her that traveling one's chosen road had its obstacles. The time for treasuring her secret tryst with Geddes was done.

"Ye canna do this, Angel." He spoke with the authority of one with staunch beliefs and the right to enforce them. "Do ye hear what I say?"

"I cannot do what?" She glanced pointedly at the stunning pieces she had produced during the morning, willing him to see the change. "Make splendid pots?"

"Nay." Iain gritted his teeth, clearly frustrated by her obviously intentional obtuseness. "Ye ken what I mean."

She took pity on him. She knew what he meant, yet no argument could justify her behavior, not even that she had fallen hopelessly, helplessly in love with the MacCallum chieftain. Even if it had been a useful reason in an argument, she wasn't sure she could speak of it. Not yet. It was too new to share. "I see nothing wrong with it," she said truthfully. "Everyone respects me, whether I am his mistress or no. 'Tis not as if anyone objects."

"I object." He raked his wild crop of red hair with one hand. "Yer sister Lucina would object. Yer mother and yer other sister, Rozalinde, would object. We canna stay here more, ye ken? We mun arrange to leave."

Angelica dipped her hands into a bucket of water, rinsing away the worst of the clay on her fingers. She must try another tack. "Are you trying to ruin my happiness?" She searched his face, looking for an answer.

"Aye. I mean nay." He spluttered in confusion. "What I mean is, 'tis my duty. No' to ruin happiness, but to ruin any improper male advances. I told ye, I'm a blight to romance. Ye think I like it? Ye're wrong, but I'll do it faithfully or Alex and your sister will have my head."

"They'll not blame you. 'Tis my decision to enjoy

the MacCallum's favors. I will explain to them, when necessary, that it is my choice."

"Ye mean ye expect to continue this behavior?" Iain cried. "He's using you, Angel. Sure an' you see that."

Angelica tilted her head to study him. "How so?"

"He's a rake, by heaven." Iain was becoming increasingly agitated. "What else does a rake want but to have a woman without obligation to wed?"

She picked up the cutting wire and ran it beneath the flagon to separate it from the wheel. She must convince Iain that her reasoning was sound rather than the choice of a stupid, sentimental female. "He is not using me. In truth, if anything, I am using him."

Iain's red eyebrows snapped together as he frowned at her. "Ye're using him? How is that possible? A maid canna use a man."

His genuine puzzlement brought a smile to her lips. "I requested his attentions because he inspires feelings in me I cannot ignore. They distract me from my work. By indulging in them, I become free once more to concentrate on my clay. Look at my work since yesterday." She separated the board with the flagon from her wheel and carried it to a shelf. With care, she lifted the flagon and lined it up with the others to dry.

Iain moved along the row, examining the statuesque flagons, the dramatic bowls, the mugs waiting for handles, the dainty jars with lids. "They're magnificent, I'll grant ye. I've never seen the like, with such thin sides or perfect shapes, but 'tis nonsense that he inspired ye," he objected. "Another person canna give ye skill ye dinna have."

"I did not say he gave me my skill. He gives me

peace. I have found at last what I need," she contradicted.

"I never heard of such a thing." Iain paced up and down the pottery, pounding one fist against his palm. "Ye'd best write to yer family before this goes any further. Seek their advice if ye'll no' listen to me."

"I have not been able to send a letter, but even if I could, I'll not ask their permission." Angelica sat down at her wheel and dipped a sponge in water. "I am of age and will do as I wish." She started the wheel and held the sponge to the work surface, cleaning away excess clay. "When we find someone to carry a letter, I'll write to them, naturally, to let them know I am well and have started the pottery, but that is all. Geddes MacCallum appreciates my work in the pottery. To my way of thinking, that is a rarity worth anything in exchange."

Iain groaned abysmally. "But Angel, I havena done my duty. I was to protect ye and I've failed."

"Oh, ho." She shook the sponge at him. "So your concern is about your duty, not about me. But you did do your duty, Iain. I've not been harmed on this journey north."

"No' harmed?" Iain turned so red, she thought he would explode. "Ye're the doxy of a notorious rakehell. That's harm, I'd say. Ye're degraded past all redemption by associating with him in such a way."

Angelica slapped the sponge into the water bucket, anger filling her. "Never let me hear you speak thus of him. I lose nothing by associating with him. He's an upstanding, honorable chieftain, and I am a free and independent woman. He hasn't acted the rogue a single time since I've been here. I think 'tis all a lie."

"I canna help it, I dinna like it." Iain rolled his eyes and headed for the door. "I warn ye, I'll no' let it be."

"Ye canna let her do this. She's an honorable maid."

Geddes looked up from the bridle he was mending as Iain Lang confronted him in the stables. The lad looked more provoked than a bear stung by bees. "I cannot do what to whom?" Though he was certain what Iain meant, he held on to his composure.

"Ye ken who I mean. Angelica, o' course," Iain huffed. "She says she's had her way wi' ye, if ye mun hear the truth."

Geddes had to suppress the grin that threatened to take over his face. "Does she now?"

"Aye, she does. She says ye inspire her work."

Geddes felt his smile slip. If Angelica had not mentioned her love to someone as close as Iain, mayhap it had been a whim of the moment. The idea dismayed him more than he liked to admit.

"But she doesna ken what she's saying. Ye've got to stop her," Iain pleaded, not noticing his silence or change of expression. "Can ye no' refuse her?"

"You think a man could refuse the likes o' her? She's too bonny for that."

Iain's green eyes turned desperate. "But ye mun. She'll ruin herself. She'll bear bastards and be a fallen woman. She'll—"

"I intend to wed her," Geddes interrupted forcefully, knowing he had played with Iain long enough. He'd made this decision before making love to Angelica, and he intended to abide by it.

"She'll be treated with disrespect and never have a home to call her own. She'll . . ." Iain stumbled to a halt in the midst of his tirade as Geddes's words sank in. "Ye intend to what?"

"Wed her," Geddes repeated succinctly so that Iain could not miss his meaning.

"But ye're a . . ." Iain stumbled over the word he'd been about to pronounce and halted again as his face turned an even more brilliant shade of red.

"I'm a rakehell and I ruin maids," Geddes supplied with a cynical smile. "Well, the rakehell has met his match, it seems. He's decided to let the Englishwoman make an honest man of him."

"Ye're certain o' this?" Iain examined him as if suspecting a trap.

"Aye."

"When will ye wed her? Posthaste?"

"Aye."

"Ye'll treat her well all the rest of yer life? Ye're certain ye wish to wed her?"

"I shall treat her with the utmost care and respect. I wish to wed her. I've never been so certain of anything in my life."

Iain dropped into a chair. "Hallelujah." He pulled off his bonnet and fanned himself with it. "For a moment, I thought I would ha' to challenge ye to a duel."

"All is well," Iain said as he entered the pottery several hours later.

Since he had left, Angelica had slept, eaten a small repast in the kitchen, and returned to the pottery. She was so excited, she could not stop working, even though it was the Sabbath and Magnus and Stone were resting. She wished to pull handles for the set of drinking mugs she had made. "Of course all is well," she agreed with Iain "You should not concern yourself."

Iain saun⸻
her, a satisfie⸻

She studied hi⸻
dering what his ex⸻

"All is well," he ⸻
Callum intends to wed ⸻

Her stomach did a flip-⸻
decide such a thing without ⸻

Her face must have betrayed ⸻
hurried to reassure her. "In all s⸻ ⸻es. I
just confronted him, and he said v⸻ ⸻hat he
intends for the two o' ye to wed. So t⸻ ⸻s it should
be and all is well." He seemed to be congratulating
himself as he picked up one of her bowls to admire it.

Why must everyone be involved in her affairs? As
the youngest sibling, she had never been free of her
parents' and elder siblings' interference. Now here was
Iain, sent to watch her by Lucina, her mother, and
Rozalinde. Would they never believe she could choose
on her own?

Besides, from all that she had observed at Duntrune
Castle, marriage between her and the MacCallum was
not necessary. "Why should I wed with him? I am
held in esteem without rushing into marriage."

"What?" Iain thunked down the bowl and turned
around in surprise.

"I see no need to wed him," she stated firmly.

"What are ye talking about? Of course ye'll wed
him. 'Tis the only honorable thing to do and he ex-
pects ye to accept."

"I'll not do anything hasty." She placed the end of
the handle against the mug's scored side and
smoothed it into place. "Where is he? I'll tell him
so myself."

"Nay," Iain pleaded, seeing that she was serious.

ants to wed ye by his own
m angry by saying nay."
ain, but I am not prepared to wed."
ummoned all the strength she had within
Though she couldn't put her finger on it, something seemed off-kilter in the MacCallum family, beginning with Lilias's recent change in attitude toward Geddes, and continuing with the girl's mysterious predictions of disaster. Geddes himself had refused to answer questions on the subject. It all pointed to one thing. Something unusual was going on, and she didn't want to plunge into the middle of it. Not if it would cause Geddes difficulties.

Although she loved Geddes and freely told him so, she wished their relationship to deepen first. It was the wisest course to take before making a lifelong pledge.

Of all his kin, Geddes chose to tell Lilias first of his plan to wed. He summoned her to the small fruit orchard beyond the castle walls. There, among the trees ladened with setting cherries, he told her his intentions. As he had expected, she flew into a frenzy.

"Ye canna wed," she cried, grasping his arms, pleading. "Ye ken it as well as I."

He held firm. "I will manage the difficulties, Lilias. I've deflowered her and 'tis the only right and honorable thing."

She twisted her handkerchief. "Are ye sure ye can manage? What if someone discovers yer secret."

Geddes tightened his jaw at mention of his deception, to which Lilias was now privy. "I mun wed her. There could be a child. Ye wouldna have me create a bastard when I could have an heir, would ye?"

"I would have ye end the feud," Lilias insisted. "That is what I would have."

"And how do you propose I do that, with Angus Kilmartin ruling from Fincharn Castle and trying to take our land every chance he gets?"

To his surprise, Lilias began to cry. "I dinna ken, brother. Everything is"—she gestured helplessly—"it gets no better and always worse. The trouble with the flag, with Angus Kilmartin, with ye."

He didn't like being lumped in the category of trouble. "The belief in the flag will keep Angus at bay. And Angel's sister is wed into a powerful Lowland family. There will be advantages to allying with them through marriage. It might discourage Kilmartin from attacking, at least until we are better prepared to fight him. I need all the time I can get to train the men and solidify our position at Duntrune."

Lilias nodded, looking hopeful though not entirely convinced.

"Geddes MacCallum, I require a word with you." A feminine voice cut into their discussion—a voice he recognized at once. "You owe me an explanation." Angel came toward them through the cherry orchard. She had changed her kirtle skirt and bodice since Geddes had seen her last. Clay streaked her hands and bare arms, as if she had been too hurried to wash. "Iain tells me that you expect we should wed. How could you decide such a thing without consulting me first?" She halted before him, looking annoyed.

He shook his head to clear it. Why would she doubt the necessity? "Of course we must wed."

"There is no need. I am satisfied with things as they are."

"*I* am not satisfied." He added a note of warning to his reply. He would not let her continue without the full protection of marriage. How could she think otherwise?

At his statement, some of the antagonism leaked out of her. "You never wished to wed before."

"People change."

"You are no longer a rakehell? Or were you ever?" Her oblique gaze reeked of suspicion.

He would have to be careful or he would give himself away. Angel was no fool. "You object if I have reformed? If you, perhaps, reformed me?"

She wavered, as if the idea discouraged her doubts as well as appealed to her feminine vanity. "I did not think of myself as a reformer."

"Lilias, you will pray excuse us." He sent his sister a stern look.

Lilias stood, taking in every word. With evident reluctance, she nodded and obeyed. As she trudged toward the castle, looking over her shoulder the entire time, he caught both of Angel's hands in his, ignoring the clay.

"Sweetheart, be reasonable. You want the pottery. I meet your requirement in supplying it. I need a legitimate heir. Let us call it a good bargain and wed." He didn't mention her declaration of love. Given her unexpected reluctance to wed him, he feared it might evaporate. Why the idea troubled him, he didn't want to know. He wasn't ready for any startling new revelations about himself just now. Life was chaotic enough as it was.

She did not pull her hands from his, but she refused to meet his gaze as she thought this over. "You will never object to my working with clay?"

"Never."

"Not even if Muriel scolds me for the dirt and dust?"

"Muriel must be kept reasonably happy, but I am not personally troubled by the dust, as long as you dinna mind eating gruel from time to time." He grinned.

She remained serious. "You will not object, not even if I hire apprentices, both male and female, and sell Duntrune pottery everywhere I can?"

"I dinna care if you personally cry it in the streets of Glasgow, as long as you are in my bed each night."

She blushed the becoming color that he loved. "But you're asking so little. What do you receive in return?"

He wished his gaze were fire, so he could sear away her clothing, baring her body to his desire. "An heir," he said, choosing the argument that most matched her impeccable logic. " 'Tis what every man needs, and I am no different. Your family connections are excellent. You no doubt bring a suitable tocher to the union, and we suit. The match is a good one."

She clearly didn't know what to say to that. It was eminently logical. She ran her tongue over her lips as she considered.

He loved the way the soft flesh traveled a sensual road along her silken lips. His control slipped, then fell away. He grasped her with both hands.

"Geddes, I'm covered with clay." She angled backward, indicating her streaked arms and hands.

He didn't care if she got mud all over him. He would make love to her in a bog if required. Smothering her protests, he claimed her soft, desirable mouth with his own.

Angelica's senses reeled. How could she resist this beguiling man? She let him kiss her, and within moments she was kissing him back until they were both aroused and breathless. Would he make love to her right here in the orchard?

To her surprise, Geddes suddenly drew back, though he maintained his hold on her. Triumph gleamed in his eyes. " 'Tis settled, then. I shall announce our intent to wed."

He had aroused her, but she had no intention of conceding the issue. "No." She pulled out of his grasp, drawing on her quickly ebbing reserve of strength. "I'm sorry, but I cannot agree just now."

"Why?" he demanded, clearly impatient.

She must give him a reason—something more solid than evasion. Yet he was the one being evasive, making her task all the harder. "Because I fear for you," she said with complete candor. "I will not wed where I could do damage. Let us leave things as they are for now."

But the set of his jaw suggested he didn't agree with her, and she didn't know what to do.

Angelica watched the MacCallum chieftain talking to Muriel in the kitchens and worried. From her vantage point in the kitchen doorway, she reviewed his positive traits—the reasons she might agree to wed him—the reasons she *wanted* to agree. He was considerate, accepting, and passionate. He set her blood on fire. . . .

It was the very reason she must refuse. The handsome MacCallum chieftain seemed to want her in typical male fashion. To him lust might seem an adequate substitute for love, but to her it was not. She knew she held impossibly high standards, but she wanted words of love.

What were he and Muriel discussing? Geddes's marriage plans? She squinted, trying to see the expressions on their faces in the fading daylight. Geddes seemed to be coaxing Muriel, as if he tried to convince her of something. Muriel appeared to be pleading with him and losing. Her broad face, usually so tranquil, suddenly crumpled like a leaf of lettuce left to dry too long. She ducked her head in seeming defeat.

Angelica must know what it meant. Though they probably wouldn't tell her outright, she might be able to deduce something. As she approached, they ceased speaking and drew apart.

Muriel smiled tremulously and embraced Angelica. "Ye'll make a bonny bride, love. 'Tis glad I am ye'll be stayin' among us."

Angelica never doubted that the woman's words were heartfelt and genuine. Muriel hadn't a hypocritical bone in her body. Yet as she embraced the stout old lady who had become her friend, then released her, she caught the look Muriel shot Geddes.

The cook clearly was happy about the wedding. Her smile was almost as wide as the mouth of her great soup kettle. Yet the smile trembled, and anxiety hovered at its edge.

"I am so sorry, but I cannot wed Geddes just now. You both know that present circumstances do not permit it." Angelica studied their faces, hoping they would discuss those circumstances if she pretended to know them, too.

Muriel drew a shocked breath and opened her mouth, as if to protest Angelica's refusal.

"She'll see reason." Geddes ignored Angelica and consoled the cook. "I'll not accept any argument against it."

"But we cannot." Angelica put aside her own feelings about the matter. "Disaster would surely follow, and I refuse to be part of it." She had no idea what she spoke of, but since Lilias had mentioned it, and Geddes had behaved as if his sister's opinion had weight, she would use it as bait to fish for the truth.

Geddes refused to acknowledge her words, but fear flashed across Muriel's face at the mention of disaster.

Angelica took the cook's reaction as a warning. She should not wed the chieftain. She didn't know why for certain, but Muriel had known Geddes for years. She was a faithful, loyal retainer who understood the family. Muriel knew something, just as Lilias knew something.

In her gut, Angelica knew something was wrong. She must make him see reason and insist they wait.

Chapter 18

Geddes had no intention of waiting to wed Angel. There were difficulties, but for once he was putting what *he* wanted first. He would wed her regardless of the consequences. He refused to live with the risk of losing her.

Angus Kilmartin's letter, in which he had demanded Angel's return to Castle Fincharn, was a jarring reminder that the risk was real, not imagined. The Master of Fincharn would not have hesitated to kidnap a visiting maiden. Geddes hoped he would think twice before abducting the wife of his rival. The decision to protect Angel by wedding her was sound.

He called a discreet gathering of clansmen and household retainers to the solar that night to announce his decision. As he waited for them to assemble, he studied his bride to be, who sat to his right. He had bidden her wear the golden-brown velvet, and she sat with her capable hands crossed on her lap, her gaze downcast.

Why had she refused him in the kitchens, and what did she know of the possible disaster? Surely she had merely parroted his sister's recent use of the word without knowing what Lilias meant. Though Angel understood him better than any of his kin, she couldn't know what he was hiding. Nor did he believe she didn't wish to wed.

She sensed a problem, and based on that, she put his interests first, before her own. She would offer herself as a sacrifice on his behalf.

Her generosity of spirit warmed him. And to think, even now his seed might be growing within her. The thought of their child, begotten in her body, roused a fierce protectiveness in him. It was unlike anything he'd ever felt for a woman.

It must be male instinct. The need to preserve one's heirs moved all men to take necessary measures. If Angel were not already with child, she would be soon. He would not relinquish the right to their offspring. Nor would he let her carry their child, defenseless and alone.

With everyone gathered, he closed the solar door and announced his plan in no uncertain terms. A hubbub broke out. Alex cheered. Georgie shouted a ribald jest. The general speculation seemed to be that he had taken the first step in becoming chieftain by returning home and reclaiming the clan's lands. Now he would seal his claim by marrying to produce heirs. A natural choice. Even rakehells needed to preserve their family holdings and bloodlines.

"I told you I wouldn't do it," Angelica said to him under cover of the noise.

"You dinna mean it, sweet. Not after the way you behaved last night." He caressed her cheek, expecting to melt her resistance.

She blushed hotly at his touch and squirmed on her stool. "But what of—"

"This is my choice," he admonished. "Can you not let me feel good about it for even a minute?"

"Oh, yes, I suppose so. A minute, then."

She gave him five. As she started up again, he supposed it was the best he could hope for. "We will speak of this later," he commanded, wondering if he should explain all to her. Yet if he did, she would undoubtedly become even more adamant in her refusal to wed him, and he didn't want that. He wanted to bind her to him now, without analyzing why.

Just then, Alex and Georgie approached. With sly winks and many elbowings in the ribs, they congratulated him, then kissed Angel on the cheek and welcomed her to the clan.

As they saluted and left the chamber, he felt a vast relief. One by one, the others came forward to voice their approval. In their faces, he read their growing confidence in him as chieftain. He was creating stability for them and they responded. It was like a blessing from on high.

In the end, when they were all gone, he was left with Angel. He was elated. She, he could tell from her face, wasn't convinced.

"I'm sorry, your moment is over," she began.

"I enjoyed it, and I intend to keep enjoying it until we wed, as well as after."

She sighed with apparent frustration. "Why must you be so stubborn? We need not wed to enjoy one another."

"No, we need not, but I choose to, and you will oblige me. That is, if you do not find my personal attentions repugnant." He knew she did not, and he intended to exploit that fact. Winding one hand around her waist, he drew her into his embrace.

At his touch, her eyes glazed over. As if in desperation, she braced both hands against his chest.

He refused to relent. Tilting her face up to his, he covered her mouth with his own.

She responded at once, melting and softening. But even as her breath came faster, she tried to push him away.

Ever resistant. The opposite of what he wished.

He released her lips and trailed his mouth to her ear, teasing the tender spot in the manner he knew she liked.

She shuddered and gripped his shirt. Clearly she did not find him repugnant. Not in the least.

"But I am concerned." She struggled, as if fighting to find words despite her arousal. "Something is wrong, and you refuse to tell me what it is."

So she was going to be blunt. He supposed he must be also, to a point. The question was, how much did he dare tell her? Too much and she would refuse to wed him. Too little and she would not believe him. Resigned to walking a narrow path, he found a stool and drew her onto his lap.

"Angel, I will tell you the truth. As my betrothed, you are entitled." He prayed fervently that he was making the right choice. "The trouble you suspect, if you understood it completely, would make no difference to you. Trust me when I say I ken you well enough to predict your reaction. You will not mind, but it makes a great difference to others, and lives could be at stake."

"Lives?" Her voice quavered. "At stake?"

He'd gone too far. Geddes cursed his mention of lives. Yet how could he not speak of them? It was the truth, and the seriousness of the risk was the very reason she must know nothing about it. Bad enough that she already knew of the false flag. The less she knew, the less she could let slip, though he did not intend to give Angus Kilmartin the chance to ask her anything. "Your fears are based on surmise, Angel." He moved to lock gazes with her. "Trust me. We will wed as planned and all will be well. Do I make myself clear?"

But she looked thoroughly frightened, and he despaired. He had tried to tell the truth, as far as he could in order to protect her. Though in the end, he had no idea if all would be well or not.

She had taken a risk and confronted Geddes, and what he had told her was frightening. Angelica felt more certain than ever that they should not wed.

There was also the other issue.

She wanted love.

Could she make do with lust and appreciation?

She wanted heartfelt declarations of undying devotion, which she would return in kind.

Would approval of her work with clay do instead?

She doubted it, yet by letting him announce their impending nuptials to his family, she had all but agreed.

And what of the undefined disaster that threatened? Geddes had openly admitted it existed. Could she learn more about it from the others at Duntrune? She vowed to ask, beginning with Rhuri. She could not let it rest.

The next morning she went to the kiln in the woods to unload the cooled pottery. She left word summoning the captain of the garrison to join her. He arrived before she had finished unbricking the kiln opening. As it was early, no others were about yet.

Rhuri doffed his bonnet, maneuvering his great gangling body in a bow. "Mistress, how may I serve?"

She put down a brick. "Rhuri, what shall we do?"

He had been present last night. Now she pleaded with him in silence to understand the meaning of her question. She didn't understand it fully herself. Did he?

Rhuri planted his feet in a wide, stalwart stance. "The same as we've been doin'. The flag is ours." He winked to indicate that he knew the secret of the false flag and would keep it.

Good, faithful Rhuri. She should have known he was one of the men keeping the flag's secret. "But we cannot keep secrets forever," she pointed out. "I would refuse to wed—"

"Ye canna refuse to wed." He seemed horrified by the idea that she would even consider it. "Why would ye? And we wish an heir, ye ken."

"Of course," she murmured, wanting to ask him many questions but not daring. His answers suggested he knew little more than she did.

"Never fear." He resumed his bonnet and prepared to return to the castle. "We'll keep Angus Kilmartin from hearin' o' things he shouldn't. And we'll give ye a bonny wedding."

"Thank you, Rhuri. You are most kind." Angelica shook her head in discouragement as he departed. If Rhuri didn't know, she doubted the other garrison members did either. That left Lilias and Muriel. They were the only ones who seemed to sense the danger, and they weren't ready to share with her. That much was sure.

Two days later, Angelica vowed to concentrate on rejoicing, not disaster, as she, Magnus, and Stone prepared to celebrate the second kiln opening. This time they had fired her fine ware along with that of the others, and she knew she would be proud of the results.

They invited Geddes to the ceremony, of course, and Iain, Lilias, Magnus's family, Muriel, Rhuri, and several other clansmen from the garrison, along with their wives and families who lived nearby on their designated clan lands.

Magnus and Stone performed the honors of un-bricking the opening. The still-warm stoneware glowed in the morning light. Magnus lifted out the first row of crocks, handing one to Geddes, one to Lilias, and one to Angelica.

They had turned all of the vases and a few of the crocks on their sides, balanced on three small stones. On the side that had faced down during the firing, flames had licked the pots, turning them molten bronze like the sun in autumn. On the top side, where wood ash had settled during the process, the stoneware was covered in shifting shades of brown, gold, and black. The effect was stunning, a light and dark that alter-nated between dazzling and intriguing. Everyone oohed and ahhed.

More pieces were unloaded and passed around. An-gelica's best work was praised, and, feeling in a gener-ous mood, she made gifts with Stone's and Magnus's approval. A big crock with a matching lid went to each clanswoman, to Muriel, and to Agnes, Magnus's daughter-in-law. A mug each went to Lilias and Iain. And to Geddes, she presented the set of flagons and matching pitcher she had promised him.

He called them magnificent, admiring both them and her with his gaze.

Warmed by the generous reception, Angelica spent the rest of the day packing the remainder of the firing along with the first firing into a cart. The next morning she, Iain, and Lilias, with the escort of three men from the garrison, traveled to Dunadd to sell their wares.

With the MacCallum clan being kin to the Campbells, she had no trouble gaining permission to sell in the market of the Campbell-protected town. They turned their cart into a stall and did a brisk business until the supper hour, when they returned to Duntrune for the night. The next day, they revisited Dunadd and sold everything down to the last piece.

Tired but satisfied, they returned to Duntrune with silver and copper coins jingling in their purses and goods ladening the cart. But despite their triumph, Lilias groused and complained the entire way. She wished to go riding, she nagged, and Angelica agreed she had earned it. They would go the next day.

Angelica set out for Loch Awe early the next morning with Iain and Lilias, but once Brian joined them, he advised them to move. " 'Twill be safer at another location," he said. "My father is restless these days and suspicious of everyone. If we meet at the loch too often, we could well be seen."

The isolated cove on the western shore was a delightful trysting spot. The waves that washed against the land were so clear, Angelica could see the sandy bottom. Elated by the sunshine and the beauty of the day, they all stripped off their shoes, boots, and stockings and waded into the water, finding it delightfully cool.

"How is your father's health?" Lilias asked Brian, her voice carrying across the water to Angelica and Iain.

"He has been most unwell, taking to his bed earlier each evening than the last. 'Tis not like him. I had the herb woman make him a tonic, but he refused to drink it. Said it tasted foul."

"Do you think he has pain?" Lilias seemed honestly

concerned about the man who was keeping her apart from her lover and perpetrating strife for her people.

Angelica approved of Lilias's new maturity. She was overcoming the self-centeredness of childhood and concentrating on the needs of others.

Brian nodded in answer, his clear, young features crinkled with worry. "He's surly in the mornings and labors for breath at times. He'll no' discuss it, but I think he has discomfort, if not outright pain."

"I am sorry," Lilias said. "If I knew the trouble, I could have Muriel concoct a remedy for him. Her mixtures dinna taste bad, and they do help. I often had fever and pain in my ears as a child, and Muriel's doses fixed me up fine. Might your father let me visit? Could you ask?"

"I dinna dare, sweet. The last time I mentioned your name, he flew into a frenzy, cursing and shouting. Changing his mind seems a lost cause."

"Did you tell him I had nothing to do with what happened to your sister, Susan? That I do not approve of what Geddes did?"

Angelica had wondered about Susan. Lilias had mentioned her once as being the reason Geddes had left Duntrune. What had happened to her? But her moment to ask slipped by as Brian continued.

"I told him, but it made no difference. He roared that he would like to see me do the same to you as Geddes did to Susan. He would never approve our marriage, and I canna wed without my chieftain's say."

Lilias kicked in frustration, shooting a spray of water arcing as high as her head. "I dinna have the patience for this. We'll end like Hugh Kilmartin and Mairi MacCallum, and ye ken what happened to them." She scrunched up her face as if about to cry, and Brian hushed her, pulling her against him and kissing the top of her head.

"Who were Hugh Kilmartin and Mairi MacCallum?" Iain asked, fishing an interesting shell from the water to show Angelica.

As Angelica took the shell, she nodded, wanting to hear of these people as well. Lilias's tone was so tragic, whatever had happened to this couple must have been dire.

"Hugh Kilmartin was my grandsire's brother," Brian began. "He fell in love with Mairi MacCallum, who was Lilias's grandsire's youngest sister. On the night of a terrible storm, Mairi quarreled with her brother about her choice of husband and ran away from Duntrune. When he discovered her missing, he realized she intended to go to her sweetheart and wed with him against his wishes, so he gave chase with his men. The rain was a torrent, and the water of the burn swollen to flood level, washing far beyond its banks and running swiftly with dangerous currents, yet she must have tried to cross anyway. By the time she was found . . ." His voice trailed off, leaving the tragic end of the story to their conjecture.

"She drowned," Lilias said flatly, finishing the story for him. "And Hugh drank himself into oblivion for the next ten years before he joined her. After her burial, the Faerie Flag was discovered missing, but no trace of it was found in the burn. If Mairi took it with her, intending to use it to join the clans, it vanished. Most people doubt she had it with her. 'Tis why Geddes still seeks it. Those still alive from that time think it disappeared after the battle and has been missing since."

The story saddened Angelica. Multiple tragedies set the two clans at odds. "Cannot King James order the clans to intermarry and end the feud? I have heard of such solutions."

Brian shook his head, as did Iain. "The king doesna interfere in clan feuds, except if the royal revenue suffers or if the country's safety is in jeopardy," Brian said.

"Or if one of his favorites is involved," Iain added.

The situation did seem hopeless, and Angelica had proposed these meetings to Lilias with the hope that they could contribute to a solution. Yet what could they do next, if Brian's father would never recognize the marriage? Nor did Geddes seem amenable to such a match.

As Angelica splashed in the water with Iain, skipped flat stones, and talked of this and that, she saw Lilias twine her arm around her sweetheart's waist and lean her head against his shoulder. She patted his arm, and Angelica could see that despite the hardship, she strove to comfort Brian. Lilias was showing new maturity, but Angelica still worried. She must warn the girl to do nothing rash.

One thing comforted Angelica as the day wore on. From listening to Brian, it was clear that not a word had leaked to the Kilmartins of the false flag. Brian would not have failed to mention it, had he heard the news.

She treasured the small fact as she carried it away from their meeting. The secret was being kept.

Angelica welcomed Geddes to the cherry orchard that evening. In the early twilight, he strode toward her through the trees, barefoot and without his plaid, to join her on the bench. She had left word at the castle that he could find her here. She intended to broach the subject of their marriage once more.

Though she did not relish the need, she welcomed his company. "On our ride today, we heard not a word spoken of the flag anywhere," she told him, wanting to share good news first. "Your clansmen are keeping the secret. 'Tis wonderful, is it not?"

"Aye." He seemed elated by the idea, grinning broadly. "Nor have I heard mention of the flag at Duntrune in days. No' by Lilias or anyone else. They're relying less on it and more on themselves. The men are gaining confidence daily at their weapons practice. Someday I hope no one will even care about the flag."

Angelica cast him a questioning glance, not wanting to ask outright if he was keeping his promise to search for it.

Ever attuned to her, he guessed her thoughts at once. "Today I spoke to an old man who was at the MacCallum victory bonfire after the Battle of Dunardry. He remembers seeing the flag on display."

"Excellent." Though they both wished the flag to be unimportant in clan matters, she was glad he was keeping his promise to Lilias and the others. She rewarded his effort with a generous smile. "Did this man see what happened to it after the bonfire?" She hugged herself, feeling the evening's chill coming on.

Geddes looked as if he wanted to be the one doing the hugging. "Only that it was placed in a wooden casket, which was brought to Duntrune." He slid closer to her on the bench. "I had heard that my grandsire kept the flag in a wooden casket. That tells us little, but at least we know it returned to the castle rather than disappearing after the battle. You see that I am making progress. 'Tis safe for us to wed." He draped his arm around her shoulders and drew her near.

As she snuggled against his warmth, the air seemed to throb with his presence, tempting her unbearably. But she must state her position clearly. "I prefer things a good deal more definite before we take such a step."

"I told my kin last night," he said, unquestionably annoyed with her. "You led me to believe you had accepted."

"I never agreed. I still don't." It sounded weak and unkind, but she must say it. "You did not tell your kin *when* we would wed. Let us wait."

Geddes narrowed his gaze for a moment, as if he meant to argue. But suddenly he seemed to relent. With his fingertips, he skimmed her jaw, evoking tingles of pleasure.

This was better. He was ready to concentrate on pleasure. She welcomed the feelings as his powerful masculinity overtook her senses.

She would not wed him until it was positively safe to do so. But she wanted him to make her blood race. With his gaze locked on hers, he trailed his fingers down her throat to the lace peeping from her bodice. His every touch evoked a promise of passion.

Their lips met, and her heart soared. She could enjoy this with or without marriage. There was all the time in the world.

"Mmmm, delicious." He punctuated his throaty whisper by loosening her laces and opening her bodice.

The fitted top gaped, and he pulled down the smock beneath it. Cool air flooded in to caress her flesh, but she was no longer chilled. As he lowered his head to her breast, took her in his mouth, and suckled, every nerve in her body came alive and clamored for more.

He moved to the other breast and teased her further. Her body cried out with sweet, sweet hunger. He alternated between her mouth and her sensitive breasts until she could bear the storm of feelings no longer. Lifting her skirts, she placed his hand on her thigh.

He did not refuse her invitation. He spread her legs, fingertips searching until he found the sensitive spot awaiting him. Suddenly she felt like a piece of clay in the kiln, white-hot and glowing. Oh, how she loved him.

He withdrew his hand.

"Geddes?" Her mind was in a fever, confused and yearning. She groped for his hand, found it, and tried to guide him back.

"I'll resume when you agree."

Her mind stumbled, refusing to grasp his meaning. "What do you mean? We were enjoying each other. Do you not wish to continue?" She coaxed his hand along her thigh.

He squeezed her leg, sending waves of anticipation shooting through her. "I shall not continue until you agree to wed me by week's end."

But he hadn't stopped yet, and she couldn't think he meant it. "Black rent?" she challenged, reaching for him in return.

He put her hand away, though he continued the sensuous dance of his fingertips on her thighs. "Aye. You mun agree."

"I'll pleasure you in return if you continue," she wheedled.

He chuckled. "Not good enough." His eyes said the rest. He wanted her, but he would not relent until she agreed.

"No," she insisted, hoping to call his bluff.

"Then I am sorry." He threw up both hands. "I can do no more for you."

"Geddes!"

He pulled her into a sitting position and straightened her garments. He really meant it.

She groped to find a coherent protest. "Geddes!" she cried lamely.

He slid to the far end of the bench. "Aye?"

She lunged across the space, caught him around the neck, and kissed him. He was clearly aroused. She felt between his legs, and he groaned in response, putting her hand away once more. She grasped his hand and guided it to her breasts again.

He rubbed gently, provocatively. "You ken the price, Angel."

"How dare you torture me." What a clever bargainer. She would send *him* to sell her pots next time. They would be rich. Except the bargaining price he used was not to be shared with anyone else. He was hers, though she couldn't have him unless she relented. She huffed in frustration.

He wouldn't stop teasing. He kissed her again and explored between her legs, making her even more eager than her first time.

Back then, she hadn't anticipated bliss.

Now she did.

Now every part of her body burned for him.

He seemed to sense it. No doubt he burned as well, for he fell to his knees between her thighs, pushing them open. His tongue darted out to tantalize her flesh, arousing her until her body hummed with feeling and logic deserted her.

"Good heavens, Geddes." She grasped a handful of his hair, so amazed by the force of her response, she needed an anchor. Her sisters had told her of this secret; he had pleasured her thus during their night by the kiln, but she had never imagined it would happen over and over, each time better than the last.

"Easy. Enjoy it," Geddes counseled.

She was helpless in his arms, able only to obey. Her head fell back, and she gazed at the forming cherries dangling above her. Her mind filled with the image of fruit ripening. She imagined her body ripening with promise as he filled her.

Suddenly she could wait no longer. She straightened and dived for the fastening of his kilt.

He laughed but let her tear away the garment. The sight of his arousal, huge and swollen, set her aching. "I must have you, my love."

"Take me and you forfeit. Marriage is my price."

"You cannot be serious."

"Aye, I am."

Indignation filled her. Furious, she lunged for him, pushing him backward on the grass. She straddled his middle and tore the closing lace from his shirt, clawing away the garment until he was naked. Strongly, sensuously naked. She draped her full length on him, covering his nakedness with her own.

Laughing, he let her. "My fiery ravisher. Am I to let you have your way with me?"

"Aye."

She guided him eagerly between her legs and pushed. Much easier this time, though he seemed even bigger than she remembered. She sank onto him, letting him fill her.

Oh, heavens, what was she doing? He had her spellbound. There was no escape.

"Say yes, sweetheart." He began to move within her.

She refused to answer, concentrating on pleasing him.

Despite his obvious response to her, he grasped her waist and lifted her, pulling out.

She nearly sobbed with disappointment. "Geddes, you're wicked."

He grinned. "I am not. I want you for my wife. Wed with me in five days."

"You win." She groped for him desperately. "I'll wed with you. Please love me now." She cried it to the treetops.

He obliged by sitting up, rolling her onto her back, and thrusting into her.

She shouted with joy as he penetrated her. He paused, braced above her, the muscles of his arms and shoulders quivering. Only then did she realize what his denial had cost him. Now hunger gleamed in his eyes as he thrust over and over, as if he couldn't get enough of her quickly enough. The pleasure was close to unbearable, blocking out everything else. Need commanded her rapt attention, and she gave in to it wholly.

So good. So right. So different this time. No pain. Only a spiraling urgency as excitement escalated. She was well past the moment of awakening; they raced together toward fulfillment. She hummed and purred as he rained kisses on her face, her neck, bringing her with him, thrust by thrust.

Her universe seemed to expand. Everything grew light and rapturous. Her senses were tuned solely to him, moving with him.

They rose to the summit together. She felt him swell within her, then grunt in ecstasy as he found his release. Shattering joy broke over her as she followed. Blinding happiness.

He wanted her enough to risk anything. She was so happy, yet so worried, she wanted to laugh and sob at the same time. She laughed aloud. Then tears gained the upper hand. She lost control, and they tracked their way down her cheeks.

"Angel, what is it?" He kissed her with great tenderness.

It did no good to tell him of her fears. He refused to listen. Yet her happiness couldn't last. Too many dangers threatened. Some of them known. Others unknown.

Eventually, if they could not find the true flag, Angus Kilmartin would tire of waiting and attack again. If they did not produce the true flag when under attack, he would know it did not exist. Or someone might tell him. Time could change circumstances and drive people to change their minds about keeping a secret.

Nonsense. The clan was stalwart. She had celebrated the signs of their growing loyalty a mere hour ago.

Yet it seemed impossible that the Kilmartin would never learn of the false flag. They lived within a few leagues of one another. Each clan knew every detail of the other's history and affairs.

No, the only way Angus Kilmartin would never learn of the flag was if he went to live on the moon. And the only way she would ever find both security and happiness with Geddes was if the clan war would end.

Chapter 19

"If she was nothing else, my mother was handy with her needle." Lilias smoothed the sapphire blue silk chosen for Angelica's wedding, spread on the bed in her chamber. "She made all her gowns herself."

Angelica forced a smile and tried to ignore the misgivings warring within her. She had made her choice five days ago in the cherry orchard. It was the first time in her life that she had let carnal cravings rule. Why she couldn't love without physical fulfillment, she didn't know, but now she must live with her weakness. "I appreciate your wanting me to wear this gown," she said as Lilias tied the laces of yet another petticoat around her middle.

"Nay use letting it molder." Lilias had a practical nature when her emotions weren't running high. "Silk doesna last forever, and this is a good ten years old."

"You are correct, silk doesn't last forever. So mayhap the Faerie Flag disintegrated after all these years." Angelica picked up another petticoat and prepared to don it. "Mayhap that is why we cannot find it."

"Nay, the magic keeps it in one piece." Lilias let Angelica drop the petticoat over her head, helped her with the ties, then gathered up the cornflower-blue tinsel underskirt shot through with gold thread. It would be covered by an overskirt of deep sapphire, its front cut open in a wide vee to display the tinsel, its hem flanked by wide bands of velvet in sea green, cornflower blue, and violet. Angelica stood still as the two layers of freshly aired and pressed silk shimmered past her head and shoulders to settle around her waist.

What a lavish delight. She had thought herself wedded to clay, but Geddes had shown her she might dress in silks like other ladies. For the first time in years, she enjoyed the extravagance.

Lilias arranged the overskirt over the underskirt and petticoats so it fell in graceful folds. "First you shall wed, then me," she said, fiddling with the skirt's ties.

"Not yet for you," Angelica cautioned. " 'Tis too soon."

"I'll no' sit by, hoping for the old Kilmartin's blessing." Lilias jerked the ties of the skirt tight. "I'll be an old woman ere he does that."

"But what would you do?" Angelica took up the kirtle bodice, the next garment in the wedding ensemble.

"Wed in secret." Lilias took it from her and held it open.

"And continue to live separately? That would not be much of a marriage."

" 'Twould be better than nothing," Lilias pointed out. "Ye're sure ye'll not wear the corset? The bodice will be tight without it."

"Nay, I cannot bear it," Angelica said.

"Nor I."

Lilias sounded too fervent to be referring to the corset. Angelica supposed she meant waiting to wed and could think of no solution to offer. Instead, she scowled at the muslin corset reinforced with wooden busks. "I declare it unfit for human use."

"I agree. Ye'll note I dinna wear such a contraption." Lilias grinned at her, and for a moment, they were in perfect accord. "Here." Lilias held up the bodice.

Angelica slipped into it, admiring the garden of blue silk rosettes and embroidery adorning the front.

Lilias parted Angelica's long hair, hanging loose down her back, and closed the fastenings of the bodice. She adjusted the wide edge of lace adorning Angelica's silk smock so that it showed all around the neckline of the bodice.

"How would you explain to Geddes if you swelled with child?" Angelica pressed Lilias, picking up one of the pair of cornflower-blue taffeta sleeves with cuts to reveal her silk smock.

"I would tell him I had wed the father."

"And then?" She gestured for Lilias to tie on the sleeve, then waited through a potent pause as Lilias performed the tying but failed to answer.

"More clan wars, I suppose," she admitted after tying the second sleeve. She flopped onto the bed, heedless of her own ivory silk ensemble with a tinsel underskirt in a fresh, deep pink. "But we already have them, and I canna wait forever. I'm aging." She hopped up to peer into the looking glass on Angelica's table, searching for wrinkles.

Angelica would have chuckled, but she didn't have the heart to discourage Lilias. She understood the fears of the young. The breaking of her own betrothal, the thought that she would forever be a spinster, had been a painful time in her life.

Awe still crowded her mind at the thought that she

would be married within minutes. What an unexpected outcome of a journey to dig for clay.

As Angelica approached the door to the castle chapel, clutching Iain's arm, Lilias walked before her, carrying a bouquet of rowan leaves and berries, the MacCallum clan plant badge. Through the door, she could see that Muriel had decked the chamber with summer flowers. Small wreaths of boxwood decorated with pinks and marigolds hung at the end of every pew. Sprays of pink and purple heather stood at the altar. Buttery light streamed from the windows, softening the scene before her. Householders, villagers, clan members, and tacksmen crowded the pews.

Across the distance, she picked out Stone, Magnus, and his family. They were turned in their seats, smiling and waving at her. By custom, the guests would have followed her and Geddes in a procession to the church, where they would exchange vows at the door, but here, there was not room for everyone to crowd into the corridor. The guests had thus been seated first.

She heard the drone of bagpipes long before she saw them. The front door of the castle flew open, and butterflies swirled in her stomach as the chieftain's procession approached. She gripped Iain's arm more tightly, and he patted her hand, offering reassurance.

Two pipers led the way, their bagpipes wailing a solemn tune for the solemn occasion. They were followed by the standard bearer, who carried the MacCallum flag from the great hall. As war captain, Rhuri came next, looking most impressive in full ceremonial costume and bearing the MacCallum claymore of state.

Geddes had been home too short a time to fill the

many other household offices customarily maintained by a chieftain, but he had recruited all his closest kin to join him in the procession. Three more men approached before she spied Geddes.

In his deep blue dress kilt and plaid, he seemed taller than ever, his strong features reflecting satisfaction. He fixed his gaze on her, his expression speaking plainly. He found her beautiful in her finery and he wanted her.

As Iain guided her forward to meet him at the door, the rest of the chieftain's procession, a daunting force of twenty men in ceremonial costume, came to a halt behind Geddes. Angelica swallowed hard against the lump of emotion forming in her throat. This would be no handfast joining, easily broken at the wish of either party. They would pledge their troth forever before God and witnesses.

The kirk minister had been fetched from Dunadd to officiate. Somber in black robes, he stepped forward to direct the exchange of vows. After, he would lead the church service.

Iain released her and stepped aside to join Lilias, and Geddes took her hand. As he tucked it in the crook of his arm, the butterflies in her stomach multiplied, beating their tiny wings, creating an unbearable excitement mixed with dread.

As a girl, she had made a wish. Let there be a man who would walk into her life, as strong as the waves crashing on the Dorset shore and just as constant. Was this that man? Or would the mysteries swirling around Duntrune cause her to lose him, as she had James?

She could not predict the future, but as she met Geddes's sea-blue eyes, as he pressed her fingers into his arm, making his claim, she cared no longer. She would have him, and he would have her.

The vows were brief and to the point. Now wed, Angelica traversed the length of the chapel on Geddes's arm. Young Jamie sat on his mother's lap, waving frantically. She smiled back and lifted one hand to him in salute. The clansmen followed, and they all sat in the front pews. First would come the church service, then the reciting of the genealogy of both her and Geddes's families. Angelica had spent several hours in the company of Alex MacCallum, writing down every family member's name she could remember back several generations. The MacCallum genealogy went back centuries, and Alex could recite it all by heart. After the prayers and sermon, he rose and proceeded to do so. Every clan member present hung on his words, seeming to delight in this custom.

By the time it was finished, Angelica felt faint with hunger. She had eaten nothing that morning, having been too nervous to do more than drink a little milk. Now she imagined the haunch of venison she had smelled roasting in the kitchens. Was she a glutton, to think of food before her husband on her wedding day?

"I'm famished," Geddes whispered to her as they rose at the end of the genealogy. "First for the feast, then for you."

So she wasn't wicked. He felt the same as she. As she smiled up at him in agreement, he turned her toward the door, and she was surprised to see the clansmen from the procession forming a double row on either side of the aisle. At Rhuri's command, swords hissed from their scabbards. Each man touched the tip of his steel blade to that of the man opposite, forming an arch.

She looked to Geddes, uncertain what to do.

"They are welcoming you into the clan and speeding our way into our new life together."

Angelica almost wept as she surveyed those twenty

brave men. She offered Rhuri a brilliant smile of thanks as they entered the arch. He grinned back at her and winked. After that, she flew through the archway on Geddes's arm, feeling borne on wings. It was a day of glorious emotion that she would never forget.

The feast in the great hall was exuberant. Food and spirits were plentiful, moods high.

Angelica felt like the princess of the hour. First she was guided with great ceremony by her husband to a special chair for the lady of the castle. Then a dozen speeches were made, followed each time by drinking to her health until she, drinking her share, was entirely tipsy. Only then did the feast begin and she was permitted to eat from a parade of dishes. Succulent venison, barley soup, swan in plumage, young leg of lamb. She waved many more dishes on past as she and Geddes presided at the high table. Although Muriel had outdone herself, Angelica couldn't manage to taste them all.

And each time someone rose to drink to her health again, Geddes kissed her while the clan applauded and whooped in approval. The occasion of the chieftain taking a bride to preserve the family bloodlines was clearly the cause for great celebration in the Highlands.

Just as she was about to indulge in a dish of clotted cream with strawberries, she was called to the dance floor. She must lead a reel with Alex MacCallum, something called the *Chez-mez* that was customary in welcoming the bride to her new home. The dance set her head spinning, as did her many partners. Every man of the clan seemed determined to dance with her.

By the time she was allowed to retire, she was thoroughly giddy. "Geddes, I am exhausted. Can we not bid them god'den?"

The intimacy of his answering smile warmed her. " 'Tis only early evening, but they will not fault me if I display great eagerness to bed my bride. I trust you are not too exhausted for that?"

"You place your trust rightly," she said with as much dignity as possible, then ruined her composed reply by blushing. Yet she felt as eager to be alone with him as he was to be with her.

He rose and drank her health again, then invited the guests to stay as long as they wished, enjoying the food and drink. It was his sign that he intended to retire to bed.

Bawdy jests were flung back and forth across the hall as Geddes assisted her from her chair and signaled for Lilias to follow.

Puzzled by this, Angelica saw Lilias descend from the dais and hurry to where Muriel was laughing and eating with the others. At a word from Lilias, the cook rose.

"We have yet to sign the kirk registry, recording our marriage," Geddes explained as he led her out of the great hall and across the corridor to the chapel. "Lilias and Muriel will be witnesses, along with the minister."

How odd that they had not signed the book earlier, whilst everyone was still at church. Yet Angelica had forgotten about it as well. Not odd at all, she supposed. Or mayhap it was Highland custom to sign the registry after.

Either way, it made no difference. The marriage would be recorded. She took the quill offered by the minister and signed her full name. As she passed the quill to Geddes, Lilias wrapped her in a hug.

"First you, then me," Lilias whispered in her ear, reminding her of their earlier discussion.

"Oh, Lilias." Angelica hugged her back, once again worried about what the girl might do.

She had no chance to think of the problem further, for Lilias released her and turned to sign the book as a witness. Muriel crowded in next to her, as if eager to make her mark.

"I taught her to write her name for the occasion," Lilias explained as she passed the quill to Muriel and joined Angelica and Geddes.

Angelica's heart warmed at yet another sign of Lilias's growing maturity. "How good of you, Lilias. I should like to see." She took a step in the direction of the book, but Geddes stopped her.

"You can look another time." His smoldering gaze reminded her of why they had left the feast early. "I am in no mood to extend this business."

Her heart seemed to still in her chest as his need reached out to her like a palpable touch. Muriel had passed the quill to the minister. He dipped it in the inkwell and signed.

It was done. Official. She smiled up at Geddes and took his arm.

As they quit the chapel, thrills of anticipation flowed through her. His gaze was proprietary, conveying his eagerness to claim her. Though they had made love twice now, this was different. They were wed.

Geddes had ordered his father's chamber cleared of all furnishings and had placed at its center a new bed. Only just constructed, it had a marvelous feather mattress but no hangings. There hadn't been time. Still, it was summer and hangings weren't needed. She would enjoy what she and Geddes had built together, both the marriage and the bed.

Geddes sent her upstairs ahead of him. He needed

to check on something, he said. She wasn't sure what to do while she waited for him—whether to disrobe or stay as she was. He didn't keep her waiting long, though. Within minutes he stood in the entry, surveying the chamber in a leisurely manner. But his gaze, as he fixed it on her, had no leisurely quality to it. His eyes glittered with lust. His masculinity was like a charge in the room, filling it with the tension of his hunger. He hungered for her. Always for her.

He banged the door shut and strode toward her, pulling her into his arms. Passion rose like a rain-swollen river, lifting her on its flood. It swept away all else, leaving her spellbound. By his touch. By his kiss.

But she had power over him as well. His muscles quivered beneath the touch of her nimble fingers as she unpinned his plaid, then reached for his tight black jerkin, unbuttoning the silver buttons, dragging it from his arms. Then he took a turn, traveling her back with quick fingers, unfastening the many little hooks of her bodice. As he drew it off, he turned her to face him, his gaze devouring her body. Without a corset, her breasts were clearly visible through the light, almost transparent silk of the lace-trimmed smock.

The need in his eyes set a fire deep in her belly. She reached for the buckle holding his sporran, removing the elaborate leather pouch and setting it aside. His kilt and boots joined it.

The many layers of skirt and petticoats were too much for her. Too many fastenings. Tangled laces. She barely managed to untie the silk kirtle skirt and pull it over her head before he was kissing her, his mouth locked to hers, alive with heat.

"Geddes, my skirts," she mumbled against his mouth.

"I see them." Ignoring her concern, he ground his hips against hers.

Despite the layers of fabric, the friction of his arousal was fully evident, rubbing against her belly. "I ought to remove the skirts," she whispered. "They're in the way."

"There are many things we *ought* to do. I tire of the word. To my mind, the only thing we *ought* to do at this moment is enjoy each other. If skirts try to stop us, then skirts be damned."

She had to chuckle as he trailed kisses across her face and down her neck. When he turned his devoted attention to caressing her breasts, she wanted to cry to the heavens, she felt so wonderful.

"Mmmm, you taste of trust, Angel," he whispered against her throat. "Delicious."

She laughed. "Now you're reading my thoughts through our kisses. How perceptive. I'll not be able to hide anything from you."

Her mind leaped at once to Lilias's secret, and she felt guilty. She *was* hiding something, and if he found out, it could ruin her blissful happiness.

Her happiness was a castle built of sand, doomed to be washed away by the advancing tide in the end.

"Look, Iain, we have almost enough ware for another firing." Angelica beamed as she showed Iain shelf after shelf of crocks, basins, mugs, and bowls lining the pottery. The excitement of the wedding had subsided slowly in the days that followed. The clan seemed to enjoy prolonging the celebration, and Angelica could not object. It was heavenly being the center of both their and Geddes's attention—especially Geddes's.

"So I see." Iain walked along the rows, examining the finished ware. "And what are ye doin' here?" He indicated the dish of powder and the measure of water beside it on her workbench.

" 'Tis my special glaze powder. My robin's-egg blue," she confided. "I brought it all the way from England and wish to surprise Geddes with it. I'm going to glaze this big bowl for him."

He surveyed the piece, with its delicate, sloping sides and its wide rim that opened outward, flat and smooth. " 'Tis stunning. What is it for?"

Angelica ran her finger around the rim. "Anything he wishes. To serve soup at the high table. To slop the hogs." She grinned.

Iain chuckled. "No piglet shall ever get near it, I trow. He'll cherish it."

Secretly, she felt sure he was right. She added water to the powder, then mixed the glaze and prepared to dip the bowl.

" 'Tis gray." Iain squinted at the concoction. "Not blue at all."

"The fire turns it blue. A beautiful color. Remember the little bowl I brought with me?"

Iain dipped a finger in the glaze and stared at the plain gray. "The fire changes it from ugly to beautiful? Imagine that."

Angelica felt as if she, too, had been through another type of fire and been transformed. The fire of passion had made her into a different woman—one willing to risk all for happiness. "What shall you do now that I'm situated?" she asked Iain.

"I would like to return to Castle Graham."

And never revisit Duntrune? Her face must have fallen, for he hastened to reassure her.

"Only for a brief visit. I'll return in a fortnight, as

there is still unrest here. I could carry letters to yer sister. She must be told of your marriage, as must your family in England. Geddes never asked that legal matters be addressed before the ceremony, but yer family will wish to settle yer tocher so that what ye bring to the union is clear. Yer family is powerful and these people must be made fully aware of it. The word will then flow to the Kilmartin and further deter his meddling."

"I would be so happy if you would take letters to my family." Angelica put down the bowl and hugged him, hoping he was right about the marriage being a deterrent to more Kilmartin attacks. "I long to write, telling them how I am."

"How are ye?" he asked, examining her closely.

"I am content," she assured him.

"Only content? No' deliriously happy."

Why not admit it? "Yes, I am happy." He raised his eyebrows questioningly, and she felt herself blushing. "Very well, I am deliriously happy. I admit it. I only hope it lasts." As his face darkened, she hurried to clarify. "The peace between the clans. I hope it lasts."

Iain nodded in understanding. "I should no' leave ye. There could be an attack."

"Not as long as we have the Faerie Flag, and I do so long to write to my family and receive their letters in return."

"I shall make all haste and return quickly," he promised.

"That would be wonderful." She beamed at him, grateful that he was as eager as she to make contact with those they had left behind at Castle Graham.

She finished glazing the big bowl and placed it in a safe place to dry. Then she dipped several more pieces until naught but a trace of glaze was left in the bowl.

"That's all of it, isn't it?" Iain watched, seeming fascinated, as she absorbed the last of the glaze with a brush and dotted random designs on a vase.

"Aye." She felt a brief stab of regret that it was gone and couldn't be replaced. "But it was meant to be used," she insisted to herself as well as him. "To give people pleasure."

"To please Geddes, ye mean. Do you think he'll appreciate it? O' course he'll like it, because you made it," he corrected when he saw her expression. "But I dinna ken if he understands what it means to ye."

"Oh, he understands. I'm quite certain." Angelica smiled as she washed glaze from the brush. Geddes understood exactly what working with clay meant to her and respected it. It was a rare blessing in a relationship. Of that, she had no doubt.

Iain discussed his journey that night with Geddes, who agreed that he should return to Castle Graham if he wished. Angelica rushed to her chamber to write letters to Lucina, her mother, and Rozalinde. Lucina would receive hers and forward the others on to England.

Geddes wrote several letters as well and asked Iain to take them to Glasgow on his way south. This would extend his journey, but only by a few days, and as Geddes insisted his business was pressing, Iain agreed. Geddes offered to pay for the service, but Iain refused the MacCallum's gold. He asked instead for supplies for the journey, insisting that the hospitality accorded him since their arrival had been payment enough.

With a stout garron pony from Geddes's stable and the company of the blacksmith's lad, who'd been itching to see the south of Scotland and could help ensure their safety from ruffians, should they encounter any, Iain departed the next day.

Chapter 20

Life seemed so perfect. Too perfect. Angelica treasured Geddes's lovemaking each night, her pottery by day. She couldn't ask for more, though she did.

Please let Angus Kilmartin not learn about the false flag. Please let Geddes find the true flag.

Impossible wishes, yet she wished for them.

Still, life must go on, and she strove to keep a routine for her days. In the pottery one morning, as she lugged in a bucket of fresh water, Stone lifted the wooden lid of the clay barrel and peered inside.

"We'll need to dig more clay soon. The barrel is empty," he said.

It was indeed time to dig more clay. That afternoon, Angelica asked Lilias to walk to the stream with her. It had been raining of late, and she wished to examine the site before they began digging, to see what tools they would need. Geddes sent two garrison guards with them. Just to be safe, he said.

They took the narrow footpath that led from the village to the burn. As they walked through the dense woods, Angelica thought of poor Mairi MacCallum, drowning so close to her home. "Where did Mairi try to cross the stream that night?" she asked, sure that Lilias would understand what she meant.

"At the ford, the place where the crossing is narrowest," Lilias said.

Angelica nodded. A track for carts and horses led from the castle to the narrowest part of the burn. They crossed it each time they went riding.

"Her brother and his men following saw her swept away by the flood."

"How terrible. She must have been desperate," Angelica said, then felt immediate concern for Lilias's own desperation. Stopping on the path, she caught the girl in a hug. "You must not do as she did, Lilias." She spoke in hushed tones so the garrison men could not hear. "I could not bear it if you drowned."

Lilias looked startled, then touched as she hugged Angelica in return. "I may be desperate, but I would never go into a burn that is too deep or running too swiftly to cross," she whispered back.

Relieved to hear the practical side of Lilias speaking, Angelica released her and they continued along the path. "If I were fleeing the castle, I would come this way, not take the track to the ford," Angelica pointed out, unable to shake off thoughts of the doomed lovers. "Anyone taking the wider track would be easily seen."

"Mayhap Mairi did come this way but found the water too deep to cross." Lilias moved ahead of Angelica as the path narrowed, then fell back in step as it widened again. "So she went to the ford. It wasn't quite as wide or as deep, so she took a chance."

It seemed like a possible explanation. "If most people cross the stream at the ford, why does this path lead here at all?" she asked.

"Because 'tis a favorite fishing place. Has been for ages. Mayhap centuries."

Angelica nodded. "Geddes did say that, but I forgot. I imagined the path was here solely so I could come to dig clay." She chuckled wryly. "How self-centered I am."

"Ye didna believe any such thing. Ye're too practical." Lilias pushed through the last of the wet foliage and into the clearing at the burn. "Oh, dear." She halted. "The rain has washed away part of the bank."

Angelica stepped around her to see that the rushing water had eaten away at the bank, digging a hollow cavern into its underside and exposing thick tree roots. Alarmed that her digging might have caused the problem, thus muddying the water used by people downstream, she hurried to remove her shoes and stockings and descend to assess the damage.

Closer scrutiny showed that only a moderate portion of clay had been washed away. Though she was sorry to lose the precious material, it would not foul the stream in the long term. The place where she had been digging now tunneled deeper into the bank, the clay supported by a thick network of tree roots. Backing out, she stared up at the bank. "Was there a tree here once?" she asked the men of the garrison, knowing they would remember farther back than Lilias.

"Years ago, aye," one of them answered, coming to stand directly above her. "A big oak. A badger family lived in its roots. Quite fierce they were, keepin' everyone away, but they left after the tree fell in a storm. The stump rotted. Ye can just see what's left o' it." He stomped around the tall grass of the uneven spot.

The tree explained all the roots they had picked from the clay. Angelica resigned herself to more such picking as she climbed out of the burn and pulled on her stockings and shoes.

On their return to the castle, she questioned Lilias

further. "Did Geddes come here when he was young? Did he like to fish?"

"Nay. Ye ken what he liked, once he was old enough," Lilias said darkly. "But Lachlan always brought a trout or two for Muriel when he'd been out. I suppose he caught them there. Everyone else did."

Angelica didn't know why, but she liked the idea of Lachlan the Peacemaker fishing in the burn, right above the clay that many years later became hers.

More perfect days followed, dissolving into all too perfect nights. Clay was dug, Rhuri's son came to work with them, and the pottery thrived.

Two sennights later, Angelica finished trimming the base of a pot. "I think I've done enough for the day," she said to Lilias, who had joined her. She lifted it from the wheel and placed it on a shelf to dry.

Lilias looked up from the clay she was manipulating on the workbench. She had rolled it, pounded it, squeezed it, and cut it. Now Angelica was pleased to see that she was sculpting something. "Muriel's prepared another feast for tonight," she said. "Tells everyone she's celebrating peace, though I know she imagines it another wedding feast. I'm near starved. I think I'll go beg some tidbits from her."

Angelica took up a sponge and began to clean her wheel. "I'd best change when I'm done cleaning here. You can get by with just a wash."

"I've clay under my fingernails. I dinna like clay." Lilias held up her hands, grimacing.

"You may not like it under your fingernails, but I think you've enjoyed playing with it. What did you make?" Angelica peered over the girl's shoulder. Lilias had shaped a flower, complete with leaves. "How pretty. I'll fire it if you like."

Lilias tilted her head as she studied her work. " 'Tisn't very good, but it might be interesting fired." She washed her hands in a basin of clear water on a corner washstand and dried them with a clean linen towel. "May we go riding on the morrow?"

Angelica had expected the request and agreed it was time. Happy with the response, Lilias flitted away to tease Muriel for something to eat.

Angelica hung up her apron, washed the worst of the clay from her hands, and entered the castle. Unlike Lilias, who had kept her clothes clean, she had clay on her kirtle skirt. After the cheery brightness of the kitchens, the darkness of the back stairs crowded around her. Emerging into the dim, silent corridor above, she was surprised to see the door to Geddes's old chamber standing open. Geddes was in the stables. She'd seen him as she'd passed. Lilias was in the kitchens. Who could it be?

She tiptoed down the corridor and peered around the door. Ross, the kitchen lad, knelt before the big chest at the foot of the bed. The lid was open, and his head was inside.

"What in heaven are you doing?" she demanded, knowing he couldn't hear her but feeling too aggrieved to hold back. Looking at things in the family solar was one thing. The chest there was unlikely to hold personal items. Searching a chest in the chieftain's private bedchamber, despite the fact that he had moved to another recently, was entirely different and Angelica didn't like it. "Have you no shame? You should not be here," she scolded, grasping his arm and shaking it.

Ross leaped a foot in the air and wrenched away from her grasp. Backing against the bed, he cowered, regarding her with frightened eyes.

Still angry, she shook her head and frowned, pointing at the chest.

He seemed to realize she was not going to strike him, for instead of bolting from the room, he offered her a plaintive, winning smile and held up the rich-toned kilt Geddes had worn at the wedding. Ross motioned to show that he wished to wear it himself.

The lad wanted to be like the other clansmen, but he could not wear the kilt. "This pattern is only for the men born into the clan." Angelica took it gently away and refolded it in the chest. Though annoyed with him, she reminded herself of his orphaned state. She should teach him, not scold him. How could she make him understand? Perhaps she could explain in pantomime.

"The kilt belongs to Geddes, the chieftain." She pointed to the garment, then indicated the height of a tall man with one hand, nodding vigorously.

He nodded, as if he understood.

She pointed to the garment again, then to him, and shook her head violently, frowning.

Ross rewarded her with a puzzled look.

She gave up. She was no good at this. "Ross, I am sorry. You may wear a shirt like the chieftain's, but not the kilt. At least not in those colors. Here, let me look for something you can wear." She pushed past him to rummage in the wardrobe until she found a shirt that looked too small for Geddes. If he couldn't wear it, surely he wouldn't mind if she gave it to Ross. She held it up to the lad, testing the size.

Ross smiled, smoothing the garment against his body.

"You may keep it." She released the shirt and stepped back, still struggling between compassion and annoyance. Why did the lad not come to her or Muriel if he needed new clothes? They had helped him before when he had indicated his need for new garments. Why did he think he could walk into private chambers and help himself?

But his pleasure in the new shirt eased her irritation. He hugged it to him as he skipped from the chamber and headed for the back stairs.

Left alone, Angelica surveyed the chamber, feeling a sudden, poignant interest in her surroundings. This had been Geddes's chamber since he was a lad, and she couldn't help but be curious, wondering if it could reveal anything about him. She knew so little of his past, despite the intimacy they shared.

She had noted the contents of the chest—winter clothing, blankets, and a wooden box, no doubt full of personal possessions. Though she would have liked to look through the chest, she would not do so without Geddes's invitation. When it was moved to their new chamber, perhaps he would share its contents with her. Until then, she would content herself with examining the chamber's furnishings—the trappings of Geddes's youth that he had left behind as a married man.

The chamber was simply furnished. Geddes had moved all his clothing to their shared chamber. A plain washstand stood in the corner, holding an even plainer washbasin and pitcher. The bed was hung in linen embroidered with bands of a single color, as befit an heir in his youth. The only personal item was a leather-bound book on the bedside table. Odd that Geddes had left it here.

But then she smiled. Not so odd. Since their marriage, when had he had a moment to do anything in bed besides make wild, passionate love to her, then fall into happily satiated sleep? Neither one of them

had even considered doing anything so dull in bed
as read.

She picked up the volume, idly wondering what lit-
erature Geddes liked. The title was foreign, so she
couldn't understand it, though she recognized it as
French, not German or Latin. The book had been
handled often, too. One section in particular had received much attention, for the book fell open to a
specific page filled with stanzas of poetry. The word
amour leaped out at her.

Wasn't this the same book she had seen in the
chamber belonging to Lachlan, the younger MacCallum brother?

She closed the book and reexamined the cover, but
it told her nothing. She opened it again and imagined
it sitting on the worktop in Lachlan's chamber. It
seemed to be the same book. The leather binding had
been brown. Or could there be two such books, and
because the title was French, she couldn't tell the
difference?

Putting it back on the table, she slipped across the
passage and opened the door to Lachlan's chamber.
No open book reposed on Lachlan's desk.

Feeling like a spy, she closed both doors and hurried
to change for supper. But throughout the meal in the
great hall, the question haunted her.

Why was Geddes, a fighter, reading Lachlan the
Peacemaker's volume of French love poetry?

Angelica sat in the solar the next evening, avoiding
thoughts of Geddes and Lachlan, concentrating instead on memories of her husband's lovemaking the
prior night. He had been incredibly passionate. On
her ride today with Lilias, seeing her young charge in
the arms of her sweetheart had whetted her appetite

for more of her husband. Each night, the pleasure they took in one another increased.

Lilias sat by the fire, languid and dreaming, staring into the flames. She had little to say, except to ask Angelica when they would go riding again. Alex Mac-Callum had been invited to join them and was playing cards with Geddes.

"Where are your shoes?" Geddes asked Angelica.

"Ross wasn't around to clean them when I got in from the pottery. Muriel insisted that one of the other lads would clean them, but they didn't have a chance. I told her to let them go until morning." She curled her toes, enjoying the warmth of the fire on them. "I hope you don't mind my stockinged feet."

"No' in the least." He trumped Alex's latest card and collected the trick. "That lad is a slippery one, disappearing the way he does."

"He's a mere child," Angelica protested as Alex played another card.

"Even children can be in league with the wrong people. I've meant to see if he has any clan that claims him."

"Mayhap I should do it," Alex offered. "You have the fields and weapons training to manage." He looked dismayed as Geddes played his own card and took the trick. "Not to mention the very simple task of beating me at cards. I believe you've won again."

"Winning at this game is entirely luck, not skill." Geddes motioned for Alex to make the next deal. "Are you serious about looking into the lad's background?"

"I can make time, since we're no' being attacked, leastwise not now." Alex rapped on the wooden table with his knuckles. "For luck," he explained.

As Geddes thanked Alex for his offer, Lilias rose to bid them good night. Nodding sleepily, she left the chamber. Angelica heard her footsteps retreat down the corridor.

Geddes put another log on the fire to ward off the evening chill. Alex shuffled the cards.

A piercing shriek rent the night.

"By Saint Columba, who was that?" Geddes sprinted for the door.

Angelica caught up a candle in a holder and hurried after him, Alex just ahead of her.

In the dim corridor, Lilias grappled with someone. The small, wiry form fought with her like fury. Before they could reach the struggling pair, the intruder kicked. Lilias cried out and collapsed to the floor. Free of her grip, the intruder dived down the back stairs. Geddes and Alex charged after him.

"Lilias, are you hurt?" Angelica put down her candle and rushed to the fallen girl's side. "What happened?" She helped Lilias to sit up.

Lilias bent over her injured leg, groaning. "When I came into the passage, I saw the tower door was open, and I knew at once that someone was up there. When I started up the stair, he came barreling down. Knocked me flat, he did, but I grabbed his leg, so he kicked me in the shin with his free foot. I hope Geddes and Cousin Alex catch him."

"Let me see your shin." Angelica fetched the candle and held it steady as Lilias pulled down her stocking. Blood welled from a gash.

Despite her injury, Lilias yanked up her stocking and jumped to her feet. " 'Tis no' bad. I must see what he did up there, Angelica. I fear the worst."

Before Angelica could answer, she tore up the stairs, taking them two at a time.

Angelica followed and arrived in the tower chamber, holding her candle aloft.

Lilias knelt on the floor before the trunk. The lid was thrown open, and the trunk was empty. Guessing that Lilias had stored the flag within, Angelica knew the worst had happened. The intruder had taken it.

The secret of the false flag was out.

Geddes and Alex returned a short time later with bad news. The intruder had escaped.

"How did he get away?" Angelica lamented. They had been gone so briefly, she and Lilias were still standing in the corridor.

"Someone awaited him just outside our gate, which happened to be partially open, as he had summoned old Dunardley and was plying him with nonsensical questions." Geddes unpinned his plaid and pulled it off, his face riddled with disgust. "That someone had a very swift horse. He snapped him up and they were gone before we could fetch mounts from the stable. With a dozen trails to choose from, we couldna tell which they took." He knelt before his sister to examine the shin she was again nursing. "Are you much hurt?"

Lilias straightened with determination. "The little monster had quite a kick, but I'll live."

"You believe it was a young person?" Alex asked.

"I believe it was Ross, the kitchen lad." Lilias described what she had found in the tower. The open trunk. The missing false flag.

Darkness settled over Geddes's face. He strode to the tower door. "How did he get in the tower? I had the only key." He yanked the key from the lock. "I kept it in the chest in my chamber."

A sick feeling rose up in Angelica. "Oh, dear." All

gazes turned her way. "I found Ross in your chamber one day, Geddes, looking in the chest. I thought he was searching for clothing." She folded into a chair, feeling a complete idiot. "How could I not realize what he was doing? I'm such a fool."

Geddes stared at her. "How did he get into the chest? 'Tis kept locked as well. I keep the key here at all times." He undid a flap in his belt and searched in the recess. "By Saint Columba, 'tis gone. The beggar must have searched my things while I slept and taken it." He looked at Angelica, his expression grim. "You're no' the only fool."

Angelica groaned. "I should have said something when I found him in your chamber. I disliked his boldness, yet I thought him harmless. I didn't know you kept the chest locked, or I would have reported it to you at once. I remember there was a key in the lock of the chest."

"So I would think I had accidentally left it there myself, if I noticed it was missing. Of course, since I havena been in that chamber of late, I was unlikely to think of the key or the chest at all." Geddes snorted in self-deprecation. "He kent that and used it to his advantage, the little monster."

Angelica wanted to sob. "I never imagined he was a spy."

At her use of the term, Lilias began to cry. Quietly at first, then more loudly until she sobbed, nigh on hysterical.

Geddes could not calm her, nor could Angelica, which left her feeling helpless. She wanted too much to weep as well. "Do you suppose Ross wasn't even deaf?" she asked Geddes, aching at the thought of Angus Kilmartin using a child for his devious purposes.

"I'd guess he could hear as well as you or me," Geddes said. "How else would he have known about the Faerie Flag and where it was kept?"

The next morning, Ross was not present in the kitchens, nor could he be found anywhere in Duntrune Castle or the village. It confirmed their fears. Ross had been a spy for the Kilmartin, and a very clever one at that.

Geddes felt he had no choice but to prepare the garrison for an attack. He left it to Rhuri to tell the select circle of men who knew the secret of the flag. He would let the rest conclude what they would when the attack came and no flag was produced. Peace was at an end.

Though Geddes did not explain to the rest of the householders and villagers the reason he expected an attack, they did not question him. They took the news stoically, going about their preparations as assigned, some looking frightened, others grim. No one sang at their work or jested or teased. Tension reigned throughout Duntrune.

Late that afternoon, Geddes issued the order that all the women, youngsters, and elderly of the household and village, regardless of position, were to sleep in the castle storage cellars among the grain sacks and ale kegs. They were to bring all movable provisions and livestock to shelter within the castle walls.

Early in the evening, he checked to be sure that Angelica and Lilias had joined the rest in the cellars. Then he and all the men of the village and garrison took up a vigil on the northeast castle wall.

"Think you they will attack here?" Alex asked him for the dozenth time.

"Nay, they'll attack the village first, as always. Only

when they find no one there will they attack here, and then they'll choose the northeast side. They ken our weakest point." He turned to the fifty men of the garrison. "But they dinna ken our strong points. Mark me." He had their attention now. "You're strong and more than their match. We have arrows aplenty. We're ready for them." He slapped Rhuri on the back. "Here is the best swordsman north of Glasgow. 'Tis the truth," he insisted as Rhuri ducked his head, embarrassed by the praise. "You've seen him best every swordsman I could find in this region to challenge him. If a single Kilmartin finds his way into our keep, he'll regret it when he crosses swords with Rhuri."

They all nodded in agreement.

"And Alex MacCallum is the sharpest bowman I've ever had the pleasure to work with. He can halve an apple at fifty paces. Do ye think he'll have any trouble stopping a Kilmartin from scaling our wall?"

"Nay, he'll stop him in his tracks," they all shouted.

"And then there's the rest of you." He strode up and down before the ranks of villagers. Ten had been chosen to train with the archers. "You'll make a strong showing, I have nay doubt. They'll never breach the castle walls."

He continued to encourage them, building their excitement to fever pitch. Then he dispersed them to their lookout points on the wall surrounding the castle. Though they would undoubtedly lose the cottages in the village, there would be no dead tonight on the MacCallum side. They were ready for the Kilmartin attack.

The attack came just after midnight. They saw the lights in the village and heard the shouting. Soon enough, Kilmartins surged through the forest, seeking more challenging sport. As Geddes had predicted, they charged the northeast side of the castle, where the wall ringed the stable yard. At the signal from Geddes, a wave of arrows greeted them.

The Kilmartins fell back, clearly surprised by the strength of the counterattack. But they rallied within minutes and attacked again, only to be met by another wave of arrows, and another.

Geddes kept the rain of arrows coming. The Kilmartins retaliated with flaming arrows aimed at the thatched roof of the pottery. Several of the arrows found their marks, and fire blazed to life in the straw.

"Hold your place. They're trying to distract us," he warned the men on the wall as he strode up and down behind them. "The fire will no' spread. We'll put it out later. Shoot at will at your chosen targets."

Every time a Kilmartin approached the wall, he received a MacCallum arrow in welcome. At length, the Kilmartin ranks fell back, leaving several dead. They had made no progress in entering the castle. Their war leader bellowed the command to retreat.

Geddes and his men sat on the wall long after, listening to the defeated attackers razing and burning the village. Unsuccessful in their attempt to invade the castle, they vented their helpless anger on daub-and-wattle huts.

The villagers chafed at the order to remain passive, letting their homes be destroyed. They wanted to fling open the gates and rush to defend their property, but Geddes was tired of slaughter. He'd seen all he could tolerate in his lifetime.

He gathered the men together in the stable yard to remind them of the tactic he'd taught them.

"What's a timber or two compared to lives? Dougal, would ye rather have a roof on yer cottage?" He singled out the shoemaker. "Or yer son here, alive and well?"

"My son, o' course."

"People come first, ye ken."

"Aye," they all shouted.

"Now we wait and keep watch until we're sure they're gone. I want every man with a bow on the wall, and every pair of eyes on the lookout. Anyone who puts his arrow in an attacking Kilmartin earns a bottle of French claret."

Such a rich prize. They leaped to obey.

By dawn, several bottles of claret had been earned, and no more Kilmartins approached the castle. It was clear that the last of them had gone home. Geddes's strategy had won.

"We succeeded without the flag," Geddes heard Rhuri telling Dougal, the shoemaker. "Do ye ken what that means?"

"He's our MacCallum," came the stout reply. "He trained us well."

They praised him in terms that amazed him. Pleased as he was about the lack of casualties, he hadn't expected this outpouring of faith.

They called him their hero. They called him invincible.

In the midst of chaos, he received an incentive to fight on.

It was morning before Angelica and the others received the signal to come out of the cellar. She hurried up the steep stairs, anxious to see what she would find in the aftermath of battle. To her vast relief, only a few men had minor wounds, and none were dead. Though the deserted village had been laid to waste, Duntrune Castle had been held by the MacCallum clan with no loss of life. The chieftain's name was on everyone's lips, and all were praising him.

Still, the blessing of the victory could not allay her fear. Such attacks would become common. They could not all live in the castle all the time.

As she stood in the entry hall, contemplating their dismal future, Lilias ran in. " 'Tis ruined. Destroyed," Lilias wailed.

Angelica clasped the girl to her, surprised to find tears streaming down her face. "What is destroyed?"

"The p-pottery," Lilias sobbed. "My flower. Everything."

With her heart in her throat and her stomach churning, Angelica ran for the pottery, praying it wasn't true. But it was. The thatched roof of the pottery had been set afire and had collapsed. Villagers had put it out, and among the soaking, charred, smoking ruins, she glimpsed broken pottery. Her dream was in ruins.

She sank to the ground and wept. Not for this single loss. The pottery could be rebuilt. She could make more pots. She grieved for the ruined village and for the vengeance of their neighbors that would be visited upon them again and again into the interminable future, with no hope for peace. She could not bear it.

She should not have come here. Continual strife would be her lot and that of her children.

Blinded by her tears, she sought Geddes, but he was not to be found in the village or among the men of the garrison.

Back in the stable yard, she gingerly picked broken pottery from the smoking ruins. The pieces that had not yet dried could be softened and reused. She found her work apron, pulled it from the mess, and spread it to her receive findings. As she sorted through the rubble, she happened to glance up. The windows of several family members' chambers faced the stable yard, Lachlan's among them. A dim figure sat there, holding a book, but he did not seem to be reading. He was gazing out the window into the trees.

Lachlan the Peacemaker. Lachlan, the romantic.

But Geddes was not a peacemaker, she told herself, unwilling to believe what her eyes told her. He was a fighter. Everyone knew that.

Chapter 21

Everyone said that Geddes was a fighter. As a lad, he had learned the ways of sword and dirk while training to be chieftain. As a young man, he had served his king with his sword. But Angelica no longer accepted these facts as all there was to know of her husband. He was hiding something.

Tell me who you are. The demand hovered on her lips. She longed to ask him, yet she dared not. No one else doubted who he said he was. What if she was wrong? By asking, she could ruin his trust by suggesting he lied.

There was one way to be sure. She could look at the parish registry. On the night of her wedding, Lilias, Muriel, and Geddes had all seemed to conspire to keep her from looking at the book after Geddes had signed it. Was it her imagination? Or would she find her answer there?

Unfortunately, the parish registry had returned to Dunadd with the kirk minister.

Very well, she must travel to Dunadd. Everyone was busy with cleanup and rebuilding in the village. She would slip away for a few hours.

The plan was good, but finding an escort was diffi-

cult. Whom could she ask? Geddes's men would tell
him if she asked them, and she wanted secrecy.

In the end, she took the two stable lads assigned to
help her clean up the pottery. Though she hated the
necessity of swearing them to secrecy, she did it anyway. They trusted and respected her, and agreed
readily. She would make it up to them later, she told
herself. She would not feel guilty about something that
was her right to know.

They rode fast, pausing only once in the hour's ride
to rest and water the horses. At the town of Dunadd,
she bought the lads hot mutton pies and bade them
wait for her in the town square, guarding the horses.
Then she hurried on foot to the nearby church.

As it happened, the minister was out calling on his
flock, as a good minister should be. The thin old man
trimming grass away from the stones in the kirkyard
invited her to wait inside. He didn't know when the
minister might return.

It could be in a minute or in four hours, Angelica
realized, and she didn't have all day. She must look
without permission in the records office. She entered
the church alone and found the small room containing
the records. Shelves of volumes lined the walls: birth
records, death records, all going back decades. At last
she found the marriage records. The latest book was
at the far right end. She took it from the shelf and
paged through it with fingers made clumsy by
eagerness.

The tenth day of June was the date of her marriage.
She had signed the register first. Here was her signature. *Angelica Maria Cavandish.* And next to it . . .

She stared at the scrawled signature next to hers.
Though she had fully expected what she saw, it still
shocked her.

Geddes MacCallum was not the man he said he was. He had told her the truth wouldn't matter to her. He was correct; she didn't mind. But everyone else would, especially the Kilmartins. They would be more vulnerable to attack than ever.

Despair descended on Geddes during the dismal cleanup, though it was punctuated by moments of elation. They had defeated the Kilmartins. In doing so, he had won a major victory in gaining respect from his kin. His clansmen had also proved to themselves their strength.

Yet they would never stop fighting Kilmartins. How could he celebrate, knowing that?

Geddes wanted comfort. He wanted Angelica's softness, but they had work to do—he in the village, she in the pottery. Once during the day, he went to the castle for a bite to eat. She wasn't at the pottery, and the few people there hadn't seen her.

"She took off ridin'," said Sim, the head stableman. "The two lads went with her. Something about finding new timbers for the pottery roof."

He didn't like her going off on her own, even with the two lads, but the Kilmartins would be burying their dead today. They would not be attacking just yet. He returned to his work in the village.

He was glad to see her at supper. The doubt and fear in her eyes were palpable, yet neither of them spoke of it. He wanted to remember her the way she'd been on their wedding night—his spellbound bride.

She came to him willingly that night, letting him make love her, making love to him in return. Before, her kisses had tasted of trust. Now something had changed. She saw too much of him and understood him too well.

Why not tell her his secret?

In the aftermath of their lovemaking, he considered it. Gazing on her innocent features as she slept, he felt the same overwhelming impulse to protect her that he'd felt the night of their marriage.

Yet he was the one from whom she needed protection. He had wed her under a false name and false pretenses. Who could forgive that?

He could not tell her. Rejection would be too much to bear at this moment. He had her trust and he wanted to keep it. Somehow he would find a way to tell her—later, when it would be easier for her to accept.

The village was in worse condition than the pottery. Angelica knew it must be rebuilt first. Magnus, his son, and Agnes were reroofing their cottage. Stone was helping them. Angelica would not take them from their important tasks. A new roof for the pottery must wait.

Knowing that she had no place to work, the head stableman offered her the use of his tack room. He and his lads moved the saddles, bridles, and other equipage to a spare stall and let her take over. She must begin by wrestling the wheels from the debris of the pottery. It was difficult work, and before she had gotten even one of them very far, the stable lads ran over to help.

Grateful for their concern and their muscle, she let them move the wheels and her workbench. She salvaged what she could of the clay, putting it back in the softening pit. Rain and mist would break it down. She could rewedge and use it again.

But the work went slowly and she grew tired. When she found a piece of the pot with the blue glaze for

Geddes, she could not prevent tears from springing to her eyes. The clay could be softened for reuse, but the glaze could not be reclaimed. The precious resource was lost to her, as was her hope.

That afternoon Lilias arrived, moody and full of suppressed rage. She joined Angelica in picking pieces of smashed pottery from the rubble and lugging them to the softening pit, but her face was set in angry lines. Feeling sorry for Lilias, feeling just as sorry for herself, Angelica called a halt to their foraging and settled at her wheel, bent on consoling herself by throwing a pot.

"Why don't you make another flower?" she suggested to Lilias, handing her a lump of clay.

Lilias snorted. "I'd rather break someone's head."

Angelica understood her charge's feelings all too well. Lilias had lived with the threat of Kilmartin attack all her life. It had clearly taken its toll on her patience.

In a sudden frenzy of energy, Lilias grasped a dowel and rolled out the clay until it was flat. Grabbing a pin tool, she began to draw. "Drawing is easier than sculpting," she muttered, holding out the slab of clay for Angelica to see.

She had etched a design much like the graceful brush-and-ink plants that she drew on paper. "Wonderful," Angelica praised, a small hope lighting the moment. "You could use a brush and glaze instead of the pintool and ornament my pottery. 'Twould be beautiful."

Lilias flung the clay on the bench. "I could, but why trouble? We're bound to be murdered in our beds some night."

Angelica didn't know what to do for Lilias, let alone for herself. They were both caught in an impossible situation, and she felt much akin to her new sister-in-law, ready to explode from the pressure.

Beauty in the midst of chaos. What good did it do?

Geddes stood at the door of the tack room, watching Angelica pull a beautiful handle for a mug. Her clever, beautiful hands stroked and stretched the clay. The handle lengthened, growing long and sleek, reminding him all too well of his body's response to her touch. In that moment, he wanted her more than ever.

Yet he was caught in the midst of insanity. He had wed her, and they would now go to ruin together. Everything they cared about would be destroyed and torn apart faster than they could rebuild it.

This was the destruction that Duntrune wreaked on everyone who sought to hold it. This was why he should never have come back. What audacity he'd had, thinking he could succeed where his ancestors had failed.

"Geddes, you mun do something." Lilias scowled at him from the workbench where she sat. "Attack Angus Kilmartin before he attacks us again."

He had not yet spoken, and this was how she greeted him. "Why? 'Twould do us no good," he pointed out.

She threw out both hands in evident frustration. "If you could capture the Kilmartin, you could stop his attacks."

Geddes shook his head. "I should hold him prisoner? His heir would carry on in his place," he said bitterly. "His son would be obliged to fight us for his father's release."

Lilias jumped to her feet and kicked the stout leg of the wheel closest to her. "He would not carry on in his father's place."

"What is that supposed to mean?" Geddes didn't like the savagery of her kick. Nor did her tone bode well. Her voice trembled with pent-up passion and a threatening note of defiance. "Lilias?" he demanded.

She refused to look at him. "Brian Kilmartin would not carry on as his father has," she muttered to the clay.

"What do you ken of Brian Kilmartin?" A prick of anxiety stung him, but he ignored it, hoping her mention of his enemy's son meant nothing.

Lilias grabbed a slab of clay and examined it closely, frowning.

"Lilias?" he demanded.

A shudder shook his sister. She flung down the clay and whirled to face him. "Brian Kilmartin is my lover," she cried. "There. I said it. He is."

Angelica had sat in silence throughout the exchange, but now she leaped up. "Lilias, stop."

"I can hide it no longer," Lilias wailed, throwing herself into Angelica's arms. "I mun tell him. 'Tis Brian we ride out to see, and I love him. I love him with all my heart."

Geddes felt like a pebble dropped from a cliff, spinning into the void. He groped mentally for a handhold on something solid, but found nothing. "Ye've given yourself to him?"

Lilias stamped her foot. "Everything is sex with you. Dinna you think there can be love without it? Nay, I havena," she shouted. "I havena given him my virtue, but I love him, ye ken." Like so many times before, she burst into tears and fled.

Geddes groped for the wall to steady himself. Nothing was sacred, it seemed. Nothing. He turned to Angelica, his face set and grim. "I should have kent at once, when Kilmartin sent your pack to me so promptly when you first came. But it wasn't the master at all. 'Twas his son, and he sent the pack because he knew you. You deceived me, taking Lilias to see him.''

He could see her visible struggle to swallow in the face of his accusation. Despite her obvious disquiet, she spoke with great dignity. "I knew that if I accompanied Lilias whenever she saw Brian, there would be no babes. But there will be no more visits now. Not since the Kilmartins know we do not have the flag.''

"That is correct. There will be no more visits. Not ever.'' He felt both stricken with grief and more furious than he could ever remember. She knew how his clan felt about the Kilmartins, yet she had encouraged Lilias in her love for their enemy's son. She still argued as if she had been right. He stalked toward the door.

"I believe there is true love between them." Her words halted him. "It was my intention to see and judge for myself. If there were not, I would have put an end to their meetings, but they are right for one another.''

He rounded on her, letting his anger blaze forth. "I shall be the judge of whether there's true love between my sister and any man she considers as a husband. In this case, there is not. If there were, I would forbid it.'' He turned again to leave.

"She might wed with him anyway. You might unintentionally force her into it, to defend her right to love where she chooses.''

He clenched his hands into fists until they ached with the exertion. "She should defer to my judgment in the matter.''

"*You* would be able to tell if she was in love?''

He turned a cold gaze on her. "You seem to think

I know nothing of love. Well, your ladyship, you will be pleased to know that until this moment, I thought I did. But now I see I was mistaken to expect someone I esteemed to hold the same beliefs as I. But that is the legacy of Duntrune, and we shall have no better than those who went before me. I was a fool to hope otherwise."

"Love doesn't mean two people agree in everything," Angelica cried, tears glinting in her eyes. "It means they work out their differences. Why are you so against Brian Kilmartin? He wants peace. Why should he and Lilias not wed?"

"Have you forgotten that Angus Kilmartin killed my father? He has attacked my people ever since I can remember, as did his father before him. I should wed my sister to the offspring of such?"

"Brian is a far different man from his father." She seemed not the least aware of his anguish. "I met him. If you would but meet him as well, you would find him most acceptable. And he is unwilling to carry on the feud. Please say you will give him a chance."

"Can *he* forgive the wrongs done him and his by the MacCallums?" Geddes knew full well the damage wasn't one-sided, though it pained him to admit it, even to himself. "Does he speak of that?"

"I . . . I did not hear him do so," she stammered.

"Then how do you know he isna setting a trap for Lilias?" he pressed, "intending to do to her what was done to his sister?"

Instead of answering his question, Angelica stamped her foot, much as Lilias had done. "*What* was done to his sister? No one will tell me. What?"

Her question cut into him, a blinding flash of pain from the past. Death. Destruction. He could not speak of it. Not to her. Not to anyone. He spun on his heel and stalked from the room, able to think of only one thing.

He must escape from the memories. Escape from the ghosts.

She had ruined everything. As Geddes left her, Angelica wanted to cry, but she held back the tears, refusing to give in to weakness. She must do something, so she went in search of Lilias.

"Tell me, Lilias, what happened to Susan Kilmartin?"

Lilias sat in her chamber on the bed, kicking the bedpost, her leashed fury frightening to behold. "Years ago, when he was but eighteen, Geddes seduced Susan Kilmartin and got her with child. He refused to wed with her, and Father supported him. They agreed he could do better than marry the daughter of the clan's enemy who was naught but a minor chieftain, beholden to the MacDonalds. Susan was disgraced. Ruined. She gave birth to a son, then died shortly after. The child died as well. Angus Kilmartin never forgave Geddes. He'd fought for the land all his life, but after that, he was also fighting for his blood kin. He killed my father for revenge, and now he would kill Geddes as well."

Angelica pressed her fingers to her temples, trying to find order in the chaos. "We both know that the man I married didn't do it." She stared pointedly at Lilias, willing her to acknowledge what Angelica had learned from the registry. "He's not capable of getting a woman with child, then deserting her and letting her die alone."

Lilias's jaw tightened. "Unfortunately, *Geddes MacCallum* did it, and that is what matters." She swiped at her eyes, apparently unwilling to speak more plainly. "And we all suffer for it. I see no escape."

The man she had wed had not done this thing. Angelica knew it, but what could she do? She might do greater damage by proving it than by remaining silent, yet it rankled her.

She went to see Magnus, hoping he might be helpful. He was sitting in the doorway to his cottage, making a new lid for a churn. She sat on the stool opposite, suddenly aware of many questions she had never thought to ask. "How did you come to write to Master Stone and invite him to start a pottery with you?"

"I kent the clay was there, but I needed help to dig and work it. I thought o' him." Magnus smiled at her in his kindly, gentle way.

Another story whose details did not add up. "But why did you think of writing to someone you had known in your youth but haven't seen for years? And the cost. You would have needed someone to write the letter, which would have been expensive in either coins or barter, and someone had to carry it all the way to England."

"I wished to dig clay from the burn," Magnus repeated, seeming not to understand the intent of her question. "The Kilmartin controlled the land. I told him my wish."

Angelica tried again. "Why did you not just dig, without seeking someone to help you?"

"When I first told the Kilmartin my wish, he laughed at me. Said I was an old man with one foot in the grave. I couldna think what he was about when he started to dig himself. But then the MacCallum returned and ousted him." Magnus worked in silence on the lid. "After that, the Kilmartin sent for me. He was right civil, urging me to dig the clay and start a new enterprise. But he was right in one thing. I needed help. I could have found help to dig the clay, but I'm too old to do all the other work alone, and no one else had the skill. So I thought o' Stone and asked Kilmartin to write for me. He took a good deal o' convincin', but he did it at last. And Stone brought you."

Angelica shivered. So Angus Kilmartin had been behind her coming to Scotland the entire time. This was what he'd wanted: someone to dig in the streambed for him. And she didn't think his only motive was the profits to be had from a pottery.

Angelica didn't sleep with Geddes that night. After his earlier anger, he seemed unsurprised when she indicated her wish to retire to her old bedchamber, to be alone and think.

In her chilly bed, she curled beneath the cold sheets and sobbed. She had destroyed his trust in her. Though he hid something from her as well, in typical male fashion, he did not see it as the same thing, and he was right. She loved him, regardless of his name. But he could not accept anyone he cared for dealing with the Kilmartins.

He had called the legacy of Duntrune deadly. Anyone who tried to possess it was destroyed.

No, her logic argued. It wasn't Duntrune that destroyed; it was the clans' fighting, and she refused to be part of it. She was a creator, not a destroyer. She would not accept the role.

With her tears spent, she rose, put on her green kirtle skirt and bodice, and left the castle by the front door. With a lantern in hand, she approached the man on night watch at the gate. The old fellow who usually kept the gate had gone to his bed, as he did each night when no battle was brewing. He was replaced by one of the younger members of the garrison.

Colin MacCallum did not question her wish to speak to Master Stone in the middle of the night. Her artistic consultations with her teacher had been so frequent and at such varied hours of late, she suspected he would think nothing of her request. Sure enough, he called one of the other men on night watch to serve as her escort.

"Hugh, here, will go part way wi' ye, then find one o' the men on patrol to see ye the rest o' the way. That way, Hugh can return to his post," Colin said.

Angelica thanked him and set out with Hugh, but once the mounted man on patrol left her at Magnus's cottage, she waited until he was out of sight. Instead of knocking at the door, she headed for the stream where she'd been digging clay. She did not wish to speak to Master Stone this night. She had something entirely different on her mind.

Walking alone in the dark was eerie, and she held up her lantern to avoid tripping. As she approached the stream, the rush of its waters reassured her, though the surrounding trees harbored gloomy shadows in which she imagined goblins or Kilmartins waiting to attack.

To work, she chided her active imagination as she arrived at the stream. Physical labor would quiet her fear. After retrieving a spade and two buckets from tools stored at the site, she removed her shoes and stockings and descended into the water.

Placing her lantern and the two buckets in niches, she waded into the recess cut by the recent turbulent waters and set to work with her spade. Her two buckets filled quickly with clay, and she had to lug them up to the bank to empty them. After heaping a pile for later retrieval, she returned to the stream.

An hour passed. Her feet chilled in the cold water, and the clay pile increased. Perspiration ran down her forehead, soaked her underarms, and trickled down her back. At the hoot of an owl, she jumped and froze, staring in first one direction, then another.

Her lantern cast little light, illuminating a tiny ring where she worked without penetrating into the night beyond. Was that a movement in the bushes by the bank downstream? She started and stared, but could make out no one in the dark.

The devil with it. Defying the menace, she threw herself into the digging.

Let me find what the Kilmartin wanted.

But it was a large bank, and she didn't know what she was looking for, or whether she dug in the right place. As the sun peered over the horizon, it seemed an impossible task. In the still-murky light of early morning, birds awoke and began to sing, harbingers of dawn.

She was so tired, so sick at heart, she supposed she should give up and return to her bed. But she could not leave yet. She must know. Mayhap another direction in her digging was warranted. She chose to dig upward, into the roof of the recessed bank above her head. It was awkward, trying to loosen the clay, then catch it before it fell into the stream or on her head, but it was the one thing she hadn't tried. She dug on as the darkness slowly ebbed from the sky and pale light took its place.

She was just about to give up when her spade struck stone.

Or was it metal?

She dug frantically, uncovering a long, flat edge of metal. She struggled to expose more of it, but the wet clay clung to the treasure, unwilling to give it up. Frustrated, she climbed out of the stream to the bank above. Once there had been a tree here. A hollow tree into which someone could have deposited something metal. Time had rotted away the remaining stump, but the roots remained. Perhaps the hollow had penetrated below the ground level.

She dug from above, pulling out clumps of grass and soil, gradually exposing remnants of the old hollow stump. Deeper she went, down into its center, through soil and debris that must have accumulated in the recess over the years.

At long last, she struck metal from above. Digging with renewed excitement, she exposed the top of a metal casket as long as her forearm. Anxious to see its contents, she climbed into the hole with it and clawed at the metal with both hands. It refused to budge.

She dug away more soil, then wedged the spade under one end and pried. The casket rocked slightly. Heartened, she fell to her knees, heedless of the mud smearing her skirt, and tore away a network of tree root. Again she applied the spade. She pried first one end, then the other. At long last, with a moist sucking sound, the casket popped loose.

Angelica hauled it from the hole and stood, torn between wanting to pry open the lid to see the contents and the practical thought that she should wash first. She was filthy. If it contained what she hoped and suspected it did, it would need to be kept clean . . .

Practicality overcame curiosity. Tucking the casket under her left arm, she put on her stockings and shoes, then descended to the stream to wash her hands.

Balancing the casket while perched on a rock and rinsing one hand was no easy feat. Then she shifted the casket to the other arm and crouched to rinse the other hand. At last she was clean. As she turned on the rock, preparing to return to the bank, a splash sounded behind her.

"Who's there?" she cried, fear churning her stomach. As she turned to look, strong hands pushed her hard. Flailing for balance, she tumbled into the stream.

The cold water closed over her head. Submerged and unable to breathe, Angelica struggled to rise but could not seem to get her feet under her. The ruthless hands held her head underwater and tugged the casket from her. Just before panic set in, she was suddenly free.

She shot out of the water spluttering and furious. A shadowy figure sped up the path on the other side of the stream. A Kilmartin, surely. The man raced away on the path beyond. He must have been hiding in the distant shrubbery since she had arrived.

Furious that she had worked so hard for the prize, only to have it stolen from her, she gave chase. She would not give up the casket so easily.

As she reached the path and pounded after him, she saw him mount a tethered horse. So he had come prepared for a speedy escape. Angelica could never catch him on foot.

Despite her distinct disadvantage, with wet shoes and stockings and no horse, she set out. She would find her assailant, for she knew where he was going.

To Castle Fincharn.

Practicality prevailed after Angelica began her journey on foot. She must have a mount to bear her such a distance, so she begged the loan of a mule from a clan family and continued on her way. The faithful animal delivered her to Castle Fincharn, and she begged a villager, with a promise of payment later, to care for him until she collected him. She would return the mule to his owners after her task was done. Though she was exhausted and dirty, she went straight to the castle on foot, still as furious as when she had set out.

"What do ye want?" the surly gatekeeper asked when she called through the bars of the yett at the castle entrance.

"I wish to see Angus Kilmartin," she said with dignity, despite her dirty clothes and disheveled hair.

"Why?" The man's insolent tone clearly suggested he thought her a beggar maid or worse.

She drew herself up in her haughtiest manner. "Tell him Angelica Cavandish is here." She spoke in the same stinging tones she had once heard Queen Elizabeth use to inform a foreign ambassador that he had displeased her. "He will understand why. You may let me in now."

Angus Kilmartin sat in his withdrawing chamber by a comfortable fire, a flagon of wine in his hand, the metal casket reposing on his lap. He did not ask why she stood before him, covered with filth and as angry as a hornet. He gazed at her without a word, his clansman in the Kilmartin colors standing behind her, awaiting his orders.

The Kilmartin looked older than ever, if that were possible. His face was a haggard, sickly gray, his scant hair plastered in an oily snarl to the top of his bald head. He was ill and old. Why did he not give it up?

Since he did not speak, she waited until the clansman had withdrawn, then began without preamble.

"You wished me to find *that* for you, and I did." She pointed at the casket he held. "Is it what I think it is?"

"None of your affair, lassie." He grinned at her with an indulgent, satisfied air. "I'm done with ye now. Depart."

His curt dismissal infuriated her. "Nay," she cried. "I'm staying until I find out what this is about. I'm tired of it. Do you hear me? You've ruined everything I ever loved, and I won't permit it." She shouted at him, behaving in a manner most rude and unreasonable. Yet she could not hold her temper in check.

He winced, apparently unused to such behavior, especially from a woman. "If ye dinna depart at once, I shall use ye to further my aims. I'm being generous, allowin' ye to go."

Angelica didn't believe he'd ever been generous in his life. "You dare not harm me," she argued. "I'm English. My family will have the Queen of England demand reparation from your king if you harm me. She will make his life so miserable, he will be furious with you."

"I dinna have to harm ye bodily to use ye." He chuckled nastily, then shouted for the clansman to return. The man entered the chamber and waited for orders. "Lock her up." Angus gestured rudely at Angelica.

The man grasped her, jerking her arms behind her back.

Pain shot through Angelica's shoulders, and fear all but paralyzed her, making it difficult to speak. "Call Brian," she choked. "I wish to speak to him."

"My son has no interest in talking to the likes o' ye."

She dared not tell him she knew otherwise. She had been a fool to come to this cold, forbidding castle, thinking to persuade a dangerous old man to change his mind. Hate had twisted Angus Kilmartin's mind past redemption.

"I found that casket for you. You've wanted it all your life and you owe me payment for it," she cried as the clansman dragged her toward the door of the chamber. It was her only bargaining token, but its value had weakened, now that he had the casket.

Deep in her gut, worry tightened like a drawstring squeezing shut the neck of a bag. Her impulsiveness had led her to make a terrible mistake.

Geddes returned from archery practice in the village to find the household as upset as a hive of bees whose queen had died. He took Muriel aside to ask what was wrong.

"Sh-she didna rise to break her fast," Muriel faltered, on the verge of tears. "I thought she wished tae sleep a wee bit longer and let her be, but I should ha' kent something was wrong. She's never been a slugabed. When I went tae rouse her, she was gone. Colin was keeping the gate last night. He says she asked to see Master Stone, so he sent her with an escort. She never came back, and she isna there now."

Geddes cursed his lack of foresight in anticipating Angel's impulse. "We will begin a search at once. I'll see to the garrison if you will enlist the aid of the household. Send a pair of maids to the village for any news of Angelica. I will send men to search the area. Let no one walk alone. Kilmartins may be on the prowl."

Within an hour, Rhuri reported evidence that someone had been digging at the burn. With his heart in his throat, Geddes raced to see for himself.

He was sure it had been Angelica, and she had been digging, but not for clay. The old tree stump atop the bank had been unearthed, and she had delved deep into the compacted rubble of its core in search of something. Two buckets stood to one side of a mound of freshly dug clay, clearly brought up from the burn. She would never have left it if it had been the object of her nighttime travail.

There was only one explanation for both her digging and her disappearance: Angus Kilmartin.

From the start, Geddes knew that the Kilmartin had had a part in bringing Angelica to Scotland. The man had given her permission—nay, had urged her—to dig for clay in the burn. He had demanded Angelica's return to Castle Fincharn. It didn't take much for Geddes to guess what Angus had been looking for. He, too, knew the story of Mairi MacCallum's drowning, knew that some believed she had taken the Faerie Flag with her that stormy night when she had quarreled with her brother and drowned in the burn. Angus Kilmartin could have been looking for only one thing in the bank.

As Geddes raced back to the castle with all speed, he knew he must set his personal fears for Angel aside. He must be calculating and objective in his decisions, but one thing was sure. Death must come to the Kilmartin if he harmed his wife.

With his purpose clear, he gathered the garrison and rode for Castle Fincharn at the head of sixty mounted men.

Angelica dozed fitfully in the tiny chamber where she'd been locked. What folly her ungoverned impulse had brought down on her. She was now the prisoner of Angus Kilmartin. The lock in the door rattled, and she struggled to banish her exhaustion and sit up.

Brian entered the chamber, his father behind him. "Angelica!" Brian hastened to her side and took her hands. "Are you well?"

"So ye do ken her." Angus looked skeptical, despite their obvious familiarity.

"O' course I do, Father. I met her when she was our guest," Brian reminded him. He grinned roguishly. "A man doesna forget a face like hers."

"Even filthy?" Angelica laughed ruefully, pushing back a mud-encrusted strand of hair.

Brian seemed to take in her disheveled state for the first time. "By Saint Andrew, Father, ye've no' been courteous to our guest. She requires a bath, clean clothing, and a meal, I'll wager. And an escort home."

In the silence that followed, Angelica gazed balefully at the smirking Angus Kilmartin. "I'm not going home, it seems, or so your father says."

Brian turned to his father. "Is this true?"

Angus nodded, a wolfish smile creasing his face.

Brian's mouth tightened. "Then I shall set her up in one of the nicer chambers, as befits a guest. Come."

He held out his hand to Angelica, and she took it. "I should like a bath, please. And I'm thirsty and hungry, Brian. Thank you for thinking of me." As Brian led her from the chamber, she glanced at the casket tucked under Angus's arm. She must find a way to regain the contents of that box.

Chapter 22

Bathed and attired in a clean kirtle skirt and bodice that had belonged to Susan Kilmartin, Angelica sat with Brian in a chamber with a big window facing south. He had brought her a tray of cold mutton, newly baked bread, and cooked turnip greens. Though she appreciated being clean and having the chance to eat, she was filled with turmoil. What would Geddes do when he discovered her missing?

She knew exactly what he would do, and she despaired. She would be the cause of a clan battle, the last thing she desired.

"Brian, what do you suppose is in that casket I found?" Though she felt certain of the answer to her question, she wasn't sure what Brian knew.

"The Faerie Flag," Brian said bluntly. "I saw it. Ye've solved the age-old mystery o' the lost flag. Ye're a wonder, ye are."

A combination of joy and panic coursed through Angelica. "I'm thrilled to have found it, but now 'tis in your father's power. From the way he holds it so tightly, I didn't think he would let anyone else see it, not even you."

"I *am* his heir," Brian pointed out dryly. "Besides, he needed help getting the metal casket open, then the wooden box within, and he trusted me to help. The flag lay inside."

Angelica could still scarcely believe it. "How can you tell 'tis the real flag?"

"There is no doubt once ye've seen it," Brian assured her. "The silk is very fine, dyed and embroidered in many colors, but its looks are no' the proof. 'Tis the feeling ye get when ye see it. I've never experienced such a thing in my life. I canna describe it."

"Try," Angelica urged, fascinated. She did not believe in magic, except for the magic of Geddes's kisses. Yet she knew Brian and trusted his judgment. If he said there was something unusual about the flag, she wished to hear about it from him.

"As Father opened the metal box, then the wooden one, I felt excited. That was natural, wantin' to see what was inside," Brian began hesitantly at first, then continued more quickly. "But the moment I laid eyes on that shining silk, 'twas as if I'd received a wondrous gift, and the gift was inside me, no' in the box. I felt full of hope when I saw it, as if I could achieve anything in the world. I need only put my heart and mind to it, and 'twould be so."

It sounded quite fantastic to Angelica. "The flag wasn't wet or soiled or decayed from being in those two boxes, buried in the dirt for more than fifty years?"

"Nay." Brian shook his head for emphasis. "Father took it out and unfolded it. The silk was whole and as sweet-smelling as if it had been packed in lavender in our finest linen chest."

That, Angelica knew, was a miracle. Fabric, especially silk, decayed over time, and the chance of water leaking into the boxes over the years would have been great. "You don't suppose the flag's power would sweeten your father's temper, do you?" she asked, hoping that as the flag had achieved the miracle of staying whole for centuries, mayhap it could accomplish another.

Brian looked doubtful. "I fear 'tis too late for that."

Just then, the cry of geese sounded outside the chamber window. Angelica glanced out and saw an arrow of geese winging their way south.

Brian started to his feet. "Lilias. She's at the loch, signaling for me."

My God, not now. Angelica's heart leaped into her throat. Dropping her spoon, she hurried to clasp his hand. "Go, Brian. Hurry. You must keep her away from here." Her moment of hope, now that the Faerie Flag had been found, was at an end. "You must keep her away from your father. Please keep her safe."

It was too late to keep Lilias away from Castle Fincharn. Minutes after Brian left, Angelica saw Lilias riding toward the castle gate. Angelica hung from her window and tried to signal the girl, but Lilias never looked up. She rode straight to the castle gate and shouted for Brian.

To Angelica's relief, she saw no sign of Angus Kilmartin. Below, Brian ordered the yett raised and Lilias admitted. With a terse order to his father's men, he helped Lilias dismount and escorted her into the castle.

The couple entered Angelica's chamber. Lilias's color was high, her hair disheveled from riding like the wind. "Geddes is coming with the garrison," she said, panting, and clutching Brian for support, so violently did she tremble. "He intends to attack. I had to warn ye, Brian. What shall we do?"

Angelica embraced Lilias, knowing what was coming.

No more bloodshed, her heart cried.

She grasped Brian's and Lilias's hands and clasped them together, holding them in place. "We must prevent the fighting and end the feud with your marriage. We must."

"But how can we prevent the fighting?" Lilias sobbed, wiping away tears.

"I have a plan," Angelica said, knowing that this was not the time for faint hearts. "If you're willing, here is what you both must do."

Angelica stood on the wall walk of Castle Fincharn, her arms twisted behind her, held in the devil grip of the Master of Kilmartin. She was a hostage, her life forfeit at his pleasure. Her heart banged at her ribs so hard, she thought it would burst from her chest.

Yet Angus could not hold her and the Faerie Flag at the same time. Though a small blessing, it gave her hope. Neither the flag nor the casket were anywhere to be seen. Her plan might still succeed.

At the head of the MacCallum garrison, Geddes faced the gate of Castle Fincharn. With complete calm, he sat his prancing stallion, his mighty claymore drawn. Buckled into a steel-plated leather jack and bristling with dirks, he was a warrior both proud and deadly. The clan's archers held their bows in hand, arrows ready to fly at his command.

"Release my wife, Angus Kilmartin, or feel the wrath of Clan MacCallum," Geddes shouted.

Angelica knew that she and Angus were both clearly visible on the wall walk. She studied Geddes's face, but at this distance she could not read him. All she could sense was his will to fight. He was prepared to go to any length for her, even take on the devil himself at the gates of hell.

Her heart thrilled to know his devotion, yet she despaired. The chance of her plan's succeeding was so slim.

The Kilmartin garrison stood at the ready in the yard behind the gate. Archers lined the wall walk, arrows trained on their foes.

Angus jerked Angelica's arms, causing her to moan involuntarily. "I have yer bride, MacCallum, *and* I have the Faerie Flag. Ye dinna stand a chance. Ye might as well put yer tail between yer legs and run home, for I shall keep her and use her as I please. Mayhap I'll give her to my garrison, for their sport."

His taunts were meant to dismay his enemy, to break his will to fight, but Geddes paid him no heed. "I dinna believe that you have the Faerie Flag," he sneered. "Let us see it if you do."

"O' course ye dinna believe me," Angus retorted. "Ye pretended so long to have the flag yerself, ye expect others to lie as well."

This time his jeering words had the desired effect. Members of the MacCallum garrison who did not know the secret gazed at each other in bewilderment. Then they turned to Geddes with questions on their lips. Disappointed murmurs rose from their ranks.

"That's right, yer chieftain deceived ye. How does that feel?" Angus mocked them. "Ye're led by a liar. Ye'd put yer faith in such?"

"Don't listen to him," Angelica cried to her rescuers, unable to remain silent. "The MacCallum has fought for your dreams and for Duntrune. He helped you reclaim your birthright. He cares for all of you. Angus Kilmartin never cared if you lived or died. *He* is the liar."

Angus jerked her arms hard, punishing her as she spoke, but the pain was worth it. The men recognized the truth of her words and responded. Yet they still seemed confused by the lie about the flag. Their murmurs continued.

"It matters naught what your chieftain did for ye." Angus sought again to sway them. "I have the Faerie Flag and I shall possess Duntrune once more."

"Let us see the flag," Geddes challenged again.

With a satisfied smirk, Angus shouted for the flag. One of his clansmen appeared in the doorway to the wall walk, empty-handed, blathering, and scraping.

"Where is the flag?" Angus roared at him.

"Here, Father," a young male voice rang out. From the opposite end of the wall walk, Brian Kilmartin stepped forth from the door. At his side was Lilias MacCallum. Between them they held a rolled flag on a pole. Hoisting the pole in the air, they unfurled a mighty banner, whole and beautiful, and let it fly free on the breeze.

The garrisons on both sides gasped as the silk glimmered and shone in the sun. The color seemed to change and shift as they gazed upon it in awe. As Angelica watched, it seemed to increase in beauty by the moment. Changing colors of pale rose, corn-silk yellow, emerald green, and azure rippled on the wind, making it a thing of loveliness and grace. Yet it was more than beautiful. A sense of power emanated from it, a heady promise of sweetness gleaming in the future, for this was the legendary flag that had commanded the loyalty of legions. This was the MacCallum heritage, brought centuries ago from the Holy Land by their ancestor, blessed by a saint and sacred to the clan.

With a roar of rage at his son's audacity, Angus shoved Angelica against the parapet and started toward the couple. "How dare ye bring that MacCallum harlot into my keep, or let her close to my flag. Give it to me. I want it in my hands."

" 'Tis not your flag." Angelica lunged after him, locking both hands around his right arm and yanking backward. Caught completely off guard, he stumbled as she pulled.

"I canna give you the flag, Father," Brian answered as Angus fought to free himself from Angelica. "For you will use it in war, and I wish it to bring peace between the clans."

"Aye, he does." Angelica grunted, hanging on to Angus. Brian started toward her, clearly meaning to help her, but she motioned him back. "As the wife of the MacCallum chieftain, I give Lilias MacCallum in marriage to Brian Kilmartin," she shouted to all as Angus shook her off. "Since they are both heirs to their clans, I proclaim the two clans joined and a pact of peace in force."

"Ye'll no' wed the MacCallum bitch," Angus shouted at his son. He jerked a thumb at Geddes. "For *he* killed yer sister."

"He did not kill her." Angelica summoned all her strength to shout at the top of her lungs. "The man below did not kill Susan Kilmartin, for he is not Geddes MacCallum."

Everyone froze. A sudden, eerie silence reigned on both sides of the wall as every man present turned in her direction. Angus Kilmartin turned to confront her. "What did you say?"

She could see Geddes turn her way as well. Because of the distance, she could not make out his expression. His eyes seemed the color of obsidian, dark and questioning. Yet there seemed to be hope in them as well. Yes, it must be hope. She would not let him down. " 'Tis God's truth. He is not Geddes MacCallum," she cried, turning to shout to them all, spilling the long-held secret. "He is Lachlan MacCallum, and to him I plighted my troth when I wed him at Duntrune."

"Ye're daft. Lachlan MacCallum is a sniveling weakling," Angus said. "He's no' capable o' lifting a sword, let alone fighting as he's done."

"He is not a weakling." The passion within her carried her words with ringing fervor out over the Mac-Callum garrison. "Lachlan has become a warrior, ready to fight for his kin, whom he loves. I believe in him with all my heart, and so do all of you who have lived with his loyalty and caring and fought under his leadership. Let that be proof to you of who and what he is."

Angus fixed an accusing stare on the man leading the MacCallum clan. "Is this true?" he demanded.

Every pair of eyes shifted to the warrior they had called Geddes MacCallum.

Angelica leaned over the wall, willing Lachlan to look at her. His gaze met hers, and in that moment she saw all the love she had longed for, shining in his eyes. He accepted that she had seen past his mask and was glad.

"Aye," he shouted, turning in the saddle to his men. "Aye, she speaks truly. I am Lachlan MacCallum, here to lead you in battle." He paused, waiting for his men to grasp the full meaning of his words and respond.

Angus recovered first. "If he's no' Geddes MacCallum, he hasna the right to lead his clan," he scoffed in triumph. "Are ye still willing to follow him?" he demanded of the MacCallum garrison. "He's a liar two times over, first about the flag, then about who he is."

"But he *does* have the right. Tell them, Lachlan." Angelica was desperate to still the murmurs of doubt that broke out among the men. She waved frantically at Lachlan, urging him to answer, hoping she had guessed rightly about the strength of his claim.

"I visited Geddes in Glasgow before I came to Duntrune," Lachlan announced to his men. "He is very ill. He told me of the trouble here, but he had not the strength to come himself. I came in his stead, knowing you had been ousted from your lands and were suffering. When you all mistook me for Geddes, I let you, because I knew what you thought of the old Lachlan. You would never have followed me in the fight."

Rhuri nudged his horse forward from among the others. "I kent that ye were no' Geddes MacCallum. No' at first, but by the time I did, I didna care. I'd follow ye into hell's teeth and back again. Geddes could never lead us as ye do."

Alex MacCallum moved his horse forward next to Rhuri's. "I should ha' kent it, but I didna admit what was before my own eyes. The heir to the chieftain has the right to lead us in battle as clan war captain. We owe our allegiance to ye."

Rhuri pulled forth his sword and tendered it to Lachlan. "I cede the place o' war captain to ye, Lachlan MacCallum. 'Tis yer rightful place." He turned to the rest of the garrison. "Do ye all join me?"

Cries of MacCallum assent rose to the skies as Lachlan accepted the sword and brandished it above his head.

Angus Kilmartin had stood in bewilderment throughout these exchanges. Suddenly he whirled on his son with drawn dirk. "I dinna care who he is. Ye'll no' wed his sister," he cried. "I've tolerated all sorts o' deception from ye because ye're my heir. But on this, I'll see ye dead first."

Brian and Lilias held tightly to the Faerie Flag,

seemingly paralyzed as Angus approached. When he was almost upon them, Brian took the flag from Lilias and stepped to the edge of the wall walk. He dropped the Faerie Flag over the side.

"What are ye doing, laddie?" Angus screamed with rage and leaned over the wall, flailing for the flag. He caught the edge of the silky fabric, but it slipped in his fingers, forcing him to lean over farther. He stretched for it with both hands, overbalanced, and slipped.

As Lachlan caught the flag, Brian scrambled to catch his father, but he was too late. Angus Kilmartin toppled over the wall.

Nausea rose up in Angelica as she heard the old man land below with a dull thud.

"Father." With a cry of anguish, Brian raced for the nearest stair, with Lilias close at his heels.

Pulling together her shattered nerves, Angelica raced after them. Despite the success of her plan, must there still be tragedy? Numb to everything else, she hurried after them, praying there would be no loss of human life.

Lachlan saw Brian burst from the castle gate, followed by Lilias and Angelica. They raced straight to the still body of Angus Kilmartin. He handed the Faerie Flag to Rhuri, signaled his men to remain where they were, then dismounted to go to the fallen Master of Fincharn. The hate kindled over the years was extinguished. Death and destruction had that effect. He would not wish it back.

Brian knelt beside his father, tears streaming freely and unashamedly down his face. He put a hand on the old man's chest, which barely rose and fell. "Father, can ye hear me? If ye can, pray, speak."

Angus's eyelids fluttered, then opened. He gazed up at his son with eyes dulled by pain.

Brian sat and lifted his father's head onto his lap, cradling him, shielding him from the sun. "I love ye, Father, though we dinna believe in the same things."

"The hell wi' ye," Angus cursed his only son.

"Nay, I've been to hell, Father, for it has been hell watching ye suffer and being unable to help ye," Brian whispered. " 'Tis over now. Rest. The feud is done. Lilias and I shall bear bonny babes, and we shall name our first son Angus Kilmartin, for love o' ye."

Tears had gathered in the old man's eyes, despite his show of defiance. Now they coursed down his cheeks as he struggled for breath. "Ye love an old man?"

"Aye, I love ye, Father. Though ye fought wi' yer neighbors, ye were ever good to me. Rest now in my arms. I'll hold ye."

"Dinna leave me." Angus raised a quivering hand and tightened his fingers convulsively on Brian's arm.

"I'll no' leave ye. I'm here for ye, Father," Brian soothed.

Lilias and Angelica both wept openly, one kneeling on each side of the old man. Lilias took his other rough, gnarled hand in her two small ones. "I'll stay wi' ye, too," she said.

Angus's gaze went slowly to Lilias, and his lips moved. "Forgive me," he whispered, his voice rasping. "For killing your father."

Lachlan was stunned to hear his enemy ask for forgiveness. Turning, he beckoned to Rhuri to bring the Faerie Flag. He settled the silk fabric over the dying man.

Brian gathered a handful of the magical silk in his hand and held it up so his father could see it. "Do ye feel the flag's blessed power, Father? 'Twill ease ye,'' he said.

Angus looked at it, and for the first time, he smiled a gentle, beatific smile. Then he closed his eyes and breathed his last.

The feud between the MacCallums and the Kilmartins was done.

Epilogue

Lachlan sat in the solar at Duntrune Castle, Angel beside him, clinging to his hand as if he might disappear should she let go. Beside him was Brian Kilmartin, and beyond him was Lilias, then Alex MacCallum, Georgie Dunaudley, and Rhuri Dunardley, their wives, Muriel, Master Stone, and Magnus. He looked with satisfaction on them, his family and friends.

"Tell us everything," Lilias urged. "We all wish to ken how ye fared all the years ye were gone."

"I went to Paris and entered the university, as planned," he began as the others echoed her interest. "But I admit I was disappointed in the subjects offered for study. Their methods of cutting people open and letting blood seemed to cause more pain than good for those who were suffering. From the first, I knew I must work for sustenance while I attended the university. I found a position in a noble household, serving at table. When the captain of the guards saw I was both quick with a dirk and honest—"

"Ye've been ever honest," Muriel put in. "This must o' been a strain on ye, pretending to be Geddes."

"And you kent from the first that I was no' Geddes," he said.

"O' course I did." Muriel preened, clearly proud of her ability to read character. "Nay matter how Geddes changed, he would never care for Lilias as ye do. I kent that at once. Ye changed as well, but in different ways. In good ways."

Lachlan acknowledged the compliment, and Angelica squeezed his hand, adding to his pleasure. He thought of how she had championed him, denying that he was capable of the things people thought he had done, and he had never been happier.

"I should ha' kent 'twas ye, no' Geddes, but ye've grown so," Alex said for the dozent time. "Ye were both mere striplings when ye left."

"People change," Angelica pointed out.

"Aye," Lachlan agreed. "Who would ever have thought that I would be eager to learn combat skills? I drilled for months in the use of rapier, sword, and dirk."

"My grandsire would ha' taught ye, same as he did me," Alex MacCallum pointed out. "He offered, if ye recall."

"My father demanded I learn, but I proved a poor pupil on purpose," Lachlan admitted. "I had to learn the value of the skill first. When I found myself in a situation where my most notable ability was serving ladies gracefully at table, I was suddenly eager to learn something else. Of course, they were the reason I had the position at all. It seems I became the favorite of the lady of the household. She suggested to the captain that I was good training material."

"No surprise there," Angelica murmured with a grimace.

"Only because I did not muddy their fine carpets or spill wine on their gowns at table or blunder into their fine baubles and break them," he said with a laugh to reassure her. "Later, I learned that the countess had rejected numerous men-at-arms for her personal guard because of their crude manners and clumsy behavior. She wanted someone who was both refined enough to .accompany her to entertainments and skilled enough in fighting to defend her and her three daughters if necessary. I and several other carefully chosen men accompanied them to all their engagements, both day and night. At one of these entertainments, I came to the attention of King Henri, who was fighting for his crown. He offered me a place in his army, training under one of his captains, and I took it, knowing that I had no future serving as a personal escort to a lady—but if the king was crowned, I might acquire land in return for service, so I threw in my lot with his. The captain saw my promise and taught me well. I put my skills in battle strategy to good use and gained some property. It seemed enough until Granduncle Simon wrote to me."

"He told you Geddes was ill and you returned to Glasgow," Angelica guessed.

"He did, and I did," Lachlan agreed, not wanting to say more about his brother, though he doubted he would escape so easily.

"How is yer wastrel brother?" Muriel asked in disparaging tones.

"Aye, we've always sent him the money that he demanded," Alex chimed in. "Claimed he was comin' home after your father was killed by the Kilmartin, but he didna. And still we keep him in style, living in Glasgow claiming to serve the king but doing blessed little soldiering."

"I went and pleaded with him to come home," Rhuri said soberly. "He would not bestir himself from his women and his drinking to return to where he belonged."

Lachlan was silent for a moment, gathering himself to tell them the bad news. Angelica seemed to sense his distress, for she pressed his hand again, as if to tell him they would bear it together.

Thus fortified, he looked at his cousin. "He didna come home because he is dying, Alex. He has not long to remain in this life."

Clearly stunned, they all fell silent.

"He looked terrible when I saw him last," he continued soberly. "He has lost weight and his face is haggard. He's but a year older than I, yet he looks a hundred. 'Twas a vivid reminder of the tenuous hold we each have on life, and the importance of treasuring each moment and each gift we're given."

He looked intently at Angel as he said these last words, and her gaze was full of appreciation and understanding, reminding him that she was the most precious gift of all. He raised her hand to his lips, and felt a wash of warmth at the loving expression in her eyes.

"Geddes clearly did not wish any of you to know the state of his health," he continued, "but by the time I saw him, 'twas evident. Since I am his heir, his physician was willing to talk to me. He said that Geddes has consumption."

They all knew what that meant. Consumption was a long, lingering illness involving a terrible wasting of the flesh and deterioration of the lungs. Geddes would labor for breath and be racked by an agonizing cough that brought up blood. Though Lachlan was angry at his brother for failing in his responsibility, he never wished such a death on him.

"Since Geddes said not a word of what should be

done and refused to let me remain with him, I chose
to come to you myself. I couldna bear the idea of all
of ye ousted from Duntrúne. 'Tis our home. You ken
why I let you think I was Geddes."

The men looked uncomfortable at this. They would
have doubted his ability to lead had they known he
was Lachlan. Even when they had thought he was
Geddes, they had doubted their ability to win, as well
as the value of trying.

Lachlan refused to dwell on what was over and
done. He had their trust now, and that was what mattered. "Just after Angelica arrived, Geddes wrote to
Granduncle Simon, summoning him. That meant the
end was near, for he had refused to have any of us
with him until then."

"Aye, he threatened to murder Lachlan if he tried
to stay," Lilias put in. The others stared at her in
surprise, and she looked back at them, a bit sheepish.
"I saw Granduncle Simon and made Lachlan tell me
of Geddes," she admitted. "I guessed about Lachlan
early on."

"Poor laddie." Muriel looked greatly saddened.
"He was ever a difficult one, was Geddes. He should
ha' let us comfort him."

"The idea that others should come from Duntrune
upset him terribly," Lachlan said gently. "He insisted
I swear to keep his illness secret. I supposed he wished
you to remember him as he'd been when he left,
young and strong. Shortly after Angelica and I wed, I
wrote to him, asking for his instructions. Iain Lang
took my letter to Glasgow on his way south."

"Iain should be returning very soon," Angelica
pointed out. "We will know how Geddes fares."

"Aye, but for now, we must bury your father with
all honor and ceremony," Lachlan said, turning to

Brian. " 'Tis only proper. You mun send word to the chief of the MacDonalds, to whom you are beholden, and if he agrees, then Clan MacCallum shall swear friendship to you and all your clan if you will have all Kilmartins swear to uphold the peace."

Brian looked abashed by the enormity of the responsibilities descending upon him as his clan's chieftain. "I thank you for your kindness to one who was so recently considered your enemy."

Lachlan felt a flash of pain for the agony of the past. "If you and I can end the feud between our clans forever, then I am willing to put all that passed behind us. Let us celebrate your wedding to Lilias here, at Duntrune, and make it a ceremonial joining of the clans. We shall pray together, dance together, and feast together to seal the bond."

Brian brightened at the offer. "I shall bring all my clansmen and they shall swear friendship to MacCallums in return for your swearing to us."

All present murmured their heartfelt approval, and Lachlan glimpsed a hint of tears in the eyes of men and women alike. Never had they thought to see this day.

Lilias was the only one who seemed done with tears. She sat forward eagerly in her seat. "Angelica, I mun hear it from your own lips. How did you ken the Faerie Flag was buried in the burn?"

Angel chuckled. "I didn't, but I knew something important was buried there. Now I'm guessing that Mairi MacCallum did take it with her the night she left Castle Duntrune. With her brother almost upon her, she stowed the casket in the hollow tree trunk, intending to retrieve it later. It must have settled in the hollow down among the roots. One of the men said that a fierce badger family lived there. They can be very nasty, so everyone left the creatures alone. With all their burrowing, the casket might have slipped even deeper. No one would have thought to search there. Once the tree blew down in the storm, it would have been covered by decades of debris." She was silent for a moment, as if considering something. "The man who told me about the badger is your cousin," she said to Georgie. "Kenneth Dunaudley."

"Verra good. You kent his name," Lachlan teased her.

"I did, didn't I?" Looking surprised with herself, she pointed at Rhuri. "You're a Dunardley. The man at the gate is your uncle, also a Dunardley. Sim Dunarchy manages the stables, the man I met my first day here is Dougal Dunardry, and Goodman and Goodwife Dunangley live in the cottage in the wood, with their grandson Euan."

Everyone applauded her recitation.

"If you ken the Dun names, you are more than ever one o' us," Lachlan said, heartily enjoying her surprised pleasure at her knowledge. "How did you learn them?"

"I don't know," Angelica admitted. "I kept meaning to write them down and study them, but I never had a chance. I guess I heard them enough to get them straight at last."

Lilias nodded with enthusiasm. "She kens the Dun names, she dirtied Muriel's kitchen floor and lived through the consequences, and she helped us find our flag. She is one o' us, for certes. What a wonder, though, that she found the flag after it was missing for so long."

"I intend to see it hung in the great hall," Lachlan said. "I want everyone to ken where it is at all times.

There shall be no future disputes over who has the Faerie Flag."

And to that, they all heartily agreed.

Angelica stood in the stable yard the next day, watching three men rethatch the roof of the pottery. The structure had been rebuilt, its dimensions even larger than before. As she talked to Rhuri's son about plans for his future as a potter, Lilias ran up.

"Look, Angelica, I painted on one of your pots with wood-ash glaze that Magnus made for me," she cried with excitement. "Do you like it?"

Angelica turned to examine the large vase that Lilias held. " 'Tis beautiful," she exclaimed, tracing with her fingertip the dried pattern that Lilias had created on the hardened clay. " 'Tis a fern like the ones that grow near the burn. I like it very much. Will you ornament more pots for me?"

Lilias grinned with pleasure. "I never thought I would like working with clay, but I love this. I can create designs, and people will pay for them and use my pieces every day."

Angelica returned the smile. "Now you begin to understand the enjoyment I receive from selling my work. We must get you some different choices of glazes so you can get a variety of effects."

As Lilias nodded with enthusiasm, two horsemen rounded the castle at a trot and halted in the stable yard. Angelica recognized a windblown Iain.

She ran to embrace him. Over Iain's shoulder, she saw the other man dismount and suddenly recognized the old gentleman she had seen her first morning at Duntrune. As she had left the castle for the village, he had passed her on horseback, looking sorrowful and downcast.

"We mun see Geddes at once," Iain said. "Is he nearby?"

"You must see Lachlan," Lilias contradicted. "Everyone knows now."

Iain and the old gentleman exchanged knowing glances.

"Did someone say my name?" Lachlan appeared from the stable, his sleeves rolled up, a horse brush in one hand.

Iain pulled a letter from the pouch at his waist and tendered it to him. "I fear we bear sad news, MacCallum."

Lachlan tore open the sealed letter and scanned the contents. His expression became grave as he beckoned to the head stableman. "I would like everyone to gather in the hall. Lilias, fetch Muriel. Tell her to assemble the household. I shall summon the garrison and send someone to the village."

Every man, woman, and child who lived close enough and belonged to the clan, either as kin or tenants or through any other relationship, assembled in the great hall within the hour. Lachlan stood on the dais but would not sit. At his bidding, Angelica took the seat to his right, as befitted the lady of the castle.

"I have just received this letter from Glasgow," he said in his strong, clear voice. "It is from my brother, Geddes MacCallum, and is meant for the kindred of Clan MacCallum. I shall read it aloud." He held the letter high so all could see.

" 'People of Duntrune,' " he read. " 'As I leave this earth, I consign ye to the care of my brother, Lachlan MacCallum. Ye all kent me as my father's tanist. Lachlan is my tanist, and ye will obey him in all things.' He signs it Geddes Euan MacCallum, as witnessed by Simon Euan MacCallum, brother to the third Laird of MacCallum, at Glasgow, the seven and twentieth day of June, the year of our Lord, sixteen hundred."

All was silent as those in the hall acknowledged the passing of their chieftain. Then Simon MacCallum, who had witnessed the document, came forward and joined Lachlan on the dais. As the clan's eldest member, his acknowledgment of the next chieftain would be respected by all. He clasped Lachlan's hand, and together they raised their joined fists high above their heads. The clan roared its approval and praise for Lachlan MacCallum.

Angelica knew that later, at a formal ceremony, all the kindred would swear their loyalty to Lachlan. He had won their respect and restored their faith in themselves, his ultimate purpose in coming to Duntrune. She was so happy for him, she could not hold back her tears of joy.

That night, in the privacy of their chamber, Angelica went eagerly into Lachlan's arms.

"Do you forgive me for pretending to be Geddes and deceiving you?" he asked, kissing her.

"There was never a rakehell bone in your body," she teased, kissing him back. "I was never deceived about who you really were. You predicted correctly when you said the truth wouldn't matter to me. And to think, when I first met you, I was looking for something you needed that only I could provide."

"And you found it, though it was not at all what either of us expected," he said with a laugh. "I needed someone who saw *me,* not what she expected to see. I am sorry, though, that I said a false name aloud when we wed. We can repeat our vows in church if you wish."

"We might do so to satisfy others, but I guessed you signed the kirk register with your real name, so I looked to be sure."

"You imp. Is that where you disappeared to, the day after the raid?"

She nodded. "Why else did you think I dared stand up to Angus Kilmartin and tell him you weren't Geddes? I would never have done it if I hadn't been certain."

Lachlan rolled his eyes. "How could I think otherwise? Well, then, I apologize for holding you spellbound that day in the orchard so you had to wed me."

"No apology necessary." She grinned, wrinkling her nose at him. "For I had you spellbound first."

" 'Tis true that when I first saw you in the burn, caressing that blasted clay, I wanted your beautiful hands on me instead. But that wasna why I was spellbound. It was because you saw through my deception."

Angelica laughed with delight. "So you admit it. I held you spellbound."

"But I held you spellbound later. You admit that."

She clasped both arms around his waist and gazed into his eyes. "You did and you do. Why must you apologize for it, or for anything?"

He sobered at that. "Because I am sorry I didn't realize and tell you sooner that I love you."

"You love me?" She gazed into his eyes, entranced beyond belief.

"Most certainly I love you, Angel."

She sighed, feeling blessed. "I'm glad you've said it. That's all I require."

"I think you require a good deal more than that," he teased. "You require that I demonstrate my love.

Often and with vigor, so you'll never forget." He reached for the laces of her bodice.

"And will you permit me to demonstrate my love to you in return?" she teased him back, reaching to loosen his kilt.

"Aye," he agreed, kissing her. "And we shall always remember this spellbound summer as the most monumental time of our lives."

Historical Note

This story is a mixture of historical facts blended into a fictional venue. The Fairy Flag, spelled Faerie Flag in this book, is a real historic Highland artifact that belongs to Clan McLeod. I found reference to it in several books, the primary one being *The Highland Clans* by Sir Iain Moncreiffe, published by Clarkson N. Potter, Inc. of New York. There's even a black-and-white photo of the flag, or actually its tattered remnants. I'm sure that even a magic flag would have difficulty remaining whole over the space of a thousand years. According to Moncreiffe, the flag was thought to belong to a Norse king who acquired it while in service as a knight in Constantinople, then later brought it to Scotland. Some believe it gained its magical powers because it was the shirt of a saint. Others say it was given to the clan by faeries, hence its name.

Regardless of its origin, I loved the idea of a magical flag that inspired the clan. At the same time, I could see all too readily how a clan might become overly dependent on its power. Hence, my story was born. However, I did not use the aspect of the legend that said the flag could only be used three times before its power was spent. Over the course of a thousand years,

I think the clan would have lost count of how many times the flag was used.

The geographic location where *Spellbound Summer* takes place is Argyll, on the peninsula just south of Loch Awe. There, as you can see on some maps, lies the Castle of Duntrune and the town of Dunadd. In fact, if you search the Internet for Castle Duntrune, you will find the official castle web site, where you can see photos of the castle and surrounding land and reserve one of the quaint outbuildings on the property for a holiday. You will also learn that the castle is privately owned and occupied by the current chief of the MacCallum family, or O'Challum, as the official web site calls it. The name MacCallum means "Son of Columba," referring to Saint Columba, and is now anglicized as Malcolm. By the way, the castle is said to have a ghost, but he came to live at the castle later in the century and so is not part of my story.

Although I love a Scots accent, I tried to go light on my use of a brogue by my hero, and of course Angelica has no accent at all, being English. You will note that minor characters have a bit more accent. In truth, these Highland Scots would have been speaking Gaelic, and Angelica would have found most of their speech unintelligible. Only a few of the educated individuals, such as Geddes/Lachlan and Lilias, would have known English and been able to speak to her, but if I had dealt with the language barrier in the story, it would have been a much longer book. I chose to enhance reading pleasure by leaving out that aspect of Highland culture.

Regarding the wearing of Highland kilts and plaids, historical documentation shows that these garments were being worn in the Highlands by the year 1600, though the regularization of specific tartans for each clan cannot, according to historians, be substantiated until after that time. In fact, the Highland Scots, when they spoke Gaelic, never used the word *tartan*, according to John Telfer Duncan in his 1984 work *The Costume of Scotland*, published by B. T. Batsford Ltd., London. Instead, they said *breacan*, of which one meaning is, Duncan tells us, "stripped cross wise." Nevertheless, we all adore a man in a kilt, and the romantic idea that the entire clan wore matching patterns is presented in this story for the reader's pleasure.

Terminology of English costume is also important. For this, I depend on my favorite book, *Costume in the Drama of Shakespeare and His Contemporaries*, by M. Channing Linthicum, published by Oxford University Press. Readers will note that I refer to gowns as kirtle skirts and bodices, which may sound odd because a kirtle was a different garment in the fifteenth century. Linthicum verifies that the kirtle changed in fashion and purpose throughout the ages, thus making this terminology confusing. During the sixteenth century, Linthicum verifies from written historic documentation that the term *kirtle* meant a garment worn by women over petticoats and farthingale as an outside dress. It consisted of a separable bodice (called a pair of bodies) and a skirt. In the opening pages of Linthicum's book, you can see a photo of a "lady's kirtle body embroidered in colored silks." Hence, the origin of the terminology used in my books.

If you enjoyed the story of Angelica and Lachlan, I hope you will drop me an e-mail and let me know at jlynnford@aol. com. If you don't have access to a computer, say hello via snail mail at P.O. Box 21904, Columbus, Ohio, 43221.

JANET LYNNFORD

SHETLAND SUMMER

The author of *Bride of Hearts* returns to the Scottish Isles...

In this spectacular new historical romance, two outcast hearts rebel against the harsh rule of the Laird of the Shetland Isles—and discover a love beyond their wildest dreams.

"Lynnford has a magical gift" —Patricia Rice

"Lynnford keeps me turning pages long after my bedtime" —Teresa Medeiros

0-451-41032-7

To order call: 1-800-788-6262

CATHERINE COULTER CALLS JACLYN REDING "A RISING STAR."

The award-winning author of *White Mist* returns with a new Scottish trilogy—and a passionate tale of disguised love.

HIGHLAND HEROES: *The Pretender*

Lady Elizabeth Drayton is to be forced into a loveless marriage to a man her father's age. But the fiery lass has other ideas. She decides to trick her father by beating her fiancé to the altar—arm-in-arm with a poor, local farmer. Little does she know, however, that once love enters the picture, the joke will be on *her*...

0-451-20416-6

To order call: 1-800-788-6262